THEY THAT DWELL
IN DARK PLACES
AND OTHER GHOST STORIES

DANIEL MCGACHEY

Ghost House
2009

FIRST TRADE PAPERBACK EDITION

THEY THAT DWELL IN DARK PLACES
and Other Ghost Stories © 2009 by Daniel McGachey
COVER & INTERIOR ART © 2009 by Julia Helen Jeffrey
INTRODUCTION © 2009 by Charles Black

Cover Painting – **'Dr. Lawrence—An Informal Portrait'**
by Julia Helen Jeffrey

Cover and interior design by
David G. Barnett
Fat Cat Design

ISBN: 1-888993-72-3
ISBN-13: 978-1-888993-72-1

Ghost House
Dark Regions Press
PO Box 1264
Colusa, CA 95932

This collection is dedicated to...

My parents and family, who, though I don't see them nearly often enough, are always in my heart and my thoughts...

My friends, not only for their advice, opinions and encouragement throughout the writing of these stories, but for the laughter and companionship over the years...

Two gentlemen who I have never actually met, but without whom these tales could never have been written—Lawrence Gordon Clark, whose BBC productions of classic ghost stories renewed my acquaintance with the master of all ghost story writers, and that master storyteller himself, M.R. James.

PUBLICATION HISTORY

THEY THAT DWELL IN DARK PLACES, first published in **The First BHF of Horror Stories** (BHF Books, 2006), edited by Christopher Wood. The revised version in this current collection incorporates material originally written for the **Imagination Theater** radio adaptation of the story, first broadcast October 30th 2005, directed by Lawrence Albert, produced by Jim French.

THE SHADOW IN THE STACKS, adapted from the **Imagination Theater** radio play, first broadcast October 29th 2006, directed by Lawrence Albert, produced by Jim French. Short story adaptation first published in **The Second BHF Book of Horror Stories** (BHF Books, 2007), edited by Christopher Wood.

THE BEACON, adapted from the **Imagination Theater** radio play, first broadcast May 13th 2007, directed by Lawrence Albert, produced by Jim French.

"SHALT THOU KNOW MY NAME?", first published in **The Black Book of Horror** (Mortbury Press, 2007), edited by Charles Black. Adapted from the script for the **Imagination Theater** radio play, which was subsequently broadcast October 26th 2008, directed by Dennis Bateman, produced by Jim French.

THE MOUND, first published in **Filthy Creations 3** (Filthy Creations Press, Autumn 2007), co-edited by Steve Goodwin & Rog Pile.

THE CRIMSON PICTURE, first published in **The Second Black Book of Horror** (Mortbury Press, 2008), edited by Charles Black.

'AND STILL THOSE SCREAMS RESOUND...', first published in **The Fourth Black Book of Horror** (Mortbury Press, 2009), edited by Charles Black.

AN UNWISE PURCHASE, first published in **Further Tales from a Ghostly Study** (Cadman & de Mauleon, 1908), reprinted by kind permission of the Trustees of the Estate of H.S. Grace.

THE WAGER, RAGS, THE TRAVELLING COMPANION, A RAVELLED TRESS, THE UNMASKING, SHEDDING LIGHT ON DARK PLACES and the introduction to **AN UNWISE PURCHASE** are original to this collection.

CONTENTS

ARTWORK

Introduction:
The Lurker in the Shadows

CHARLES BLACK

When I decided to start the *'Black Book of Horror'* series of anthologies one of the aims was to give some newer writers exposure. So I was delighted when Joe Morey of Dark Regions Press contacted me asking to be put in touch with Daniel McGachey. At the time, Joe mentioned an anthology invite, but I wasn't at all surprised to learn later that a collection of Dan's stories was in the offing. What did surprise me was being asked to contribute an introduction for it.

So here I am writing what will undoubtedly be the weak link in the book. But don't worry I'll keep it brief; in fact I urge you to skip it and get stuck in to the stories rather than waste time reading this—they are that good.

Still here? Oh well, don't say I didn't warn you.

I first met Dan at a select club, the members of which have a taste for the horrific, macabre and weird; many of whom recount tales of that nature. One evening several of us were gathered in the Guthrie Room and Dan told a tale so chilling that it had such an effect on one member that he quite literally sha...er, well perhaps I better not go into the details. I will add that the poor chap was later found dead, although whether he died of fright or embarrassment at his earlier reaction is unclear. Anyway, I was most impressed by Dan's story!

I see the *Black Books* as a modern day equivalent of the old *'Pan Book of Horror'* stories, and despite popular opinion of them being full of the nasty and disgusting many volumes would contain at least one traditional supernatural tale. As an aside it's interesting to note that two authors in particular associated with that series—Alan Temperley and Martin Waddell—went on to become authors of children's fiction whilst Dan has gone in the opposite direction, although originally writing for children's comics he would try and give his young readers the heebie jeebies whenever possible. Not for nothing has he become known as a scary bloke.

So when I began compiling my first anthology, I wanted at least one traditional period ghost story and I knew I had to have Dan involved. And he didn't disappoint. He contributed *"Shalt Thou Know My Name?"* a story set in the world of academia. It was very Jamesian and proved very popular with the book's readers.

Usually in these introductions there are very brief details of the stories you are about to read. Personally I prefer not to know what I'm in for, so I tend to leave reading the introduction until the end. And thus I'm not really going to go in the specifics of what awaits you. What I will say is that these stories are set in the same milieu, and often share connections although they all stand alone. Many of these tales contain somebody telling a story. And much like the Sherlock Holmes stories, they contain hints and references to other tales, some of which appear here. Hopefully the others will be told at a later date. Mention is made of Dr Lawrence's travels abroad, and I hope one day to hear more of those. I wonder perhaps if he made the Black Pilgrimage to Chorazin.

In his bio Dan mentions some of his loves in *'the frightening, fantastical and mysterious,'* and these influences are clearly evident in his work except perhaps Lovecraft. Dan's take on cosmic horror is another thing I'd like to see in the future. But it's a love of the writings of M.R. James that comes through the strongest—what is it they say about you never being further than twenty feet from a rat? I don't think Dan is ever further than that from one of his many copies of the *'Ghost Stories of an Antiquary'!* Even in the few stories of

Dan's that I've had the pleasure of reading that have contemporary settings the Jamesian elements are noticeable. So as well as enjoying the stories you'll be able to see how many references you can spot, whether they were deliberate tips of the hat or not.

Will these stories still be read in 70 or so years time like the works of James? Well despite the current lack of interest in the horror genre from the book buying public at large, I wouldn't at all be surprised if they were. After all stranger things have happened.

Well, there we have it: my first introduction to a collection, and probably my last, but almost certainly this will be the first of many collections from Daniel McGachey. So pull your chair closer to the fire, make sure you have you favourite tipple to hand, settle back and enjoy this debut collection by a writer who quite rightly deserves the title *Master of the Macabre*. But keep a wary eye on the shadows; you never know what might be lurking there...

…there were some rusty stains on the pages, dried but unmistakable.

The Shadow in the Stacks

I don't know if I've spoken before of my old friend, Dr. Lawrence, the folklorist. It was he whose researches took him, some years back now, to the library of Saint Montague's—one of our older and, I must add, more forgotten colleges.

The library itself dates back several centuries, and houses many original texts that in other, more conveniently situated and oft-frequented libraries, had become lost or damaged over the years, while other manuscripts were peculiar to that area. As such, they were jealously guarded and, with the college reluctant to the point of rudeness to entrust them beyond their own precincts, Lawrence was forced to decant himself and his studies to rooms within that locale, allowing him daily access to the treasured tomes.

The nearest settlement, Greymarsh, is hardly the most inviting town for visitors. But Lawrence being Lawrence, this was entirely to his liking. "If I am to gather the fables and folktales of antiquity," he would declare, "it's better to have the truth of it, and not some sanitised version that has been formulated to please tourists."

And, doubtless you are now imagining that one of these ancient volumes yielded some tale of long buried horror, which I now intend to share. In which case, I should tell you that, while long buried is an apt description, this wasn't a tale to be found within the pages of any book.

In his capacity as a visiting scholar, Dr. Lawrence had developed a fine working relationship with a Mr. Perdew, one of the assistant librarians. It was he who entrusted him with the somewhat fantastical story Lawrence passed onto me, and which I now intend to recount.

His researches had been proceeding apace, in many ways thanks to Perdew's excellent knowledge of the library's stock. Still a young man, Perdew had retained the enthusiasm of youth but, through experience, had developed the wonderful knack of knowing just when to display an interest or offer an opinion on Lawrence's work, and when to hold back and allow the doctor to pursue more solitary trains of thought.

It was only when he expressed a desire to seek out certain of the more elderly texts, some obscure parish records from early in the previous century which were not kept on display among the main collection, that Lawrence saw Perdew's affable eagerness to help falter.

He seemed somewhat reluctant, a little vague about where the records may be kept, while all the time his eyes kept flitting toward a door in the far corner that, as Lawrence had already learned, led to a basement stock room. He hummed and hawed and said that he'd see what he could do, all with the intent of putting the scholar off his goal, it seemed. Baffled, Lawrence chided, "Come now, man. You're not afraid to go rooting about in the cellars, surely?"

At this, Perdew bridled, his face beetrooting, as he seized a key from behind the desk and made for the door with a determined step—one which became decidedly less determined as he neared the doorway. For a few moments he stood, the key held out toward the lock. Yet he did not press it home and turn it. It was only as Lawrence approached to enquire if he was all right that he realised the assistant librarian was trembling, his entire body shaking as though a current of electrical power were passing through it.

He scarcely seemed to notice as Lawrence gripped his shoulders and led him back to a seat, prising the key from his numb fingers. There was no doubt that he was in a state of terror and, once his eyes showed a flicker of recognition toward Lawrence, the doctor gently pressed him to tell the cause of his distress.

"Perhaps I must, Dr. Lawrence, sir," he admitted, weakly. "And, as I know you to be a man of honour, I can trust you."

"Of course," Lawrence assured him. "You may speak freely of anything in front of me."

What he told Lawrence was, he claimed, something that he had never previously spoken of to anyone, for fear of losing his position, or of being accused of losing his grip on reality. It was an incident he recalled from a few years earlier, not many years after he had taken his post in the library.

"All had been well, and I was as content in my job as any man could hope to be," he revealed. "Until one cold morning as I arrived outside these doors, ready to open up for the morning's students, only to find the place full of activity and my way barred."

«« ——— »»

"Something's happened, sir. A disturbance in the night! I don't know that I should let you in." The old porter, a man named Gordon—though I was never entirely able to work out whether this was his Christian name or surname—was clearly agitated as he placed up signs alerting the students to the unexpected closure of the library.

"No-one's been hurt?" I queried. "There has been no fire? The walls aren't set to come tumbling down?"

Mr. Gordon shrugged, as though incidents of fire, flood, or the very crack of doom were little concern of his.

"Then I really must be let past. There are certain rare and irreplaceable volumes which I must see are made secure."

"They haven't been taken," the porter said, with heavy meaning. "If you are referring to..." and here, the fellow became conspiratorial, bringing his bewhiskered face closer to my ear, as if he imagined that any of the chattering students thronging past would pay two college employees the slightest notice. "If you are referring to those... 'Items of Uncertain and Curious Origin,' Mr. Perdew. Them ones what came out of the pit?"

As anyone remotely connected with the college, indeed, practically every soul on the entire campus and in the surrounding villages, could not help but be aware, the recent renovation work in the library cellars had turned up something, as Gordon liked to put it, of uncertain and curious origin.

There is a corner of the cellar which the students have, as far back as I remember, referred to as 'the haunted crypt,' insisting that the air in that spot carries 'the chill of the tomb,' and that strange noises, scrabblings and scratchings might be heard there. And, even though no student has had access to the cellars since they had become the storeroom for some of our rarer volumes, the rumours persisted, as such stories frequently do. It was here that the discovery was made.

Workmen, brought in by the Dean to begin construction on a new annexe that he planned to have named in his own honour, had been persuaded to raise a few flagstones in the cellar, mainly to satisfy the Chief Librarian's assertions that the chill and the sounds could be explained by the presence of a subterranean stream, possibly even a centuries-old sewer, dating back to the time of the ancient castle onto whose ruins the college had been grafted.

Much had been whispered, in the day or so since then, about the odd parcel that was found in the dry hollow, which occupied the space in which my superior had assumed a stream to be located. On my way to my rooms, as twilight gathered the previous evening, I'd heard mutterings of treasure, of a hidden chamber, even of a human skull. But the truth of what was found there was neither as spectacular, nor as straightforward.

"Books? Is that all? But we have books already! It is a library, after all!" The Dean had been summoned within minutes of the find but, even in this short space of time, rumours had begun circulating and, judging by his dissatisfaction, he'd already been rather taken with the notion of a treasure chest. "Was there nothing else?" he urged, hopefully.

"Apparently not, Professor Clark," I informed him, to his ill-concealed displeasure. "Just these half dozen volumes, found in a sort of oilskin sack, according to the foreman."

"They're ugly enough," he muttered, then, straining to lift them, he added, "and heavy enough." And, as he turned the pages, the look of annoyance grew, mingled with a hint of incomprehension. "What gabble is this?" His finger jabbed at the rows upon rows of cramped figures. "Is that even writing? Worthless!" And, with a scowl, he threw the book carelessly into a heap with the others.

"Actually, sir," I gasped, swiftly examining the leathery brown binding for damage, "judging by their age and condition, I think these may prove to be of inestimable value."

Professor Clark's piggy eyes lit up in the folds between his bulging cheeks and his coppery, unkempt eyebrows. "Valuable, you say? Then what are you leaving them lying around for? Have them put under lock and key. Grief, man, there are common labourers and Lord knows who else swarming through here!" He was still talking even as the door swung shut behind him, "Tell the librarian to come see me whenever he sees fit to return." And he had departed happily, his greedy little heart full of joy.

That had been the day before, and our next encounter was less joyful.

The local sergeant and a constable had arrived by bicycle, which is a sight easier than a horse and carriage to navigate through the twisting avenues of the university. As my fellow assistants looked on aghast at the tumbled volumes and scattered pages, I spied the Dean, the Bursar, the Chief Librarian and these policemen sitting opposite that white haired night porter. None of them looked happy with whatever Gordon was telling them.

It was the Dean who noticed me first. "Perdew! Over here! Sharply, now!"

What followed was an interrogation. What time had I left the library? Had the books been locked away? Where had I gone? Had anyone been loitering? Was the building securely locked?

"Who else knew of the discovery?" demanded the Sergeant.

"Practically everyone. It was all round the college."

"But who had actually seen the objects?"

"Only the Dean himself, the workmen, the other assistants," then I recalled one other. "Oh, yes, and old Harkwell."

"You showed these valuable artefacts to an outsider?" croaked the Dean. "And why was this man informed?"

As I explained, a swiftly despatched note, entrusted to the care of a fleet-footed first year, had brought the equally swift arrival of Mr. Harkwell. The old bookbinder had been called upon many times over the last fifty years, when overly rough student handling had caused the books to buckle and burst. Although near blinded by age, his knowledge of the various bindings and papers were so ingrained that he could tell, by smell and touch, just the right materials.

However, even this expert craftsman was at a loss. "The texture, it's not leather, I am almost convinced," he muttered, fingers caressing the spine and cover of the smallest volume, which he rotated under his prominent nose, like a man savouring the aroma of a fine cigar. "There's a certain familiarity about the smell but, as loathe as I am to be defeated after all these years, I must admit to it, Perdew."

The old craftsman looked so crestfallen by his failure that I felt duty bound to offer some measure of dignity back to him, insisting that I had all faith that he would find the answer, and bundling him off with the small tome on which he might continue his researches.

"You wish me to take this? You're entrusting it to me?" he asked in a mixture of surprise and delight. "You are a scholar, Mr. Perdew. Something of which this college is in sadly short supply."

"But," quaked the Dean, when I had explained my reasons for summoning the bookbinder, "can this man be trusted?"

I almost laughed at the notion of the eighty-seven year old Harkwell running rampage through the library. Fearing that I might be reduced to helpless mirth, I asked to be excused to help attend to the tidying up.

"Yes, you may go," the Sergeant replied, looking suddenly weary. "I doubt if this old...ahem...if this gentleman has anything to say that might interest you."

I was somewhat surprised. "I've always found Mr...er... Gordon most helpful."

"My thanks, Mr. Perdew, sir," said the old porter, and he lifted his cap to his head specifically so that he could doff it in my direction. "That is my aim, to help in the smooth running of the college and its faculties and facilities."

The Sergeant sneered. "Helpful, eh? All right, then. Tell this gentleman what you witnessed, then. Let's see how helpful he finds it."

The old man shrugged. "I don't know as I'd say that I'd actually witnessed it, sir, as I couldn't rightly attest that I saw anything too clearly. Rather, it was what I'd say was in the nature of an impression that I had.

"I was on my regular rounds, just checking in, and I'd not even had the time to turn on the lights when I felt it. That queer, unsettling sensation that some strange eye was regarding me gave me cause to turn my head sharply... though, perhaps, I might be glad that I wasn't sharp enough to catch full sight of what I believe to have been just behind me.

"The impression I had was of something crawling just out of sight, into the darkness. Something that was red, and peculiarly glistening. Red and wet, like something that you might see in a butcher's display..."

It was at this point that the Sergeant lost control of his temper and, in language I won't repeat here, questioned the college's policy of employing soft-headed individuals obviously in their dotage. Gordon, paying no heed to the insult, merely said, "My people is country people and, in the country, if you want to eat meat, you got to prepare the carcass first, and that's what I was put in mind of. That was my impression. But then, before I could think more on it, I saw the mess in here and raised the alarm."

The Sergeant left soon afterwards, his mind seemingly set on the notion of high-spirited students indulging in a spot of vandalism, and, obviously unwilling to expend any further concern on the matter, opining that it was an issue for the college to deal with internally and, if he had any advice to offer, violently.

The authorities may have lost interest, but the same could not be said of the students, and by the time we had restored some semblance of order and could reopen the doors a considerable crowd flocked in, many of whom I had never once spied lifting a book, let alone setting foot within the library. That long day consisted mainly of fielding the same questions about the disturbance, while also having to politely listen to a variety of theories to the nature of the criminal. "Only a ghost could have entered without opening the window," was one. Another was, "Whatever it was that came out of the ground, it wasn't alone!"

By six o'clock that night, I was exceptionally tired of the students and their comments, and I was so looking forward to closing up for the night that I eagerly cantered after a fellow I had glimpsed disappearing amongst the stacks, with an, "Excuse me, sir, but we're closed," on my lips.

"Chasing shadows, are we, Perdew?" smirked a younger colleague of mine, adding, as I looked blankly at him, "There are no students here. I saw the last one out not five minutes ago, and I've locked the door against any last minute browsers."

He was right. There was no-one else to be seen, apart from my fellow assistants, slotting books on shelves or extinguishing the lamps in the reading rooms. The row into which I had been about to follow the figure was empty.

"A shadow," I agreed. But, if that was so, why had it seemed so...so red?

I spoke nothing of this to my colleagues, convincing myself that some delayed shock from the morning's excitement had triggered my imagination, as it had certainly heightened my own curiosity. As I bade the others a good evening and began my routine check of the locks—though the action was considerably less routine on this night—my mind turned once more to the unearthed, and seemingly unearthly, books.

Had the damage done here been wrought by someone who desired them? Was it someone who perhaps knew something of their origin, and of the significance of the strange inscriptions that filled the pages? And how determined was this seeker to claim his prize? Would the locked safe in the library office stand in his way? Indeed, would anything or anyone come between it and its quarry?

'It'? Surely I meant 'Him'?

I was suddenly chillingly aware that I was alone in the darkened room where the very objects that this possibly mad intruder sought were to be found. I didn't linger beyond the time it took to grab my hat and overcoat and make my way to the main door. But, before I had reached for the door handle, my heart had leapt into my mouth at the sudden loud rapping on the window, and the dark shape that waited beyond the frosted glass.

My breath was escaping in bursts and gasps. "Who..?"

"Mr. Perdew?" came the muffled voice. "I've a message for you. The lady said it was urgent."

It was a student, wrapped in scarves and mittens against the chill, who placed into my still trembling hand a note, summoning me to Harkwell's home above his workshop. Normally I savoured these visits, as the old fellow's book-shelves carried many well-preserved volumes even older than some in the library, and his collection filled both his house and his shop. Each visit felt like a chance to step back into an almost forgotten world, but the grim look on the messenger's face left me with uneasy thoughts as I has-tened into town and through the winding streets.

My fears were confirmed when I saw the distraught housekeeper, who hurriedly beckoned me in upon my first knock, and up the worn and narrow staircase. "Oh, Mr. Perdew, sir, but I don't know what to tell you or where to start with it, but I should warn you before you see him, sir. I'd be remiss if I didn't."

"Warn me, Mrs. Trenchard?" I asked, nervous of what I may hear in reply. "Warn me of what?"

"He's not..." Here, that good woman paused, fussing to tidy her usually immaculate grey hair as she struggled to find the right words to answer. "Well, you may not know him. He may not make any sense."

"Mrs. Trenchard, it's you who isn't making sense. Not know him? I've known old Hark... I've known Mr. Harkwell for years."

She gave me a look of almost sympathy. "Not like this, you've not. The doctor says it was a fit or the like. His heart's not strong enough to go moving him, but he was determined to see you. Wrote your name, what I could read of it, his hand trembling so."

"Wrote it?" I demanded, my anxiety and puzzlement growing by the second. "Can't he speak?"

Mrs. Trenchard's reply was a piteous wail. "Oh, sir, to see him! And him only eighty-seven!"

The reason for the housekeeper's distress became obvious as she opened the creaking door on a dimly lit room, and pointed a shaking hand to what I, at first, took to be an empty bed, heaped with discarded linen. Then I saw the pallid face amongst the folds, and I heard the voice that attempted to speak. "Per...dew... Lost... Gone..."

I rushed to the bedside. "Mr. Harkwell, what has happened to you? How can I possibly help you?"

Again he croaked, "Lost...tried to stop...book...red...so red..." Though his voice was weak, his grip was strong, and he grasped my hand, guiding it onto a bundle of fabric. I recognised it as the cloth which I had used to wrap that small volume in when I had presented it to him the day before. "Gone..."

Then the realisation of what Harkwell was trying to tell me struck home. "The book? Someone has taken it? Should the police be summoned?"

Harkwell let loose a howl that tapered off into a weak cough. He shook his head, vigorously protesting against the thought of the police. I could get no more from him and made to close the door and leave him to his rest. But his arm raised up to me, pleading. "Light... Please... Not dark..."

"I'll open the curtains," I told him, horrified by the look of fear in his bleary eyes. "Will that help? Just a little, for you must rest."

As I allowed the light of the streetlamps into the room, his eyes darted, seeking out every corner, as though he didn't entirely trust every shadow to fully retreat.

Finally, satisfied, he sank back into a fitful slumber, and I left him to sleep.

Mrs. Trenchard, looking somewhat more composed and back to her normal, practical self, with only the red rims round her eyes to let slip the strain she was obviously under, was waiting for me in the hallway. "I found him when I came on up this morning," she told me, leading me to the door of Mr. Harkwell's inner sanctum. "In here."

The scene that was revealed made me gasp, though it was one that was all too familiar. "His study! His books..."

The housekeeper indicated a clearing amidst the debris. "Lying amongst them, I found him. He must've brung them all down upon himself when he took his tumble."

The room was awash with papers and books that I had always seen lovingly presented and preserved. It was as though a storm had blown itself into being in the room, and had spent its wrath on the books and their bookcases, before dying away.

"Such a mess," Mrs. Trenchard grumbled, shaking her head, "and where I'm to start with it, I don't begin to know."

I picked up one of the scattered books. Its spine was twisted, its leather binding half wrenched off, and there were some rusty stains on the pages, dried but unmistakable. "Blood?" I muttered.

I hadn't been conscious that I'd said the word aloud but the housekeeper spoke up then, saying, "If it is, it's not his, thank the Heavens and All who dwell There. He had a bruise or two, but no cuts.

"Unless," her voice rose in alarm, "there was someone else here? Some burglar who attacked the old Mister? I heard there's them what's after rare books loose in the area."

"News does travel," I said to myself, knowing full well that nothing escaped the ear of Mrs. Martha Trenchard. "But could anyone have gotten in? Was there any sign of a break in?"

"Apart from himself and the mess, all was as it should be. But, if there had been someone else..." She paused, a troubled look fixed upon her face, leading me to prompt her to continue. And when she did so, it was reluctantly. "If he'd surprised someone in the dark, it would explain the feeling I had when I'd found him on the floor, here. That, if he'd had the strength, if he'd had the voice, he would have been screaming!"

It was clear that someone desperately wanted those peculiar volumes, to have attempted robbery at both the library and in the bookbinder's home. Whoever it was had now achieved partial success. The book Harkwell had been working with was gone. My first instinct was to discover why these books were so keenly sought. If there was some clue to be found amongst those ostensibly jumbled scribblings, I had to at least try to locate it. I had to see just what it was that we had set loose in unearthing them.

I returned to the library through darkening streets made even more gloomy by my own mood. From the safe in the office, I chose a volume at random, before carefully locking the others away.

My eyes were aching within minutes of trying to decipher the cramped writing that filled the pages but, in time, I confirmed a suspicion that the garbled text was a mixture of languages: some Latin, some Greek, Anglo Saxon, even Danish and runic. I had a hard task ahead of me, but I was equipped with both a library's worth of textbooks to verify the more obscure languages and a healthy dose of stubbornness.

But, even amongst these alien phrases, there was a name that I recognised, which leapt out of the page. Startled, I whispered to myself, "I've heard of you, 'Nicholas Hobsgate'! So these books belonged to that ancient sinner? The worst of men."

«« —— »»

At this point Dr. Lawrence felt compelled to interrupt Mr. Perdew's narrative, for the assistant librarian was not alone in recognising that unsavoury name. "The worst of men? Your description says little, yet succeeds in saying it all. As an antiquarian, I have certainly encountered Sir Nicholas Hobsgate before, though not, I'm very happy to say, in person.

"Indeed, it is rather difficult not to have encountered 'Old Nick' when researching this town's past. I've seen his name in print many a time, in other places scored through, as if some would hope to erase his name, and to edit him and his deeds from the town's past.

"From what my own researches have found, from what little has survived censorious hands through the centuries, Hobsgate was, by inheritance, the lord of the manor...by reputation, a necromancer, a black magician of vilest habits, a murderer, and defiler of tombs. Though I doubt that this was even the half of it!"

Perdew nodded, scarcely attempting to hide his revulsion at the mention of the name. "It's a better world for the fact that he's been in his tomb these past centuries. I just wish his notebooks, for lack of a better term, had been buried with him, and had never surfaced from where he'd obviously concealed them in the bowels of his castle. But they had." And, with what Lawrence would later describe as a wearily haunted look clouding his eyes, Mr. Perdew resumed his account.

《 《——》 》

Thus it was that I found myself seated in the Chief Librarian's small office after an inordinate amount of time had passed, copying by lamplight some of the more intriguingly obscure passages from the books. All the while, I kept myself company by mumbling and muttering to myself as I read, *'Thus, all of the subject may be used, the fat for candles... the hand of glory... the fluids to be drained... the sk...'*

The faraway chiming of twelve broke into my concentration, and I was distantly aware of a sudden pang of hunger as, to quote Mr. Poe's poem, *'I pondered weak and weary o'er many a quaint and curious volume of forgotten lore.'*

Like that poem's narrator, I nodded nearly napping. Yet it was not the sound of a tapping at the chamber door which jolted me back to wakefulness. It was another sound, like footfalls: soft, shoeless footsteps, but there was another quality to them. A quiet, wet, sucking sound, as if, with each step, the feet momentarily stuck, congealing, to the floor.

Roused, I lifted my head. Something was perched on the edge of my desk. Something that moved suddenly as my eyes lit upon it...a scuttling, spidery movement, all joints and angles. Though, by the size, and by its red, glistening moistness, it seemed more like a crab, or something else from the depths of the sea. Or the depths of a nightmare, I realised, as I saw the arm that led away from it, sinew and muscle fading back into the darkness beyond the ring of lamplight. I could tell the rest of the figure was there, however, by the glints of teeth and eyes, lipless and lidless.

What I was then aware of was the harsh scrape of a chair on the floorboards, the sound of my own stumbling footsteps, and the thud of books falling to the floor as I tried to steady myself. My voice was a gasp of horror that seemed to issue from somewhere far off. "No! Please!"

The only reply was a wheezing, wet breath.

Even as I cowered away from it, I could sense that this visitant had no interest in me. It gathered the book from my desk and clasped it to its raw chest. The strange tenderness of this action must have registered through the fog in my mind, as I at once felt a rising wave of nausea and terror that forced me to my feet and away.

Truth to tell, my flight from that midnight library is lost to memory, as is the remainder of that night, and whether I slept or paced or raved in my rooms, I have no recollection. What I do recall is finding myself surrounded by the greasy remains of every candle in my possession, which littered every available surface, in an attempt to banish every shadow from the place.

It was a knock at the door which brought me to some semblance of sense and, when I could force my shaking hand to turn the key and open the door, there was a familiar face waiting beyond.

"Mr. Harkwell? Are you..? Shouldn't you be resting?" My voice was a whisper, my mouth was dry and I had a sudden thirst. As I sought for water, the old man entered in the wheelchair that had obviously carried him from his front door to mine.

"My good fellow," he said grimly, "it is you who looks in need of rest." And I was suddenly alert to how my unshaven and unkempt appearance was causing him concern.

"Well, I could certainly be resting, after pushing this blessed wheelchair," wheezed Mrs. Trenchard, though, despite her protests, I could see she was more than happy that Harkwell had mustered the strength to set out on his journey. "Why you couldn't send for the young gentleman, with his strong legs, instead of having me wheel you this distance..."

"I did send for him, Martha," the old man rasped. "The messenger could get no reply. That's why I worried so." Signalling that he no longer needed her assistance, the old man wheeled himself round the room, allowing his house-keeper to take a moment's rest.

His eyes immediately fell on the burnt-out candles. "So, you saw him too, did you?"

I hadn't the energy to pretend otherwise. "What...who was it?"

Harkwell grimaced. "Someone who had the misfortune, many years ago, to encounter Sir Nicholas Hobsgate.

"You never examined the diagrams in that book before passing it to me, did you?" he surmised.

I shrugged. "I scarcely had time for more than the merest glance."

Harkwell shivered, and he had to gesture for Mrs. Trenchard to leave him be as she attempted to adjust the travelling blanket around him. "You didn't see, and I am glad that my eyes are failing from what I could perceive. It was more than enough, seeing glimpses of demons and imps and the tortures of hell, listed alongside instructions and ingredients, as though it were some grisly magician's cookbook. But, frightful though these creatures were, the image that lodged in my mind was the diagram of the knife and the victim, and the instructions on where to cut and where to peel."

A vague memory of my nocturnal reading bubbled up. 'All of the subject may be used, the fat... the hand... the fluids... the skin...' Good Lord, the skin! 'The skin may be employed for binding enchantments and sealing their powers...'

Harkwell continued, his distaste evident, "I've read of such practices, of course. Who hasn't? In legends and tales of awful and ancient rituals. But to hold an actual example of it in my own hands; it is more than I ever thought possible in all my years in my craft, and more than I would ever wish to again encounter and endure in whatever time I may have left on this earth.

"That binding that had me so puzzled? Well, before my nocturnal guest made his presence known, I'd made my enquiries and I'd had my researches done. I know what it is, and that is why I'm glad I've never encountered it before."

And before he had even told me, the image of that wet, red hand came to my mind, and I knew just why this creature sought the books so fiercely.

"If it were left to me," Harkwell told me, "I'd put them back, in the dark, where they should've stayed!"

But I didn't have to put them back. That night, I left the remaining volumes in full view in the open safe and the door to the office unlocked. I didn't need to wait. I knew the visitant would claim his goal.

Indeed, even as I turned back to extinguish the lamps, I saw some dark shadow move rapidly between the office and that corner door. And even in the darkness, I saw those white, grinning teeth and the heavy bundle it clutched to itself. And I also saw where it was no longer raw and red, where brown and wrinkled skin had been pressed and moulded to the form, in rough, ragged patches.

By morning, the books were gone, and the library was in uproar yet again. Yet the Dean was a rational man, with no stomach for flights of fancy.

"All this ridiculous talk of ghostly burglars and cursed books among the students must be stopped. This all smacks of some prank to disrupt the building works. Yes, that's it. A prank. Those ridiculous red prints on the safe? The books were placed in the ground by troublemakers with intent to provoke the kind of gossip which they're now causing. Valuable? They didn't even take the pages, just ripped the covers off! Grief, man, you've been taken in by forgeries! Should the ringleaders be found, they shall be dealt with most severely!"

Thus, our unimaginative Dean concocted his own flight of fancy, which I think he might even have believed, though he did swiftly alter the site of his proposed building works.

As to the hollow in the cellar floor, it was filled in as quickly as the workers could be summoned to carry out the task. They reported that it had been disturbed, somewhat. That some of the clay had been clawed at—that possibly some subterranean creature had emerged to cover up the entrance to its burrow, for the narrow tunnel beyond the hole had apparently collapsed in on itself.

Something had returned to the darkness.

«« —»»

As Mr. Perdew's account came to a close, Lawrence felt obliged to offer him some reassurance. "It is a remarkable tale, my friend. Though I can see why you have chosen not to spread the story. But, the pit is sealed; the visitant has what he came back for. You must put these things to the back of your mind, as nothing more than an unpleasant memory. Can you let fear prey on your mind still?"

He looked at the doctor as if he had failed to grasp the point of anything he had yet been told. "This isn't fear," he said. "Not in the way you mean it." And he turned toward that corner door, beyond which Lawrence could easily believe something might lurk.

"I do not often think of it," he told the scholar, "though it sometimes forces its way through in my darkest dreams. I do not even know if it lies down there, cocooned in that hollow beneath the cellar floors, or if it has returned to some other unknown grave. I do not know if it lies easy, or if it is awake still. I merely know that I do not want to disturb it further.

"I hope that it has found some peace now, and some comfort—that it is at rest finally...in its own skin."

The Mound

As was his habit each evening before retiring, Mr. Elmsmore stood at the balcony of his upper floor study and looked out over the grounds of his estate. This open air ritual was a necessary pleasure before bedtime—his wife being of that breed of woman who cannot abide tobacco smoke in the house. Through the haze of his own smoke, the scene he was forced to gaze upon was no hardship to endure. To the West he could survey his avenue of yew trees leading to the fountain imported, at no little expense, from Italy, and the walled garden. To the East, there was the orchard and summerhouse, wherein he would sometimes risk a cigar or pipe. Straight ahead, beyond the yew walk, was the rose garden. He had, at one point, considered a hedge maze, but an old school friend of his had once had rather an unpleasant experience in a maze, so Mrs. Elmsmore's roses had won their place.

Few things, particularly at this late stage in his life, gave Mr. Elmsmore as much pride and satisfaction as surveying this vista that had been so radically transformed during the first few years of his tenancy. Admittedly the actual labour in reshaping the overgrown wasteland had not been his, but the vision and the planning were all his own. He had conceived the design, chosen the flowers and plants, and had been on hand to guide the gardeners and grounds-men at every stage.

It struck Elmsmore that no living soul knew his gardens as thoroughly as he; that he was familiar with each individual blade of grass on the perfectly smooth and even lawn and, though he never much favoured roses, with every petal as well as every thorn in the rose garden. He prided himself that he was so keenly attuned with his privately grown Eden, he could instantly spot the slightest irregularity, be it the beginnings of a wilt in the shrubbery, or the first speckles of blight on the foliage.

It was, therefore, with a combination of acute surprise and indignation that his passing eye detected the first inkling that his lawn was not so perfectly smooth and even after all.

In the silvery moonlight that spilled out across the lawn, just there, to the left of the yew alley, was a ridge of shadow that could only be cast by some irregularity, like an upraised hummock. It was rather too distant to distinguish just how high and how long this hummock might be and, in truth, there was only just the merest sliver of a shadow to suggest that it was even there in the first place. But that sliver may as well have been a sliver of wood piercing his skin and nagging dully away, for the irritation it gave rise to in Elmsmore was such that he abandoned his hitherto savoured smoke unfinished and returned indoors with his temper considerably sharpened.

Of course he would speak to Galton, his head gardener, first thing in the morning to ascertain the cause of the disturbance and remedy it immediately. But the morning was a long way off, and sleep was elusive and only fleetingly attained.

Mr. Galton, a sturdy, solid sort of fellow, with a smile rarely far from his lips, and hands that were never free from the grime of honest toil, shook his head in puzzlement when Mr. Elmsmore had described the situation. Out of the possible causes, he could discount moles, of that he could guarantee and Elmsmore had no doubts whatsoever to the man's vigilance. The grass had been freshly cut so he could not imagine it being a shadow cast by some overgrown clump. "Perhaps it's some natural reaction below the soil," he ventured, as he and his employer strode out across the lawn. "Maybe some build up of natural gases? You never can tell with some of them newer fertilisers, Mr. Elmsmore, sir."

But Elmsmore was not listening. He was fully engaged in trying to pinpoint the spot where the problem lay. It was to the left of the nearest yew, just slightly forward, as he pictured it, and he pictured it all too clearly. Yet here he was, approaching that very spot, now standing directly above it, now circling around it, finally squatting as low as a slightly arthritic knee and a waistline that had expanded by slow but steady means since his retirement would allow. And all the time Galton watched him closely, with only the slightest hint of bemusement showing itself in his amiably obedient smile.

Of the hummock, or mound, or whatever the irregularity may have been, there was no trace. Not in the place where he was certain he had sighted it. Nor was it in the area immediately surrounding the spot. Had he, in fact, seen anything, or were his eyes beginning to succumb to age as much as his knees were? A triumphant memory of the preceding Saturday's golf match against his godson and some other younger associates drove that suspicion from his mind.

Perhaps he had simply been fatigued, or the smoke from his cigarette had gotten into his eyes. Yes, those struck him as two perfectly rational explanations and Mr. Elmsmore was not possessed of the type of mind that allowed a rational explanation to go by without seizing upon it.

Thus, happy that everything in the garden was, if not rosy, at least regular, Elmsmore went about his daily routine of being a man of leisure. Yet, as content as he should by rights have been at dismissing this unwarranted deformity from his view, there remained a lingering doubt that his eyes had, in fact, deceived him. And this doubt lingered long enough to evolve into solid certainty so that, by the time of his evening cigarette, he was avidly scanning the lawn for telltale shadows. It would have been difficult for Mr. Elmsmore himself to declare whether it was a groan of disappointment or a gasp of relief when, at last, his eyes fixed upon the shape on the grass.

That was why he had been unable to locate it! The blasted thing was more in line with the alley itself, and just a little closer to the house than he had recalled. He was surprised that they had managed to avoid stumbling across it on their way to and from the wrong spot, as it seemed that much longer and steeper than he had previously believed, with edges that were rounded, like a definite mound, long and narrow.

He made sure to take mental note of where it lay in relation to what was behind and to either side of it, before returning indoors for another night with some sleep but little rest.

Mr. Galton, who had slept a sound night, was somewhat surprised to have his breakfast interrupted by an urgent summons to step lively and follow his employer, who scarcely allowed the gardener time to gulp down the last of his tea before stalking stiffly off toward the yew alley.

When Galton caught up, he found Mr. Elmsmore looking even more perplexed than he had when the two had parted the day before. Yet again he paced and peered, prodded the ground and, for one alarming moment, Galton even feared that the retired gentleman was going to throw himself on his belly in the still dew-damp grass, the better to examine the ground at closer quarters.

"It seemed to me," Elmsmore said uncertainly, having obviously decided to keep his dignity intact and his suit-front unblemished, "that it was coming from the direction of the summerhouse, but I can think of nothing there to cause such a thing."

"Nothing there now," was Galton's response, though he clearly regretted voicing the thought the instant the words had passed his lips.

"Oh, that? Why it was only an old well, just like any other. Rather more stagnant than some, perhaps, but that's why we drained and sealed it."

To this Galton nodded, though he might have added that it wasn't Mr. Elmsmore that had attended to the drainage, or had subsequently been sickened by the stench of the putrid water for days afterwards. Nor was it his employer that had hauled out the mass of bones that had lain festering down there: mostly sheep that must have wandered too close to the crumbling edge of the well, though weren't some of the bones too large for a sheep? But of these unpleasant memories Galton said nothing, venturing only that the noxious waters that had fed the well might have taken a new course below the lawn, and there was no telling what influence such sub-terranean motion may be having on the soil above.

Another rational explanation was therefore seized, though from Elmsmore's mood as the day progressed and nightfall loomed ever closer, we may assume that he seized it with a less than steady grasp. And, were we to view him as he stood upon the balcony, his nocturnal cigarette smouldering to ash between his fingers, we would observe a dazed expression fix itself upon his face. And, were we to follow his gaze, our eyes would alight upon the mound, which was clearly not in line with the yews and far nearer the house than he had described it.

In fact there was little about the raised portion of lawn that corresponded to his mental picture. Whereas before it had seemed like a narrow ridge, it now appeared both wider and longer than a man. Even as he calculated this, Mr. Elmsmore instantly had the impression that what he was looking at was, in fact, a grave—an unmarked burial mound that, night after night, approached that degree closer to the house or, and Elmsmore would never normally be described as a superstitious man, encroached upon one of the house's inhabitants.

The next morning saw Galton left to finish his breakfast uninterrupted, for Elmsmore had no wish to embarrass himself further by insisting on the existence of graves that crept stealthily across nighttime lawns and dissolved away by the light of dawn. And so he trudged, quite unaccompa-nied, to the place where he suspected nothing out of the ordinary would remain to be found, and left moments later in the same way.

In the days that followed, Mr. Elmsmore's temper was as short as his nightly vigils were long. Though he spent hours staring out across the darkened grounds, he consistently failed to pinpoint the precise moments when the mound would either emerge or subside, either by arriving at the window too late, or by nodding off as dawn tinged the sky, during which moments he succumbed to the most horrible dreams, wherein he felt the blackness of the tomb closing in on him.

His subsequent exhaustion was shown most dramatically in that moment when he lost his temper with his wife who, after apparently sharing his alarm at the disruption to their idyll, had laughed it off dismissively the instant she was assured that her roses were in no imminent danger. The marriage, which had long been an affair of polite tolerance and vague affection rather than anything closer, became distinctly cooler after raised voices crossed the dining table and Mrs. Elmsmore, despite a token placatory effort from her husband, decided that a long weekend with her city cousins would be in order. It is undoubtedly for this reason that whatever befell Mr. Elmsmore remained undiscovered for quite so long.

It was Galton who first sighted the curious bulge in the shadow of the bush by the porch. "Why, look here, Roberts," he said to his assistant, "if that isn't the very disturbance His Nibs was insistent upon us dealing with? Well, no wonder we couldn't find it. It's practically in the house, nowhere near where he indicated. It's a shame he's not here to see it, but you fetch the spades, and we'll have it sorted out nice and proper for his return."

It was frequently Mr. Elmsmore's habit to disappear into the city for days at a time, for, though he was retired, he still held several consultancy posts that might call upon his services at a moment's notice. It was on a business trip such as this that Mrs. Elmsmore had naturally presumed him to be upon returning and finding no trace of him in the house. But, several days having passed, and not a word of his return having been received, had made even that redoubtable lady anxious. For it was surely anxiety that had brought about the creeping sensation that something unwholesome was festering in their safe haven. Of course she confided none of these fears with any of the staff.

Mr. Galton, who was not one given to entertaining nameless fears, was nevertheless glad of some hard, honest labour with shovel and soil, following a number of days spent dealing with unexpected moulds and withering on a fair few species of plant, as well as some wanton vandalism to the fencing adjoining the neighbouring farm. And his sleep, which always came easily after a long day's efforts, had been disturbed more than once by some distant noise, as though a fox had gotten into a farmyard, or the dogs had got scent of something they did not like.

Here though, was something to get your back into, and the two men set about it with gusto. The soil was loose and shifted easily, and Galton and Roberts were soon digging deeply, until something hard jarred the edge of the younger man's shovel. The dirt on the object was easily rubbed away and it was revealed as a torch, now quite twisted and useless. How it had come to be there, neither man could fathom. A quick dusting away of soil confirmed that it had been Mr. Elmsmore's own torch, and that it could not have been in the ground more than days given its lack of rust.

If he had been carrying a torch, reasoned Galton, he had to have gone out after dark. And, with a horrible jolt, the gardener recalled that night just the previous weekend. It was just as the moon had peeped out over the big house, and Galton had been walking back toward his cottage when he'd heard a noise that he'd put down to the wind shrilling in the trees. He attempted to shrug the memory away but, when he thought more closely, that sound had sent him scurrying home all the quicker, and it now struck him as more of a cry than the shriek of the wind: a cry of horror, and something much worse that followed it.

With a moan of apprehension, the gardener dropped his spade and pulled Roberts back, away from the pit. But it was too late, for the younger man's last lunge had unearthed something white and pale and quite still, and, torn about and encrusted with dirt as it was, it was instantly recognisable to both men as the remnants of a human hand.

By the time the village sergeant and two constables had done and a doctor had been called out to attend to both Mrs. Elmsmore and young Roberts, the whole mound had been excavated and Mr. Elmsmore, what there was of him, was exhumed and taken for examination. The digging had also uncovered a shovel, its shaft splintered into matchsticks. This discovery, along with the torch, gave Galton an all too clear idea of his employer's last act: striding out in the dark, determined to root out the problem once and for all.

What had awaited him in the dark, Galton could not say and refused to speculate upon. But, in his dreams, he saw the face of Mr. Elmsmore, the mouth wide in a scream that was choked forever by the soil that filled the shrieking maw. And he saw the torn clothing, and the torn flesh it no longer concealed, and the bones within. And he recognised the marks on those exposed bones as something he had witnessed once before, on those other bones they had dragged from the well. Then, as now, they were clearly the marks of teeth.

But, worse than the images that refused to fade, there was the memory of the sound that he had heard in the wake of that wind-borne cry. Quite simply, it was the sound of gleeful, gurgling laughter.

And the question that he feared to have answered was not, "What was it that had awaited Mr. Elmsmore at the heart of the mound?" It was, "What is it that has been let loose?"

The Beacon

The sea's rolling crash and the gusting shrieks of the storm roared in Dr. Pardoe's ears as he scrambled across the shingle and the slippery rocks. Not for the first time, he caught himself wondering why he'd ever left the city for such a spot. In a city there was order. Here, nature gave no heed to order, at least not that imposed by man. Of course, following a dozen or more years as junior partner in a handful of practices within the city, he had welcomed the chance for advancement. On his arrival, a few months prior, he'd thought himself fortunate to be stationed in such a beautiful seaside town. But he'd swiftly discovered that beauty can be deceptive and tempestuous; indeed, the tempest that now bore down on that stretch of coast was more than amply proving the point.

The doctor cursed softly, though he might have yelled his oath and gone unheard, as his foot slid and he felt his ankle bend badly. But a rough hand grabbed his and righted him again before he could do himself any genuine injury. When the moon momentarily glimmered through scudding clouds, Pardoe saw that it was Caleb Finn who had caught him. A good man, Caleb, according to all who knew him, and, in a town the size of Bleakfall, that was everyone. He'd been one of the first to rally the locals, just as soon as it had become clear that there was something badly wrong off the coast on this bitterly blustery night.

*When I looked back, I saw her, crawling with
what strength she had left in her, on her belly…*

Pardoe would have thanked the man, but that fleeting moon had also revealed something further down the beach. Though the wind whipped his breath away as soon as he opened his mouth, he called out, "Bring that lantern round, man! I saw something," before racing toward the dark shape he had perceived.

Caleb, used to being heard over blustering winds while out at sea, yelled back to the men that followed in his wake, "Get that light to the doctor."

Pardoe was pointing, "Look! Look there! On that sandbank!"

Once a lantern was thrust into his hand, Caleb saw the shape the doctor meant, but still he shook his head. "On a night such as this, it'd take more'n a row boat, Dr. Pardoe."

Pardoe raced on. "If there's one survivor, that's one more than I'd hoped for!"

Caleb was at the doctor's shoulder as they reached the small wooden vessel, beached on the ridge of sand. He let the lantern's beam play across the boat's interior and both men groaned. There was no-one there, and nothing but a sack or a length of canvas—a sack which moved suddenly, causing Caleb to let out a gasp of, "Something's alive under there." But it was Pardoe's hand that whipped away the torn sacking to reveal the ashen face of the boy who cowered, shivering in the bottom of the boat.

"Please, no! Keep away," cried the youth as he made a lunge for the rough covering fabric.

The doctor gripped the boy's wrist, gently drawing him out of the waterlogged vessel. His voice was soft yet clear over the dying wind, "You're quite safe, I swear. Come out from under there, into the light."

The words jolted the lad into sudden alertness, and he sat up abruptly, a look of anxiety flashing in his eyes. "The light," he cried. "I have to get to the light!"

"That's it," soothed Dr. Pardoe, beckoning for Caleb to hand the lamp to him. "Into the light, where I can examine you."

The youth, giving no indication of having heard him, struggled to his feet, though he was too weak to remain standing for more than a few seconds. "No-one's seen to the light. If there's a storm..."

"If there's a storm?" Caleb echoed. "If? Is he blind and deaf?"

But the doctor waved him to be quiet, hissing, "It's shock. The poor lad's traumatised."

The youth attempted to regain his feet, though once he had reached them he merely stood swaying. His voice was desperate as he insisted, "If I don't get back, there'll be hell to pay. I must get back!"

Dr. Pardoe followed the boy's gaze down the length of the beach and out to sea. "Back? You can't go back to the ship."

The youth turned sharply toward him, his voice rising. "A ship? They aren't safe in the fog. They need warned!"

Something in the tone made the doctor pause, before asking, "You were on the Alexandra, weren't you?"

"No, sir. Not on a ship. I was at Drearcliff."

The doctor gaped. Could this lad really have come from Drearcliff? To have survived on such a night, over such a distance? He almost laughed. Drearcliff was the lighthouse, which clung to its rock some six miles out to sea.

"Hold that lantern steady, doctor," grunted Caleb, thrusting his face forward to look closely at the youth. "Hang on, there. Is that young Arthur Flannen? What are you doin' here, Arthur? Why'd you risk comin' out in a storm like this, lad?" The lad, Arthur, merely stared dumbly. "What's the trouble out on the rock? Where's old man Vernon and Fred Douglas?"

Dr. Pardoe lightly eased himself between Caleb's insistent questioning and the barely conscious boy. He used his most soothing tone, the one he used for panicking first time mothers, or the mothers for whom he had only the worst of news. "Arthur, is it? Can you tell us what happened, Arthur?" He could see from the boy's eyes that his mind was far away, yet, even so, he persisted, "Arthur?

"Can you hear me, Arthur?"

But, for the boy, it was not the doctor's voice that he heard, nor was it the shriek of the storm that whistled in his ears, or the chilly fog that swirled and glistened around him.

«« —»»

"Arthur?"

My mind had been wandering, and it was with a start that I heard my name called. I tried to fan away the white, misty vapour that was all around me.

"The kettle, Arthur! If I'd asked for a roomful of steam and a dry mug of tea leaves, you'd be doing a fine job," chuckled Mr. Douglas.

"I must've been dreamin'." And I pulled the kettle from the grate and poured a couple of mugs. "Sorry, Mr. Douglas."

Mr. Douglas shook his head, and he added an extra sugar or two to his tea. "How many more times? It's Doug. Just Doug. We can't be getting all formal out here."

Just as he said it, the door to the crew quarters opened, and Mr. Vernon strode in, checking his pocket watch and nodding to Mr.... to Doug. "That's the quarter to the hour and a mist rising thick, Mr. Douglas."

Doug gave me a sly wink. "Well, not all of us are formal."

Mr. Vernon nudged Doug's feet down off the table, where he always rested them when he was reading. "And we're not all lazing about with our noses in books, letting others wait on us hand and foot."

I handed the old man his mug—four sugars, just as he liked it. He thanked me, saying, "You're a good lad. Don't let that be your downfall," before scowling again at Doug.

I'd been stationed out at Drearcliff lighthouse for near two months, just about time for me to hand over to my relief. Truth is, this was my first time in such a job, but it wasn't too big a chore, and I was lucky with the men I was stationed with. Vern... Mr. Vernon, that is, was steeped in the tradition, conscientious and as solid as the rock the lighthouse sat on.

"What's this you're ignorin' your duties for, Mr. Douglas?" said he, picking up the book and flicking through it, pulling a face and saying, "Not more ghosty stories, Doug?"

Doug took the book back and placed it on a shelf, saying, "Don't you go worryin' about that, Vern. You just leave the reading to those that can."

See, that was Doug. He liked to act as if the world was all a bit of a joke, though he was always ready to muck in when called upon. Good thing, too, since Mr. Vernon would have taken bad against him otherwise. But the two got on, in their way.

"Aye, well," Vern told Doug, "it'll be you reading your name in the report if I don't see you looking a bit more lively. I don't know, you and your ghosts."

Doug settled himself back in his seat again, smiling, "Don't need no other ghosts with you haunting this place, eh, old un? Should've taken you out when they got rid of the oil lantern up there!" Then he turned to me and said, looking all serious, except in his eyes, "I'm telling you, when I used to go on watch, I had to light a match to tell if the lamp was lit."

But Vern just ignored him, taking a long sup of his tea, before saying, "I've never had no complaint over them putting in the electrics, and you know it, Fred Douglas. But that generator downstairs takes more coal than my back can handle. One of you will have to go and top her up."

Not that Doug was paying any heed. "I was just getting to a good bit in my story, here. See, the squire in his big old house has just caught glimpse of somethin' in the moonlight, creepin' across his lawn. Somethin' that belongs more in a churchyard than a country garden..."

I felt kind of strange, listening to Doug's story, so I tried to make my excuses and go to get seeing to the coal. But Vern must've spotted that I wasn't feeling right in myself, because he asked me if all was well, saying, "You look like you've..."

"...Seen a ghost?" Doug was grinning and pointing at his book. "Just like the old squire?"

Vern gave him an evil look. "Now, don't you let Doug's daft stories scare you, son. That's all they are, stories. Can't see what joy he gets from 'em, but folks is folks, and tastes is tastes, I suppose."

It wasn't that, I told them. "I can tell the difference between a story and what's real."

But Doug was smart. He'd guessed what was in my head. "And you're wondering if the tales you've heard about this place are real or just stories?"

Of course, I tried to laugh at the idea. "Who said I'd heard any tales?"

There was no getting past him, though. "If you hadn't, you'd be the only one who's ever visited this stretch of coast and not heard them."

Vern nodded. He had that look in his eye that folks get when they're thinking of other times or places. "I was here with old Turner, who gave the job up when they took out the candles and started using oil for the lamp. Well, he was probably going a bit soft in the head—bit like Doug, here..."

"Funny," Doug muttered. "No, really. Most amusing, Vern."

"But he'd heard stories, Turner had, from back when even he was a kid. This has always been a fearsome spot. Many's a ship has sailed treacherous seas a thousand times over and still come to grief here. From pirates or smugglers, to the odd show-off with more money than respect for the waves and the weather. That's why it's reckoned the sea here's haunted. There's so many dead down under them waves, there's bound to be them as comes back. And when they do, they come back angry!"

Angry? I couldn't understand why they'd be angry.

But Doug had his notions as to why. "They're angry because they reckon they died too soon! Some died so sudden, they don't even know they're dead. They're still out there, drifting, trying to make it back to a shore they'll never reach. I reckon that'd make them more than angry. That it'd drive any soul mad, living or dead!"

Vern was nodding away. "Turner told me there were ships seen riding them waves that had gone down to the bottom years before. Said he'd seen the skull an' bones flying, and seen crews that weren't much more'n skull an' bones theirselves! That on the worst nights, through the wind and the roar of the water, you could hear the crashes of them ships as they hit the rocks, and the screams of them onboard, going through it all again and again, and never able to escape those final, fearful moments."

In my head, I reckoned I could hear distant crashes, ones that echoed over and over. So what Doug said next near made me jump. "Like an echo, they are, sounding down through the years."

Vern was walking back and forth, now, and I couldn't keep my eyes off him. His voice had gone low, like what he was telling was a secret. "Some nights, I'd be stood up in the lamp-room with him, keeping an eye on the wicks, and he'd go tense, like a dog sensing something us folks can't hear. "Listen, Vern," he'd say. "The damned are sailing tonight..." Most of all I'd just hear the blusterin' of the storm but, on some nights, I would be lying if I said I didn't hear what sounded to me like cries of mortal terror and the splinterin' of timbers."

Those words stuck in my mind. "The damned are sailing..."

"Mind you," Vern said, his voice normal now, and him laughing to himself, "he did also say he saw a mermaid once, crawl out of the sea onto the rocks, so I wouldn't take what Turner said as gospel."

Doug was laughing too, though I wasn't sure if it was at Vern's story or the look on my face. "Aye! He put it about he had the second sight. Ended up breakin' his neck when he was blind drunk."

"Now, you shouldn't mock them what's gone, Doug... Mind, if he'd had the sight, he'd've seen that flight of stairs before he hit the bottom."

I had to join in with their laughing. Aye. These were all just daft stories!

Then Vern clapped his hands, the way he always did when there was work needing done, and it was business again. "You get up there to that lamp, Doug. Should've been on watch five minutes since."

Doug saluted, then bowed down low. "Going, your Majesty! Arthur, you'd best get that coal shovelled before he has you walk the plank."

"Aye, aye, sir," said I, and went out of our quarters and onto the stairs. I was near down to the furnace when I noticed the smell. Like the sea, but somehow gone foul. I was wondering what could be the cause, and I can't have been paying much attention to where I was going, because it took a minute for me to realise that something had passed me on the stairs! It just slid round by me, like a shadow, or something damp and slippery!

In seconds I was back in the crew quarters, with the other two looking at me like I was mad when I tried to tell them what it was I saw. Vern turned on Doug, snarling at him, "Look what you've done to the boy, with your ghosts!"

"You and your phantom pirate ships, more like!" Doug came back. Then, to me, trying to calm me, I suppose, "It's just like you said, Arthur. Just a shadow. The lamp can send funny shapes past your eyes."

But that didn't explain the smell, so Vern joined in, saying, "Imagination! You were thinkin' of ghosts and the like, and your mind done the rest."

"He's right, Arthur," Doug said, calm again now. "There's nothin' there. Besides, we're more than a half dozen miles from land. It's not like anything's going to come prowling here, is it?"

I thought on this, and I had to reckon they were right, and I was just being daft. Just an ignorant, superstitious country lad, thinking I was seeing things. So, when I heard it, I bit my tongue and said nothing to the others. It was only when Doug, all tensed up, asked, "What was that?" that I was set to admit that my ear had caught that distant pounding, like something striking against wood, not once, but regular and becoming more rapid, more persistent. There was only one thing it could be. There was something at the door!

Doug, even though he'd heard it, wasn't having this. "It can't be the door! We're miles offshore."

But, when we listened, amongst the wind and the pounding and the generator chugging away below us, there was a voice, and it was pleading, "Help me, please..."

It was Vern who came to his senses first. "The boy's right, Doug. It is the door!"

"We'd better go and answer it," I told them, for all that time we were stood there, I could hear that beseeching voice. "There's someone there, and they're needing our help!"

"You're right, Arthur! Good lad," said Doug, moving all of a sudden. "Keeping the head! Good lad!" And he went for the flare gun, telling Vern, "If it's some of your perishing pirates come to loot us for treasure, they're not getting my tobacco, my tea or my biscuits!"

Then we were running down the stairs, down to the ground level, where the big, old generator rattled away to itself, and the furnace made everything glow redder than them pits we were always warned about in Sunday services. But when we reached the bottom, we weren't running anymore, and Doug was whispering, "It's gone quiet." And it had. There was no pounding at the door, nor no voice crying out to us. After a minute, listening as we all were, he whispered again, "I reckon it was just the wind. It can make some peculiar noises, it can."

Vern's voice was hushed too. "I never heard wind do that before," he said. Then, "Besides, if it is the wind, why are we whispering?"

"Well, it's..." Doug said, all quiet, till he saw Vern grinning at him. "Funny, Vern." Then we were at the door, bracing ourselves against it to stop the gale blowing through and putting that furnace out.

When the bolts were drawn, we let the door open a crack, and even through that tiny gap, the din of the wind and the waves was something fierce to endure. But we opened it further, half expecting...well, I don't know what we were expecting to see.

Finally, it was Doug that yelled, "See? Nothing there but the fog."

"Please..? Help... I saw the light!"

The voice... Her voice came out of that mist, and it seemed to drown out the storm and the waves. At first, we couldn't even see her, then two dark eyes and a mouth formed out of the fog, and a hand was reaching out, damp and cold. She was all in white, and pale from the cold. Her hair so blonde and fine, it scarce showed up against the haze, and it wasn't till she was near over the threshold that we saw it was plastered to her white skin, soaking wet from more than just the mist.

"Lord help her," Vern gasped, "she's been in the water!" Then he was giving orders. "Get her upstairs, quick, into the warm. Blankets and hot tea, Arthur! Doug, get on the telegraph and find if any ship's reported in trouble or gone down! She can't have swum all this way! I'll check if there's a boat or anyone else dragged theirselves ashore!"

But Doug's eyes were fixed on the shivering girl who'd washed up on our doorstep. "Miss? Was there anyone else? Miss?"

Her voice was soft but clear. "So cold," she said. "I came to the light."

Vern nudged Doug, telling him, "You won't get anything from her in that state. I'll go out an' check."

Doug passed him the lantern and the flare, saying, "Good luck, Vern! And careful!"

Vern was already in his oilskins and heading outside, but he winked back, "Always am, Douggie! That's how I got to be so old! Now close this door behind me, but don't bolt it. I don't want to be out there any longer'n needs be!"

I heard the wind dropping away as Doug closed the door below us. The girl followed me up toward the crew quarters, her bare feet soft and wet on the stairs. She hardly seemed to be watching, or even to know where she was or where we were going, and when she stumbled, I had to grab hold of her arm. Lord, she was cold!

"So cold," she said, as if she'd heard my thoughts. "I had to get to the light. So dark..."

Trying to sound more reassuring than I felt, I told her, "You're safe, and we'll soon have you warm and dry."

Her laugh, when I said this, wasn't a nice sound to hear. "I'll never be dry again."

Once we were in the quarters, I opened up the grate on the range to let more heat into the room, and Doug found us some old blankets. They were rough and worn, but they were at least warm. So I wrapped them round her shoulders, and sat her down in a chair, saying, "Maybe you can tell us where you come from, Miss..?"

"Alexandra..."

Was that her name? I repeated it back to see if it'd help get some sense from her. "Alexandra?"

But she wasn't looking at me. "On the rocks," she whispered. "All drowned... Alexandra..."

It was Doug who reckoned he knew what she was saying. "The Alexandra's that yacht: Lord Livermere's one. I've seen you with him, haven't I, miss? What's your name, now?"

"Madeline."

《《——》》

"That was the name she said," the shivering lad in the boat insisted, and when he repeated the name, he shivered all the more. "Madeline."

"So, she come back, did she?" rumbled Caleb. "Thought she would."

Pardoe, aware once more that he was a stranger amongst a community in which it might take years for him to be fully accepted, waited for the fisherman to explain. "Lordship's pretty young lady. You must've seen the two of them in the park, doctor. Her in her bonnets and laces, him with his dandy airs and city clothes, and that stick of his with the fancy gold head, twirling it like a parasol, like he were in Paris.

The doctor, whose work didn't leave him much time to stroll in the park, nonetheless had an idea of who was meant. "Though wasn't the gossip that she'd left him? Run off and married some rich Italian, or some such thing?"

"So they say," grunted Caleb, "but she had a passion for him, strong and fierce. I heard her myself, sayin' nothin' would come between them, so it's no surprise she came back."

"In time for this tragedy," reflected the doctor. "The poor wretch."

"Think o' them other poor wretches, doctor. She was lucky to get out of it alive."

"Lucky?" repeated Pardoe. "It was little short of a miracle." Then he turned once more to the shivering lad, urging," Did she tell you how she'd managed it, Arthur? Did she tell you anything at all?"

Arthur nodded, his numb lips stuttering over the words. "She told me her name. Madeline..."

《《——》》

I'd wrapped her up as well as I could but the poor lass wasn't getting any warmer. I tried to coax her to take some hot, sweet tea, but it was like she stared through me, through the walls, into the storm that had brought her there.

"Telegraph's not working," Doug complained. "Something's got into the wiring. I'll have a look." And he started trying to shift the heavy machine.

I'd never trusted the machine, myself. I'd heard electrics can do bad things to a man. "Maybe you ought to get the manual?"

"I've read it, cover to cover. Twice."

"You like your books." I'd never much been one for reading. Didn't have the brains for it.

"When I get peace to read them," Doug admitted. "You'd have thought that wouldn't be too difficult on a rock in the middle of the sea, wouldn't you?"

"He reckons that's why he came out here." The voice from the door near made us both jump. We never even heard Vern come up the stairs, but there he stood, dripping wet. "Lookin' for peace to read his books, he was. Not ghosty stories in them days. Text books. Medical."

"Are you a doctor, Doug?"

"I look like one, don't I?" he grunted, still trying to shift the telegraph.

"He was doin' the training," Vern told me. "A university lad, this one."

Doug tried to wave Vern away, saying, "I didn't finish the course. Never will now. I'll be stuck out here till they carry me off the rock in a crate."

"Aye, well, Dougie," Vern said, smiling in that gentle way of his. "I reckon you've saved more people by bein' 'ere than you ever would've done as a doctor."

"Well," Doug said, pushing past and going out, looking a

bit red in the cheeks, despite his trying to hide it. "I'd best get a screwdriver and have a look inside this thing."

"You do that, Doug. On your way, lad," said Vern, then he turned to me and his smile was gone. "I need to go back out there. I reckon I saw something."

If there were more survivors, I wanted to help, but Vern told me there was no need, that he'd just come back for a brighter lantern, and that I was to see to the furnace. So I went, and I could just hear Vern, as I went, asking the girl, Madeline, if she was cold.

Shovelling that coal was hard work, right enough. With the lifting and the heat from the furnace, you'd be coated in sweat within minutes, normally. But there was a chill in the air this night that weren't shifting.

I'd just stopped to catch my breath when there was a clatter on the stairs, and Vern came round. He looked to be staggering a bit, and he was mumbling something to himself. I asked if he was ill, he looked so green in the face, but he just shoved past me, that look of something far off in his eyes again, muttering that something was not right, not right at all... Then he was gone, out into the storm, slamming the door at his back.

I'd never seen Vern look so fearful. In another man I'd have reckoned it was the storm that had got to him, but he'd kept things turning through worse than this, I knew. Yet there was something, and I had the notion I'd best go check all was well above.

When I stepped into the quarters, Doug was hunched at the machine, working away at a panel in the back. I asked if he'd seen Vern, but he shushed me, pointing to the figure curled up in a chair. "I think our guest's sleeping. I only just got back. Vern gone off again, then?" But he didn't wait for an answer, and was taking off that loosened panel. I was going to warn him against electrical shocks, but what he found inside was a shock of a different kind.

"All the wiring rusted through," he said, peering in close at the slimy, brown mess inside the cabinet, then drawing his head back quick, his nose all wrinkled. "And that smell? Salty. Like it had been a long time in the sea."

I had an idea that smell was familiar, but there were more urgent things, so I let it slip. "If the telegraph's broken, we'd best send up a flare and let the mainland know there's a ship down."

Vern had the launcher, so Doug set off for the stairs. "See if herself can tell you any more, like where the Alexandra went down, and how many was aboard."

I was suddenly worried for him, going out on his own like that. Vern had looked like something was after him. But Doug just laughed. "More of your shadows? I'll see if I can shout him back from the lamp-room! It's past time someone checked the lamp." And he went, leaving me with the girl, who should've been sleeping, but didn't rest.

"Is he drowned?" she cried, sitting up suddenly. "He must be!" Then she grasped her head, as if it hurt something vicious.

I tried to calm her and her fears for his Lordship. "We don't know that! He might be alive, still. Are you sure you're all right, now? You need to sleep!" But before I could get her settled back, I heard Doug calling from above.

"I can't sleep, and I don't want to be alone," she was insisting, but Doug's yells were getting all the more frantic, and I had to go to him. When I went, she was still talking, not noticing that I'd left her. "So cold. So all alone... Can't sleep!"

In the lamp-room, the great light turned on and on, but no sign of Doug was to be seen. Then, beyond the glass, outside on the platform, a figure was shown up dark and solid as the beam passed it. What was he doing out there? He knew how dangerous it was in these winds! But when I tried to tell him, his answer was, "It ain't safe anywhere, Arthur. Come out, lad. Come see!"

I didn't want to go out onto that narrow metal ledge. It barely felt safe enough on a calm day, but in this weather, it was suicide. So I begged him, my voice hoarse from trying to be heard, to show me what he'd seen so we could both get back inside!

"I saw what Vern saw, an' I know why he ran! She didn't come back alone, Arthur! There are more of them out there!"

51

The joy I felt nearly made me forget my own fear. "Vern found more survivors? We need to get down to help them!"

But Doug held me back, his grip tight, digging into my arm, before I could reach the door. "Don't open that!" His eyes were savage. "Don't dare!"

"But, if they're alive..."

"They're not alive," he screamed. "That's what I'm telling you! None of them! I've seen them out there! Look! Through the fog! See them? The sea's boiling with them! See, there? Crawling across the rocks!"

He'd grabbed me, pushing me to the railing, so that I had to grip with all the strength I had in me not to go over. He was pointing, down, amongst the dark rocks and the white masses of foam. Was there something? No! "It's just a shadow..." Then I remembered: the shadow on the stairs, and that reek of mould and decay!

Doug had me in his grip, but he was struggling to keep his footing, and I quickly broke free. I grabbed for the door, and the fury fled from him. Instead, he was crying. "Don't go back in there, son!"

But I knew that it was what I'd feared all along. There was something already inside! I couldn't stay out there. We had to go to Miss Madeline!

But Doug was begging now. "Leave her, Arthur! It's too late for her! We have to stay up here with the light!" I told him not to talk crazy, but he wasn't in any state to listen. "You're the crazy one, if you go back in there. The damned are sailing, and they are angry! Maybe they're angry with us for not saving them! Maybe they resent those who didn't succumb to the deep..."

"Those are just stories, Doug! You said as much yourself!"

"Maybe they don't like that we stop others from joining them down there. Perhaps the dead need company!"

I wanted, needed him to stop talking like that. Then, again, I saw some movement down below. I tried yelling. If it was Vern, maybe he could talk sense into Doug. But, no, it was just the fog rolling by. It had to be! And I needed to get in and see to Miss Madeline. I couldn't leave her alone down there. Alone with whatever else was inside already! "But I'm not leaving you here like this, Doug," I told him. "I don't want you dashed over, onto the rocks or into the sea!"

But Doug, poor, maddened Doug, was already lashing himself to the rails, yelling back, "Don't you panic over me. A strong belt and a sturdy set of railings'll see me fine."

I promised I would come back for him. I promised him that! But I didn't understand what he meant by his answer. "You might come back but will you still be you?" And I left him, screaming into the storm, and went down to who-knew-what?

"I was waiting," she said, when I went to the quarters. Doug's shouting had to have scared her. That had to be why she was cowering there, in the dark, crouched up and shivering. "So cold. So very cold…" So I thought.

"There's…" How could I tell her? After what she'd already been through, it might've scared her to death. "Well, something's happening, Miss. I don't know what it is, but whatever it is it's bad. Now, there's blankets. Here, I'll…" You could near see through her fancy dress, the way it clung to her. So I just pushed the blankets toward her so she could wrap herself, and told her, "You have to stay here. I'm going to turn this lantern up so it's lit up full. You aren't to let it burn down."

I was at the door before she turned to me. "Where are you going? Up to the light?"

"I've got to go below, see the generator's working and check the door is…well, just to check. You should be resting, but I need to ask you to keep your eyes open and watch for anything…strange. Even if it looks like only a shadow, I want you to yell down to me."

"Down? Down below?"

"That's right," said I. "Now, wrap yourself, like I say. You're still soaked through. I'll see if I can get some heat going. And don't let that light go out, like I said. I'll be back in no more than a minute or so."

And I left her, mumbling to herself in the dark.

The chill that filled the place was seeping in from the open door. I thought of going out and looking for poor Vern, I truly did, but the wind was like daggers, and the fog was a thick, grey curtain. I had to put my shoulder to the door to shut it, and it was freezing to touch. And the mist that curled round it was almost liquid, oozing and writhing and full of shadows. But, before it had finally closed to, there was a noise from above. It sounded like Doug, but what was it? A yell? A scream?

When I'd got back up, the quarters were dark, the lantern gone. I'd left my own down below and was cursing my carelessness when I saw the strange light approaching down the stairs, then the shadow that filled the doorway.

My breath caught in my throat, then I let it out in a laugh when I saw the gown and the pale hair, like a halo on one of the angels in the church window, only the face it framed was hidden in the dark. But, for a moment, I'd thought... Well, I can't say what I'd thought. Instead, I asked her, "What were you doing up there?"

"I went up with him before," she said, her voice still soft, remembering, "once, twice...a hundred times. It was our place. Our secret. Where no-one would intrude."

"In the lamp room, Miss? What were you doing? And I told you to keep that lantern up full, didn't I? I can barely see a thing... Miss Madeline?"

"I wanted to tell him there. I thought he'd be happy."

Her words had no meaning for me, and it was my own words that hit me with a force like the storm outside. "Can hardly see? But where's...?" Then I felt the panic. The lamp had gone out! There was always light on the stairway from the lamp! I yelled up to Doug, tried to run, but she was barring my way.

"He wasn't happy. Not at all! He said I'd ruin him!"

"What happened to the lamp? You were up there! The generator's working, so where's the light?"

But still she didn't hear me. Her mind was somewhere else. Some other place. Some other time. "Fire in his eyes! Blazing! Hateful! The words he used! Curses! Threats! I saw, then, that there was never really love there! And I wasn't fool enough to try to cling onto him. I would go. He'd never see me...see us! But the storm was in him, a fury I'd never seen. "But that won't be it, witch," he cried. "How long till the demands on my money and on my title...for something that likely isn't mine?" His words numbed me, so I never even felt the blow. I was so cold then...

"So cold and so dark. But we had a vow. We'd made our solemn oath that nobody could part us. But he said that I was a plaything, and nothing more! I was his to use at his leisure and discard when he saw fit, and I no longer amused or entertained him!"

I moved to shake her, to break her out of her trance. But then she turned and looked at me! And I saw!

I saw her face...what there was left of it, bloated and blistered and the colour of seaweed. Dead and bloodless, and the only living thing about it was some sea-dwelling thing with claws and legs that scuttled back into the dark between her hair and the broken bones.

Her voice had changed, too—become a croaking whisper. "It's so cold in the water. Cold and dark and deep... But our vow will not be broken! Our oath binds him to me, and what cannot be undone will be his undoing. Let's see how that amuses him, to be by my side forever more...Down in the cold and the dark... We'll never be warm again. But we'll never be alone!"

And there was the thing she cradled in her arms. That thing that had never even truly lived! The thing that let out a cry: a wet, gurgling squeal that my own scream couldn't drown out.

I turned and I ran, and they were waiting, those shadows on the stairs! Only they weren't just shadows no more but people, or what was left of people. Rotted and wet and moving upwards. Up to the light!

Then came the voice, and it said to me, "Go! You don't need to stay here." It was Vern! He was among them, and I knew then that he'd gone, either into the sea or his heart had given out, for he was one of them now. "It's her, Arthur. Her passion! Her love and her hatred. That's what's drawn them—drawn us, us that doesn't rest easy in the deep. You go. You don't belong."

When I looked back, I saw her, crawling with what strength she had left in her, on her belly, using one arm to claw her way up the stairs toward the lamp-room, the other to cradle her squirming bundle. The darkness at the top of the stairs parted for her, splitting into more of those shadows that followed in her wake, then swallowed her up.

I ran, not caring about the dying generator, not thinking about Doug, be he alive or dead, and I just kept going till I was out, into the boat we kept tied alongside, and into the storm.

Something bumped alongside the boat. I looked over the side and I saw Vern, face down, floating. I could do nothing for him now, so I kept on rowing and, when I looked up toward the lighthouse, I could see them all there, all those shades and shapes, fillin' the lamp-room, blotting out whatever light there was...

Then there was the noise, the crashing and the screams, timbers splintering and yells of panic! And I knew this wasn't Vern's phantom echoes. This was a ship of the living running aground. Those screams, the cries for help in the dark, were real! There was no light, see? They'd swallowed the light in a dark sea of shadows! There was nothing to guide them.

Then the sky exploded, turned green...

《《——》》

Pardoe held a blanket round the shivering boy, trying to comfort him, but knowing that it was to no avail. "It was the distress flare from the Alexandra. In the sky. It was sighted from the shore. We came to help."

"No help for them," burbled the boy, his eyes focussed on something distant. "I heard them screaming for help, then getting quieter, then nothing. Just the water... It's so cold and dark and deep. So cold..."

Arthur Flannen's voice faded to a whisper, then was still. The doctor gathered the blanket as snugly round him as he could, reckoning sleep was the best thing for him, "After what he's been through."

"Then you believe his story?" urged Caleb, though there was no trace of incredulity in his own voice.

"He believes it," was Pardoe's only response. "But, there's only one way to find out what happened on Drearcliff. We have to go out there!"

By morning, after the storm had calmed, Caleb Finn's fishing boat made swift progress to the island, and they were soon pulling alongside. The crew remained on board as the doctor and the fisherman went ashore alone, neither man disposed to share their suspicions of what might be found once they reached that isolated tower.

There had been no word from the rescue boats, but this was no surprise to Caleb. "No-one came off Alexandra alive and hung on this long! And no answer to the telegraph from Drearcliff."

"If their machine's broken," Pardoe pointed out, "like the lad said..."

"That's if anything he's told us is true." By the light of day, the sturdy fisherman seemed less inclined to give the same credence to the story that he had on that darkened beach. So, the two trudged across the rocks in grim silence, until Caleb, shielding his eyes against the bright sunlight that had followed the storm, pointed ahead, announcing, "There! Look above! That's Doug!"

The doctor grinned in relief, squinting to see the figure on the platform high above them. "He is there, waving us on. Beckoning us in. But why does he stand at so odd an angle? Can you see?"

And with a groan of horror, Caleb saw. "It's his belt! He's lashed himself to the railings. And he ain't waving. He can't wave, poor devil. It's the wind caught his arm... That's no way for a man like him to have died!

"But this means the boy was right, Caleb. They did go mad. And if he was right in what he told us..." The rest of the thought was left unsaid.

The noise of the generator was a painful, arthritic wheeze, and it was clear to both that the furnace was nearly burned out. Resolving to attend to it before they left, they ascended the winding staircase, to see what awaited them above.

Even before they'd opened the door to the crew quarters, both could tell, by smell alone, that something was badly wrong within, and when the door was opened, the stench that flooded out was rank and rotted.

Dr. Pardoe was careful to keep the handkerchief pressed tightly over his mouth and nose with one hand, while he pointed with the other. "There, in the corner!"

They approached the pallid, hunched and bedraggled figure in the chair with caution, until Pardoe, close enough to be sure of his suspicions, told his companion, "She can't hurt us, Caleb. This girl didn't crawl from the sea tonight."

Caleb Finn was a strong-willed man, with a strong stomach, but he looked away quickly, his gorge rising. "If that's what Arthur saw looking back at him, well... I'm not sure I wouldn't have run screaming."

His training coming to the fore, Pardoe allowed the handkerchief to drop from his face as made his examination. "Grief, man, from the look of her, I'd say she'd been in the water for weeks."

"Two weeks," confirmed the fisherman. "That's how long since his Lordship said she'd run off. And all this time, she's lain in the deep, drowned."

But a brushing aside of some of the bleached strands that clung to the head gave Pardoe a clearer view of the young woman's demise. "I don't know that she did drown. Her skull's fractured. Look here."

"I'll not, if it's all the same," Caleb declared. "You don't reckon it was from hittin' the rocks, though, I can tell."

Having started out in a big city, Dr. Pardoe had been presented with little choice but to become adept at tracing the causes of violent death. "I'd say a heavy object delivered this blow. I might even venture to say it was a large, ornately carved cane head. In which case, it's murder. Two lives taken if that bulge in her belly is more than just gasses!"

Caleb heaved a great sigh, stating, "And now the murderer's at the bottom of the sea too. There'll be no justice for him."

"Not justice, no," admitted the doctor. "It's a harsh justice that takes innocent lives to bring down the guilty, and leaves someone's sanity in the balance... Maybe it's my sanity in the balance with what I'm reckoning! Don't you see, Caleb? It's as if her passion had turned her into a beacon for the other unhappy, angry dead to follow. Her need for revenge drew them out of these haunted waters, like moths to her flame... Mad, I know, but, however this ill-starred woman got here, her presence caused the light to be dimmed, just as the Alexandra most needed it, and brought death to her murderer!"

Caleb again recalled that overheard vow. "She always said nothin' would come between them."

"Then nothing will," resolved Pardoe. "Give me a hand, if you've the nerve for it. Having her here will prove nothing any inquest is going to accept. Into the sea with her. We'll never find her lover's remains, but I reckon she will. After that, neither time nor tide will separate them."

And after they were done, and their grim cargo was claimed once more by the waves that had carried her there, the two men looked back, toward the land. "That poor lad might recover," Pardoe said, "but I doubt he'll want to speak more of this. The inquest will say a fearful, tragic accident struck the Drearcliff beacon: that something in the food or in the drink caused the men to lose their minds."

"You mean," said Caleb, grasping for some kind of answer that would let him sleep easier that night, "maybe something in the water?"

"Yes. I'd say you were right, my friend," Pardoe told him, though he was less certain. In years to come, perhaps, he might grow to believe that they had hit upon the explanation. That some taint had gotten into the food or the water. That the poor creature's remains were simply washed up on that rock. And that the young lad, already poisoned and half-mad, as well as scared practically insensible by the legends of that place... Well, who knows how a discovery like that might have made him act?

But in his heart, he feared that there was another explanation, one that was contained in those very same words: that there was, indeed, something in the water.

"Shalt Thou Know My Name?"

As a collector of folklore and accounts of legend and superstition, my old friend, Dr. Lawrence, has long made it his duty to seek out the unusual and arcane, and for him such a find is generally cause for celebration. What is by and large less pleasing, indeed, often uncomfortably alarming, he once told me, is when the unusual and arcane seems actively to seek him. Lately, even his own rooms at the college have apparently provided no safe haven.

He had barely begun to make an in-depth study of a most interesting text, accompanied only by the reassuring crackle of the fire in the hearth and the soft whisper of the pages as they turned, when his musings were rudely disturbed by an insistent clamour.

Over the loud and frantic knocking on the study door, Lawrence heard a familiar shrill voice raised to an unfamiliar level. "Lawrence! Are you in? Open up if you're there, man!"

He laid aside his reading matter with a rueful sigh of, "So much for Night thirty-seven. How I'm ever to get through all one thousand and one at this rate..." but got no further with the thought when the pounding at his chamber door grew louder and the voice on the other side grew yet shriller, causing him to hasten his steps across the room in order to silence this commotion before it roused every fellow who lodged along the same corridor.

"Lawrence? Dr. Lawrence!"

Lawrence turned the key with a mutter of, "Hold on there, would you? I'm coming as fast as I can," though he had no very real desire to face the owner of that strident voice.

"Lawrence, thank providence!" cried his visitor when my friend finally did open the door, and the look of relief that flooded his face may have softened Lawrence's response just a little from the retort that he had been formulating.

"Dower! Are you trying to knock a hole through my study door? I have quite enough ventilation as it is."

Mr. Dower, for that was indeed the name this caller rejoiced in, looked at Lawrence and past him and all around himself in quick succession, while demanding, "Are you free to talk? You are alone, aren't you?"

"Well," Lawrence began, rather taken aback, since in all the years he had known Dower he could never once recollect hearing of him making a social call. In fact, from the description he gave me, social is not a word anyone could ever equate with this man, Dower. "Well, I suppose…"

"You suppose?" Dower practically spat the words, his eyes narrowing with a look Lawrence could only ascribe to suspicion. "You are either alone or not!"

"I was," Lawrence replied icily, before realising that bickering in the corridor would only prolong this encounter, not hasten it to a conclusion. With an inward sigh, he pushed the door wider and stepped back, saying, "Do come in, Dower. It is, as always, a pleasure."

"What?" exclaimed Dower, the barely disguised sarcasm obviously registering even in his agitated state. His tone softened as he entered the study, though he paced so furiously that Lawrence feared he would wear a threadbare patch in a rather attractively decorative rug of Eastern origin that he had won in a wager with a particularly eccentric baronet. "Oh, I am sorry, Lawrence. You must think me mad to make such a fuss in your own study."

"Mad? Not at all," Lawrence replied, closing the door and allowing himself the whispered addition of, "Insufferably rude, most definitely!"

In that instant the softened tone was gone and Dower cried, "Are you talking to someone? Is there some other here?"

Lawrence had already made for the brandy and he offered Dower a glass, while surreptitiously doubling the size of his own measure, should the remainder of this visit prove as trying as its opening moments. "I was simply asking if you would care for a drink..." Dower accepted eagerly, draining the glass in a single gulp. "...which you obviously would. A top up?"

This too was accepted with alacrity, though Dower had never been known to be a drinking man. Indeed his attitudes toward partakers and his strict temperance were the subjects of several cruel, though not entirely inaccurate jibes in those bars frequented by the college men. "Thank you," the visitor croaked, his face blooming with the warmth of the drink. "I needed that, I truly did. And, again, my apologies for bursting in, and for burdening you."

"Really," Lawrence said, taking a sip from his own glass, "you haven't burdened me."

Dower fastened him with a serious gaze, saying, "No, but I am about to."

"Oh," said Lawrence, suddenly thirsty, "perhaps I'll have a top up myself."

Dower stopped pacing for just a moment, declaring, "I would recommend it. I cannot imagine that what I have to tell you will not affect your nerves."

Dr. Lawrence shuddered, despite the fire's warmth. "Has it grown colder in here? Oh, no, I see, Dower! This is some joke. A prank to raise the hairs on the back of my neck with some spookery. Well, I warn you, I'm rather hard to impress in that respect, given the superstitions in which I'm daily immersed." He waved airily at the shelves that took up most of the wall space, each one crammed with tomes and tales from times and cultures both near and distant.

Dower nodded, with barely a glance toward the books. "Indeed, this is why I come to you."

"Very well," said Lawrence, seating himself and indicating that his guest also should take a chair before the fire, if only to spare his rug from further wear. "The fire is lit and the brandy is pleasant. Let's have your ghost story, then. It'll serve as an amusement."

Dower sat and the expression on his face, the shadows cast by the flickering of the flames, and the low tone of his voice combined to eerie effect, well suited to the telling of ghostly tales. "There is a ghost involved, yes, or a daemon or whatever you may call it. But, answer me this, Lawrence; when have you ever known me to joke about anything?"

The eye that regarded my friend as he posed this question was one in which he had never yet seen a trace of humour. "You have a point. Make yourself comfortable and begin, then." Lawrence stood, eager to break from his visitor's gaze. "I'll fetch the brandy closer...and maybe I'll just turn up the lighting a little."

As he sat once more, glass refilled, Lawrence found that the hiss of the gas and the crackling fire combined to create a warm and convivial atmosphere, though it was not a feeling that would last as Dower's tale progressed. Yet, for the moment, he sat back and made himself as comfortable as possible while his guest began his preliminaries.

"Now, I know full well my reputation. "Dour Mr. Dower" is the usual remark, and I admit that I have never been one for levity. Personally, I do not regard a soberness of spirit as any flaw, but I am evidently in a minority on that count. I never have been popular company and have never sought to be. This goes back as far as my boarding school days and continued throughout university life."

Perhaps Lawrence's expression betrayed the fact that none of this was news to him, for Dower nodded and said, "What I have just admitted does have bearing. But, I shall begin by telling how I found myself on a working visit to Seachester..."

««——»»

Seachester is a picturesque coastal town, if somewhat untroubled by modern conveniences such as flat roads, adequate transport or comfortable hotels. I had taken myself there for the purpose of seeing what might be found amongst trunk loads of antique volumes deposited with the local museum following the death, at one hundred and two years of age, of the last member of a very old and long established family of landowners.

Even as I describe the place, I still seem to smell the salt in the air and to hear the waves and the cries of the gulls. But, as I do not propose to reminisce about the town itself, I must let these sensations fade, to be replaced by the musty smell of too many old things gathered in one space. The waves are drowned out by the scratch of my pen's nib on paper and the dull, echoing tick of the museum clock. To me, such sounds are the sweetest music, as they are the sounds of my diligent toil. Typically, though, it was not long before a voice broke in upon my quiet work.

"How are you getting along, Mr. Dower?" The speaker of these words, the curator of the museum, stood grinning expectantly, rubbing his hands together and bending altogether too close to my ear.

"Slowly, Mr. Burnstow," I replied, adding pointedly, "and I am not aided by your solicitous interruptions."

The intention of this remark was seemingly lost on the fellow, as was the faint but distinctive jangling of the entrance bell to the small building which housed Seachester's only museum. Instead his grin widened even more as he looked at the piles and packets of papers I was attempting to sort through. "Old Squire Hesketh was never the tidiest of men, which can't make the work much easier." Thankfully, before he could continue stating this blindingly obvious piece of observation, there was an impatient ringing on the desk bell and with a cheery, "Oh, excuse me, sir. I'm wanted at the desk," he shuffled off in search of a fresh victim on whom to inflict his presence. My work was frequently hindered by the ever-present Burnstow, so I was not in the least sorry to lose his company. But, mere moments later, I encountered a yet bigger disturbance.

The museum was a quiet building, quieter than most as, apart from Burnstow, I had not yet encountered another soul within its precincts in those few days in which I had been based there. This, I imagine, was why the curator was forever interrupting my work, though I imagine Mr. Burnstow's interjections may well have been the reason behind the lack of customers in the first place. But the point I make is that the building was quiet, thus the voice that issued from beyond the bookcases that obscured my view of the main desk seemed unnaturally loud and garrulous, and my every attempt to ignore it was in vain.

"You see, my dear fellow," this newcomer was declaring, "my job is much akin to the life of the crow. One pecks and pecks at the dirt around oneself until, voila, one finds the worm. And I feel there are worms aplenty to be found here— worms grown fat and ripe after being buried away in the dark for so long!"

This nonsense continued until I could only declare the situation as intolerable.

"As I said, sir," Burnstow wheedled, "I'm afraid someone is already examining the Hesketh archive at the moment."

"Well, I'm sure if I just have a word with him," began the overconfident reply, raising my hackles yet further. I could already picture the owner of this voice—brash, arrogant, smug. I knew the type only too well.

Burnstow sounded anxious. "Mr. Dower isn't keen on being disturbed." I could not help but marvel that the curator was incapable of heeding his own advice.

There was a brief pause. Then, "Dower? Well, well, speaking of worms... Perhaps I'll just take a stroll round your fine museum."

It was more than I could bear. What was this din? I sought out the curator to have words with him.

"I do beg your pardon, sir. It was a gentleman...not that I'm suggesting you aren't a gentleman, of course, sir. Enquiring after the Hesketh papers. I'm afraid his manner rather overwhelmed me. A very cheery sort."

"Good cheer seems to breed noise," I observed.

Burnstow's brow furrowed as a thought surfaced. "He knew you, sir. When I mentioned your name, it struck me that he recognised it."

"He knew me? And did you get his name?"

The curator shuffled toward his desk, muttering, "He left his card. Was most insistent that I take it. Here we are. Well, well, it's not that often we get two learned gentlemen visiting our little museum."

He brandished the card triumphantly and my heart sank as I read the name printed on it in a florid font, *'Edgar Bright Esquire.'*

«« ——— »»

It was here that Lawrence interrupted Dower's account, "Bright? Wasn't he the fellow they found..?" A grim memory took shape. "Of course. Seachester! I knew I'd encountered that name recently. That was a gruesome business. My dear chap, I should have realised you'd know Bright, really. You were both undergraduates at Rhodes House, weren't you?"

Lawrence remembered well the exuberant fellow and his flamboyant ways. He scarcely struck him as the type of associate Dower would relish. "I only crossed swords with him once. Literally. It was a heated debate at mediaevalist society function, over an infamous duel. The only way to settle the matter was to re-enact it with a rolled up newspaper and a five iron. In fun, of course. But I proved my point and he accepted my interpretation of the historic event."

Dower laughed. It was a noise Lawrence had not heard him make before and it was not a pleasant one. "Accepted it? Yes, I imagine he would. He was always very good at accepting the theories and notions of others. And not always when they were offered."

It took only seconds for the implication of Dower's words to settle in. "Are you suggesting plagiarism?"

"I am not suggesting any such thing," his guest replied angrily. "I am stating it as a fact! I loathed the man, and finding that he was on the same mission as I filled me with fury."

«« ——— »»

"Mr. Dower, are you quite well, sir? You've grown very pale." There was concern in Burnstow's voice, even if that foolish grin of his seemed never to be far from his lips.

My own voice, if it even came, was lost to me, as I was aware only of footsteps approaching from one of the small side chambers, and an all too familiar and hateful voice that crowed, "No need to worry, old fellow. You run along now. Probably just the shock of running into an old friend. Am I right, Dower? Surely you haven't forgotten your chum, Eddie Bright?"

I did not turn to acknowledge this most unwelcome arrival, and instead concentrated on watching the reluctant curator slowly wander away with the vague pretence of putting some books on a few shelves.

"Dower?"

"I haven't forgotten," I replied coldly, turning now to face him. "How are you, Bright?" It was a ridiculous question, as I could judge from his expensive clothing and his easy grin that he was doing undeservedly well for himself.

"Splendid," he confirmed. "I have a new book shortly to be published."

My reply was instant. "Really? Who's it by?"

For a few brief seconds the smile faltered around his lips in a most satisfying manner and his eyes darted to Burnstow at his shelves. Then, with a laugh, he clapped my shoulder. "Touché, Dower! And you? We haven't heard much of you in the academic journals. Still grubbing away, I see. I should have known you'd get here first. You always were an eager little chap."

"I am rather busy, Bright," was my lame response, and I turned to walk away.

Bright, never one to take a hint, continued in his well-remembered arrogant tone, "Eager but dry as a stick. Don't you ever relax? What say we have a chat about old times? I saw a most inviting looking public house across the square."

I spun round sharply, fighting to stop my voice from rising to a shout. "No! Thank you, no. I really do not think we have anything to 'chat' about, do you? You and I do not have any old times that bear discussion."

Bright attempted an appeasing smile, "Oh, now, surely..."

But I cut him off with a quiet threat of, "Unless you would have me talk loudly enough that anyone might overhear, of how you once sought my company and declared friendship..."

"I was merely being companionable to a fellow student," said he, defensively.

"You lured me from my studies and urged me to..."

"To live a little," he insisted. "You were young. You shouldn't have been closeted away with nothing but dusty books for companionship."

I glared at him, unhappy memories washing over me. "Live a little? Yes. That was the phrase you used. 'Try this.' 'Try that.' 'Live a little.' 'Just one more glass.' 'Just another tankard.' Oh, yes. Under your guidance I lived a little." I was no longer concerned with keeping my voice hushed. "You plied me with drink till I was insensible, then watched over me as I thought I would surely die."

"I watched as a caring friend would," he said, affecting a wounded nobility. "I fetched you water and broth and mopped your brow."

"And kept me bed-bound while you had the run of my rooms and access to my work. My work! My thesis paper, with the deadline mere days away. And, while I sweated and shivered, you were hard at work, copying it all down. While I was still weak and poisoned by excess, you submitted your own version of my paper."

Bright sounded dismissive as he said, "Dower, we had enough of your fantasies at the time," but there was a glimmer of worry in his eyes as he glanced toward Burnstow.

I would not be silenced, though. "Was it a fantasy that I submitted the results of months of research and was accused of cheating? Oh, you may have couched your facsimile in more elaborate and fanciful terms, yet the work was mine and I was the one accused of stealing it!"

"I spoke up for you, didn't I?" he replied hotly.

"And had the board of the college convinced that I was an inveterate drunkard who was scarcely able to control his own actions as he cheated and stole."

By this point, Mr. Burnstow had looked across, with a plea of, "Gentlemen, please! Think of the other visitors...if we had any other visitors..."

Bright, aware now of our approaching audience, replied breezily, "You're entirely mistaken, my dear Dower," before adding, under his breath before the curator could draw closer, "And, even if you weren't, there is nothing you can do to prove the claim. So, were I you, I'd just keep quiet about it."

"I cannot prove it, true," I responded, equally quietly, "but can you disprove it? If that curator you are working so hard to charm was to suspect what I know, how would that affect your dabblings here?"

For the first time, I saw Edgar Bright admit to defeat, as he sighed, "I would ask you not to joke about it, but I see that there has been absolutely no change in your humour over the years. What would you wish?"

"That you find whatever flimsy and facile treasures you need, and give me and my studies a wide berth."

He nodded, placing his hat on his head and moving toward the door. "So be it. I'll bid you good day, Dower."

I waited until he was at the door before responding, "Goodbye, Bright."

As I have already said, and as most who have met me already know, I'm a far from jocular person. Yet to finally see Bright's unbearable confidence falter and the smugness slip from his face made me almost dance with joy. Indeed, it put me in such good humour that, when I had returned to my work, I leafed merrily through the mouldering papers and laughed with uncontrollable mirth when I found one that I would ordinarily have discarded as some piece of local superstition.

Yet, on this day, this paper put me in mind of a joke that I might play, should Bright make his presence too closely felt.

Yes, you may very well be surprised. Can this really be dour Mr. Dower playing a joke? I admit that my mood must have been unusually heightened. Yet, as you must surely see, the joke has worn off.

It was hardly an amusing jest to begin with and the outcome was far from comical. For it was this joke that led to Edgar Bright's violent and unnatural death!

Please. I know the questions that must be forming already, but I beg of you, let me tell the tale in my own way in my own time. I can only apologise if I occasionally slip ahead of myself, or if the chronology of the events becomes distorted. Or, indeed, if my account seems to stray into realms normally reserved for lurid fiction. But, as you will discover as the tale progresses, the stress I am now under makes it sometimes hard to keep a clear mind.

As you are surely only too aware, if anything is more of a hindrance to an historian than a lack of recorded evidence, it may just be an overabundance of documents, papers, dockets, inventories and receipts, all of which require sifting and sorting and assessing. And, clearly, the last of the Hesketh line had hoarded papers like a miser hoards gold.

I found this particular document by chance, as I was attempting to make order out of the chaos of papers that had been thrown carelessly into one of the old trunks. The entire mass had been heaped and crammed in, not with thought of preservation, it now seems, but more with the intention of concealment or confinement.

I had scarcely noticed the page since it was hidden between the folds of an old newspaper, and was in such poor shape that it was practically in the waste-paper basket before I realised that there was writing on it.

It was a leaf torn from a book of prayers from the middle years of the century before last. I had seen many like it before, naturally. But it was what was written on the other side of the page that caught my eye. In a spidery, untidy hand...yes, spidery, that is entirely the apt term... Well, in this disorderly hand, the marks near faded and invisible in places, I shall tell you what I read.

'Some shall call me wicked for writing these words in a book of prayers,' it began, 'but, I, Meriel Pearson Hesketh, in the hours approaching my death, have no use for books, and no recourse to prayers. I have been given the book, they say, *that I might repent my sins as the judgement approaches, but I shall not be hung in their noose nor locked in their madhouse, and these are surely the only fates that may await me. In my grandmother's day, it would have been fire or ducking in the pond that must follow. Perhaps it is best that I leave only a son and no daughter and that I am last of my female line.*

'For the crime that I am charged with, and the crime of which I am guilty, is one that goes against all laws of man and church. I, Meriel Pearson Hesketh, like my mother before me and her mother and all the mother's mothers in my line, am guilty of witchcraft.'

Meriel Pearson? The name seemed faintly familiar to me, but the details were vague. Had I fleetingly encountered that name as I trailed through these endless papers? I rifled through them frantically, the urge to know more strong inside me. Then I had it!

'The trial against Mrs. Meriel Hesketh, formerly Pearson, continues on this day, with much that is unusual and uncanny being spoken of.'

The local news sheet, little more than a few loosely bundled pages, dated Seventeen Hundred and Fifty Four. And surely I had spied some bound transcripts.

A confession of witchcraft and a trial. More a tale for our celebrated Dr. Lawrence, with his myths and mysteries, which is why I bring the tale to you now. I wasn't remotely interested in this type of matter. Normally, at any rate. Normally I'd have dismissed it. Give me facts, not fables. But something in the tone struck me as ominous and strange. The gaps in the tale filled me with curiosity and, if there was more to be learned, I wished to know it. I was like a man in the grip of an obsession...though, I now wonder if *possession* might not be a more accurate description.

But I must return in my tale to that dingy museum, where I was so utterly engrossed in trying to decipher a most peculiar word...was it, *'Arch'*? Perhaps, *'Arachnid'*...that I had no idea of anyone approaching until Burnstow loomed down at me, asking, "Mr. Dower? Still busy, sir?"

That word, could it be, *'...necron...'*? Curse the man, could he not see that I was deeply involved in deciphering this name? Did I even know that it was a name at that point? Why would he not go? "What? Burnstow? What is it?"

"I'm about to lock up for the night," said the curator, and I was suddenly aware that he was dressed in his outer clothing, and that the sky beyond the windows was darkening. But surely it was too early to lock up? Yet there it was on the clock, a few minutes to six. "Good grief, where has the day gone?" I cried.

Burnstow shrugged, "You looked so absorbed, sir, I scarce wished to bother you. And after your friend's arrival seemed to disturb you so..."

My friend? I had completely forgotten about Bright's arrival. "Has he been back?" I demanded. "Well? Tell me, man!"

Burnstow looked uncomfortable. "I believe I may have caught sight of him passing outside on more than one occasion. Should I be on my guard against him, sir?"

"What? Oh, no." Already a thought was forming itself in my mind. "No. Indeed not," I assured him.

The curator looked at me uncertainly. "Are you quite all right? You have a strange expression on your face."

"Oh, I'm quite in the pink, Burnstow," I smiled. "But, no. I don't think you need worry about Mr. Bright."

This did not seem to convince him. "But if he is in some way disreputable..."

Then justice will be served, said a thin, hard voice in my darkest thoughts. But I said nothing of this, instead turning back to the contents of the late Mr. Hesketh's trunk, with the words, "A few moments, if you please, Mr. Burnstow, and I shall bid you goodnight."

"Do you require assistance in tidying these away?" he asked, but I shrugged the offer away.

"No need. I shall be here at first opening tomorrow, and I have my doubts that anyone should attempt to make off during the night with some old pages and dockets. There is nothing of interest in them, anyway." Then, as he drew away from me, I called out to him, waiting for him to turn back before adding, "And, should Mr. Bright enquire again, you may tell him that. Nothing of interest at all!"

Again those questions form. Nothing? What was I trying to hide? You are eager to know more of what I had discovered. And so, you see how easily the trap was baited.

Pausing only to scribble a few notes and place them with my day's work, I wrapped my coat tightly round myself and shivered in the gusting wind outside, before setting out into the gathering gloom. But it was more than cold that made me shiver. It was the excitement of my discovery and the use to which I intended to put it.

You have realised that I had found something of importance, of course. What I had were fragments, no more, but with enough connective strands to allow a narrative to form. I had found a meagre type of journal and had read, in the hand of Meriel Pearson, married into the Hesketh family, how there had been two families of wealth that had vied over which was to own more of that area. The words are still clear to my recall.

'Sannox has his mind set on the grove, my Nathaniel says. It's an age-old dispute. Bartholomew Sannox argues that the grove and the trees in it are rightfully his, while Nathaniel swears the land is Hesketh property. In truth, I know Nathaniel to be right, for I know the land was once my family's land. Not the Pearsons, but the land of my mother's female kinfolk, way back when. It was bequeathed to a Hesketh in dark times and if I could but prove it I would. But those times aren't to be spoken of.'

And I read of how the dispute grew more bitter.

'Our labourers have fled, in the midst of the harvest. They say they won't be put upon by the thugs that has been set upon them. Though he denies it and calls them scum, I know they work for Sannox. I seen him talking to their leader, and I seen the coins in the leader's hand. Sannox aims to ruin us by force, but there are forces more than he knows. Nathaniel tried to have it out with him but Sannox calls him an ill-bred peasant. He writes down Nathaniel's words, lording his educated ways. He says he's keeping an account and that it'll be evidence should Nathaniel take action.'

There were appeals to magistrates to settle the matter, without success, court appearances, brawls, quarrels and assaults, until the matter was taken out of Hesketh's hands.

'The grove is gone. It burned and Sannox's hand is the one that lit the flames. Them few trees what didn't burn have been felled and piled. The heart has been burned out of the place, and the heart has also gone out of my poor Nathaniel, who is beaten and broken. He is a decent man who has tried to stand up against a foe with no human decency. But, being as he is so inhuman, we shall see how something even less so than he shall despatch with him.

'I have mixed the draught, as my grandmother's grandmother described it and as the knowledge has been passed down. I shall drink of it and dream and, on awaking, I shall know the name that I need to aid me.'

I read how imbibing some distillation of herbs and roots had lead her to dream of the hidden identity of some monstrous being. And I read of the frightful spectre that, it was said, had been summoned up against that landowner.

'In the courtroom they told of a great wind that gathered up in the courtyard of Sannox's grand house, and which stirred the leaves and branches that littered the ground. And these appeared to gather up in the air and take on a form, like that of a scarecrow but growing thicker and more solid and more like a living thing. And it fastened itself upon old man Sannox and rained blows upon him. And his wife spoke of how, as the blows fell, the outer clothing of leaf and wood fell away... and what horror it was that was revealed within. And, as she told it, there were screams in the court and cries of terror. And I know why they cried out, for I seen it, that dark avenging thing, in my mind. I seen it as the leaves fell away. Something dead and decayed, but full of dark movements...'

《《——》》

Dower shuddered and Lawrence silently refilled his glass, his own thoughts racing through accounts and legends, "Many is the ancient belief which held that to have knowledge of an entity's true name gave the possessor of such hidden knowledge control over that entity and called it to follow in his wake and do his bidding."

Dower nodded, gravely, "So the story went. As I read it, *'It was I who left the name for Sannox to find, chalked on the stone that broke the ankle of his prized steed. I know he took note of it in his evidence book. Now he has accepted it in. He has prepared the invitation, and it always answers the summons to its name.'* So it went."

Lawrence asked, already knowing the answer, "The words of Meriel Hesketh's confession?"

"As I read it," admitted Dower, "and as Bright read it also."

With a degree of dawning horror, Lawrence asked, "You let him find the name?"

Dower jumped to his feet, pacing in agitation, his voice rising in desperation. "There was no name there! I constructed it myself, from fragments of words that Meriel Hesketh had scrawled in the margins around her final confession. In one or other of the ancient languages—something about spiders—about death—something about time. I merged these words into a suitably imposing name and left it to be found. I took the notes that seemed of value and left the dregs for Bright to find. If he were to take this nonsense, the ravings of a delusional peasant, and attempt to publish them with this invented word, he would be exposed for the sham he was. He would be the joke, you see?"

But neither man was laughing.

《《——》》

I had not gone to the museum until late that next day, leaving the bait in plain sight to be found. When I did set foot in the place, there was the curator, Burnstow, positively bursting with some piece of tittle-tattle.

"Sir, while it's far from my custom to pry," he wheedled.

I could not resist a barbed, "Yet, pain you as it does, I know you force yourself."

"But it was your acquaintance, Mr. Bright, sir," he continued, oblivious to my remark. "He was here. Or rather, in there, sir, where you were working."

"I trust you sent him on his way."

"I'd no need, sir. I'd been through in the back, you see, and when I came through... Well, as soon as I saw that the door was open I went to speak, thinking it was you, sir, as you're so diligent in your studies. But I'd scarce cleared my throat to make my greeting when he came scurrying out, as if in fright. When he saw that it was me he laughed and said how it was a gloomy business surrounded by old bones and such like, and how he needed some air. Then he was gone, and didn't even wait for his companion."

This news unsettled me somewhat. "I did not know he had company with him."

"Well, I didn't meet this person but, just as Mr. Bright came through, I thought that I saw something shift behind him and, when he went, I reckoned I'd heard someone laugh in the darkness. But, then, I was so distracted by Mr. Bright's peculiar nerviness and his sudden departure I forgot to look. And when I remembered, there was no-one to be seen. Though how they got past me..." The curator shivered and shook his head slightly. "Maybe I was mistaken and what I heard was the rustling of your papers as Mr. Bright ran off. I do hope everything's in order, sir."

"Oh, yes, Mr. Burnstow," I replied. "Everything's quite in order."

My happiness that all had gone to plan must have been evident, as Burnstow remarked, "May I say, sir, it's a change to see you smiling so?"

I was indeed smiling. The trap had been sprung. Burnstow's interruption had almost spoiled matters; though I was sure Bright would have recovered his wits sufficiently to offer a bribe to ensure his silence. For, then at least, I believed his panic was due to him being almost caught in the act of theft. I was rather pleased to imagine his discomfort.

But, though I wished Bright to suffer, I had no idea of how much suffering my actions were to bring about until I saw Edgar Bright again. Or, at least, what he had become. But it was not until the next morning, as I left my lodgings, that I was to witness for myself the effects of my joke.

"Dower. Thank God! I thought I had missed you," yelped

the shambling figure who nearly bowled me over on the doorstep.

"Bright?" I was startled more by the change in his appearance than his sudden presence. "What are you doing here? I told you to leave me be! I am in no mood for your pretence at friendship, not after the night I've had."

His response was practically hysterical, though whether it was a laugh or a sob I could not judge. "The night you had? Did you sleep?"

In truth, I had slept all too deeply. And my dreams had not been pleasant ones. Full of half glimpsed night-things and...dark movements. The dream, only dimly remembered yet refusing to be wholly forgotten, seemed to cling to me, like strands of some dark web.

Bright let out a cry which was unmistakably a sob. "I don't think I shall sleep again."

As I said, his appearance was dramatically altered. Instead of the puffed up, dapper and arrogant Bright of old, he looked appalling! His eyes were rimmed with red, his face was furred with stubble and his clothing was disarrayed. There were also cuts and grazes on his face and hands, as if he had come off the loser in some scuffle. Had he been drinking? I took a step back, warning him, "If you intend cause a scene or threaten me..."

He stumbled toward me, his hands outstretched. "I must know what it is."

"What what is?" I demanded, though a dark suspicion was already lurking. I dismissed this thought, though, insisting, "Speak sense or step aside."

"Dower, I must know! What is it that's after me?"

I shrugged him off, insisting that I had no idea of what he might possibly mean.

His next words chilled me. "Something dead..."

'... *dead and decayed, but full of dark movements,*' were the words of Meriel Hesketh that seemed to be whispered in my mind from across the centuries.

Even though I knew that the revelations he might make would terrify me, I flung the door wide and ushered him into the hall, saying, "Come inside, Bright. Tell me what you mean."

Once inside my rented room, Bright looked fearfully round the evidence of my studies lining the walls and taking up much of the available space. "Books? So many of them."

"Never mind the books. They cannot hurt you," I told him.

He laughed shrilly. "And I bet Bart Sannox thought leaves were harmless." But he did not laugh when he flopped exhaustedly into a seat and looked up imploringly at me. "What was it? What did Meriel Hesketh conjure up? What did her witchcraft summon?"

I was surprised, and I confess a little frightened, at the coldness in my own voice as I looked down at him and prompted, "If you know of this, then I must assume..."

"Yes," he sighed. "I admit it! I copied those papers that you had been looking at. I couldn't resist it. You were clearly hiding something. What if it had been something of value? I'd have used it properly, sold it to an eager audience. With you, it'd have been collated and filed and forgotten: preserved for a posterity of no interest."

I shook my head slowly. "And this is you asking for assistance?"

His voice cracked as he finally said words I had waited many long years to hear. "I'm sorry. For copying your notes, now... and then."

I leaned closely to him, demanding, "You will finally admit to it?"

"Yes! I'll admit it! Whatever you ask," he sobbed. "But, please! This isn't the time! Something is following me!"

He stopped suddenly, looking round himself, as though something might have concealed itself in the room, waiting for its moment to bear down upon him. When he had satisfied himself that we were alone, he continued, struggling to keep his voice from trembling, "I first became aware of it in the museum. I thought someone was watching me, spying on me as I worked. Several times, I turned to face this watcher, half expecting to find you at my shoulder, quivering with rage, but there was never a soul there. Yet still I heard whisperings and movement and glimpsed something. Only glimpsed it, yet I felt sure it was always close by me. After an hour or two of this worsening feeling of something closing in on me, I left the museum.

"I hurried back home. All the way along the narrow lanes and unlit avenues I sensed a storm about to break at my back, a gathering darkness and a fearful and violent force set to be unleashed upon me.

"I slammed the door, locking it, just as the storm's first howls reached my ears. Just in time. But, whatever tempest I may have escaped, there was worse awaiting me that evening. Some..." He took a ragged gulp of air before he could continue. "Some presence had been in my rooms! There was a great mound of books and papers piled high atop and around my desk. Something in the arrangement made them seem placed and precise, as if stacked by hands other than human.

"As I searched for other traces of this intruder, I became aware of some other presence in the room. There was no harsh breath to betray it. Instead, the sound was of a whispery scuttling, softer than the scratching of rats in the walls, yet amplified in the unnatural silence following the storm outside. The room shifted and distorted in the glow of the swinging lamp. Shadows lengthened and shrank back. And, within these shifting shadows, I was suddenly all too keenly aware, other things moved."

Yet again Bright's words seemed to echo those committed to paper by that young woman in her prison cell those many years past, *'Darkness within the dark. Shapes blacker than the shadows. Shapes that move.'*

Even as I recalled these phrases, Bright's next words made me start, they were so in tune with my thoughts of the instant. "Shapes that move! Shapes that run! There! And there!" He was whirling and pointing, his eyes wide, his words jumbled in his terror. "More there! From every corner, larger than mice but with more legs. Moving toward that mound of books. An infestation of crawling, creeping things!"

I had no brandy to hand, and I could scarcely leave him alone in this condition while I fetched a bottle of the landlady's sherry, so water was all that I could offer, and I thrust it upon him, insisting, "Bright, calm down and drink this! You are safe here!"

His shaking hands spilt more than he managed to get to his lips, and all the while he babbled on, "In a daze of horror, I leapt forward... just as the pile of books leapt at me!" He cowered back from the bookshelves, tears springing from his eyes. "I saw it between the pages as they fell away..."

I tried to reason with him, but I could see that all reason was gone and only horror remained as he cried and gestured and sought the words to convey the darkness that had engulfed his mind.

"...creating motion... Motion toward me! Unstoppable, unrelenting... I ran screaming into the night and kept running till I could no longer breathe. I collapsed and fell into a daze, but it was a stupor with dreams. Such dreams! No matter how hard I run, it will never rest until it has me!"

I had to try to get through to whatever semblance of rationality might still be present. Grasping his shaking hands, I urged, "I can help you. I know! I know what you must do!"

"Nothing can help me against that! Listen! You hear it? It's speaking to me. *'Shalt thou know my name?'* You hear it?"

The wind was rustling the leaves outside the window and even I had to admit that they stirred like something furtive. And, when I turned my head back, Bright was gone, the door flapping in the wind behind him. I ran to the door and tried to call out to him, "Bright! Come back, man! It can't hurt you!" Whether I believed that, I cannot say.

The wind was fierce and stung my eyes and throat and, as it intensified, it truly did seem to be filled with whispering voices. As I shielded my face I was sure that I saw Bright disappear into an alley that lead to the seafront, while rubbish and papers were whipped up in a frenzy at his back. I thought only the mad or foolish, like poor deluded Bright, would be out on such a night. But in the gloom I seemed to see another figure, though it may only have been a jumble of rags or a grey mass of discarded and sodden newspapers thrown up by the wind.

But, really, did I fear that it was something summoned to follow in his wake? Following, but not to do his bidding! You see, I did know something! Something that might help him!

I had also read that there are further laws, if control is to be maintained. Sacrifices must be made and tributes laid. Yet I had not left the pages with that information upon them for Bright to find. Imagine, then, that you have presented control over such an entity to someone with no knowledge of these other, vital laws.

It... the entity would turn on them. It would be like a wild beast in captivity, ever prowling, testing the limits of its confinement. The captor would become the prey. It would claim its tribute one way or another.

I tried to tell him. I can still taste the salty wind and hear its rush as I called to him, "Bright, It can't hurt you! I can stop it, Bright!" If he even heard me, I cannot say. Nor can I honestly say why I did not follow after him, though I shudder to think that the sound I heard as I closed my door on the storm outside was not the wind rising but a distant scream.

Of course, the death was reported and naturally Mr. Burnstow had much to say on the subject when I returned to the museum to pack up my belongings. "They said that when his body was finally found and dragged from the sea that something had gotten to him: crabs or some such creeping scavenger."

Could this be true? When they'd dragged him from the foam, he had only been in the water for a matter of hours. But Burnstow had his answer to this. "Well, there are mysteries in death as well as in life. But, it is a truly a sad day for us, sir. And you're to be leaving us too?"

"Yes," I told him, feeling that some sort of explanation was necessary and that a lie would suffice. "I have... business to attend to, elsewhere."

Burnstow nodded, the grin returning to his lips if not to his eyes, "Life does go on. For some, at any rate, I suppose. Let's be thankful that some departures are less drastic than others."

《《——》》

Dower stopped his pacing and stood before the fire, his back to Lawrence. "The implication was that it was a suicide. But, if he truly died by his own hand, mine was the hand that guided his."

Lawrence prompted him, "By dagger? By bullet? By poison? That would have been murder, but by pen and ink and paper?"

Dower turned to him, stating, "By writing its name, he called it forth. Yet by not offering it the sustenance it needed, the prescribed sacrifice, it was not bound to his control so it took payment in due. I held back that knowledge. That is my guilt!"

"Well," said Lawrence, after a moment's silence had passed uneasily, "you promised me a tale."

"More than a tale," insisted Dower, reaching into his jacket pocket. "I have the proof here! You see?" With a rustling sound, he drew out a folded sheet of paper.

"What's this? A confession to murder?"

Dower shook his head wearily. "No, but a death warrant, nonetheless, signed in my own hand." His voice remained dangerously low as he continued, "The first time I wrote it, I was spared a visitation. At least, spared a visit outside my dreams, as I had made an... an offering... of Bright. This time..."

"You've written it down, haven't you?" Lawrence cried, appalled. "You've written the name of the being down." He could make out Dower's neat and precise writing quite clearly. '*Arachrononec...*'

"No!" Dower crushed the paper into a pellet and threw it into the flames. "Don't read it! Into the fire with it! Let it burn like Meriel Hesketh's words burned. As she herself would have burned if she hadn't sealed her own demise."

"She escaped the witch-finder?" Lawrence asked, surprised. "How?"

Dower reached once more into his pocket, explaining, "She eluded him by summoning her own executioner. Her journal is burnt to ashes in my study grate, but I've brought you this."

It was a news sheet, just a few yellowed and mouldering pages, from which Lawrence read, *'Let it be known now that Meriel Pearson Hesketh, complicit in the unlawful death of Bartholomew Sannox by means of witchery, was this evening found dead within the confines of her locked cell. Her body was badly torn about and the wounds were such that she was scarce recognisable as a person, even one bethought possessed of evil. No sign of human entry has been found into the cell but the jailer has sworn oath that a 'dark shape or shade' did seem to him to be present around the jailhouse in the hours leading to the death of the witch.'*

Lawrence held the page out to Dower, though the visitor showed no interest in taking it back. "She admitted in her journal that Sannox was the sacrifice, and the entity did depart after claiming him. But she had called it back yet one more time. This time, it would not have far to look for its prey. *'Already I have dreamt it.'* Those were her words."

Dower stared into the flames, his voice more even than it had been since his arrival. "It is my reckoning that some things are not found but find us—that some instruments we think to use to our own ends are using us to achieve aims of their own. I went back to Meriel's final confession, looking for the words I had found scrawled there and which I had used to create that dreadful name. There was no writing there! I feel I was used to call this thing forth once more to our world. And Bright was the cost. I know what must come for me. You see, Bright described it, shortly before it caught him up."

《《——》》

As he prowled and paced in my room he never stopped speaking, even when it seemed that his voice would desert him. "In a daze of horror, I leapt forward... just as the pile of books leapt at me! I saw it between the pages as they fell away, the books dropping like a shedding skin. What stood there was a corpse. Little more than a skeleton, though it was given the illusion of solidity by the masses of web that sheathed and festooned it, webs of unnatural thickness and strength, many of them ancient, hanging with the dust of decades long gone.

"How did the witch girl put it? *'It is grey and gaunt, and whatever life it once lived it was not as human life.'* Yes! That was it!

"Through the curtains of webs I could dimly spy something that moved, something that might once have been mistaken for a spider, yet one grown huge over the years. Whatever it was, it was dark and many-legged and it moved within the hollows of that desiccated form with purpose and intent.

"And the wind seemed to change, the whispering voices shifting. *'Shalt thou know my name?'* they had demanded, even though they already knew. For now they answered, *'Then thou shalt see my face!'*"

Meriel's words were in my own mind as Bright shrieked those words at me. *'Something dead and decayed, but full of dark movements... I have seen its face! It has no face! Just the skull beneath, and the things that crawl within!'*

Bright continued his description, barely giving himself time for breath. "Things that moved, acting like puppeteers, controlling through the merest twitches of countless strands of web, radiating through the cadaver, coiling in their thousands through and around the bones like silken muscles, guiding them, creating motion... Motion toward me! Unstoppable, unrelenting..."

««——»»

Dower paused, and in this silence, Lawrence was aware of the wind outside.

"Sannox's crime was the destruction of the grove! Bright's was the theft of my notes! For me it won't come clad in the form of some rustling thing of leaves or paper. It will be an entity of darkness, inky-black and full of spiders."

Although the paper had long since curled up and burned in the grate, Dower's gaze remained fixed on the flames. The reflected firelight seemed to be the only spark of life in his eyes. When he left, it wasn't racing out into the night like poor Bright, hurtling blindly toward his brutal fate. He went calmly, his terror seemingly spent in the effort of telling the tale. His parting words, much gentler than his opening words, were, "My apologies once more, Lawrence. I hope... I pray that I have not burdened you."

When Lawrence told me of this visit, a week had passed and he hadn't seen Dower since that night. Nor had anyone he had spoken to and he can be found neither in his rooms nor at his studies. My friend had no doubt that he will be found but, whether what is found will be recognisable, he would not speculate.

As of the night of Dower's visit, he did tell me this. As he sat to write what Dower had told him, endeavouring to jot it all down while still fresh in his memory, Lawrence began to attempt a phonetic spelling of that daemonic name he had heard described. Even as his pen traced the letters, he became aware of some movement around the edges of his vision, and he turned to see the most enormous spider creep slowly across the bookshelf and into the darkness.

Fair enough, you may say, all studies in old buildings have their spiders. But, my friend assures me, he was not entirely convinced that it had only eight legs.

As Lawrence says, "I wonder now if Dower's need to confess was truly at his own volition, as I also wonder if he hasn't, indeed, burdened me with a terrible knowledge!"

Suffice to say, what is left of the tale remains unwritten.

The Wager

The hour was late when, through wreaths of cigar smoke, Vincent Style spied a face that he knew of old. That face wore an expectant expression as its owner pushed a reasonable pile of chips across the table, murmuring to his immediate neighbour, "Always been my lucky number, fourteen." But, with the spin of the wheel, that expression fell into one of gloomy resignation, accompanied by a rueful, "I didn't say it was always good luck, I suppose."

Style offered a sympathetic nod. "It's Cardew, isn't it?" And he proffered a hand, his name, and the belief that they had attended school together. "Care for a drink to drown your sorrows?"

Cardew accepted the hand, and the offer of a drink and, as they made their way to the bar, with the glimmerings of a smile he added, "I wouldn't go talking about drowning, Mr. Style. With the river so close, you might give me ideas."

Two whiskies were ordered from Stevenson, that most excellent barman; Style judging from Cardew's slouch that they had better be large ones. "Best put them on my account. No offence, Cardew."

"None taken," said he. "I'm afraid that I can ill afford to be offended. Or to return the favour."

The apology was waved away. "Oh, no need. I'm not staying. It's getting on. Your health."

Cardew returned the toast, mock horror in his voice.

"What, you? Leaving a club on the same day you entered it? Have I lost my senses along with my purse?"

"Not at all," Style shrugged, although he was forced to admit his reputation to be one earned on countless nights over countless tables. "Thankfully the money I've lost also remains countless. Some tallies are too alarming to keep."

Cardew nodded, "Yes, but you've won it all back many times over, from what I've seen of you. Our days as pupils at St. Robert's may be ever more distant, and I may have been a few years ahead of you, but as I recall it, it didn't take long for your reputation to spread throughout the entire school. Until you were almost expelled for running that card school during choir practices, that is."

The memory forced a grin to Style's lips. "Luckily for me I'd worked out that the Padre wasn't averse to risking the proceeds of the collection plate on a bet or two himself, and 'persuaded' him to let the matter slip."

"Cunning," said Cardew, raising his glass. "And your skills haven't deserted you."

Style had to acknowledge the fact. "True, I have had my share of luck, thank heavens."

"Luck?" his old schoolmate laughed. "There's a name for your type of luck, and it has little to do with the heavens. Quite the opposite."

Style joined him in his laughter. "Well, I'm not going to be foolish enough to lay claim on the luck of the Devil, lest he decide to come looking to demand its return. Although..." and here a dangerous thought struck him.

"Although?" Cardew prompted. "I know that smile. I've seen it many a time, just before you've alleviated some poor soul of his life's savings."

"Well," said Style, "let's face it, it would be an interesting wager."

Before Cardew could give his opinion on the matter, another fellow known to both joined them, rather unsteadily it has to be said, at the bar. "What wager's this?" the newcomer demanded, before nudging Cardew somewhat roughly in the ribs. "I'm surprised you can afford any kind of bet. Thought you'd been cleaned out, old sport."

Cardew grimaced, none too pleased at this new associate's presence, or his lack of manners. Nevertheless he forced a smile, thin-lipped as it was. "Ah, Wheeler. Style was just talking about what a worthy opponent the Devil would make."

Wheeler, never less than flamboyant, and rarely more than half sober, flung up his arms and, in doing so, splashed the dregs of his champagne across Cardew's shirt-front. "Oh, what rot! A flutter with the Devil? Rot, I say!" Then Wheeler wheeled, airily flapping his arms to indicate the club and its patrons. "This is a house of commerce, gents, where the addition or subtraction of sums of money is the only reality. So let's have no more of this superstition. And let's have plenty more of Stevenson's excellent whisky."

Stevenson placed two glasses atop the bar, but a nod from Style stayed his hand before he could add a third. "Not for me," he apologised, though he was far from sorry to be parting from Wheeler's company. "I must be going."

"Off to take on Old Nick?" Wheeler brayed, before shaking his head as if at some private joke, and adding a scornful, "You'll be telling us you've found the Club Tenebrosa next."

The implication of his words was lost on Style at that moment and he simply explained his wish to get home to his wife.

"Of course!" Cardew laughed. "That's the reason for this reformed character heading home before midnight. I had heard you'd been made an honest man."

"I don't know that I'd go that far," remarked Style, though his smile suggested otherwise.

Congratulations were offered, as were further drinks, since Wheeler had never been known to let an opportunity for celebration pass. "You've had enough for one night," Cardew suggested. "For one week, if we're being honest. You might want to slow down."

Wheeler was hearing none of it, however. "I'll slow down when my wallet is empty, or my thirst is quenched, and not before. We're celebrating! Style here has just got himself hitched to a charming young lady. At least, I assume she's charming, Style?"

Style agreed that, yes, she was charming. And lovely. "And, for reasons that entirely escape me, quite devoted to me," and with that he made to leave.

"You run along to her," Wheeler slurred. "That sounds much the more sensible option than going looking for the Tenebrosa."

What was this place the fellow kept mentioning? "A gambling club? If it is, I've never heard of it."

"No," Wheeler affirmed, "you wouldn't have done. It's very select. Membership by invitation only."

"Really?" Despite his irritation at the fellow's babbling, Style found that his attention had been caught. "And where, if I were to be invited, would I find this astonishing club?"

"You wouldn't. The Club Tenebrosa would find you."

Cardew's exasperation with this nonsense was evident, yet Wheeler persisted. "That's what the talk is. Well, I say talk. Whispers would be more accurate. Though it's surprising what people will let slip in your presence when they think you're insensible.

"It was in some public tavern, somewhere rather less select than here, where the prices were less select also, and the drink was as rough as the clientele. I'd laid my head against the bar for a moment or two—just to gather my thoughts, you understand—so I never saw the gents who were discussing the matter. But here's what I gathered. They say that only members know how to find the club because it moves between locations, never in the same place two weeks in a row. The members are informed the morning before the each meeting as to where is to take place."

"Informed?" demanded Cardew. "How?"

"They said something about messengers..." and the shudder that went through their inebriated companion made both men look at him warily. "It's so vague, but there was definitely something in their tone..."

"No doubt some hired thugs sent out by the club's proprietors," noted Style. "What else did these talkative fellows say?"

"There was something about a game."

"In a gambling club?" laughed Style. "How shocking!"

But Wheeler's expression was devoid of humour. "A very particular game. One that could gain you that which you hold most dear."

"In what way?" was the obvious query raised by such a statement.

In reply, Wheeler shrugged. "As I told you, it's all very vague, and I was rather the worse for wear. Besides, it's a story. Nothing more."

Now it was Style who seemed to lose his sense of humour. "I can tell when I'm being lied to, and you are clearly holding something back." To Wheeler's incredulous look, he continued, "If you were being totally honest your eye wouldn't be twitching in such an alarming fashion. It's a classic tell. If I were you, I'd give the cards a miss tonight. As it is, I shall follow my own advice and give all of these dubious pleasures a miss for the evening." With this, Vincent Style took his leave, though not before turning back to add, "And, fear not, Wheeler. I shan't go looking for any mysteriously wandering clubs."

Wheeler ceased examining his reflection in the mirror behind the bar, looking for tell-tale twitches, saying, "I'm glad he dropped the matter. I wish I'd never raised it in the first place."

Cardew expressed his surprise that the man appeared honestly to believe in this infernal club. To which, Wheeler admitted, "I'd prefer not to believe. Better yet, to forget I'd even heard talk of such a place. There was more to the story, you see. But, knowing our Mr. Style's inability to resist a challenge, I thought it wise to draw a veil."

"And you did so most discreetly," Cardew said, knowing that the ironic tone would be lost on his drunken fellow. "But, really, you make it sound as if the members gamble with their lives."

"Oh, no, their lives would be one thing. No, this was something much more dreadful entirely!"

"That which you hold most dear," Cardew mused. "A rare thing to gain."

Wheeler murmured his agreement into his glass. "But a far greater thing to forfeit."

It was a month or more before Ernest Cardew and Vincent Style met once more, outside that same club. Cardew had barely had time to exchange a pleasantry with Louis, the doorman for this establishment for as long as anyone could remember, before a breathless Style hared across the street, entreating him to hold fast a moment.

Good gracious, he knew Style was keen on a flutter, but there was surely no need for such rush. "Where have you been, man? I thought I was going to have to send a messenger..."

These words caused Style to draw up short. "A what? No. No. I see. Have you a moment?"

They had all evening, but Style insisted that he had little stomach for cards and dice. Fortunately Cardew knew of a nearby bar that served a more than adequate brandy, and, once ensconced there, he awaited an explanation for the other's peculiar agitation.

"You remember our meeting last month? And what that fellow Wheeler was talking about?"

Cardew remembered clearly. "Poor fellow. An inveterate drunkard. After you left he practically lapsed into a stupor, and started mumbling about trolls or ogres, or some-such fairytale nonsense."

"It's not nonsense," Style muttered darkly.

"What are you talking about? And what are you looking around for? Are you expecting company?" But Style merely took a long draught from his drink. "This cannot really be about this club that Wheeler was rambling about. The superstitions of sailors and actors are no match for those of the gambler, eh?"

"There is more than superstition in what he told us," snapped Style, much to the amazement of his companion, who had never once seen the other lose his composure, even when the cards seemed set against him. Style recognised this, saying, "Forgive my nerves but the weeks that have passed..."

《《——》》

It was Wheeler and his damn stories. Like yourself, I tried to put them down to a combination of drunkenness and some silly tale that had grown legs. As I say, I tried, but unlike you, I didn't have much success, and the idea of a secret gambling club consumed my imagination. Even at home, with my darling Constance, who should have been filling my every thought, I found my mind wandering, and had to gently be nudged back to reality.

"Vincent, are you quite all right?" she asked one afternoon, ceasing her piano playing to look intently upon me.

I apologised, lamely suggesting, "I must have been carried away on the wings of the music." My pretence was obviously poor, as she then enquired as to which particular piece had swept me away. "It was the Elgar. Or the Debussy..? I cannot say. They were all wonderful."

"You are a terrible liar, Vincent Style," she told me with the pretence of severity. "I haven't played any Elgar today, and my Debussy is badly in need of practice."

"On the contrary, my dear," I reminded her, "I am a very good liar. If I weren't, we'd be considerably worse off than we are."

She laughed, then. "It isn't the done thing for the husband of an heiress to boast about his gambling. There are those that might think you married me only for my money."

Then I insisted that they would be fools to overlook her beauty, her intelligence and her warmth as the real reasons I had fallen in love and begged her to marry me.

"I hope this isn't you demonstrating your abilities as a liar," she scolded.

"If you don't believe me, I'll step aside and admit defeat, and Walter Fellows can claim you."

"Silly. You know Walter was never a match for you after you won my heart."

"I won it, did I?" said I with an unwise grin. "To the victor, the spoils."

She didn't return the grin. "When you say it like that, you make me sound like some sort of prize in one of your wagers."

"That's not true," I maintained, taking her in my arms. "But if it were, what a prize you would be! The most perfect, shining jewel. The one prize that might put all others in the shade."

Yet still, my preoccupied manner weighed upon her, and I had to reassure her that nothing distracted me from her. "If I seem lost in thought, it is only because I can barely believe how happy and content a man I have become."

I had never lied to my wife until that point. She knew about my gambling and was content that it continue, if on a rationed footing. And I genuinely was content—more content than I'd ever thought possible—but for one nagging thing. Could such a club exist in London, and yet remain secret amongst the twilit fraternity I knew only too well? I had to find out. And, if anyone would know of such an establishment, that would be Jasper Dyson.

You wouldn't know the name. Dyson doesn't...didn't frequent the type of establishments you would be comfortable in. He said he found the pace there far too genteel, though he is a gentleman. Or was. Like so many of noble birth, he had gravitated downwards.

"We don't see the likes of you here so often," he announced, raising his voice over the grunts, yells, cackling and catcalls that filled the air in that broken down dockside pit where I found him. "Slumming it, are we, Mr. Style? Or have you developed a taste for the more exotic spectacle?"

As I was swift to point out, there's nothing exotic about watching two poverty stricken dock workers punching one another unconscious for a crowd of braying ghouls. This brought an unpleasant smile to his flabby lips, and he said, "Would you care to say that a little louder, Vincent? I'm sure the lads would be happy to instruct you in the bareknuckler's arts, and lift your wallet to pay for the lesson. You didn't come here for that? Well, should you care to hang around, there's always the dog fighting to follow. These poor souls aren't even top of the bill. Tragic, isn't it?"

"I'm sure your heart is breaking," I countered. "I was just looking for the one man I know even less capable of resisting a wager than me."

Here I had his interest. Leaning back in his chair, he

asked, "And what would be the purse on this hypothetical wager?"

"If you prove the victor, enough to buy back your membership to every club that's barred you."

"That is a pretty penny," he admitted—a gross understatement of the matter. "And tempting. I must admit the yelling and the bloodshed round here become mere background details, but the smell is another matter. Though, as you can imagine, I can't match the offer."

I informed him that it wasn't money, merely information I sought from him.

"Pardon my suspicion, old boy, but any information that'd see you risk your wallet and throat in this rookery has to be something very special indeed. And if it's that special, what makes you think that I'd give it up so cheaply, if I even knew it in the first place?"

"Well, aside from your pathological inability to resist a bet, no reason at all." And I made as if to depart from that filthy den. "No, no, you're right, Dyson. I was foolish to come here."

"Come now, Style," he smirked. "A man of your wit and intellect surely isn't going to try such a blatantly obvious trick to pique my curiosity?"

"Then you're not curious? In that case I'll leave you be."

As a man already gripped by an unassailable curiosity, I recognised the same in Dyson, as he urged me to stay. "If I have the information it is yours. Deal?"

"Without even knowing what the wager is?" I enquired.

In reply, he thrust out his hand to me. "You're a man of honour. Deal?" And with a shake of his damp, fleshy paw, we had that deal, though Dyson had stipulations. "Since we're both clear that all accounts must be settled in a timely fashion..."

"Quite clear."

He relaxed again, letting his corpulent frame settle back once more. "Well, then, what's this knowledge you seek?"

"You have, of course, heard of the Club Tenebrosa? I gather it meets tomorrow night, and I would like to know where."

His relaxation was short-lived. His pig-flesh pink jowls turned white and, with a gasp, he blurted out, "Who told you of..? I mean, I have never heard of..."

"Such a place," I told him, "if it does exist, is surely known to a man whose tastes... no, whose obsessions, are with any form of gambling. Come, Dyson, you even took bets on the time it would take your own mother's funeral procession to reach the church."

"I cannot give you the information you're after," he insisted, a fumbling hand putting a flask to his lips.

I stood, looking down on him. "Then I prove the winner, since my wager was that you could not prove that such a club exists. However, as you cannot settle your account with the information I seek, some other arrangement must be made!"

He cursed me, roundly. "You treacherous jackanapes! For me to even have had a hope of winning I would have had to give you your prize."

"But since you do not have the information," and I leaned low to emphasise the threat in my words, "and since all accounts must be settled in a timely fashion..."

His own voice was low, with fear rather than menace, beady eyes darting as he whispered, "I can't give you the information, as I won't have it myself until the morning. They don't deliver the word till just before dawn."

"They? The messengers?" A nod. "To your lodgings or here?"

"To my lodgings, of course. They wouldn't come here. Why? You surely can't..." Then my meaning sunk in, and his voice became a high whine. "No, no! You can't be there when they arrive. I mean, I've never seen them, and I don't want to, either. If you must know, I'll bring the message to you!"

Why was he so alarmed? "Surely if you're a member, you could invite a guest or, perhaps..."

"There are rules," he hissed. "You can tell no-one where you found this out. My involvement ends here, and it is not to be mentioned!"

I agreed, telling him that I would be waiting the following morning for his word, before tossing a pouch of coins at his feet. "A little gratuity, just to be going on with. The rest will follow once I've seen the proof. Don't make me come to demand this back!"

He made no move to snatch it up, though I could see other greedy eyes, alerted by the rattle of coins, looking on. "I don't know if money'll be much use to me now. Please, just go, Style. I can't be seen with you!" He was nearly shouting now. "Go!"

And I went, glad to be away from the dingy cellar, with its echoes of knuckles pounding dully against scarred flesh, the bloodthirsty chatter of the crowd fading, but not fading quickly enough.

Come the next morning, home seemed so far removed from that pit of savage spectacle that a curious chill coursed through me when a reminder of that encounter materialised there. It was Constance who made me aware of this, telling me over breakfast, "I thought I'd glimpsed a dark figure on the path. It isn't the postman, I don't think." And she stepped daintily out into the hallway.

"Perhaps it was just a shadow from the trees," I called. The lies were coming easier, for I suspected I knew precisely who was calling at that hour.

"I was wrong," said she, returning with a slip of paper in her hand. "It must have been the postman. I wonder why he didn't knock. It isn't a letter. See? No envelope or stamp. Just a slip of paper with a word on it." I had to fight the urge to snatch it from her hands as she looked at it, puzzled. "'Alhambra'? What does that mean?"

I attempted to make light of it, suggesting that it was possibly some advertising gimmick, or one of the local children playing a game. But, "No. The figure I thought I saw wasn't a child. I'm certain of that. It was too tall. Too large and grey."

Seeing her shiver so, I went to stoke up the fire, declaring, "This ridiculous note can go in the grate. We're not going to be put out by meaningless scribbles. 'Alhambra', indeed?"

As you may recall, the Alhambra is a theatre near the river. At least, it was. Disused now, following a fire. What better place for an infernal club to meet? The building had once been magnificent. Even with streaks of soot round the window frames and boards across the doors, it still had a dilapidated splendour about it when I stepped out of the cab that night.

After knocking once, twice, a third time, I waited so long at that doorway that I began to suspect that old Dyson had played me for a fool. There were few cabs in that part of town, and it was hardly the safest area to walk through. So, I was pleased when the door swung open and a dim red light spilled out.

Pleased? If only I'd turned tail and fled!

The dark-eyed man who opened the door was dressed in the neat, black outfit of a servant, and he proffered a long-fingered hand to take my invitation.

"I'm afraid I don't have it," I informed him. "It got burned up. But I'm sure you can overlook that."

He betrayed neither surprise nor suspicion at my excuse, merely saying, "It is most unfortunate, sir."

"Actually, I'm more the guest of another member. Frightfully nice fellow. Can't remember his name."

I think I was the one to betray surprise when he said, "You will be referring to Mr. Dyson, sir." Ah, so he knew, then? "The club's rules are most strict on members discussing our proceedings with outsiders. Mr. Dyson realised that he had made a mistake in telling you. This much we do know."

"Isn't there any way I can persuade you to bend the rules a little?" I was considering reaching for my wallet, which was well stocked on this evening.

"There is no need. Please, won't you come in, Mr. Style?"

I was led by this man—what was he, a butler, I suppose—through the darkened foyer. Even though he carried no lamp, I could follow him easily, as his black garb appeared to stand out darker than the gloom around him, and there was a strange rustling to his stiff movements.

I tried a friendly approach, saying, "Don't be too hard on Dyson. I did rather trick the old reprobate. The very notion of such a place became a sort of mania, I suppose, ever since…"

"Since Mr. Wheeler told you of us," he interjected. "It is quite understandable."

"Then Dyson really did tell you everything."

"Mr. Dyson is no longer an associate of this establishment, Mr. Style. Not in the accepted sense, though he has moved into the club's employ. His place has been taken. Your actions have merely accelerated a process."

What was this? Was he telling me that I was in line for membership? He assured me that he was. "Your reputation has reached the Founder and our Proprietors from many different sources. A man of your talents and interests is always going to find a welcome here."

"Why, thank you," I stammered. I was finding it hard to process what was being said. "But, the Founder? Then you aren't the owner?"

"Merely a servant," he confirmed. "I oversee proceedings for the Founder. He is rather busy on many matters. Now, please, make yourself at home. Meet the other associates, and play whatever games take your fancy. But be ready for the main game at midnight."

Main game? I was even more intrigued, but of this he would only say, "Midnight. All will become clear then." Then, as we reached the doors to what was once the auditorium, he bowed rigidly, before opening them with the words, "Welcome to the Club Tenebrosa, Mr. Style."

I must confess to some disappointment as I took my first look around the club. True, they had somehow transformed what should have been a burnt-out shell into a semblance of its former glory, candelabra filling the auditorium with dancing light, and velvet draperies hiding the worst of the damage; the gilding looking like carved ebony, and scorched cherubs peering out from every corner.

Yet, for all the novelty of these surroundings, what I found there was little more than those very types of amusement I was already tiring of in other gaming establishments. The cards and the roulette wheels, the piles of chips and the dice. The clientele, though, were a different matter entirely. Notable, in many cases, or should I say notorious? Some internationally renowned, some the vilest scum in London.

At any table you might find a duke engaged in a hand of trumps with a lumpen misfit who wouldn't pass muster in a doss-house.

"A veritable rogues' gallery, isn't it?" crowed the languid young fellow who joined me then. "I found it a little unusual on my first night. My card." The name I read there was *'Quentin Frye'*, the address was a prestigious one. I offered my own card in return, enquiring as to how long he had been a member. "Oh, no time at all, really. Not compared to some. A few months and the novelty hasn't quite worn off. Actually, I don't know that the novelty ever does wear off. Look at Lord Norvell, there. Eighty-five if he's a week, been coming here since his university days, I understand, and still in awe of the whole thing."

The club had been around that long? I was sure the fellow who had shown me through had said that the Founder was still active. But when I raised this query, young Frye's tone was guarded. "I wouldn't know much about that, Style. One never likes to pry too far into these things."

"But it's just like any other club," I protested. "The same games. The same risks and chances. What's the big attraction?"

"Oh, you'll see," he assured me, returning to the tables. "At midnight."

The amusements were humdrum enough, and I would have left in boredom if it weren't for the intrigue of this midnight game. And so I played a few desultory hands of poker and rolled a few dice... quite profitably, I might add. Wine and fine cognacs were freely available, yet I noticed that few of my fellows were partaking, in an effort to keep their senses sharp for this challenge that awaited at the midnight hour.

Come the hour, I was keenly anticipating some new delight: some exotic new diversion. And when twelve chimed, and the heavy curtains parted on the dusty stage, the butler striding forward and beckoning to the crowd, I eagerly joined the flock. One by one they filed onto that bare stage, and, one by one, they took a pair of dice and rolled them. Those who scored highly took their position in line again, while those who scored badly left the stage.

When my turn came around, I accepted the dice from the butler, though not before dryly asking, "Is this the great gamble? Simply the roll of a pair of dice?"

There was no smile, little emotion at all in his face, yet I was aware of some goading tone when he said, "Isn't that the greatest gamble of all? There are no tricks, no tells and no tactics, and the only opponent is fate. Will you gamble, sir?"

Very well. I'd wasted most of the night already. What more was there to lose? I rolled. The score was high, and at the butler's prompting, I joined the front ranks for the next round.

Again and again we rolled, and again and again the ranks were diminished, until only three of us remained. Myself, a Mr. Crow, who had the air of an undertaker about him, and who had just scored an unpromising five, and Frye, whose hand was trembling so wildly it was a wonder the dice didn't fly out into the orchestra stalls. Yet he threw well, as the butler intoned, "Nine. Mr. Frye, you are guaranteed a position. Mr. Style, sir."

I whispered an oath for luck, then let loose the dice, urging them on under my breath.

"Four. Mr. Crow and Mr. Frye are tonight's finalists." There was desultory applause that matched my mood as I joined the other unfortunates. It was a mood which darkened even further when that black-clad man informed us, "You may go. You will receive your next instructions at the assigned time."

Even as the rest shuffled off, I tried to hold them back. "Surely we're staying to see how it turns out?"

"You have seen," Quentin Frye told me, though his voice was strangely lacking in triumph. "It's between us now, Style."

But two winners? That surely couldn't be right? There had to be one more throw of the dice. But, as the butler informed me, "The dice will not decide matters now. This competition is between these two gentlemen. If you would follow the other associates, you will find transport a suitable distance from these premises, and our messengers will inform you of our next meet in due course."

What could I do? I left feeling incredibly irritated at the waste of an evening, dismayed at the banality of the proceedings, determined that I would waste no more time on such a ridiculous venture. Of course, I was curious as to how this midnight game was to be resolved. What man would not have been? To this I answer, they should be very grateful that they had not allowed curiosity to lead them to that place. Be grateful that their lives, or at very least their sanity, had never been put in the balance.

I could scarcely contain my own curiosity. So, my first port of call was to have been with the very fellow who had gained me admittance to the club. But of Dyson there was no sign, not in any of his ghastly haunts. The butler had referred to him as having become an employee of sorts. I could hardly credit the notion of Jasper Dyson working for anyone or any cause apart from himself and his own greed. But the fear in his eyes as he'd talked of the club had me convinced that he had fled.

As I left the last of these cesspits of depravity, my ponderings were interrupted by the sound of shambling footsteps, and a voice that croaked harshly, so much so that I struggled to make out the words, "All accounts must be settled." Was it Dyson? I had no chance to find out before the footsteps shambled off.

That unsettling encounter with a dimly glimpsed shadow in an unlit alley should have been enough to dissuade me from pursuing my goal. But it only lent fuel to my inquisitiveness. As the week progressed, I became so consumed by it, I made little effort to hide my agitation, pacing the floor at home, prompting my wife to beg of me, "What has gotten into you? You've been highly strung since you went out on Saturday. You've barely sat still from one moment to the next. You've paced and prowled, and you've scarcely glanced at the newspaper, which you normally devour from cover to cover."

"I'm afraid the news bores me," I said, and the unkindness of my words to her still stings me.

Her next words got through to me, though. "And you've scarcely glanced at me. If there's something I've done, I'd prefer to know it."

How could I let her fret so? "Oh, my dearest Constance, there's nothing that could diminish how I feel for you. I'm sorry if I've been distracted. It's work, nothing more. I'll be in a better frame of mind by the weekend."

Yes, the weekend. Saturday, when the next meeting was due. I had to go back!

I'd suggested Constance should visit a cousin in the countryside, who had conveniently come down with some illness or other. Thus she was gone when the message arrived which led me to my destination—The Gallowhill Hospital.

Again, that dark butler greeted me at the door, telling me, "We are most pleased that you could join us again."

The building felt as diseased and broken down as those poor souls it had once housed, yet I strode through its corridors excitedly, resolute that I would be satisfied in my curiosity. There were the faces from the week before—most of them, at least—and there were those same tedious games of chance. But these were not what took my interest that night.

My acquaintance of the previous week was there, though his bright-eyed enthusiasm seemed somewhat diminished as he refused my offer of a drink. "Is something the matter, Frye?" I asked. He looked positively ill.

His reply was a distant, "I'm fine. Just...fine..."

"Oh, I see. Been celebrating a little too freely over last week's victory, were you? I take it you were the victor? I don't see your worthy opponent amongst the crowd."

"Yes," he echoed, "The victor," before wandering off. I watched him slip through the throng like the ghost of a broken man. Clearly something had occurred to that brash young fellow in the intervening week. Would that I had taken this as a warning, but to the curious sometimes no warning will suffice.

But my curiosity was not to be laid to rest that night as the dice were once more against me.

Another week passed, another message brought me to another location, to a makeshift casino in what I think may have been an abattoir, and the next week...just last weekend, to a mausoleum.

Sacrilegious? Yes. Yet there we were, the gathered obsessives, cramped and crowded between the tombs and slabs, frittering away our lives amidst the gloomy symbols of our mortality. A sarcophagus lid bedecked in green baize as a table, red velvet hangings barely concealing those places where the tomb's walls had crumbled and the empty-eyed faces of the dead peered through.

And at the sound of a distant church bell, and the rustling that heralded the return of the butler to declare, "Gentlemen, it is time," we commenced.

And yet again the ritual, the numbers diminishing, those still in the game growing nervously expectant. Until, with a roll of ten, I heard the butler announce, "Mr. Style and Mr. Frye are tonight's finalists."

Again, the others were dismissed, to await their next instructions. With a grin, I offered my hand to my opponent, declaring, "This must be a fated challenge, Frye, old boy! I wish I had your luck, though. Two wins in a month."

He ignored my hand, growling, "You don't see it yet, do you, Style?"

Before I could ask him just what it was that I was expected to see, the butler strode stiffly forward. "This competition is now between you two gentlemen. The deadline is one week from today. And, be warned, there is a penalty should you fail to bring the contest to a satisfactory conclusion."

What conclusion? Frye was right. I didn't see it. What was the wager?

"It's between us," Frye said. "Don't you understand? One of us has to decide it. One of us has to kill the other."

"What?" I fear I was laughing. "Oh, what nonsense is this? Kill one another?"

Yet the butler's usual lack of emotion made it clear that there was no joke here. "Those are the rules, sir. One or other of you gentlemen, before the next assembly of the club, must take the other's life. The survivor will resume their membership of the club. The other will leave a position clear for a new associate to take their place."

"This is madness," I protested.

"These are the rules," he repeated. "They have been the rules since Sir Nicholas and the Proprietors laid down the club charter."

"Sir Nicholas? Oh, this enigmatic Founder of yours?"

"That is correct, sir."

I was growing angry at the insanity that I was being forced to endure. "Who founded this club over sixty years ago, at least, but is still keeping a watchful eye over things?"

A stiff nod. "The Hobsgates are a very old family, Mr. Style." As ridiculous as it sounds, Wheeler's jest about being 'off to take on Old Nick' now struck me as ominous, and I demanded to see this Founder and these Proprietors. Yet he stood implacable, stating, "In the fullness of time, I am sure."

"Time? You think I'll be wasting any more of my time with these childish games? You may tell your Founder that I resign my membership."

"That is not the procedure." The very blandness of his words now seemed a threat. "All accounts must be settled."

Hah! That was precisely what I'd told Dyson. Though a realisation came with the memory. "What have you done with him? I don't remember telling him about Wheeler. How did you know where I'd heard of the Club Tenebrosa?"

"Mr. Style, the Proprietors have eyes and ears everywhere."

"If they do," I retorted, "they'll hear me when I say that I'm done with this idiocy, and they'll see me when I walk out of the door!"

But it wasn't the servant who stepped forward to bar my exit. "You can't walk away," Frye told me. "Even if you walk out we must complete the competition. There are penalties, otherwise."

"Let me guess," I sighed. "I'll forfeit my very soul?"

To which the butler replied, "We have no interest in that. The penalty will be the loss of that which you hold most dear. Now, gentlemen, you will go your separate ways. Carriages are waiting outside. We will not tolerate any indiscretions on the club's own doorstep. After that, you have the rest of the week to fulfil your obligation."

I stood my ground, ready to argue bitterly over the ridiculousness of the situation. So much so that the butler said, "Please do not oblige me to summon our messengers to assist your departure."

At which point a white-faced Frye gripped my arm and started to drag me away, saying, "No. We're going! Style, don't argue. It's time to leave!"

Even as I reluctantly followed him, I turned back to yell, "It's not going to happen! You can't turn one of us into a murderer!"

Yet the look that glimmered in the butler's dark eyes seemed to say, "Would you care to bet on that, sir?"

《《──》》

Ernest Cardew looked across the table at his companion, waiting for him to reveal the punchline to the joke. When none was supplied, he heard himself declare, "It's insane! What sort of gain is there for a club to have its members murder one another?"

Vincent Style, who had grown alarmingly animated in his telling of his tale, now wore a distant, thoughtful look, though clearly the thoughts were dark ones. "There's a larger, more sinister game going on that we can't even see. But it sees us!"

"Unseen forces?" Cardew pondered, imagining agents of the club acting as spies.

"They knew about Wheeler," Style seemed to confirm. "How could that be? Dyson might have gone to them of his own accord, pleading forgiveness. But Wheeler never knew where to find them. Or did he seek them out, as I did?"

With a sense of shock, Cardew realised that Style did not know about Wheeler. "I thought you must have heard. The funeral was last week. Most of the club were there. It's why I'd thought to contact you. Shortly after he left us that night, he must have stumbled as he walked home along the river-side. Lost his footing somehow. He was found drowned. But not for some time. A dreadful sight, I gather. Swollen. Colourless."

Style's jaw was slack, his eyes wide, as he muttered, "Then it's true? The faces! Those dead eyes... The messengers!" He stood sharply, his chair falling back behind him as he raced for the door, his muttering rising to a babble. "I can't do it! Is he here? Do you see him? Tell him I can't!"

Despite Cardew's calls for him to stop, to come back, by the time he had reached the door he had lost sight of Style. Could that have been him at the corner, by that dim alleyway? No, there were two...no, three of them. Though Cardew couldn't say that he much liked the look of those last two: so grey and ungainly and misshapen.

More weeks passed before those two gentlemen were to meet again, though the surroundings were less convivial than a casino or tavern. And there was no pleasure in their greeting as Cardew swung back the heavy door and heard it close behind him, before looking down on the man who blinked back at him uncertainly, whimpering, "Who is it? Is it you, finally?"

Cardew reassured him of his identity, telling him, "I came when the messenger arrived."

There was a spark again in Vincent Style as he demanded, "Messenger? Did you see? Was it one of them?"

"You sent the message. You asked me to see you," Cardew urged, before taking in Style's appearance. "Grief, man! So much changed in just a few short weeks!"

"You remember what I said then?" Style asked, eagerly. "About the club?" Remember? How could Cardew forget such an outlandish tale? "I was right. It was him. Sopping wet, and the other, twisted, the neck crooked, eyes bulging. He was like that already, when Constance saw him on the path. Constance!" It was a sob as his wife's name left his lips.

"Style, you aren't making any sense," Cardew pleaded. "You must try to compose yourself!"

But Style merely repeated that name over and over, "Constance..."

《 《——》 》

Constance saw him again. I remember it. We were returning home from dining out—I confess, I had been finding as many distractions as I could to fill my time, following that Saturday—when she pointed suddenly from the carriage window, declaring, "There's that man again, I'm sure of it."

"Man? Which man, where?"

"The fellow who delivered that peculiar message," she said. "Look! There, on our pathway... No, he's gone. But, perhaps I was wrong. This one seemed less crooked, though there was something still so odd and pallid... Where are you going?"

I was already out of the carriage, sprinting to the house, but not before insisting that she stay put and let me deal with it. And all the time my mind was screaming, "Not here! Not now!"

Despite my warnings, Constance had followed me down the pathway. I would have urged her to turn, to leave, but as she observed, "There's no-one here. Whoever the poor fellow was he must be drenched. Odd. There's barely a cloud in the sky." Yet the footprints we both saw glistening before us looked like whoever had left them had dragged himself out of the river.

As soon as I could get the door unlocked, I ushered her inside, but not before snatching up the scrap of paper that was waiting in the hallway, the two words scrawled upon it blotched and smeared by the damp hand that had delivered it. But I wasn't quick enough. Constance saw it, insisting on some explanation, despite my protests that it was nothing.

"It's another of those inane messages. Let me see! *'Five days'*? What does this mean?"

"I haven't the faintest notion," I shrugged. "It's silly, like you say."

But my Constance was smarter than that. "Vincent Style, I've known you long enough to have learned all about bluffs. Is this about your gambling? Is it a threat? If you've got yourself into debt then tell me. You know I can settle any payment."

"Bless you, my dearest Constance," I would have began, only the words *that which you hold most dear* came unbidden to my mind. Instead, I said, "There really is nothing the matter. I'm just a little out of sorts. Besides, you've also known me long enough to know there are very few situations I can't get out of on my wits alone."

"I know it," she nodded gravely. "I just sometimes wish that you didn't."

Truth was, as the days passed, my wits seemed to be deserting me, and I became more and more aware of a strangeness enveloping me; a fleeting face peering at me from a doorway, a glimpse of a figure passing as I'd turn my head, the sound of stumbling, wet footsteps, and the echo of laboured breathing. Ever since I'd left that grotesque club. Others, too, shifting at the corner of my vision. But I knew the faces I saw. Grey and bloated! One clammy and damp, the other twisted and gaping.

Wheeler. And the other... Dyson! Had they dealt with him for telling me where to find them? Or, in his terror, did he do the job himself? And had they now set his phantom on my trail?

If only those had been the worst. I am a rational man! I do not believe in such things. But there were others. Faceless. Formless. A shadow in the gloom at the foot of the bed. A darkness that pressed against the windowpane before dispersing. But a darkness with a voice... Nothing more than whisperings in the wind or in the rustling of a page, but insistent. Urging! Urging me to seek out Frye. To settle it once and for all!

Could I have meant to actually go through with it? To hunt him down and kill him? I try to tell myself that my reasons for seeking him out were motivated by a desire to help him. To help us both. I knew that if I were to take my tale of a club founded on the murder of its members to the authorities, it would be looked upon as deluded ravings. But, if we were to act together, perhaps we might be believed.

Yet, as I hurried toward that prestigious address, I was already filled with the suspicion that such an act of betrayal would require more protection than all the authorities in

London could provide. No, I cannot convince myself that my actions were governed by anything more noble than self-preservation.

If Frye was in any way entertaining the kind of thoughts that I was beginning to nurture, I thought it only prudent to confront him before he could act upon them. And, should this intervention have led to circumstances where a decisive act of self-defence had proved the only solution...

Yes, I know what I am admitting! But it's amazing the justifications a desperate man will fabricate. You see, the very fact that Frye had survived a previous game was ominous in itself. He had killed, and might kill again! I had to make sure of his intentions, and stop him by whatever means. Whether or not I could have gone through with it...

The house was quiet and dark, and the ease of my entrance had me suspecting a trap. But there was no hidden ambush waiting to greet me. Indeed, what did greet me was the smell. Sickly and cloying, and leading me to Frye. Dead!

The blade that had fallen from his cold fingers had almost congealed into the redness which pooled beneath the desk where he lay slumped. The note, prised from under his lifeless form, confirmed what I had prayed were just my own delusions, brought on by the madness of the situation I'd foolishly sought out.

'They are there even as I sleep. They never leave me or let me have peace. Whispers... Threats... I cannot deliver another unto them. So, if they be proof of the existence of Hell, may this refusal to grant them their whim gain me forgiveness for another unforgivable action.'

To my shame, I felt only elation. Frye's actions had decided the bet. But the joy lasted only until the next morning, when I awoke to a horror on my doorstep. Again, it was Constance who found it, complaining, "It's another of those nonsensical notes. *'One day,'* this time. Do you think we should call in a constable?" But I was gone before she could ask me anything further.

The mausoleum was empty, with no sign that anyone, bar the rats, had set foot inside it in years. I don't know what I had expected to find there, if I'd even expected to find anything: a clue, perhaps? Something tangible! But there was nothing save darkness and decay. "It isn't fair," my cry echoed around the chamber. "Frye forfeited the wager! I won!"

In answer, two sets of shuffling footsteps drew closer. The thing that had once been Dyson whispered, "All accounts must be settled."

And Wheeler, what was left of him, burbled wetly, "That which you hold most dear."

I didn't wait for those two ungainly messengers to emerge from the darkness in the arches, though I was aware of the rope that still dangled at one's throat and the look of terror still etched into that dead, grey face. And of the reeking liquid that still clung to the other. In the brief seconds before I turned and fled, these images must have seared themselves into my memory.

Yes. I fled. I went home. Out of my mind, I ran back to my poor, unsuspecting Constance! I urged her to hurry. To pack whatever items she would need for us to travel quickly, before frantically checking that the windows and the doors were shut and locked. "We can't just go off travelling," she protested. "Vincent, what on earth has gotten into you?"

We didn't have time. I couldn't explain, but she wouldn't be budged. "It's happened, hasn't it? You've wagered more than you can afford to pay out! I trusted you! And what kind of people are you gambling with, to have filled you with such fear?"

I barely heard her words. My head was full of whispering voices. Insistent, *'Do it!'* Wheedling, *'There's no escaping.'* Threatening, *'All accounts must be settled!'*

"I'll explain," I promised her, as if I could ever hope to explain, "once we've left London far behind us. You needn't pack. We can pick up whatever is necessary on the way. It won't be for long. I just need time to gather my wits. Now, please, come with me. I've left a coach waiting outside."

I unlocked the door, opened it wide, but still she would not come! "It can wait all night, as far as I care. I'm not moving till you tell me what's at stake!"

If I could just make her see. "What is at stake is that which I..."

"...which you hold most dear," a distant, damp voice cut in.

Did Constance hear it? Did she hear the shuffling on the pathway? Or Dyson's choked reminder that, "All accounts must be settled"?

And did she hear that other, newer voice? The one that threatened, "It's between us now, Style"? It was Frye! He was one of them! They had taken him for forfeiting the game.

I slammed the door, begging Constance, who was naturally terrified by my frantic manner, to stay away from the windows. "Who is out there?" she demanded.

They were coming. But I had nearly a day left. I roared out my defiance. "You can't claim her! There are rules! You won't touch her. You... won't..."

"Vincent?" Constance had run into my arms, clasping my face in her hands; my dear, sweet Constance, staring beseechingly into my eyes, looking for answers. And then I had it. I knew absolutely how to beat them. It was so laughably simple I could scarce believe I hadn't thought of it sooner! Oh, where were my wits? Of course! I took her to my breast, telling her, "Nothing is going to hurt you. Nothing, I swear."

"You've been acting so strangely," she insisted. "It isn't like you. You're always so rational." Yes, rational. That I was! I had been so hopelessly blind those past days, but, at that moment, I had never been more rational. I hushed her, murmuring into her ear, "It's going to be perfectly all right."

What she said to me then, that I was holding her too tightly, perhaps, I cannot be sure. There were those other voices, urging and demanding. But I'd outwitted them. I simply patted her head, cooing, "It'll be fine. There, there..."

They weren't going to take her and make her one of their instruments. I'd worked it out, you see. Like I should have trusted I would. It just needed that moment of clarity of thought. And then I sat with her in my arms, all through that long night, until a whole day had passed.

It was the sound of the key dropping from the lock that took my gaze from her sweet face. But I didn't have to look up to see who had entered our home. The strange rustling of fabric, louder even than the rush of wind in the open doorway, told me that the black-clad butler had ventured forth from the precincts of that club of the damned.

"Locks, Mr. Style? Surely you have learned not to underestimate us."

"I rather fear it is you who has underestimated me," said I, standing to meet his dark gaze. "For I've beaten you. Your rules are null and void. I am the victor, and it is you who must pay some form of forfeit."

Again he parroted those same words about procedure, adding, "You took the wager, yet you failed to live up to your part of the arrangement."

He talked to me of rules and procedure? "How was I to know that the arrangement meant murder? And, even if I did, Frye took the matter out of my hands! What chance did that leave me?"

"Come now, Mr. Style, a man of your interests knows that one should assess all the variables and risks before accepting any gamble. One should, at the very least, know the rules of the game!"

"But what is the game?" I had to be told. "It's like no game I know! For pity's sake, the result's the same as if I'd taken that blade to Frye's throat myself. I've won! It's only fair! And the prize I choose is to know what benefit there is for you in this game! Who is it for? Whose entertainment? For that miserable gathering back at the club?

Was that a trace of surprise in his expression? "The associates have as much say in the affairs of the Club Tenebrosa as the ball has control over which pocket of the wheel it shall land in, or as the dice have in which faces they will show when thrown. The club does not exist for the amusement of humanity. When Sir Nicholas established the club and its charter, far further back than you could possibly imagine, it was designed to cater for a far more exclusive clientele, with far darker tastes. After all, our Proprietors too must have their entertainment.

"You may not think you know the Proprietors, but they know you. They have followed the proceedings most closely. Some are impatient. You may hear them occasionally, even in your domain, urging on their favourite."

Those hideous whispers, in my head? In my dreams? If they could be in there, then they must already have known... Whoever they were...whatever and wherever they were, they must have known that I'd outwitted them! They must know that I've won!

«« —— »»

"I've won," Vincent Style insisted. "They couldn't take her from me!"

"No," Cardew agreed, his voice cold as he gazed upon Style's hope-filled grin. "You did that yourself. You killed her! You put your hands round your wife's neck and you killed her!"

The grin faltered, before Style could explain, "So they couldn't claim her."

"They?" Cardew spat. "My God, listen to yourself, man! There is no 'they'! And what of this Quentin Frye, if he even existed? Did you kill him also?"

"He lost. I won," Style explained, and, to Cardew's worsening horror, he began to laugh. "I won!"

And if Style did kill Frye, wondered Cardew, what of poor Wheeler and this Dyson? Two of them? He could not help but think back to those figures he had seen, grey and shambling? No, it was madness to think that way! And there was enough madness in this place already, even if Style was unable to see where he was, in this grim cell in a bleak sanatorium, where he was liable to remain till the day he died.

But, even as the guard arrived to let him out of that miserable place, he turned back to his former friend, saying, "I don't know what happened to you, Style, or what you have seen, or think you have seen, but I hope something can be done for you, I truly do."

But Style, in his madness, only protested, "Why won't you listen to me? I won. I did! I won." And he was still protesting even after the door had slammed shut and Cardew's retreating footsteps were long faded.

But there were other ears to hear his words, as a rustling sound filled the cramped cell, and he looked up to see a black-garbed figure before him, who told him, "Really, Mr. Style, these claims of yours are most irregular."

Some of Style's old attitude was present in his retort, "When did you come in? I didn't send for you."

But the butler had more pressing matters to discuss. "All accounts must be settled, and it really will not do, for the sake of the Club Tenebrosa's reputation, for you to continue to claim that you have found a loophole."

Style stood up from the stained pallet that answered for a bed, and drew himself up to his full height, before asking, "Why don't you just accept it? I outmanoeuvred you. I took Constance from your reach before you could claim her into your service."

"It is you who must accept that you have lost," the butler insisted. "We have already taken what is due."

This made no sense to Style. "That which I hold most dear, you said."

The butler nodded stiffly. "I said it, and I meant it, as laid down in the rules. But your wife was never at risk. She never was that which you hold most dear. That has always been your rational, clear thinking, intellect. Your wits, so to speak. And now you have truly lost them. Goodbye, Mr. Style. You may consider your membership terminated. We must make room for new associates. And there are always many more out there, their curiosity, intellect and vanity drawn to us by the mystery, the drama and the risk, all eagerly awaiting their turn to accept the wager."

And as the rustling noise faded, and Vincent Style found himself alone once more, there was only one answer he could find to the butler's insinuations. And even though these words would soon be lost amidst the cackling, the screeching, the cursing and the sobbing from a hundred identical cells inhabited by a hundred different lost souls, still he insisted, and would continue to insist, "I won. I did. I won! I won! I won..."

...all Lawrence glimpsed of the canvas was the fleeting impression of a hand, clutching and veined, bathed in a glow of blood red intensity, the fingers contorted almost into claws.

The Crimson Picture

On those infrequent occasions that my good friend, Dr. Lawrence, can be prised away from his antiquarian researches for an hour or two of leisure, his tastes incline rather more to the jollity of the music hall, or the thrills of the picture palace, than such loftier diversions as the opera, museum or art gallery. Museums are, after all, where he spends much of his time as a matter of daily course. While the art gallery holds little pleasure since, after so many years of peering at figures woven into illuminated manuscripts, frozen in stained glass, or poised as gargoyles on church roof or crypt, he occasionally feels them peering back at him. As for the opera—of that he will only offer the cryptic response that the shrieking is altogether too reminiscent of things he would prefer not to be put once more in mind of.

It was something of a surprise, therefore, when the porter knocked upon his study door and presented Lawrence with a card inviting him to a private viewing at an art gallery located at an exclusive address in the city. Why such an invitation should come to him he could not fathom. Was there, perhaps, some mix up? Maybe there was a similarly named fellow in the arts faculty? The porter assured him that there was not and, feeling ill-suited to assist in the solving of the puzzle, took his leave; grumbling all the way of how he knew exactly who was who in the college, and why shouldn't he know him, after all those heavy old books and musty packages, some from suspiciously foreign sounding places, he'd delivered over the years?

Lawrence turned the perplexing matter over in his mind and, while doing so, also happened to turn the card over in his hands, and there, in rather fussily elaborate hand-writing, he had his answer. It read;

My dear Lawrence,

If you remember your old classmate Drayton with any affection, kindly join me at the address on the front of this invitation at your earliest convenience. The matter is a peculiar one, and such was always your forte.

Sincerely yours,
H.D.

"Horace Drayton," Lawrence recalled, casting his mind back a good number of years to a classroom filled with eager—though some not so eager—young faces. His mind's eye affixed itself to one particular face, capped with a tangle of unruly black curls and smudged with a stripe of green paint on the side of the nose that no amount of rub-bing with a spittle-flecked finger would shift. "Ah, yes, he always was the artistic one." When a second glance at the front of the card showed his name, not as the subject of the current exhibition, but as the proprietor of the gallery, it tended to confirm the rest of his memory: that Drayton's enthusiasm for art had outstripped his ability. But he had always been a determined lad and, in spite of his sadly deficient facility, that determination to surround himself with the type of work that brought him such pleasure had clearly been strong.

There was, then, some admiration in Lawrence's smile of greeting and approval in the firmness of his handshake when, after both train journey and tram ride, he presented himself at the address on the card and was shown directly to the proprietor's office, there to be met by Horace Drayton.

Although several decades had now passed since last they had set eyes upon one another, there was no mistaking Lawrence's former associate. The hair may have been greyer and more styled and anointed, but it still looked set to spring at any moment into wild curls. Indeed, so little had changed that Lawrence could not help but look for a tell-tale smudge and, in next to no time, his gaze had Mr. Drayton nervously rubbing at the side of his nose, asking, "Is there something on my face?"

"Not at all," beamed Lawrence, the friend of childhood memory now complete and in the flesh before him. "I'm merely amazed that so little has changed for you after such a long time. Well, yes, the clothes are finer and better cut than the old uniform, and this office is a sight more comfortable than the upper corridor dorm, but you seem hardly to have aged. Some of us have felt the full force of the years," and here his hand strayed to his own prematurely whitened hair. "Yet look at you! Tell me, you don't happen to have an enchanted portrait of yourself tucked away in an attic, like the fellow in that Wilde story?"

At this, the signs of strain showed themselves with such rapidity on that smooth and youthful face that, for one moment, Lawrence thought that Drayton was indeed going to admit that, yes, he did possess such an object. And his next words did little to dispel that notion.

"There is a picture I would like you to look at. Whether or not it is enchanted I cannot say, although that seems altogether too benevolent a word. But, such things were always your area of interest. Perhaps you might tell me if there is indeed something unnatural in it. I'll confess it, the thing fills me with the deepest dread even to look at it...or have it look back at me." With which sentiments Lawrence, thinking again of those saintly faces in glass or hellish minions in stone, could only sympathise.

"Perhaps, though," Drayton conceded, "there really is nothing there and it is only fancy on my part after hearing the incredible story that goes with this work. But then, when you have heard the tale, you too might also see a fathomless horror in every swirl and whorl of paint."

"Then there is a story behind this intriguing summons?" queried Lawrence, his interest, as ever, piqued by the mere suggestion of some fresh piece of lore to add to his already compendious store of uncanny chronicles.

"There is certainly a story," sighed the gallery proprietor. "But I shall not be the one to tell it. I think it better that you hear it, in all its detail, from the one who told me. You might find it unbelievable. I know I did. At least, I wished that I did. But he swears it is true, that the events he describes happened to him and, when you hear it and see that picture... I mean really look into the heart of it..." His voice tailed off and a sickly look etched itself across his features.

"Very well," said Lawrence, "and when am I to meet the narrator of this remarkable tale?"

"Shortly. He lives not too far distant and I told my assistant to fetch him the instant you arrived." Rising from behind his desk, and bidding Lawrence to follow, he ventured, "Perhaps it will be of use, while we await him, for me to tell you of the circumstances whereby he shared his testimony with me."

"Indeed so," Lawrence agreed and he followed his old schoolmate from the office and back into the plush gallery area.

"As you can see, we are host to quite an exclusive exhibition at the moment," declared Drayton, a trace of pride beginning to replace the frown of worry on his face, as he threw his arms wide, indicating the walls bedecked with canvasses in their ornate, gilded frames. Lawrence glanced politely at the gaudy landscapes and stern portraits, though his attention was reserved for the unfolding account. "Some of the most prestigious names working today are grouped under this roof. It has been a long and complicated process in arranging such a gathering. But not every piece is here simply because of the fame of its originator. As you may gather, my own hoped-for-talent never flourished, alas. But there are those whose faculty did take hold, only to find it hidden by undeserved obscurity. By mingling the celebrated masters with these deserving cases, it was my hope that their lights may be allowed to shine a little brighter."

Drayton selected a lavish catalogue from a side table and opened it to a certain page, before handing it to his guest with a sigh of, "There is one picture which I wish I had never brought before human eyes."

The title in the catalogue was given as, *'Unknown Subject – A Portrait In Crimson – Oil On Canvas – Artist Anonymous.'*

"But this cannot be right, surely?" Lawrence said, perplexed. "If you hope to showcase some neglected talents then withholding the name of one whom you would wish to celebrate seems hardly helpful."

"Ah, yes," Drayton accepted, "but that was to be my surprise. You see, officially the artist's identity is unknown; the work is unsigned. But I know him. I have an old friend who made a name for himself for a short time some years back. I've displayed as much work of his as I could find room for in the past but, of late, he has not enjoyed any great success and has sold off most of what he once produced at a pittance merely to keep body and soul together. So, as soon as I first set eyes on the portrait, I recognised my friend's handiwork, even if the style is somewhat more...fantastical than his more acknowledged work.

"How splendid, thought I, to have found one of his forgotten commissions. Would it not be a grand surprise for him, on receiving an invitation to mingle with artistically minded persons at the opening of an exhibition, to then discover that his own creation was to be the centrepiece that would direct the limelight once more upon him?"

Here the proprietor paused and, turning to a young man who was taking great pains in the delicate adjustment of those scarlet ropes in their brass holders that would keep the evening's patrons at a safe remove from the paintings, said, "Ernest, could you run along and fetch that newspaper?"

The lad scurried off toward the reception desk and Lawrence prompted, "And were you correct? Was your friend surprised?"

Drayton laughed, a humourless bark, and when the youth returned with a folded over newspaper, he merely tilted his head to indicate that Lawrence was to receive the journal. When it was handed to him, the first thing that caught his eye was the headline, *'Commotion at Exhibition Opening.'*

"Ah," Lawrence nodded, "I skimmed this just this morning, though, of course, it was before your summons arrived, and I had no idea that it was connected with you at the time. Someone going berserk and attempting to slash one of the paintings, if I remember right? Then I must surmise the intended target to be your mysterious crimson picture."

"You do remember right and surmise correctly. This is the very painting here," Drayton said. They had come to a halt before what was clearly a large canvas, though its subject was obscured by the red silk which hung over it. "And the man who attacked it, or, at least, attempted to attack it, was the artist, Hector Jardine."

On seeing Lawrence's blank look, the gallery owner supplied the information that Mr. Hector Jardine had enjoyed a measure of celebrity for a series of landscapes, "Where," Drayton explained, "the figures were as much a feature as the landscapes themselves, humanity and nature, joyful, fruitful and alive."

But, before he could present a comprehensive discourse on the artist's life and works, a lilting voice cut in, declaring, "I am hardly surprised that your guest has not heard of me, Horace. My fame, such as it was, was minor and fleeting."

"Hector," exclaimed Drayton, rushing forward to greet the speaker. "I'm so very glad you could come."

"I'm surprised that you would want me back here after my...after the incident." The new arrival on the scene was stooped, though not from age as Lawrence judged him to be several years younger than Drayton and he. Yet the face, seen at closer quarters when the man came forward, was careworn and the eyes weary. His clothing, though evidently expensive, was showing signs of fraying and, from the style and cut, it was apparent that his fleeting moment of prosperity had been some years previous. The general impression was that here was a man worn down and beaten by some terrible burden. He looked utterly incapable of the violent outburst with which he was credited. Yet, by all accounts he had smashed a champagne bottle and made to slash to ribbons the painting beneath the silk.

"This is the fellow I told you about, Hector," said Drayton, presenting a somewhat guarded Lawrence to the placid looking man who was, nevertheless, apparently capable of random eruptions of fury. "He may be able to help, if you were but to give him your account."

"You haven't told him?" Jardine's words were a reluctant sigh.

"I thought not to," Drayton explained. "At best, I could sketch in the basics but, were you to tell him what you told me last night, you would paint a much more vivid picture."

The artist allowed himself a wry smile at Drayton's carefully selected phrasing. But it was gone from his lips as the proprietor made a move to lift the covering silk from the painting. "Please, leave it covered, I beg of you. If I am to gaze upon it as I tell the tale, I fear I may have the urge to finish what I was prevented from doing last night!"

Nodding, Drayton allowed the silk to drop back, so that all Lawrence glimpsed of the canvas was the fleeting impression of a hand, clutching and veined, bathed in a glow of blood red intensity, the fingers contorted almost into claws. Despite being still in his overcoat and scarf, he found himself shivering as he pondered that if this mere corner of the piece was so powerful in its grotesquery, what dreadfulness must the rest of the painting possess?

By the time Lawrence's eyes were drawn once more from the square of silk before him, he found that the artist had placed himself on a chair facing directly toward the covered canvas. Thus seated, he began, without further bidding, to share his most singular confession.

«« —»»

My story begins conventionally enough, I should imagine, when, as a young man, I had defied the wishes of my parents by embarking on a career...no, a calling, as an artist. They had entertained every expectation that I would enter one of the professions: either legal, as my father's kin tended to be, or medical in the footsteps of my maternal grandfather. But the law held no interest for me, and I was more inclined toward capturing an impression of the life essence than studying the science of it.

Thus we find me eating when I can afford it, attempting to sleep through the hunger when I cannot; the rest of the time spent painting, practising, honing whatever gift I may have possessed. Oftentimes it was a choice between food and fresh supplies of paint. It was an easy choice. "I will eat tomorrow," I reasoned, "but I cannot guarantee that I will be inspired tomorrow so, today, I paint!"

Sometimes my mother would send me money, insisting that I accept it that she might rest assured that no son of hers was going to become destitute. You see, my parents may have been distant and reserved, proud, even, but they were far from the heartless monsters that one reads of in melodrama and tragedy. There was no disinheritance, no banishment or estrangement. While they may not have entirely understood my passion, the money was there should I have need of it. But it was I who refused to take it! My pride, you see: my determination that I would succeed on talent alone.

But pride doesn't put a roof over a man's head or food in his belly, does it? Consequently, when I was neither painting nor sleeping, I took what employment came to hand. Not jobs requiring hard, intense labour. As anyone looking at me could tell, I've hardly the build or stamina for it. Besides which, would I dare take on a task that might damage my hands and prevent my painting? No, the work was mainly in restaurants and public houses. In one or two, the landlords would even allow me to display some of my work and I actually earned small commissions from the customers. Some were looking for a likeness, usually of a sweetheart or child. Others might offer a few pennies for a sketch in pencil or chalk. I accepted all requests, no matter the fee. After all, while money was welcome, the chance to practice my skills was a matter of necessity.

But the man who was waiting for me on that October

night, as the last of the regulars left and I prepared to lock up the bar, was not a customer I had ever set eyes on before.

I was not even aware of his presence until he spoke. "You are the artist, I presume?" Yet his curiously assured voice suggested that he already knew the answer. He was tall and lean, clad neatly in black from head to toe, in clothes that seemed to attract neither dust specks nor wrinkles. He carried himself precisely, almost as though unused to walking, as he moved to indicate one of my pieces on the wall. He scarcely seemed to glance at it, however, keeping his eyes firmly upon me. His eyes, like his clothing, were intensely black.

I confirmed that the work was mine and he went smoothly into his proposal. "My employer has instructed me to request your services for a particular commission."

"Your employer?" I ventured, but the question was left hanging.

"Indeed. My employer has taken an interest in your talent. He believes that you may have certain skills which might, given the right direction, be nurtured."

Suddenly I understood. This black clad stranger with his precise manner and courteous tone was a servant, a butler in all likelihood, to some wealthy individual who, unless either my ears or my instincts were failing me, wished to act as my patron! I was instantly full of questions. Who was my apparent benefactor? Where had he heard of me? Had he seen my work before? Had someone, perhaps my enthusiastic friend Horace, been spreading the good word on my behalf?

Again, I was to receive no answer. "Mr. Jardine, even were I privy to my employer's private thoughts, I would not be at liberty to discuss them. I merely need to know if you will accept a special, private commission."

"Of course," I almost cried. "When?"

"Tonight."

"Tonight? But it's almost midnight already! I've been working practically since dawn."

At my protest, the servant bowed his head stiffly and strode toward the door. A few more seconds and he would be gone. There was no time to hesitate, though I may now wish that I had slammed the door at the wretched creature's back and forgot about him, his employer and the offer. But, of course, I did no such thing.

"Another time when I'm less tired," I pleaded, practically racing him for the door. "I merely worry that your employer will not get my best work when I'm so worn out!"

He paused and I think I may even have detected a smile when he said, "That is most thoughtful of you, Mr. Jardine. However time is of the essence, and my employer has certain requirements which must be met. Any potential impairment in the quality of your work will, I assure you, have already been factored in. And the inconvenience to yourself has also been considered, and this will reflect itself in the purse that is on offer.

"If, however, you are unable or unwilling to undertake the work at the specified time, we shall part company now and the offer will be rescinded."

"Unwilling?" I said "Not at all! Unable? I should hope not. If you will but tell me where I am expected, I shall go there directly after I fetch my equipment from home."

But of this, he informed me, there was entirely no need. "All the tools of your trade are prepared and awaiting you. My employer is very particular, and he has certain preferences for the treatment and preparation of the canvasses he acquires, and in the mixing of the paints that are used upon them. Now, if you will follow me, Mr. Jardine, there is transport waiting to take you to the allotted venue."

On locking the door, I was taken aback to see a dark carriage with two black steeds between the shafts awaiting me just outside the tavern. The streets in that part of town were never busy, certainly not after dark, and I felt sure that I should have heard such a vehicle pull up. But I had more on my mind than mysteries that likely didn't exist, and so I eagerly climbed aboard.

The interior was as plush as any I'd seen. Rich, red velvet cushioned the seats and curtained the windows, and a comfortable journey seemed promised. Whether it was to take me near or far, I wasn't to be told, as the butler did not join me inside and the carriage sped off with me onboard alone, my mind still reeling with questions that seemed fated to go unanswered.

Such was my reverie that I lost track of time and only came to myself when the carriage slowed and finally halted. Before I could reach the handle, the door was opened and there stood that same black-eyed servant, indicating that I had reached my destination.

Beyond him, I could but dimly perceive the grey steps leading up to the rectangle of a dark door. Stepping down from the carriage, I glanced up and saw that I was being hastened toward a tall, narrow townhouse, anonymous amidst a long row of identical buildings. There was no streetlamp near enough to allow me to take in much in the way of detail, apart from the fact that no light seemed to burn within any of the rooms save the harsh yellow glow from one of the windows high above me.

Even as I observed this, I was escorted through that dark doorway. It opened onto a panelled corridor, wherein stood a woman in the traditional sombre, colourless uniform of a housekeeper. The passage was lit by the lamp that she held aloft for us, which, as she stepped aside to allow us entrance, sent our shadows scampering ahead of us to be swallowed up by the gloom that lingered deeper into that house.

"Is everything in readiness?" the butler asked, as he swung the outer door closed in our wake.

The housekeeper nodded, "Mr. Jardine should find everything that he requires."

"In which case, you may show him to his studio." The butler then turned to me and said, "The studio is purely makeshift, until our employer is assured that you will accept his sponsorship beyond this one initial sitting. However, I do think that you shall find it more than adequate for your needs. If you would go up now, I shall be with you presently to ensure that all is to your satisfaction." And with that, he disappeared from view, taking neither lamp nor candle as he went to whatever task awaited him in the gloomy bowels of the property.

Left alone with the housekeeper, I had little choice but to follow her up the winding staircase or else be left in the dark. The lamp's glow revealed lighter patches on the panelling where pictures had at one time hung and had never been replaced. This, coupled with the realisation that I had seen no form of furnishing or decoration save for curtains at the landing windows, did make me ponder as to what kind of art lover would own such a property. But I swiftly dismissed my concerns, reasoning that the house may have only recently been purchased, which would also have explained the air of neglect and the chill that seemed to hang in the atmosphere.

I again tried one or two of the questions which had gained no answer from the butler, but the housekeeper's response was the same. "I must inform you that, even were I privy to my employer's private thoughts, I would not be at liberty to discuss them." Her tone was so flat and the response so identical that I had a brief fancy that my patron's staff were practically automata, programmed with the same set of responses to any given circumstance. And, while normally I liked to pride myself on an artist's instinct in finding the essential character in the features of an individual human face, here in the shifting illumination, I found it hard to gauge anything from her neutral expression, even whether she was young or old.

We had reached the uppermost floor and I followed the rustling of her skirts as she led me along a narrow passageway with a sloping wall, toward a doorway round which a rim of bright light might be seen. Surely, before I entered that daunting studio, I could persuade her to tell me something of my assignment. "I take it that it's a portrait that's expected of me?" I allowed myself a chuckle, "Well, it'd hardly be a landscape at this time of night."

"A portrait, Mr. Jardine, yes," was her only response.

"And who, may I ask, is to be my subject?"

But she merely opened the door, so that she stood as implacable as a black statue against the light beyond and, as I hesitated, intoned, "If you please, Mr. Jardine, it is almost time to begin."

The long room was an attic, with a large window set into the sloping North wall and a long series of skylights in the flat roof. By day it would be filled with natural light; what better for an artist's studio? But, of course, I would be painting under starlight and the sky above me was made all the darker for the stark electrical lighting which, following my climb through murky darkness, gave off a glare of such brilliance that I almost winced.

An easel was set up in one corner by a table, upon which were arrayed brushes, charcoals, pencils, jugs of water and jars of spirits, and more paint than I could have afforded after a month's bar-keeping.

However, my attention was reserved for the figure who was seated upon the large, lustrous, high-backed chair, practically a throne, at the centre of the room. The clothes of the richest fabrics, the elegantly coifed hair, the glittering, jewelled rings upon several fingers of the hands that either clasped the arm of the chair or rested upon the elaborately sculpted golden top of the ebony cane; everything about him suggested a man of noble breeding.

"Is this he? Is this my patron?" I asked the housekeeper, aware that my voice was reverently hushed as I did so. Then, all too aware that I had no idea who had brought me here, "How should I address him?"

"My instructions are that you are here to paint, not to talk. You must start the painting immediately." And, indicating a bell that would summon her should I require anything, she withdrew, leaving me with my silent sitter. Suspecting that I was being put to the test and not wishing to fail at the first hurdle, I took up my pencil and, as wordlessly as the man before me, I began to draw.

Despite some effect of the lighting that seemed to leave the centre of the room in a column of vague shadow, my progress was rapid. It was a matter of moments to sketch in that classical face—broad and handsome yet, to my mind, a shade too haughty and self aware. There was arrogance there in the downward turn of the mouth. And the eyes...but the eyes were closed. Was he bored or perhaps asleep? It was, after all, now beyond midnight. Whichever it was, I was grateful for his stillness. There were no distracting movements, no sudden shifts in posture to throw out that which had already been delineated. With no idle chatter and no need to pause for the model's comfort, I was applying the broad strokes of paint before the hour was out. Indeed, my own rate of progress spurred me on and made me entirely forget how tired I had been not so long before.

Almost before I was conscious of it, I had begun picking out the details: the folds of expensive material, the ruby tie-pin, the bead of moisture on that wide, pale forehead. Had I noticed that unusual pallor previously? How could I have failed to when it stood out so starkly against the heavy blackness of the clothing and the jewels that appeared to glint so wetly? How had I missed the clamminess of the skin, or the straggling limpness of the blond hair that framed that slack, blank face? Could I really have first thought him handsome and proud? There was no pride there—no thought at all.

As this realisation struck me, so too did the awareness that I had now been watching him, indeed scrutinising him in minute detail for over three hours and at no point had I seen him move. Even a sleeper makes some unconscious movements. And it was at that moment that I became suddenly aware that the portrait I was painting was that of a dead man.

《《——》》

The artist paused in his narrative, as Drayton, seeing how unpleasant the tale was in telling, had brought him a glass of brandy. He accepted it gratefully, as did Dr. Lawrence when more glasses were filled.

"A dead man," mused Lawrence, "propped up and clothed as though alive? As I recall it, in the early days of photography, families suffering bereavements frequently had a photographer make a memento of their departed loved one. One might surmise that this were a more antiquated variation on the custom, though your grim expression tells me this is too logical a theory."

Hector Jardine drained his glass and sighed, "As morbid an explanation as this would have been, it would have been preferable to the reality behind my task that night. But the truth of the matter was not to be quickly forthcoming, even after my frozen dread at being alone in that strange attic with this displayed corpse had finally thawed enough to allow me to ring for assistance."

«« —— »»

The housekeeper answered my summons so swiftly that I could easily believe she had been standing motionless in the corridor just outside the studio awaiting the bell. "May I bring you something, Mr. Jardine?"

"You can get me a carriage and let me out of this mad-house," I cried, waving my hand in the direction of the ghastly seated figure. "If this is some kind of ghoulish prac-tical joke, I want nothing to do with it! And, if it isn't, per-haps the police should be involved!"

"There is no need for such alarm, Mr. Jardine." It was the butler who said so, though, apart from an odd rustling sound that I'd taken for the wind outside, I had not heard anyone enter.

"You would have me paint a cadaver's portrait and you tell me that there's no need for alarm?"

"I can assure you," he soothed, "that even as we speak, the person whose likeness you paint is very much alive."

"But why is he so still? Why does he look as he does?" I did not dare approach for a closer inspection, but the housekeeper did, taking her lamp into that curiously light-less area. In the glow I saw that same handsome and ruddy face I had first perceived and, though it may have been but the flicker of the flame, I believed that I saw movement there: a fluttering of eyelids or a trembling of the lips.

I laughed then at my ridiculous fears. I had hardly slept in twenty-four hours and, given the combination of this, the dizzying thrill of my unexpected good fortune, and the curious effect of such unfamiliar lighting, perhaps my eyes had been deceiving me.

"Do not let his condition trouble you. He is quite at rest." The servant's voice was just as smooth as before and I accepted the ease and reassurance that it brought me. "Your work is proceeding admirably. Please do not let us delay you further." Then he and the housekeeper departed.

For the first time, I think, I stood back and looked at what I had thus far wrought. There was the corpse, pallid and glistening. This would not do! With fervour, I threw myself back into the portrait, determined to obliterate the hideous visage which I had allowed my imaginings to impress upon my subject's own features.

My eyes must still have been adjusting to the electrical lighting, as each stroke that I applied to the canvas appeared to me to shimmer and writhe. Already the sky above was paling and on and on I painted, scarcely casting a glance at the unmoving figure, allowing my hand free reign to paint what I instinctively felt was there.

The whiteness of the skin was erased, overlain by a greenish grey sheen, as wet and slippery as a fish's belly. The cheeks sagged and bloated, the eyelids were puffed and purple, the mouth was merely a drooping slash across the swollen jowls from which the grey slug of a tongue threatened to topple.

The fingers that gripped the cane were distended and as fat and pale as uncooked sausages and they bulged around the corroded rings. There was a terrible wetness about him, too, that pooled out around him in a ghastly puddle. And, from this it almost seemed that a pair of sopping arms might emerge to clasp him and drag him down into impossible depths.

The blonde hair swam round the dome of the head like tendrils of bleached white seaweed. And the eyes? The eyes were finally open and they stared. But they stared sightlessly and lifelessly!

I almost fell back from the canvas when I saw what horror I had inflicted upon it. But a firm hand grasped my arm and I was propelled gently yet steadily into a chair while a glass of wine was placed into my other hand.

"Congratulations, Mr. Jardine," said the butler. "You have succeeded admirably, and my employer will be most satisfied."

I made to indicate the canvas but the housekeeper had already removed it from its easel and was carrying it out of the studio. Instead, I managed to gabble, "I know you think me foolish after my panic during the night but I fear that your employer may be ill." I waved my hand feebly in the direction of the still seated figure, though I did not dare look where I pointed lest there be any real resemblance to the image that I had depicted.

What he replied surprised me. "Mr. Jardine, you are at a misapprehension regarding the identity of your subject. Who he is need be of no concern to you. Suffice it to say that he is acquainted with my employer and that your work here tonight serves as his reward for certain deeds he has undertaken." While this was the nearest to an explanation I had received in my time there, I was loath to imagine who would want such a reward and what had been done to earn it.

The morning light had bleached the sky above us and, with a groan, I contemplated the prospect of a long day ahead of me in the public bar. But the rustle of notes in a leather wallet held out by the butler suggested that such employment might be unnecessary, for the immediate future at any rate. "You have also earned your reward," he told me, "and you will be similarly rewarded for each future commission."

Here, indeed, were riches, but the proceedings of that night had left me uneasy about accepting such strange sponsorship. I had always strived to evoke the essential beauty in life. Never before had my vision been opened up to such darkness. The words pained me but say them I must, "You may tell your employer that I must decline his patronage."

"You are in error, Mr. Jardine," he said. "The correct term, I believe you will find, is 'our employer'." And, as he said it, I realised for the first time that I had the wallet grasped tightly in my hand.

I sat numbly in the carriage as it drove me homeward through the now busy streets, not even bothering to part the curtains to look out at the reassuring bustle of life I heard from all around me. It seemed all too clear to me that I had accepted a deal which no sane man should ever contemplate.

And, when next I saw the face of the man that I had painted that night, my estimation of his being of noble birth was confirmed. He was a lord in some coastal spot, wild in his ways, and his likeness appeared in the newspaper above a story detailing how he and a yacht loaded with his friends had been lost in a storm and dragged down into the depths of the sea.

《《——》》

"A coincidence," suggested Drayton, though his tone was more one of forlorn hope than any genuine scepticism.

Lawrence who, to my knowledge, has read much in the way of modern theory on the phenomena referred to in certain of the more arcane forms of lore, wondered aloud, "Or, supposing, a case of foreknowledge. You say that you painted what you 'instinctively felt'. A precognitive fugue, possibly? There are numerous accounts—a child refuses to travel on a particular train that is shortly afterwards involved in a terrible crash—someone meets a long-lost cousin out of the blue only to later find that the cousin has died in a distant land."

Yet Jardine remained doubtful, shaking his head. "You see, I sensed that something else was guiding my hand. Something other. Perhaps something with no form of its own. It was there that first night and it grew stronger on each subsequent visit I was compelled to make."

"You returned? You say it as if you had no choice," put in Lawrence. "You talk of a deal, as though you had some contract. Yet you signed nothing to bind you to this patron."

"It was a sense," the artist replied. "A sinking feeling that I had somehow allowed myself to be wound up tightly in the strands of some dark web: one whose spider I could not see, yet whose presence I could feel perpetually lurking close by."

Dr. Lawrence shuddered, having of late developed such an intense dislike of spiders that the mere mention of the word was practically unbearable to him. "Please, Jardine," he urged, "Continue."

"Very well," said the artist, pausing only to add, before resuming his account, "but you're wrong when you suggest that I had signed no contract. I had signed something. For I always sign my work."

《《——》》

Before the full realisation of the unnatural realm which I was gradually infiltrating was upon me, however, a full day and night of sleep and a full purse did much to diminish the strangeness I had experienced, till it had only the power of a dimly remembered nightmare.

In an effort to dim these memories yet further, I worked, making my first purchase fresh canvasses. I had, for months, been painting and repainting on the same frames, each new piece obliterating an earlier work. But no more! I had canvasses and paint and the luxury of time to devote to them. I was as happy as ever my friends had seen me. "As cheerful as a lad who's got back from playing truant to discover the school's ablaze," was how Horace put it, reasoning, "That can only mean you've been playing host to the muse. If you have anything ready, I may have an empty space on one of my walls."

I showed him one painting, then two, then a dozen. "These are extraordinary!" he exclaimed. "The vibrancy! You might almost smell the blossom in this meadow, or hear the rustling of the grass in this view of the park," and more such flattery that it would do me no service to repeat. But I will repeat the criticism. "There are no figures to give them a sense of place or scale. But I would certainly consider any one or two of these when they're ready."

And, when they were ready, Horace was as good as his word and they were exhibited. Though I had held back my own words, unable to tell him what had brought about my change in fortune and what also stayed my hand from capturing the images of the people who should, by rights, have been populating my landscapes.

It was as they were hanging in this very gallery that I met Margaruite, the young woman who might have been...no, who was, outside of painting, the one love of my life. And the one love that did not turn on me!

She had, in my hearing, praised the lifelike quality of a group of children whom I had included indulging in a game of chase in the woods on the edge of the park. When her companion, the elderly dragon to whom, I later discovered, she was secretary, companion and, it seemed, general skivvy, had moved out of earshot, I gently told this enchanting young lady that they were no more real than the cherubs in a churchyard.

"And how would you know," she retorted, unwilling to encourage this lunatic who accosted women in art galleries, "unless you were there when the picture was painted?"

"Oh, I was there all right, and I know that these children, in fact every last person depicted here, exists only in the mind of the artist, he being me."

This seemed to delight her and she was radiant when delighted. "You painted this? And that one, also? And you're not lying to try and turn the head of a country girl new to the city? And all of these people came out of your imagination?"

I told her, "There are many things lurking in my imagination," and I even managed to smile as I said it.

Horace, I know, remembers Margaruite well since, from that point, she was a frequent visitor to the gallery and, from there, to my studio. She also painted: vivid, bold, colourful pieces, full of a vitality that I envied. Yet she would let no-one see them but myself. Horace will also remember how we laughed and talked, and how she encouraged my every effort and the plans we had. Such plans!

Then, one night, as I made my way back from a long session in the studio transferring that day's sketches of a country lake to canvas, there, in the street where I lived, a black carriage was waiting.

So many months had passed since that strange night that, after an initial cold jolt on seeing the vehicle, I became convinced that its presence there was a coincidence, and that it had no connection to my prior experience, and I hurried past it to the safety of home.

The sight of the butler waiting on the steps of my building proved me sadly wrong and, as he took a pocket watch from the folds of his black waistcoat, I knew that midnight must be close at hand.

As the carriage sped on, with me yet again alone inside, it did occur to me to attempt discovering something of my destination. But, when I parted the curtains, I found darkly frosted windows that stubbornly refused to be budged. All my scrabblings were for nothing and, when he once more opened the door, the butler glanced at the glass with glittering eyes that appeared aware of my attempts.

Under the moon that glowered down on us that night, the townhouse looked gaunt and decayed and once I was again in the care of the housekeeper I noted, by her lamp's light, that the banisters and the corners were thickly coated in dust and hung heavy with cobwebs. I swear I even saw strands of the stuff within the dark pleats of that woman's dress and amongst the tresses of her hair, as if, since last I had seen her, she had somehow remained still and frozen into position, dutifully awaiting my next appointment at that skulking property.

The studio was as before, but with fresh canvas on the easel and fresh paints on the table. And, naturally, a fresh subject in the chair. On this night it was a woman—one who, with her features skilfully accentuated by cosmetics and her perfectly presented face framed by silken, shimmering hair, should almost certainly have been beautiful had there been any spark of life about her. Yet she sat as still and as rigid as the drowned lord.

Did I even think to run, as I should have? No! I stayed and I painted and as I did, the sensation grew in me that not only was this woman dead but, if I did dare approach her and lay a hand on her cold flesh, there would be nobody there at all, just the dispersing shadow of an image projected from some distant source.

But I did not approach her and, after a while, I did not even see her. And, by dawn, I had a completed portrait of a corrupted hag—her decaying flesh streaked and daubed by powder and make-up which did little to conceal the ugliness etched in every line, but turned her into a grotesque parody, a mummified circus clown. And her neck, which twisted at an angle that no neck should ever twist at, was bare and bony, since that long and shining hair of hers had been pulled back sharply from her head—clawed by what appeared to be a branch, but which might have been a shrivelled arm with its stick-like fingers so enmeshed in her hair that she dangled limply from it. And her eyes? They bulged piteously in horror, shock, and a final, ghastly realisation that I was glad I could not share.

"What kind of reward is this?" I demanded of the butler, as the canvas was once again spirited away.

"A reward for vanity," he suggested, "providing, in art, a mirror that shows only the truth within? Would such an answer relieve your turmoil? But why should such matters trouble you, Mr. Jardine? What you paint is simply the truth, even if those it portrays cannot yet see it. But they will, in the fullness of time."

Then he gave me my money and I accepted it, and I was driven home, where I slept and I arose and I painted bright, hopeful scenes, and I made my plans with Margaruite and I never once told her of my nocturnal occupation.

It was at this time, when my days were filled with such happiness and success, that I was called for most frequently by night. Eventually the butler did not even appear and I simply climbed aboard the carriage when I found it waiting for me. By this stage I'd already stopped accepting the wages that my employer arranged for me after each visit.

I cannot tell you how many of these portraits I undertook. I had contemplated arming myself with a flask of alcohol to help blot out the faces before me but, the worst of it is, I didn't even need it. I had become an expert, you see, at not recognising those put up for my attentions as people. They were objects to be detailed and that was all. But, traces still remain, even now.

Some of these faces, or faces that seemed familiar to me, I saw again in reports of tragedy, horror, execution and death. Always death! Here was the murderess, found broken-necked, hanged by her own hair; the thief entombed and asphyxiated in the vault he chose to rob, the huntsman savaged by his own dogs or something worse, the drowned lord's debaucheries drifting slowly to light... It troubled me less when the person seated in that chair was old and in the twilight of their life but, at least once, I think there may have been a child!

My other life, that which was lived in daylight, was as successful as it had ever been. My work was exhibiting and selling. I was the consummate showman, unveiling master-piece after masterpiece, triumph after triumph, and I was fêted and befriended by all, it seemed. I had even persuaded Margaruite to show Horace some of her paintings. And when she announced, "He actually likes them," she appeared to find the notion preposterous, exciting and terrifying all at the same time. "He wants to put them in his latest show. I'll be next to you!"

"Where you belong, always," I told her.

"I couldn't be prouder," she smiled. "You know how I adore your work: how you can capture the mood of a moment, and how the people in them all appear so alive." And she was still smiling when she said the last words that I would ever have wanted to hear. "You should paint por-traits! I wish you would! I wish you would paint me and make me look as alive as your other paintings."

The horror in my face was plain to see, and the effect was instantly wounding to that poor girl who could have had no idea of the thoughts that screamed in my mind. She was hurt, then angry, then confused and, all the time, I was thinking furiously. I swear, I even contemplated thrusting my hand into the fire to give me a way out of this impossible task. Would that I'd had the courage!

But, my rational mind protested, I was my own man and this was no commission. And hadn't there been something about the mixing of the paints and the preparation of the canvas for those sponsored paintings: some glamour, might you call it, in those instruments that affected the portrait produced? But I would use normal paints and regular canvas, paid for from my own earnings, not from my patron's purse. And I would not be painting her by midnight. And as a fool can easily persuade himself of anything if he tries hard enough, I agreed.

"May I move now? Is it finished?" Margaruite had scarcely been able to sit still during that long afternoon. And, when I told her that I was done, she leapt forward, crying, "I must see!"

"Please," I tried to hold her back, too exhausted to be effective against her joyful enthusiasm. "Margaruite, please don't!"

"Oh." The sound, as she made it, was so hollow that I would have wept if I'd had the strength. Then, when she turned from the canvas to me, there was a glimmer in her eyes and an edge in her voice which I had never known before. "Is this some strange form of joke, Hector?"

"I'm sorry," I mumbled, "I'm sorry I can't explain... What I see when I look at you..."

"This is what you see when you look at me?" She dragged me over to the canvas, making me look at what those dreadful hours had achieved. "You see nothing?"

"No..." How could I tell her? What could I say?

She was crying now, pointing at the dull emptiness of the canvas. "You see nothing when you look at me? Because there's nothing there! The canvas is blank!"

I cannot tell you what I saw when Margaruite posed for me that day. The memory is buried away in such a deep and dark place that I will not even approach it. But I couldn't put it down on the canvas. I had tried to paint the warm and smiling face that was in my memory, but something else kept forcing its way to the surface, so overwhelming in its intensity that I could only allow my hand to trace it in the air rather than preserve it on the canvas.

Margaruite looked bewildered as I slumped before her, as vacant as the portrait I had failed to paint. "Is it something that I've done? Are you trying to tell me something?"

No, I thought! Not done...not done yet!

"Why are you shaking so?" There was fear now in her voice, anger softening into concern. "You've been so distracted these past few days. Are you ill? What's wrong?"

"Go!" I yelled it. "For God's sake, Margaruite, just go!"

I could see that she didn't understand, but I could do nothing to make her understand. And, even if I had, what I had done on those ghastly night sittings would surely have damned me in her eyes! "I cannot look at you! Please, go!"

That was the last time she and I were ever together. Call me a coward if you will, but how could I spend my days and nights with her when I had seen what I had seen? When I knew how her days would end?

The carriage came for me that night but, on this occasion, it was I that awaited its approach. The butler had taken the journey with it. And, just this one time, he sat with me inside as the waiting house beckoned.

"I'd thought that it was the paints," I protested. "Something in the preparations..."

"Ah, but once you had worked with them and mastered the technique, you may have found yourself possessed of talents that you had never utilised before," said he. "After all, while the artist has a clear effect on the medium, perhaps the medium may also have its own effect on the artist."

"Then I'll have no more of it! My commission ends now!"

"Of course, Mr. Jardine," he agreed, stepping out of the carriage before that decomposing townhouse. "No-one has compelled you to remain under our employer's patronage. But there is the matter of tonight's appointment, and I gravely doubt that you would wish to miss the chance to paint the one responsible for your recent experiences."

And so I followed that stiffly-moving housekeeper—with her lamp that no longer worked, and her face so veiled in webs that she wouldn't have noticed anyway—up those steps and into the studio to finally encounter the monster that dwelled within.

After that night, the black carriage has not come back.

I forced myself not to run back to Margaruite and, when she left to return to her hometown, I no longer had the agonising pleasure of watching her from afar, while trying desperately to convince myself that I could forget what I had seen, or that the knowledge would not pray on us both until I had to share it rather than go mad. I still hope that I was wrong and that what I had thought I saw was no more than the projection of my own terrors. But what if my own terrors are what shaped events for all who I painted? I pray not. And I hope that she is happy, and that her life without me has been a good one.

My own life has been a struggle since then. Horace was right; the paintings needed figures. But there are no figures in the park at twilight or dusk. For these are the only times when I feel that it is safe to paint, lest a memory of a passer-by become part of the composition and some hellish fate make itself apparent.

Yet, still, I paint. But only I see the results. They are not for exhibition. I do not display my work anymore.

Not until now...

《《——》》

All eyes turned to the silk-draped square on the wall. The artist's story seemed at an end but the very presence of this object was itself the subject of a mystery that only Horace Drayton could put to rest. It was Lawrence who posed the question. "Where and how, exactly, did you find this picture?"

"That's just the damnedest thing," Drayton pondered, furrowing his brow. "For I didn't so much find it as..."

"It found you," supplied Lawrence, this almost seeming to confirm a suspicion he had been entertaining. "And, through you, it found Jardine. But how was it brought into your orbit?"

"A woman," said Drayton, hollowly. "A stiff, strangely-spoken woman. She said that her...her employer had instructed her to dispose of it, and that she was to take any price for it, and that it might, perhaps, be particularly rewarding to one of my visitors. Then she was gone. A servant, I thought, from some wealthy family, for she was met at the door by a man in butler's uniform and carried off in a massive black carriage. You see, this is how I know Hector's story to be true. And...as she climbed into the carriage, I thought that I saw some other within—a darker shape within the red, velvet darkness. A shape that seemed to smile."

"Could he have been here?" murmured Lawrence in horrified excitement.

But there was to be no answer as, with a halting step, Jardine had moved to the shrouded painting. Then, with the lingering traces of a showman's instinct, he grasped the silk and, with a cry of, "They brought it here to be exhibited? Then let us look on it one last time. Let us all look upon the face of the monster," he tore the covering away.

When he told me of his experience, Dr. Lawrence still found it hard to put into words what he saw depicted on that crimson canvas, but the impression he gave was of something bellowing, insane and infernal. He spoke of those clawed hands that gripped the arms of the throne with such force that the wood should surely splinter. He said something of a gaping chasm of a mouth that seemed to shriek its silent madness into the air around the painting, so that it shimmered like a heat haze of hellish intensity. He also made mention of the veins and arteries that stood out tense on practically every inch of exposed flesh and that appeared to pulse with livid ferocity.

And, finally, he whispered of the eyes. And, as he did so, his face was ashen and there was a tremor in his voice. "Those staring, maddened, baleful eyes that saw everything! A gaze that appeared to find me and crawl all over me like..." and here he had to force the words past his lips, "like thin-legged red spiders! It held me, almost seeing within me. Into the heart of who I am. Into my very soul! And these eyes saw so much more than eyes are meant to see that they were bleeding wet, red tears."

"This is your work?" Lawrence demanded, looking at the artist with a mixture of pity, chilling horror and, hard to credit, fascinated admiration. He could scarcely believe that the painting before him was the work of this gentle man, or of any man. "But it's unsigned. You said that you always sign your work."

"It is signed," Jardine moaned softly, "I had forgotten... forced the memory from my mind, just as I had done with all those blank, oblivious faces. But I remember it, now that I see it with my own eyes. There! Signed by my hand...but the signature is the artist's own!" And as he slumped back into his seat, he pointed a shaking hand toward the lower corner of the canvas. There, a symbol, almost like a coat of arms, appeared to be etched into the arm of the throne beneath the monstrous subject's left hand; and was that the shadow of some other, yet more ghastly hand, that seemed to lurk there?

Lawrence dropped his glass, numbed by the full significance of what he was seeing. "You said something else guided your hand. Something with no form of its own, working through you!"

"What does it mean?" urged Drayton, still squinting at the symbol, which appeared to him to be an arch or gateway framing a bestial form—possibly a goat but, more likely, a satyr or hobgoblin. "Whose insignia is this?"

Dr. Lawrence, who had encountered a similar symbol with alarming regularity in some of his less orthodox studies, had his suspicions but, whether or not he would have risked sharing them even he doesn't know. For, at that instant, there was an agonised grunt from Jardine, who had flung himself rigid in his chair.

"It's the strain of telling that ghastly story again," cried Drayton, rushing to his friend. "I should never have asked him! We must do something!"

But, with a final spasm and a noise that might have grown to a scream if there had been air to power it, there was nothing any human agency could do for Hector Jardine. The boy, Ernest, having heard the commotion, was sent to fetch a doctor. All Lawrence could do was assure his former school friend that Jardine had seemed relieved in the telling of the tale and the sharing of his private burden.

When the doctor was done, his first diagnosis, though it would have to be later verified through post mortem procedures, was that Hector Jardine had died, almost instantaneously, from a brain haemorrhage. And, as the pronouncement was made, Lawrence could not help but think on such a death, the crimson fluid filling the brain, enveloping it and drowning it. And, as he experienced this image, he turned his eyes between the crimson picture and the mortal remains of the painter: his eyes wide and staring, his mouth gaping, his hands clutching so tightly that the doctor struggled to prise the clawing fingers away from the arms of the chair. And, in that instant, he saw that this indeed was the work of the artist's own hand, a final self-portrait.

When the artist had been removed and the portrait covered once more, the two former school friends sat sharing a silence, until Drayton murmured, "She is alive, you know. Margaruite, I mean. But I think I know what Hector saw. She had an accident, you see, after they had parted. That's why she went back home, where there was someone to care for her while she adapted to her condition. For she's blind.

"She has learned to cope with it admirably. She was always strong in spirit. But for Hector, a man who lived by his sight more fully than any of his other senses, can there have been a more horrible fate for him to await for a loved one?"

"Maybe not," Lawrence agreed, "but given what his eyes had witnessed, might there not also have been a degree of jealousy amidst the horror?"

All that remains to be said is that, though Jardine is dead and the portrait burned, there are frequently works by centuries-dead artists found mouldering away in their hiding places and long forgotten vaults. As Lawrence somewhat worriedly expressed his thoughts on the matter, "Who knows when any of us might find ourselves in some unknown gallery in some unfamiliar place and what face we might discover in a dark and dusty canvas, staring back at us with all too familiar eyes?"

*Even though many were ancient, and as grey as tombstones,
there were countless fresher additions, reds and greens,
blues and golds, of wool and linen and silk.*

Rags

There was rain enough in London. So why he'd come hundreds of miles to experience more of the wretched stuff, Belstone couldn't fathom. In London the rain was just as wet, but at least there you could, if you were unlucky enough to be caught out in it, shelter in a shop doorway or under an awning. Such escape wasn't an option for him presently, up to the knees of his tweeds in sodden grass, or bracken, or gorse, or whatever they called it here, with no sign of a shop, or any other building, in any direction. No sign of anything, if he was honest—not even the fabled Highland scenery his friends had raved about during that endless journey in its series of evermore comfortless trains.

When the proposition of visiting Scotland had first been mooted, Belstone had imagined supping malts in a snug tavern, with maybe a stroll around a nice castle and a few nights in a warm hotel. It had apparently been a shock to him that Scotland extended beyond Edinburgh, which had the taverns, the castle and the hotels, or that the Highlands actually were high with not much more to them than land— land that was alternately rocky or boggy, on which you either stumbled and cracked your shins or which you were sucked in up to your knees and had to sacrifice your newly purchased boots to in order to be released. True, there was the odd tree—some very odd ones, from what he had not long ago encountered—and there were the mountains. But those trees offered little protection from rain that fell in sheets, and the mountains, if they really existed, were hiding somewhere in the fog. Ah, the fog—something else he could have stayed at home for.

"Still," as Bewley had observed only that morning, "if the Highlands were good enough for our late sovereign, God rest her, they're good enough for a junior clerk like Jeremy Belstone, esquire." How anyone could have been so cheerful in the morning, particularly on a morning like this, was a mystery to Belstone. He was almost glad that he'd somehow managed to lose sight of Bewley, and the rest of them for that matter, though he was still quite mystified as to how he'd managed it. He'd only stopped for a few minutes to catch his breath after his latest, severest fall. They'd had little sympathy and simply told him to catch up, which is easy to do when you're not the fellow with only one decent leg, another that grumbles and aches with every step, and a hefty knapsack that keeps falling apart, despite your best efforts to mend it. Clearly there was no code of ethics amongst salesmen, when they were prepared to bandy claims like, "You wouldn't find better quality for love nor money, guv'nor," about such shoddy goods.

Well, you wouldn't find Belstone anywhere north of Hyde Park after this miserable holiday was over, he swore inwardly, before limping in the direction he hoped was onward. Map reading wasn't a skill he'd ever had to acquire to summon a cab to take him between office, club and home. If Wynngrave had only kept his word and brought along his motor car, he pondered gloomily. But neither car nor Wynngrave had materialised, and he'd sent word that he was otherwise detained; though the name of whoever she was that was detaining him was omitted.

Even when the rain ceased, on likelihood owing to a shortage of moisture in the heavens, the wind blew savagely down the valley. And, by the time the grey sky had begun to turn black, Belstone was sure of a number of things: that the Highlands were better left to the Highlanders, that he was certain to be bedridden with the cold, once he was actually back in the vicinity of a bed, that his friends were laughing at him in the bar of some hotel, and that he was going to spend his last mortal hours sore, wet, tired and irritable.

Then salvation wobbled into view as he tottered his way over the crest of a rise; one that might have been one of those mountains of renown, the effort it had taken him to scale it. While what he'd ideally hoped for were the lights of some town large enough to boast a station with trains back to civilisation, he was more than happy to take the low stone building with its crumbling chimney and thatched roof. As he made towards it with as much speed as his, for all he knew, broken ankle and precarious baggage would allow, it occurred to him that this must be one of those "bothies" he'd been told about at length the day before. It was too small to be a cottage for even the people who chose to inhabit these backwards areas, but, as a resting spot for weary travellers, it seemed a godsend. Truthfully, he was relieved that he wouldn't have to fall on the mercy of some grizzled country type who probably didn't speak the King's English, so it was with fresh vigour that he hobbled onwards.

The door seemed more like a token gesture than any serious impediment to either elements or intruders, so full of gaps and holes was it, and he stood a moment in the low entrance, peering into the gloom within. Any hope that his fellow hikers were there was dashed by the lack of chatter or an expertly arranged fire to warm the interior. Still, he had matches that were miraculously unsoaked, and the flame glinted on the glass and metal of the oil lamp hanging by the door. A tentative shake revealed that there was oil still in it, and he soon had sufficient illumination to survey what there was to be seen. Which wasn't much at all.

It was a rough, roundish room, with a dirt floor and wooden bunks, piled up with straw and bedding that looked more like sack cloth. Hardly Belstone's dreamt-of hotel, but at least the roof wasn't leaking, and there was even a bundle of firewood next to the arched grate. There would be warmth, something he hadn't much counted on, even if he'd been able to put a flame to the makeshift walking stick that had done so little to support him up until now.

Half an hour later, with the hearth aglow, his sodden clothes steaming before it, and Belstone now kitted out in the merely damp replacements from his damaged knapsack, things looked much brighter. The contents, or half the contents, of a hipflask had certainly helped achieve that illusion. Even the nagging throb of his injury felt somehow distant, and his thoughts were now of the luxury of a straw covered bench with a sacking pillow. It was a thought that fled when, from one of the shadowed bunks where the fire's glow didn't reach, something sat up.

Belstone rose to his feet so quickly that he forgot his twisted ankle, until it gave out from under him and he dropped once more, scurrying back as effectively as his hands and one of his legs would push him.

Crouching on the bunk, the old man wheezed, no doubt laughing at Belstone's discomfort. The shadows and firelight joined in their efforts to make his face practically indistinguishable from the rough, crumpled blankets.

"I'm... I'm sorry," Belstone was finally able to gasp out, not certain why he was the one apologising when this unexpected presence was the one that had nearly caused the clerk to die from fright. "I didn't know there was anyone there. I didn't mean to wake you."

The old man nodded, still not quite sitting up, saying, "You didn't waken me, sir. I was waiting to find out how you fared."

"Well, you might've said something, at least," griped Belstone.

"I might, but you seemed to be coping on your own, so I thought to just bide till the moment was apt."

The man's accent was hard to place, but the tired creakiness of his voice might have been the cause. And, thought the Englishman, at least I can understand him, not like some I've met on my way.

"You've done a damage to yourself," said Belstone's fellow boarder. At least his eyesight couldn't have gone, though a near-blind man could've seen he was hurt. Still, he told him of the tumble he'd taken, coming down a precarious outcrop, and how his foot had jammed itself between the rocks and the shaft of a none-too-steady stile.

"Then you came from the East, for that would be Beel's Elbow you described: the rocks by the stile." Belstone confirmed this, with absolutely no authority on the truth of the matter. But it had been a statement rather than a question, and the fellow sounded old enough to remember when Beel, whoever he may have been, had first found part of his anatomy immortalised in stone. Feeling that some other explanation as to his presence, an alien in this rough landscape, was required, the clerk spoke of his arrival from the great Southern city, of his job and his prospects, and of what a shower of bounders his, by now former, friends were.

It was difficult to tell if the old man was interested, listening even, or asleep, but when Belstone finally ran out of pejoratives for Bewley and the rest, he said, "If you came to be here from the East, you passed Cloutie Well."

"Did I?"

"The Cloutie Well," his companion repeated.

"Cloo Tee-Well?" Belstone echoed. "Well...ah-hah...a well's a well to me, I'm afraid. I don't know their names." A thought flashed home. "There was one, though. Most peculiar. It was in a small grove of trees that I stumbled upon it—literally stumbled, what with the leg. I couldn't tell you much about the well, except that I wouldn't have drunk from it," and he remembered the yellowy green, murk-filled water. "But it was the trees that caught me off guard. I'll not forget them in a hurry."

"That's Cloutie Well, most certain," the old man told him. "Or do you not know that a "clout" means a cloth?"

"Yes, that's it! There were cloths and rags. An extraordinary sight. Hundreds, thousands even, tied to every branch of every tree!" Belstone thought back to how startling it had been, to thrash your way through bare, dull branches, and be confronted by the sight of these "clouts" flapping in the wind, as if an unimaginable horde of birds of every species and colour had come to rest in those branches and were beating their wings in unison. The noise had been astonishing, as every gust of wind had caused the tattered adornments on each branch to rustle and crack. But it had been the colours that had overwhelmed him. Even though many were ancient, and as grey as tombstones, there were countless fresher additions, reds and greens, blues and golds, of wool and linen and silk. Even in his beloved London, hub of all life, he had never experienced such a riot of colour and sound and movement. And, if he was to admit to it, it unnerved him a great deal. There was something about it that didn't seem right. That didn't seem natural. "Why is that?" he finally asked.

"You don't know, and more's the pity you didn't at the time," he was told, "for if you had but done so then, you might have bathed your injury in that well. And, were you willing to surrender a stocking or a handkerchief for your pains, all would be progressing nicely for you. But it's too late now."

Belstone, who had already surrendered one sock to the marsh that had claimed his boots, could make no sense of this pronouncement. And he was of a mind to say so when the old man spoke on.

"They have no Cloutie Wells in your part of the world, for I observe you are an Englishman. No, they're of the Celts and the Picts. There are a few of their kind hereabouts, for I've heard tell of one on the Black Isle, North of Inverness, and others to the West and even in Ireland. They're places of healing, oft since they were blessed by some saint or holy man. Some go further back still. Of this one, it's been said for centuries that a pilgrim, travelling to spread the Good Word, found himself between townships and struck with a fever."

Considering the filthy weather, Belstone found this no stretch of the imagination.

"With no fellow traveller to aid him, and miles ahead yet to be walked, he dipped his shawl in the well, praying for those waters to soothe his brow. As he prayed, he hung that garment from one of those Ash that ring the well. And as it dried there, the fever abated. So he, spreading words of miracles as he was charged, told tale of the healing waters, and some have known it as the Pilgrim's Well ever since. And any with an ailment would come to that place, dip the hem of what they wore in the water to so anoint the afflicted portion, then hung that which was soaked from the trees, as an offering that their ills might be taken."

Belstone, who was aware that all places, especially the remoter ones, had their traditions, still voiced surprise. "But some of those rags couldn't have been more than a few years old."

"There are some newer than that."

"You surely can't be telling me that people round here still believe in such things?" But the silence that followed from the dimly lit bunk confirmed that surely he was. "Then tomorrow, I shall paddle in the well, and hang from the trees by my toes until I'm cured."

This jest didn't cause the old man much amusement, and Belstone's own cackle dried in his throat.

"The well is for those that believe in its powers, and those that don't are best to stay clear, and let it alone." There was a threatening tone in the man's voice that brought the forgotten chill in Belstone's bones back to the fore again. Another mouthful from the flask ought to have seen to that although, when he proffered the same, the old man extended no arm to accept it.

"It was an Englishman," he said, and Belstone almost felt an accusation aimed at him, "who found out why it's best to avoid the well if you are an unbeliever. This was in the time of the Clearances—an act of violent spite by a parliament safe hundreds of miles away in London. Thousands of good people wrenched from their homes, and sent to survive or starve in unfamiliar places, while foreign lords claimed their lands, their wealth and their bloodright. It was a punishment, and some of those that punished did so with a passion for it that verged on madness.

"One of these men went by the name of Lord Walter Stourmont, and it was to this spot he descended. His determined aim was to wipe out all traces of the local way of life, and to fashion the landscape he had invaded into his own realm. The land he took as his estate was this land, and all around us. And that land contained something he saw as an offence and a reminder of the traditions of the rightful heirs to his new kingdom. There were still native folk left: a few who were lucky enough to be allowed to bide in their own homes, and unlucky enough to have to pay rents to, and toil for, that man who cursed their very being. Obedience was demanded, and a lack of it was most cruelly rewarded. Still, even these cowed people couldn't be compelled to do Stourmont's bidding when it came to stripping the clouts from the Ash trees.

"Such a fury may you never experience, than was felt at the great hall. The workers pleaded with him, if not for their sakes then for his own, to let the well alone. And he, for his part, flogged them, beat them, and worse. But still, though they begged for his mercy, they refused to enter that clearing and remove those tatters.

"His lordship had never had to carry out any task for himself, but never had he been so disobeyed in the completion of such, so he had to set an example. Reckoning these people feared the well's power, he thought on how much more would they fear him if he confronted and removed that power. So he gathered those that had defied him, the ones no longer able to walk after his tortures being carried by their kin. There he made them watch on, as he spat in the waters, and as he tore every rag from every branch and trampled them into the ground. And when he was through, he faced them. He expected their screams, their pleas, but they just looked on him with such pity for his ignorance, that his fury rose even fiercer.

"Some, those very few that were loyal to the English lord, made claim that the seizure he had then was because of his rage, but those that knew the well knew different."

Belstone, who had found himself captivated by the outlandish tale, had to be told, "What did they know?"

The old man gave no response, but the expectant silence had the Londoner feeling like a schoolboy, standing before an impatient master waiting for him to supply the answer. "Well, they knew...or, rather, they believed, that if those rags were hung to remove all ills, the one that is bold enough to take them down will gain those self same ills? That every sickness denoted in every piece of cloth would transfer onto him, and be visited upon him."

He may have nodded. It was hard to tell, for Belstone's eyes were aching in the firelight's wavering glow, and the pain had returned to his leg. But he focused on the horror of that fate, and the question it posed. "If this were true, it strikes me as a uniformly unchristian punishment to be taken from a blessed shrine."

The man in the bunk coughed, and it was followed by a rattling sound in his chest. His words, when his laboured breaths forced them out, were hoarse. "Some wells are older than the days when the pilgrims found them. Some were thought sacred by the Pictish folks, with their Earth spirits, and some are older even than that."

"And Lord Stourmont? Did he pay the price?"

"From that day till the day of his death, weeks, not months later, he never once left his stolen hall. What few people saw him were so affected by the sight, they could hardly speak of it.

"What was whispered of was a living corpse, though living was hardly the word for that lame, pitiable creature that festered in its bed, unable to move on withered limbs, unable to see out of dimmed eyes, unable to put food or drink into a belly that was aflame with agony. Even before it died, unmourned, the people must have gathered in that clearing among the Ash. For every last scrap of every last rag was hung once more from the trees."

There was silence then, save for the intermittent gasps of breath, and the old man appeared to be asleep. Was it the firelight that made his skin look so yellowy green and tinged with a murky sheen? And were those hands that clutched around the edges of the sacking blanket withered and gnarled and covered with welts? Or had his story taken hold of Belstone's fatigued mind? He felt the tiredness that had hung upon him all day spill its banks, and he slept a sleep that was disturbed by the pained coughs from the opposite bunk, before sinking deeper into a slumber filled with dreams of fluttering motions and vivid slashes of colours, and dark forms that crouched in murky depths.

When morning came, Belstone rose stiffly in its grey light, full of aches and not in the least rested. He tried to arrange his belongings quietly, so as not to awaken the old man. There was scarcely a sound as he moved, despite his imagining that his limbs must be creaking and groaning as he stumbled around, eyes not quite focusing in his new-found wakefulness. More than that—there was no sound at all. Not even a fitful breathing from the far bunk.

A dreadful thought seized him. The storyteller had started off weak, and he had faded as the night wore on. Had the effort in telling his story proved too much? Had Belstone spent this last, lonely night asleep with a corpse in the room?

With numb fingers, he pulled back the rumpled sacking, uncovering the empty bunk beneath. There was only straw to give the appearance of a form below. Perhaps the fellow had rallied and left at dawn, headed on for wherever he had been destined before stopping to rest for the night. But the straw had no trace of being bedded down or flattened by a sleeping body, and even a man emaciated by age and illness must have left some impress. Yet there was no sign of his ever having been there, only the scraps of rags, ancient, faded, and mouldering, that lay entangled in the straw.

Shortly afterwards, Belstone left the stone hut, not heading West, as he had the previous night, for his destina-tion, should he reach it, lay to the East. He had no choice but to go back. His leg was useless, despite the splint he had fashioned the day before from a branch of Ash. The bonds round it were still tight—those scraps of material he'd plucked from the tree to fasten it there still held—although so many others had torn and been discarded, or had disin-tegrated at his touch.

His baggage lay abandoned at the bothy, but those other strips of cloth that he'd knotted around it to patch it up were clutched in his hand, even though the welts there made it painful to grip. His fading sight caused him to stumble, and his withering arm did little to break his fre-quent falls, but Belstone moved on. He would crawl there if he had to, and he had to, to see to it that every last scrap of every last rag was hung once more from the trees.

The Travelling Companion

It wasn't Mr. Endicott's habit to frequent any of the auction rooms to be found crowding that part of town. But, on the afternoon to which we can trace the beginnings of his strange narrative, having found himself with time on his hands before his scheduled train, there seemed little harm in stepping inside one of these establishments for half an hour or so. Filling idle time between journeys was a regular hardship for Endicott as his livelihood, centring on the buying and selling of various items to businesses both large and small, demanded that he travel frequently. His hefty bag of samples, not to mention the second case containing those personal items required for overnight stays, meant that he had little desire to add to his burden. Even so, he found some enjoyment in browsing through the miscellany on display around the cavernous room. No little time was spent in amusing himself with attempts to imagine the character of those individuals who either offered or sought such objects as a stuffed alligator, a solitary, and therefore redundant, wooden bookend in the shape of a gargoyle, indifferent portraits of other peoples' relatives, or any number of items whose precise function defied categorisation.

Nonetheless, amongst the lots there was something that caught Endicott's fancy. It was nothing grander or more exotic than a bundle of books bound by a black ribbon. It occurred to him that some of these might look pleasing on

How horrible indeed, thought Endicott with a delighted shudder, before returning his attention to the unfolding story and the dark revelations yet to come.

one of the shelves at home. Not that he was himself home often, but it always cheered him to return to well-stocked bookcases, and he would often dream of a time to come when he might find the leisure to read each and every volume in whichever order he saw fit. Endicott was a voracious reader, which sat well with him considering his bachelor existence and the many hours spent in transit with little else to occupy his mind. So it was that he turned to the catalogue which had been thrust upon him as he had entered, and sought out the details for *'Lot No. 169,'* hoping that it would consist of something more interesting than agricultural reports or the collected poetic musings of some elderly country curate's wife.

'This fine and varied collection of volumes,' began the catalogue description, *'was amongst the effects of a noted bibliophile, now sadly passed. It comprises a selection of medical, liturgical and philosophical texts,'* even a cursory listing revealed that these were not ideal light reading matter for a five hour train journey, *'plus a single collected edition of ghost stories by an author as much noted for such matter as for his renowned scholarly works.'*

Here Endicott the casual browser became Endicott the eager prospective purchaser. He was a keen consumer of fiction, in particular those tales that took his imagination far beyond the confines of workaday routine. Detective stories or adventures set in mysterious foreign climes were firm favourites but, above even these, stories of the uncanny were the most favoured and savoured. Time seemed to pass quicker for him in the company of vampires, witches and the unquiet dead. Often he would purchase annual anthologies or magazines whose covers promised ghoulish terrors aplenty, only to find but a single example amongst the contents: barely affording enough entertainment to last him to the outskirts of the city. Therefore a collection entirely made up of ghost stories—and he thought he had identified it as that pleasingly thick volume in brownish leather amidst the more worthy tracts—seemed just the thing.

Endicott's lot, as luck, or perhaps fate, would have it, was called unexpectedly early. He had just begun to fear that his need to be on a particular Northbound train would necessitate his leaving before he could at least put in an offer. But an assistant had sidled across to the florid of face and bombastic of manner auctioneer during the closing stages of the sale of a battered looking phonograph and, with much gesticulation and whispering, handed him a note.

"Due to a last minute request on behalf of the seller of certain of these fine items, ladies and gentlemen, I am obliged to proceed next to what was given in the catalogue as Number 169—namely these most attractive and erudite volumes, which would be rightly domiciled in the library of any gentleman or well-educated lady of refinement. What am I bid? Yes, sir? The gentleman towards the back of the room with the luggage. I don't believe we've seen you here before, sir. Any further offers for this veritable cornucopia of learned thought? Any more bids? Well, it does seem that it's first time lucky for you, doesn't it, sir? Sold! And if you would just see the clerk about payment that would be... Oh, ho! What's this? Madam, would you kindly desist from causing a furore on my premises?"

At approximately the instant the auctioneer's gavel had struck the wooden desktop, there had been a separate clatter, this from the back of the room. A tall and somewhat striking woman, swathed in a long, dark coat, had rushed in, brandishing a pocketbook. All heads turned, so all present saw the look of furious indignation on her face when she spied the lot that was being carried from the display table beside the auctioneer's podium. With a swift and steady stride she was at the desk, causing much swivelling in seats to follow her progress. Her grievance, as all soon became aware, was over her understanding that several dozen lots were due to have been put up before the items in question, and that it was highly unorthodox and unprofessional to change the order as advertised in the catalogue. By what right had they made the substitution? Indeed, a request from the seller? And how had this request been made, and who had delivered this note? Here the auctioneer seemed grateful for some respite while the assistant who had taken delivery of the missive was summoned, and this unfortunate underwent similar interrogation. The upshot of this was the revelation that the instruction had been passed to him by that same black-clad fellow who had arranged the sale and had delivered the books, and that he had seen him neither arrive nor depart; these vague details appearing to confirm some unspoken suspicion in the aggrieved woman.

Regardless of the entertainment this unexpected drama afforded, Endicott was aware also of the pressing need for him to make his payment and collect his purchases. However, to do so he would be forced to interject himself into the debate that now occupied the attentions of the auctioneer, his assistant, and several other members of staff. He had his cheque written out and in his hand as he approached the eye of the storm, ready to thrust it into any hand that could take it before snatching up his bundle and departing. It was a commendable plan, which faltered only because the auctioneer happened to observe his approach and, clearly desperate for an end to the current distraction from the day's business—or at least for another soul on whom to deflect the lady's ire—announced, "Why, here is the very gentleman who purchased the lot in question. Perhaps if you were to discuss the matter with him privately, in less crowded surroundings, an...agreeable settlement might be reached to both your satisfactions."

Knowing that a discreet exit was now out of his reach, Endicott found himself adopting the manner he invariably found effective in dealing with obstreperous customers. The smile never left him as he took his first opportunity to examine this formidable female at closer quarters. He was faced with a very confirmed countenance, the expression intent and the eyes shining. Striking had been the word that had first sprung to his mind upon her noisy arrival, and it still seemed the most apt. Something in that face defied his attempts to categorise her as beautiful or ugly, young or old, as if her features were obscured as though behind a veil. What was clear, however, was that she was not in the least happy, despite the smile that she attempted when she turned to regard him. It recalled for him the type of smile that he'd always imagined a cat might wear on first spying a mouse venturing its whiskers outside a hole in the skirting board.

Nestling between them, where the assistant had hastily deposited them on the table, was the object of both their attentions, the neat stack of bound up books. Endicott glanced at it, wondering what it was about them that so attracted this woman. As he returned his gaze to her, he noted that she too was eyeing the books with a glimmer of some unidentifiable but intense feeling in her gaze. Perhaps there might well be a compromise reached, since there was only the single volume that held his interest and, as the price had been reasonable, he would be happy to make her a gift of the remaining books to avoid any further delay.

Even as he resolved to do so, that lady said, in a more mellow and honeyed voice than that which she'd employed with the auctioneer, "Sir, I realise that you have no part in this unfortunate confusion, and that you have bought these books in all good faith, but I must tell you that it is imperative that you allow me to buy you out of your contract with the seller. If it helps you in reaching a favourable decision, I can promise you that there is only one part of this package that I seek to obtain, and you would be more than welcome to the rest."

Some internal voice informed him that this 'one part' was certain to be the selfsame part that he wanted. Sensing his reluctance, the woman nodded toward the cheque which he still held in his hand, though her eyes never strayed from his. "Sir, you will not lose out on the transaction. See, I have in my purse enough to double what you have pledged. No? Then I can offer to triple the sum and leave you with a profit and nine tenths of what you would have paid for."

Somehow Endicott, who generally had a healthy regard for accruing a profit, found himself disinclined to take up this offer, particularly when it was confirmed that the collection of ghost stories was indeed the desired item. He voiced his regret on the matter even as he presented the asking price to the auctioneer's assistant. His only explanation was that he very much desired the book for his own collection and had no wish to take her money. Was this reaction, he would later consider, simply because the book, whose contents were as yet unknown to him, had caught his fancy? Was it possibly because he suspected that the urgency of her entrance and her overly generous offer of reimbursement suggested some hidden value and potential rarity to the book? Or, if he were honest with himself, was it that deep down he had perceived something namelessly unnatural about this otherwise handsome woman that in some way repelled him?

"Blaggard," was the unexpected retort to his entirely justified refusal to be budged, and she strode briskly off before he had time to find a rejoinder that was suitably brusque whilst also being fit for a woman's hearing. It was only after she'd gone that the assistant made his timid approach, one eye on the door lest she return with reinforcements to storm the sales room, and handed him his bundle, neatly wrapped in brown paper, and a receipt *'with thanks.'* And as the assistant bade him a good day and other such pleasantries, including an admonition that he take care, it occurred to Endicott that the perceived insult might just have been a misheard instruction to, "Be on guard!"

Engine smoke, raised flag and whistle were the sights and sounds that quickened Endicott's already rapid step upon reaching the station, and he barely made it into the compartment without a bruise or a stumble as the locomotive moved off. Some jostling saw his baggage stowed safely overhead, and a vacant seat by the window accommodated his breathless collapse. That entirely unnecessary business at the auction rooms had almost thrown his schedule to the winds, but he took no small pride in the fact that he'd never once missed or even had to put back an appointment, and he had no wish that today should set a precedent. He allowed himself a smile of self-congratulation for having lost his breath with good purpose, before making a cursory inspection of his fellow travellers. A married couple in late middle age, a sharp-featured sailor with hands and wrists that were blue with old tattoos, and a plump and sleepy nursemaid filled out the compartment. It was too early in the day for the commute of office workers—a pity as there were potential customers amongst that class of traveller, but it couldn't be helped. So, satisfying himself that there was no business to be done, he turned his thoughts to the parcel in his lap.

Having untied the knots and unfolded the paper—watched closely by the tattooed sailor who quickly lost interest on seeing nothing more exciting than some old books—he took time in sampling pages at random from each and every one. As he feared, they were uniformly uninspiring, dreadfully dull, in some cases unintelligible, and unlikely to ever be retrieved from his bookshelves, should they even make it that far. No matter, he still had the book of ghost stories to investigate, having deliberately fed his anticipation by leaving its perusal to last. Finally the time had come to savour his prize, his hope being that its contents would prove dreadful in the correct sense of the word.

It wasn't as old as the others, he noted, with none of the mustiness or discolouration of pages that comes with elderly books. In fact it looked practically unread, neat and tight in its uncreased leather binding. There was a satisfying stiffness to it as he opened it to the title page and read, *'Delve Not Too Deeply and Other Ghost Stories'* and the author's name, *'Dr. H.S. Grace.'*

Now that was promising. He was familiar with the author and regarded highly those stories of his that he'd read in various magazines. Yes, there on the table of contents, *'A Book of Curiosities'* and *'The Stolen Animus.'* He definitely knew these titles from the pages of *The Strand* or *Pearson's, Pall Mall Magazine, Blackwoods,* or any one of the pile of periodicals that he'd combed over the years for just such treasures. One or two others amongst the dozen or so listed struck a chord, but he was relieved to see that this was not to be purely a nostalgic revisiting of familiar chills. Here were other previously unseen titles that held promise. *'A Passing Malediction,''The Daguerreotype'* and *'The Legacy of Mr. Dylan'* all excited his curiosity.

Despite his earlier chagrin at being delayed, he now considered that, all in all, his idling for an hour in the sales room had proved a good morning's work. This little compilation of horrors would provide hours of necessary entertainment, and would make a rare travelling companion. And now was the ideal time to make its acquaintance so, making himself as comfortable as a second class compartment permitted, and selecting one of the stories which he had enjoyed once before, Mr. Endicott began to read.

'You are invited to picture one of the larger country houses with which the Southern counties are so compendiously studded,' was what he read. 'It is rather in the continental style, with pillars and ornamentation, though these are a more recent feature, I would hazard, and the altogether more severe and sombre aspect of the original building may yet be perceived skulking amidst the adornments, rather as the skull may be glimpsed through the flesh. It sits aloof and isolated within the perimeters of its own park, with only a considerably smaller structure, styled in the perceived manner of an ancient temple, to keep it company. The house glories in the name of Altingley Grange, and it was to Altingley that, on the advent of his first and twentieth year, Simon Eaves first ventured. And it was here that he was greeted by his one surviving relative, an uncle on whom he had never once set eyes.'

On perusing these opening lines, even though it must have been a good half dozen years since he had previously read the tale, Endicott felt vivid details of the narrative coming back to him; of the welcoming, ever pleasant relative, the one that was a trifle too welcoming, too pleasant; of the secret ceremonies in the disused temple; of the discovery of the corpse that wasn't a corpse after all, but a mannequin of sorts, and how it was connected with the uncle's concern that young Simon be hale and in the peak of health. Despite the familiarity of these surprisingly well-remembered details, he read on with no less enjoyment. Here now was the description of that mannequin—'the horrible doll-like form of pale wax that sat in silent contemplation of him, dreadful curiosity etched on its almost living face. A living face with dead eyes. How horrible it had been to find it crouching behind the curtains, as if it had crept through the window in order that it might lay in wait for the candles to be snuffed out and for the room's occupant to fall into an unwary and unprotected sleep.' How horrible indeed, thought Endicott with a delighted shudder, before returning his attention to the unfolding story and the dark revelations yet to come.

Unfortunately for him and his attempts at concentration, that drowsing nursemaid by his side had chosen this time, just as the horrors were beginning to emerge, to begin muttering and groaning in her sleep. It was just as he'd reached the passage about the dagger set to pierce the sleeping nephew's throat that she cried out and awoke with a start, glaring at Endicott as if he were somehow responsible for her interrupted nap, before realisation that she had drawn the attention of all in the compartment brought a blush to her round cheeks and an apology to her lips.

"Should you have any trouble getting back to sleep," smile Endicott, handing the young woman that inevitable book of poetry which had crept into his purchase, "I'd recommend the epic verse, 'On First Walking out in the Deanery Garden' as just the remedy." He left her bemusedly flicking through the pages and returned once more to Altingley Grange and the wicked uncle's necromantic plot.

Our hero lay drugged and drowsing, on the verge of falling victim to his Uncle Hugo's attempt to capture the life's essence of the healthy younger man and 'by means of certain rituals gained from a lifetime's profane study, transfer it to within the form of that monstrous doll, thereby keeping it supple until that moment when Death's fleshless finger would beckon he who had thus far eluded it by the sacrifice of innocents. Upon that moment, his own soul would fly from his body into the mannequin's form—a form that would prove immortal, as surely that which has never lived can subsequently never die.' And then the moment when young Simon awakes, thanks to the drug having been half-spilled by the comedically vocal housekeeper and then topped up with pond water, 'what, mercy's sakes, had to be drawn from the bottom, and me near going over and in up to my neck, simply to find some of a sufficient green and unhealthy hue, so as to match what was left there of that old bottle's nasty contents.' The confrontation, with Uncle Hugo's previous misdeeds exposed, and the moment when the doll, baulked of its sustenance, turns on the occultist, '*Its fingers growing pinker and more suffused with life, even as the face above the throat they gripped grew paler and became frozen in a mask of death.*'

Much, after all, as Endicott had remembered it, and it was a delight to reacquaint himself with the tale. He turned the page, eager to commence the next story, only to find that Simon's ascendance to master of the house, thanks to the uncle's gruesome end, didn't quite mark the end of the story. There was more to follow. '*As his first duty as lord of Altingley, Simon Eaves ordered the immediate destruction of that relic of Hugo Sylvanus's experiments. It was with much distaste, accompanied by the not unexpected grumbling and lamenting, which made this distaste evident to all within earshot, that old Corbett carried the rigid figure across the garden, where the bonfire he had prepared for the usual detritus was set to be put to a more formidable use. Shortly afterwards, Simon himself stepped out across the lawn to enquire of the figure watching the flames as to the progress in eradicating all trace of the doll. But as he gained on the blaze, his foot struck against something protruding from the pile of leaves awaiting disposal. A glance revealed this to be one of Corbett's boots. Country ways were still quite alien to Simon, but he reckoned it unlikely that the man was standing barefoot out of doors. It was then that he noticed that the foot was still inside the boot, and he saw the leg that disappeared into the mass of dead leaves. The figure by the fire turned to him. The clothing was scorched, and globules of pink wax had congealed across the shirt front, having dripped from the face that was now half gone, a glassy eye hanging down one cheek. The face might have been ruined but the homunculus still had hands, and they could still grip, and they found the heir's throat before he could even open his mouth in a futile attempt to scream.*'

Even as he read these words, Endicott was jolted by a scream—one that wasn't choked off by horrible hands of wax. The nursemaid had succumbed to the turgid poetical ramblings and resumed her dozing. Clearly she had also resumed her nightmare, but what the subject of her disturbed dream was, he was not to discover. A glance toward the window had revealed that his destination was close, and he set about preparing his baggage, consigning the rest of his bargain to the bottom of his samples bag, and finding room in a deep pocket for the pick of the bunch.

The day's first appointment was concluded successfully, and he had received a very respectable batch of orders to take back with him. Yet, despite this, and the conditional promise of repeat business should the goods match his words of recommendation, Endicott left the premises of the small firm feeling unsatisfied. The cause of this dissatisfaction was not the deal that had been struck, but the realisation that he had been a touch distracted during the course of the meeting and had not, therefore, presented either himself or the products he offered to the best of his abilities. What had caused this distraction he could not recall, and he was decidedly disgruntled as he returned to the station to await the train that would carry him to the next town and his next appointment.

Having first ensured that there were no sleeping nursemaids in the compartment, he boarded, made the usual arrangements with his baggage, and sat in moody contemplation. It was to little avail. He couldn't think what had left him off form, and wracking his brains further on the matter would only serve to worsen his mood and make his next meeting a repeated, if not worse, performance. What was required was distraction, and it came easily to hand. Within minutes his irritation was entirely forgotten, and his mind was in a mountainous foreign region. It was in this high and distant spot that an English traveller had come into the possession of a mediaeval bestiary—one whose potential value he had omitted to divulge to the foolish old priest from whom he had practically stolen it. Though possibly the old man was nowhere near as foolish as the traveller believed, and knew far more of the book's rarity than he'd let on, for the weird and ungodly creatures depicted within those pages were proving to be uncomfortably more lifelike than the book's new owner could ever have wished.

It was another of Dr. Grace's tales with which Endicott was familiar of old, yet the unpleasantness and ferocity of the demons released from the illustrations still came as a surprise to him. The descriptions struck him as so vivid that he couldn't believe that he'd recalled the story's earlier passages so precisely but had forgotten such details as *'the scaled hand or claw that reached out from the dark to place itself with alarming delicacy upon Dr. Nesbitt's shoulder,'* or the invitation to *'Imagine, if you will, a being that combines the angular scuttling of the most fearfully long-limbed spider with the gliding sinuousness of a serpent, and you are part way to understanding the horror of the entity. In whatever region the long gone Brother Osric had collected this specimen, Nesbitt was convinced that it was not one governed by the same Creator as had fashioned the world he had, until moments before, thought that he knew. And he prayed that when he left this world, as seemed hopelessly imminent, that what lay beyond was not dependant on the Mercy of whichever malign deity had wrought such an abomination.'* Endicott closed the book on the unhappy Nesbitt's demise with the nagging feeling that duping a scheming cleric didn't really deserve such a harsh fate, and that some form of rescue ought to have come. But the time to ponder further on this was to come later, for here was his next stop, and here he put unleashed beasts out of his mind.

Night-time found Endicott in a familiar room in an oft-frequented inn, having successfully secured contracts with all but one of the half dozen companies he'd called upon that day; his one failure owing to an overly parsimonious managing director, and not to any fault on Endicott's part. A spot of reading before bed might have been in order, but the establishment's usual excellent meal had left him feeling sluggish, and an early rise the next morning called for sleep. For these reasons he was quickly abed and not, he told himself, because the memory of those descriptions of taloned hands and clacking, fanged jaws made him in any way wary that it would be a disturbed night's rest should he read more from the pen of H.S. Grace before retiring.

Going by his disposition the next morning over breakfast,

Endicott's hosts suspected that a disturbed night had, without a doubt, been the case, despite his assurances that he had, in actual fact, slept. He drew the line at saying that he'd slept soundly, though he couldn't put his finger on why that might have been. He could recall no unpleasant dreams—no dreams at all, now that he thought about it—but he had awoken with a feeling of what he could only describe as unease. However vague and inexplicable this feeling was, it had left him in no mood for uncanny stories that day, and his trip North, with the consequent Southbound return in the evening, was entirely unremarkable.

"Aha! There we have you," was Endicott's exclamation when, on donning a particular overcoat after a few days, he found a bulky little object in his pocket. "I'd forgotten about you. Well, you'll do nicely for today," and he returned the book to that pocket as he set out on yet another day's travels, though on this day his various destinations were all within the city, so omnibus and tram were the prescribed modes of transport.

Nerves were never normally a source of concern for Endicott, but on the day in question he was evidently out of sorts, judging from his reaction as he sat on the omnibus bringing him back from his labours. Between appointments he had already read of curses passed on to sceptical victims, and of a piece of music written by an unknown hand that, when played on the right instrument, attracted the attentions of a particularly odious elemental force. So perhaps he had some reason to be jittery, especially when, from behind him somewhere, there was a noise. It was the sound of movement, quiet but most certainly there. He tried to focus on the book, but it was difficult enough with the lighting so low and dusk gathering at the windows. He was forced to read the same sentence three or four times before he grasped the sense of it; *'It was on the third night of Mr. Dylan's residency in his new home that the first signs of the crisis which was to loom so large made themselves known in an unexpected and ominous manner.'*

Could he hear that movement again? In the darkness behind him? Endicott felt a tingling at his nape when he remembered that the upper deck had been empty when he'd taken his seat, and that no-one had boarded since then. For a moment he wondered if someone might have fallen asleep back there, slouched down in their seat, or if he'd simply failed to spot a fellow passenger under the lamplight's ineffectual glow. Then, with the next sudden flurry of noise from behind him, he wondered no more, his head twisting in alarm to face whatever approached so furtively, with such a soft and slithering sound to its motion.

It was a newspaper, nothing more, probably discarded by some office worker as he'd made his way home from his paperwork. The first sound, Endicott now realised, would have been when the motion of the vehicle as it had turned a corner had dislodged the paper and it had fallen to floor. Yes, he was sure that it had been at a corner when he'd first detected it. Those further sounds were clearly the result of the steady rocking of the omnibus causing the forgotten periodical's gradual slide down the aisle toward him. He should have felt more relieved, he considered, but this relief was dampened by his concern over why such an innocuous happening should have his heart palpitating so. This anxiety was in no way alleviated when he plucked up the newspaper to be faced by a headline declaring, '*A CRISIS LOOMS!*' These words seemed all too recently familiar to him. It must be coincidence he attempted, none too successfully, to assure himself.

Early in the evening though it might have been, the streets between the terminus and his lodgings were dark. And, while it wasn't yet cold, Endicott huddled in his overcoat as he walked beneath the glow of the already lit streetlamps. He turned and glanced upward, uncertain why he did so. The entirely unwelcome memory of a similar gloomy walk for the protagonist in that story of the malediction swam sharply into focus, and try as he might—and he most certainly did try—to disregard them, the words were as clear to him as if he had the page held before his eyes. '*Have you ever walked under a streetlight and had it go out above you unexpectedly? It happens more often than you might think. Less frequently so with a second lamp's glare guttering and dying out, although this too may just be coincidence, the fault of some blockage within the gas supply, or some other mundane reason that you might be able to convince yourself of. However it is never as convincing when a third goes dark, and by the fourth you too might well find yourself running in desperation, too fast to even stop and look back. If you ever find yourself in that position, take this one piece of advice from one that has experienced just such a fearful, dreadful walk. Do not turn your head, and do not look above you. For you might, as I did, discover that the lamp above you is still burning but its light is not reaching you, it cannot reach you, as it has been blocked out by the vast and awful thing that hovers between it and you.'*

No, this simply wouldn't do! Endicott was a rational man, so he knew that no creature composed of shadows could be looming over him if he once more turned his head to the heavens. But Ibbotson, who had spoken those lines in the story, had been a rational man too. It had been his very rationalism that had provoked the rival Professor Bracemyre's act of diabolism in loosing the fiend upon him. "Diabolists and fiends? Really!" The realisation that he had even inwardly been contemplating such details bolstered Endicott slightly. After all, he had no hated rivals. At least, if he did he knew of no travelling vendor of office goods who employed occult powers. Cheered, he found himself whistling in a bid to raise his spirits yet higher. Until, that is, he remembered that other story with its shrill summoning call, and what had answered that call, and he walked the rest of the way with only the sound of his own footsteps for accompaniment.

The doorway to his own building had never seemed so welcoming, and he came close to dropping his key in his eagerness to be inside. As he was in the process of closing the door again, something drew his eye. That something was black and flapping, and it skittered out of sight as it left the pool of lamplight at the end of the road. A few seconds later and there it was again, dark and spindly, under the glow of the next lamp. Whatever it was, it was getting closer, appearing to flop and roll, moving on what alternately looked to be a multitude of skinny limbs that scraped sharply across the pavement or membranous wings which carried it wildly through the air. It was only three lamp's distance away before Endicott's frozen hand regained a connection with his brain that urged it to close the door and keep the thing out. The hand obeyed, but not quickly enough, as the dark thing had gained in momentum. And as it reared up into the glare of the lamp directly across from the doorway, he saw it for what it really was.

"An umbrella," he laughed. "Just a broken, black umbrella, swept along by the wind. And there it goes, off again!" And he was still laughing over this, as well as over his own ridiculous terror at two such innocent events in such close proximity, a few hours later while he finished the last morsels of his supper and prepared for bed. In fact the laughter only ceased, and ceased abruptly, once he'd settled and switched off the bedside light. Here, drowsing in the darkness, the clear thought struck him, "But there was no wind tonight." Sleep was not easy following this realisation, and the dreams that came with it were less easy still.

Nightmares, even those which are so vivid and realistic whilst being endured, are often not so readily recollected in the light of the following day. This was true of Endicott's nightmare; or had it been not one nightmare but a succession of them? For the disjointed fragments that he was able to cajole back to mind as he took his morning shave came to him as a series of hideous sketches. In the first of these he found himself moving urgently through a great labyrinth of towering bookcases, with no indication of whether what he sought was the point of exit or whatever it was that lay waiting within the ever darker recesses of the maze. If a particular book was the goal he could not say. Each and every volume he seized from the shelves, be they large or small, thick heavy tomes or slim editions, upon opening revealed precisely the same contents—contents that were somehow familiar to him. Just as the point of recognition was to be achieved, however, it faded again, as did most of the type upon the pages, the words of each paragraph he attempted dispersing almost as soon as he had begun to peruse it, leaving only certain letters which formed some sort of message. What that message might have been was to remain obscure, though, as the awareness of something else moving within those book-lined corridors, something that drew closer with each rustling step, overwhelmed him. Just as his thoughts grasped the idea of flight, the memory of the maze retreated, and his next recollection took him far from the claustrophobic tunnels and out into the open, vast and wide landscape of the countryside. Through endless fields he ran, seeking the source of that plaintive, desolate melody that vibrated in the air all around him. He knew with utter certainty that whoever was playing that particular piece of music must be made to stop, just as he knew that he was not the only seeker after its source. For, parallel to him, he saw the form of that scarecrow, which no longer stood motionless in its field but was moving with awful speed and purpose. And the final memory was of darkness. Not the gloom of an unlit room or moonless night. This was an absolute, solid blackness that wrapped itself round him, and which had taken an uncomfortably long time to dissipate when the dream had ended and he'd opened his eyes. So inescapable and limitless was this darkness that even then what was, after all, nothing but a memory of a dream was so oppressive that he had to shake himself. And, on recovering his senses, he was startled to see his own face looking back, the reflection in the mirror pale, and the razor that he still held at his throat.

Dreams and their interpretation were not subjects which he'd ever set his mind to before, but the basis of these night thoughts was clear to him. Those corridors of books had their origins in the haunted library of the old priory, the inheritance of which had precipitated that crisis for Mr. Dylan. Likewise the thing with the outward appearance of a scarecrow was from the story with the haunted musical score. Then there was the *'dread fate of being cursed to eternal darkness'* conferred upon rational Dr. Ibbotson who, despite ostensibly vanquishing the shadow-form set upon him, had ended his adventure blinded by the light which his own desperate attempts at magic had conjured up to burn the beast out of existence.

"Unhappy fates tend to await even the most undeserving in Dr. Grace's stories," Endicott found himself musing. Often these fates were delivered in the nature of little more than cruel jokes. He thought again of the mannequin's despatch of the hitherto victorious Simon Eaves. It not only struck him as unfair, but also abrupt, and it sat ill with the rest of the story, as if tacked on as an afterthought. The memory of his distinct surprise at this unexpected ending had Endicott rifling through those stacks of magazines that he'd stored for the sake of a particular article or story. He soon located the number in which he had first read 'The Stolen Animus.' Turning to the final paragraph confirmed his suspicion.

Not a trace was there to be found in the magazine's pages of the mannequin—possessed no doubt by wicked Hugo's unquiet spirit—gaining a brutal revenge. Young Eaves was left interred as master of Altingley Grange, his uncle correspondingly interred in his grave. And Endicott had no need to seek out that other edition where the bestiary tale had first seen print, as he now plainly recalled that there had, after all, been a climactic confrontation between Brother Osric's collection of demons and that elderly cleric, whose guilt over deserting his guardianship of the tome had spurred him to act just in time to save the Englishman from being rent apart.

Such significant alterations to the text gave him cause to wonder if poor Mr. Dylan had, at one time, been fated to outlive his legacy, or if Dr. Ibbotson had faced a brighter future. Squeamishness on the part of the magazine editors seemed an unlikely reason for the omission of Eave's demise, or for the insertion of a less troublesome destiny for Nesbitt. Certainly he had read equally bloodthirsty tales within the pages of their journals. It wasn't until he had again taken up that leather-bound collection—his intention being to make comparisons of the two versions of 'The Stolen Animus'—that, on flipping it open, he found inscribed on an inner page. *'A selection of original and previously published stories, with revisions, compiled and published privately in a limited edition of XIII, as a gift in return for services ren-*

dered.' Below this was printed an insignia or crest, but Endicott had little knowledge of heraldry, and there was no further indicator of the compiler's identity.

Explanation for the source of at least some of his discomfited feelings had been found. And Endicott couldn't help but consider that the stories hadn't been improved by these revisions, and that something more pleasing, more entertainingly terrible, had been lost. Whatever the case, his opinion was now that a change of reading matter was called for, possibly a novel of crime and detection. Something from the realms of the natural, not the supernatural, at any rate. He would be sure to snatch something from the shelves before departing.

Eastwards was the direction of travel this morning, and his earlier than anticipated awakening saw him prompt in catching his train. The compartment swiftly filled up around him, with a mother, grandmother and placid child of five or six opposite him, a gentleman farmer concealed within a fog of his own pipe smoke seated at the far window, and only the spot next to Endicott unoccupied. Even the most peaceable child can, when confined for too long, become a shrieking banshee at the drop of a hat, so Endicott thought to take advantage of the current calm and commence his adventure yarn.

Nestling in his pocket, however, was not on the yellow-backed novel which he was expecting, and his fingers closed on that familiar leathered hide of H.S. Grace's limited edition. Had he still been in that frame of mind in which he had awoken, he might have regarded this substitution with more alarm than vexation. But his resolve to put aside such thoughts was strong. His memory may well have been that he'd selected another book, leaving Grace's ghosts behind in its place, but it was entirely possible that his earlier plan of doing just that, coupled with fatigue, had conjured up the scene.

"It appears that you're determined to be read at all costs," he sighed, provoking curious glances from the other passengers and some amusement from the child. He offered a flicker of a smile in return, then turned his attention to the suburban houses that rolled past the windows under a dull, slate-coloured sky, while the book remained closed in his lap. There is, though, nothing quite like the dull monotony of a lengthy journey through only too frequently viewed terrain to lend even the most fantastical of notions an air of mundanity. Therefore his fancies of the night before were soon shrugged off, and what had begun as idle flipping through the pages and surreptitious readings of random passages had very soon evolved into an intense absorption in the stories before him.

Some tension came as he reached the final page or so of each tale, a sense of dread when he turned the page to be confronted by the closing paragraphs. He put it down to a growing irritation that the child opposite, who had remained so mercifully contented for so long, had chosen to grow restless only after he had found something on which he wished to concentrate. When the artistically minded Mr. Carpenter had first captured the image of the ruined façade of Glavering Manor and had set about preparing the daguerreotype that gave the title to the episode, the infant had begun fidgeting. And when the image of the derelict mansion had, night after night restored itself, even as Carpenter's own surroundings fell into creeping decay, and that fearful inhabitant of the house first began his steady progress toward the spectator, the child's whining became impossible to bear. Despite the attempts of both mother and grandmother to placate her, she had grown louder and more animated. Such was the pitch of her wailing that, by the point at which the visage of the mad earl, Francis Glavering—'so hideous an image of depravity and malignancy and dread'—had blotted out the view of the house, and his leprous fingers had begun to find purchase on the picture frame, Endicott was openly glaring at the unhappy family.

"What is it?" both females begged of the child, concern evident at this unexpected distress. The child was no longer squirming and, after a sobbing intake of breath, simply repeated the same question, "What is it?" Impatience flashed in the mother's eyes. Was her daughter mocking her? But the grandmother shook her head firmly against this idea. This was no silly game. The little girl had grown terribly pale and her reddened eyes were staring straight ahead. Both relatives were by this stage looking at Endicott with baffled alarm, while he, himself, shifted uncomfortably, entirely at a loss to identify anything he might conceivably have done to cause such upset. That same question, "What is it?" was repeated and repeated, becoming more frantic, until a tiny finger was raised to point across the compartment. It was here that he saw that she wasn't pointing at him, but at the empty space by his side. He turned, almost convinced that he would find a spider dangling close by his ear, but there was nothing there to be seen.

An uncomfortable minute or so passed, during which time Endicott attempted to disregard the crying, the desperate soothing noises, and the impatient muttering of the farmer, and returned to his reading. When the next station was reached, the women hurriedly retrieved their baggage, bundled the trembling girl into a thick coat, and struggled to force a mitten over that accusing finger. Even as they clambered out onto the platform, he could still hear that inane demand of, "What is it? What is it?" But as they bustled off, almost dragging the child who was still craning to see behind her and into the compartment, her question changed to, "And why is it saying such awful, horrid things?" The peculiarity of this query was enough to make Endicott look sharply to the vacant seat beside him. The farming gentleman had obviously been similarly affected, as his eye met Endicott's in the act of casting a doubtful glance at the same spot. It may have been being caught out in this that brought a dark frown to his features and caused him to turn away so quickly, muttering through his clenched teeth.

The seat opposite was once more occupied when Endicott turned back, and the man clad entirely in black looked on him with dark, amused eyes when he started slightly. As the station master slammed the door shut and waved the driver off, this newcomer, an elderly vicar as was quickly realised, nodded toward the book he still clasped. "Something enlightening?" he enquired. When Endicott, a little reluctantly, informed him that it was a book of ghost stories, the old man's smile widened. "I suppose I should not approve but, after all, there are demons aplenty and the risen dead within the pages of that Book from which I draw comfort." The smile widened yet further as Endicott laughed and admitted that he hadn't thought of it in quite that way before. There was an intenseness in the older man's eyes, made starker in contrast to the pale, papery skin that creased around them, and they reminded him of someone, but of whom he couldn't think. "And do you believe in such things? In ghosts and demons and uncanny visitations?"

Considering this question, Endicott swiftly became aware that it was a subject on which he could be less clear cut than a few days before. Seeing his hesitation, the reverend gentleman continued, "I have sometimes pondered on whether I might see some evidence of that saying of there being *more things in heaven and earth*' before I depart to witness that final proof. I believe, though, that I have already been given my answer." Endicott found himself leaning forward in his seat, intrigued enough to hear more. The farmer evidently didn't share his curiosity and remained glaring gloomily out at the grey clouds from within the similar fog of his own smoke. "As it is said, *'A sad tale's best for winter, I have one of sprites and goblins.'* It is not a story I care to share often, but when one finds the proper audience, a sympathetic audience..."

Here, an encouraging nod from Endicott prompted the old man to proceed. "Harewynd is a small parish, and I like to think that I know most of my flock well. Certain of my parishioners—I will not divulge their names out of respect, I trust you will understand—were of a mind to renovate the house which they had acquired, and the wife had her eye set on something rather grandiose. It was the stained glass window that had been rescued from a local abbey. This window was rather an ugly one, I must say, and I have no idea what the abbots and flock of that long-gone building must have thought when they gazed upon it, but I fear that their thoughts were never entirely holy. I was called upon by that lady and her husband to view it only after the incidents began. Both were fearfully agitated. They had seen things, they said, that they never should have seen. My first suggestion was that there was something wrong with the optics—that the different hues and thicknesses, and the warping of the aged glass had distorted that which could be seen beyond it—but if these things happen, what are you going to do about it? But their assertion remained that what they had seen was certainly no mere twisted view of their own neighbourhood, but a vision of things that moved within a distant vista. I'm afraid that there was little that I could do or suggest that might help them, beyond prayer and the removal of the offending window. Now there is nothing any earthly soul can do for them after what I fear they believed they witnessed drove them to. And as the Maker has 'set his canon against self-slaughter,' I fear even that my prayers are in vain. But pray I must, for them, and for myself. Yes, for myself, in repentance for not doing more to their aid while I could. And also for not admitting that, when I looked through and beyond that glass, I cannot deny that I too believed I saw something that moved to summon me to join it on the other side."

In the few moments that had passed while the vicar concluded his narrative, Endicott's sense of unease had grown considerably. His expectation had been of some innocuous tale of an inconsequential glimpse of something unexplained: the type of stories that psychical researchers appeared to find of inordinate interest, but which left him cold. The cold he now felt was of a different measure, and he could hardly credit that the words which he'd heard were the actual words spoken by that gentle clergyman. Yet there he was, in black and white directly opposite him, a forlorn smile not reaching his intent eyes. He was more than a little relieved when the old man bade him good day at the next station, though a persistent disquiet remained even after the train had resumed its journey.

Needful of distraction, he returned to his reading, but the title that he alighted on made him pause. 'In a Distant Vista' were the words that matched those spoken not a few moments before. He smiled wryly at the coincidence. That same smile was still on his face, fixed and no longer amused, shortly afterwards when he had finished the story. There was no coincidence at work here. The stained glass window purchased by Mr. and Mrs. Ordish and the gradually altering view beyond; the spectral landscape and its arachnidially awful inhabitants whose grim rituals drove the Ordishes to their maddened deaths—all was as he'd just heard it. And here, too, was the vicar of Harewynd, with his quotations from Shakespeare, and his *'demons aplenty and the risen dead.'* No, there was some trickery afoot, but to what purpose? No-one held any grudge with him, and he'd given no-one cause for the type of malice required to generate such a scheme. Who, in fact, even knew that he would be reading such a tale?

Groaning, he recognised instantly that he'd recently crossed paths with just such a person. And with that knowledge came the realisation of just who it was that vicar had reminded him of—with the same intent, dark-eyed gaze—it was the woman from the auction. Possibly this faux-minister was a relative, at the very least a cohort. The woman, baulked of her trophy, had turned on him... Was that a line from one of the stories? Good Lord, he was even beginning to think in Grace's prose! She had cursed him. How else could he explain the irrational fears that had grown and which now gripped him? Fears of dangers like curses? Of course, it couldn't really be a curse, but from the way that her eyes had gazed so intently into his as they'd haggled, he couldn't quite rule out mesmerism of some sort. He knew that it was possible to place a suggestion in someone's head that might cause the unsuspecting victim all manner of strange unconscious feelings. If she had done this to him, his course was set. Such a process would require reversal and, to achieve this, he would have to seek out and find that woman. It seemed a hopelessly difficult task, for he hadn't even the slightest idea of her identity, and had grave doubts that she would wish for him to locate her. But, as futile as it may yet prove, he had to make at least some effort. And he was conscious that there was but one place in which his investigations could begin.

"Aha, now I recognise you. It's good of you to drop by and visit us again so soon, sir." Judging by the expression on the auctioneer's face, his words and his sentiments were thoroughly mismatched. When—on the morning following his return from that none-too-successful venture East— Endicott had presented himself at the sales room before commencement of the day's business, the auctioneer had clearly retained no memory of him at all. But it only required a fleeting glimpse of the book and a mention of 'the woman' to bring prompt recall. "That was a rum business, sir, wasn't it? Though these rooms have seen many a rum customer over the years. Still, all went in your favour, sir, and I trust your purchase has brought you great pleasure? No? Well, that is a shame, but the sign above the door states quite clearly our policy on refunds. Not what you're after, sir? I'm afraid I can't help you there, as I've no idea who that lady was. She didn't go so far as to make a formal introduction, what with her being so anxious about that lot of yours, and I'd never once set eyes upon her here before. No, sir, nor since. Yes, I'm certain on that, as I'd most surely remember that one again. Anyone asking after you? Not a soul, sir, and I assure you that, even if there were enquiries, the discretion of our customers is highly thought of here, sir, and the answer would have been the same to anyone who asked. Why, as a matter of fact I did happen to know the learned gentleman from whose collection those books came, since much of that same collection was made up of books that were purchased right here. Though not that one you have there; I don't recollect having seen it pass through here before it came up in that posthumous lot. Anything suspicious about his death, sir? Now why should you ask a thing like that? No, he was taken from us entirely by natural causes, though I'd venture some of those causes must have been self inflicted. No, now don't mishear my meaning. He hastened his end by living life rather too well, I believe. Anything suspicious, indeed? Although, if anyone were to go that way... Yes, sir, he was one of those rum customers. As to who offered these volumes up for sale; to that I'd refer you to my prior statement concerning discretion. No, sir, I'm afraid my honour upon the matter is the one item here that can't be bid upon. Good day to you too, sir."

Night-time pressed unheeded against the windows of Endicott's lodgings, and, by the light of every lamp available, he reread words that he'd already read more than once before, attempting to decipher... To decipher what, he couldn't really say. The visit to the auction house had thrown out the theory which he had convinced himself must be the truth. His identity couldn't be known to the woman. Unless, that was, she had followed him when he'd left with his purchases that day. But his movements must surely have made pursuit difficult, if not quite impossible? Even so, the idea of it had made him conscious to the possibility of anyone following his progress as he made for home. He had, of course, observed no-one following. That is to say, he'd seen no-one. Yet he wasn't convinced that there hadn't been some follower treading close behind him all the same. Even with the door bolted behind him, that feeling didn't dissipate, indeed had grown stronger, as he'd sat reading in a solitary confinement which felt far less solitary and altogether more confining than he could bear.

During that long afternoon—an afternoon on which he was only vaguely aware that appointments were being missed elsewhere—he'd read the remaining contents of the book. His previous relish in a well-wrought tale of suspense was long forgotten as his mind had flown from his study, and he'd read, along with the unfortunate Mr. Tewkes, the maddening secrets inscribed within *'Mistress Amber's Journal'*; he'd rested in the study chair whose carved armrests muttered murderous imprecations to the poor fellow who sat between them; he'd witnessed the awful effects of the pestilence released by the disinterred relic of an unholy pilgrimage; he'd followed in *'the dragging, rattling steps of the dust-clogged feet'* of the Templar knight, as it had brutally regained its sword from those who had so foolishly ignored the warnings to leave it buried. He'd read all of these things and more and, when he'd read to the final page, he'd returned to the beginning, intent on reading the dozen stories again. It was only on this revisiting that he encountered the story which had somehow been missed before. At a point approximately halfway through the book he found it—'*Delve Not Too Deeply.*' Had the pages somehow been gummed together? A cursory inspection revealed that this was not so. It was possible, just, that he'd skipped two pages in his previous haste, as this tale—the same one that had lent its title to the collection—was little more than a vignette. Eagerly, but without enthusiasm, Endicott read the thirteenth story.

"I understand you to be an author of stories, in particular ghost stories," said the visitor who stood in my study. If it was intended as a question it was a redundant one, since he evidently knew precisely who I was. However, to humour him until such point was reached that I had found the means to make him leave, I admitted that, yes, I was regarded by some as a writer, and that, again yes, my speciality was the type of tale alluded to, for I have never cared to try any other kind. To this my visitor nodded. At this point it may be expected that I furnish some description of this unexpected and uninvited guest. I can merely say that he wore no colour save for black—a black that matched his disconcerting eyes—and that he was unfailingly polite, despite his presence being as unwelcome as it was inexplicable.

The proofs of my latest effort towards the type of entertainment already mentioned had arrived that morning from my publisher, and I had been scrutinising these for omissions or misapprehensions caused by my handwriting—all too common as my hand is quite unforgivable—when, upon looking up at some unfamiliar rustling noise, this stranger's presence was first brought to my somewhat startled attention. I had heard no knock upon my door, nor opening or closing of the same, yet the door was firmly closed and here he stood, as large as life, although here the similarity ended as his movements, expression and vocal tones carried little of the animating spark. Was he some novice servant of the institute in whose service I toil? If so, he had seemingly none of the training which those other excellent men possess in abundance. I would have spoken sharply to him for entering without the expected protocol, until he spoke the words with which I commenced this account and something in his manner left my protests quite forgotten.

"It is concerning the narrative with which you are now engaged that I am commissioned to address you." My suspicions to his status as a servant had been correct, yet his tone left me feeling little in the way of victory over my deduction. My eyes strayed to the typesheets on my desktop. They bore the title of the tale which you are now reading yet, for reasons that will, alas, become apparent, the events described are entirely different. But, as the contents have bearing, I will note that in the original manuscript that curious warning was the one that went unheeded—as all such warnings are in stories of this type—by Mr. Tarrant, the archaeologist, in his impetuous endeavours to uncover the lost tomb and secrets of a most unpleasant necromancer. As you might suppose, he is disturbed in his progress. Someone quite unknown to him has already been digging there, and the nature of the tunnels suggest that this predecessor has been digging from the inside out! Now you have the gist of it, but the method by which it had become known to this emissary and to his 'employer' was less apparent. That this employer had "certain interests within the field of literature" was the response, one which suggested without directly stating that whoever had set this black-clad figure upon me was tied-in with the publisher somehow. In this case, my supposition was wrong.

Some remarks upon my 'method', if it can be so called, here seem appropriate in light of the emissary's next assertion. Whether my stories are based on truth, I must answer, 'No.' They are based on no experience—certainly not my own and, to my knowledge, no-one else's. But it may be the case that researches undertaken for another, non-fictional, work, had brought to light certain accounts which then supplied a kernel of inspiration. For, when the writer of uncanny stories encounters a legend of a notorious practitioner of the dark arts—one whose mausoleum has vanished as mysteriously as he himself had lived—might not that writer be forgiven for allowing his imagination to deal with the matter as it will? Apparently forgiveness was not in the mind of my visitor's master.

"When dealing with any old family, there are invariably things long-buried that it may be wiser not to dig up. My

employer feels that you have overstepped certain bounds by appropriating an unfortunate incident from a long and distinguished history. It would grieve him to have to take actions against you in this matter." I agreed that it would grieve me also. His curt nod suggested that this was wise thinking, but I was then only considering the tiresome business of writs of defamation and legal entanglements. It is only now, as I put pen to paper, that the full implication of his allusion to 'actions' gnaws at my resolve to persevere. But I must be firm! Thinking to end the matter swiftly, I agreed to the suppression of the story, as to alter it by removing the offending passages would serve to cut the heart from it. His reaction surprised me. "My employer has no wish to censor you and your work. He begs of me to convey his deepest admiration for your efforts." I will admit to some vanity, even as I attempted to dismiss my works of fiction as trivial. "Not in the least. My employer is firm in his belief that you have done much in your works to open the interior eye of the deserving reader to the prospect of formidable visitants and forces." If this was the case, what then was the purpose of his mission? Surely not to make a man of advancing years blush? His employer clearly had some call to make upon me, and I was anxious to know what it was to entail. "As the personage for whom I act as an intermediate has provided you with a ghost story, he feels it only fitting that you supply him with the same in return."

A commission? If this was so, it was without doubt the most unorthodox manner of going about it that I had ever encountered. I attempted to inform him that I did not usually accept commissions, that my published corpus comprised of pieces completed for my amusement and that of friends, and that publication, and any subsequent small notoriety this had gained me, had only come about owing to pressure from those same friends to see the stories preserved in a more legible form than the scrawled pages tucked away in my study's bureau. Of all this, I am now sure, he was already aware, and he was insistent upon the demand for quid-pro-quo. Thoughts of lawyers stilled my objections, as did the amusing notion that here I had, in essence, been presented with the very basis for the required story: a mysterious commission undertaken for an equally mysterious patron of the arts.

In short, I agreed to the demand, although I confess that I stopped short of making it a gentlemen's agreement, as I was far from enamoured with the idea of clasping that stiff, pallid hand. But I was not yet privy to the full terms. "The story is to form the centrepiece of a collected edition. You would oblige us if you were to select twelve of your existing tales, either published or in draft form, to accompany it. My employer has every confidence that you will choose those which you judge to be the most alarming." Here my protest was that my publisher would be most unhappy were I to follow this course, and once again those lawyers paraded through my thoughts. These concerns were dismissed with the news that this was to be a privately produced collection of a very specific limited number, and with assurances that it should never be made widely available. "There are certain associates to whom my employer wishes to bequeath the final work. He feels that talent such as yours requires the right audience, one with the proper sympathies to that which you set out to capture in your words. If you are agreeable, there is but the matter of a contract to be signed." Time to consider this arrangement did not appear to be on offer, and a neatly folded document was removed from an inner pocket and placed before me. Had that time been available, I may well have reflected that, as someone who has read both Marlowe and Goethe, I should be wary of signing anything of so enigmatic a nature. But it looked to my eye simply to consist of the usual legal flummery; 'I the undersigned...', 'The terms herein enclosed...', 'In matters pertaining...', 'Should these terms be breached...' and so on. Nothing in the wording seemed untoward, and I appended my signature to the bottom of the page. In this action I was premature, however, as there were yet terms that had not been made clear. The matter of revisions to the existing texts was now raised.

That I have often described my dabblings in fiction by using such terms as 'trivial' and 'of little consequence', I admit, and, in comparison to some of my other works in diverse fields, I stand by these claims. But I am also of that nature that seeks as close to perfection as may be attained in all of my pursuits. Such stories of mine as have seen print or reached an audience have been the result of a great deal of effort in achieving just the right effect. If that effect has not been gained to my satisfaction, the results are unseen. There are many that I have actually written down, and they repose in a drawer somewhere. They were not good enough. But those that I had seen fit to share with an audience larger than myself and my own inner ear, I considered complete, and to tamper with them would be, I felt, disastrous. Evidently this was not a view shared by my visitor's employer, and the relayed opinion was to the effect that there were still droplets to be wrung from the sponge with regards to the element of horror. I argued against blatancy. This argument was not unforeseen, and it appeared that the emissary had not come alone, for he moved stiffly to the door, informing me, "There may yet be someone who can persuade you of the validity of the request." To my mind the 'request' had become a definite threat, and I experienced a degree of panic over the nature of what was to be revealed when the door was opened.

If you imagine that beyond that door awaited something monstrous—some hideous face, perhaps with some of the flesh still upon it, peering in from the gloom, or maybe a fearful toad-like thing that slouched into my study—I must disappoint you. But I think such a revenant would have instilled less terror in me. What stood there was simply a man, with nothing malignant nor decayed about his aspect, and no reek of the cemetery about him. Just a man, as alive as you or I! And this was what filled me with unyielding terror, for it was a man who could not possibly be alive. Here stood a figure who I, and only I, knew, for that knowledge of him came from my own imaginings. It was Tarrant, the archaeologist from that story whose mere conception had lead to this whole situation, made suddenly incarnate. Dismiss from your mind the notion that some imposter, a person of sufficient physical similarity to the subject of my tale, had been pressed into service in a bid to alarm me, for I am not given to providing detailed descriptions of those who inhabit my fictions, preferring to let them find form within the *imagination of the reader. Yet this arrival was, to the life, the figure who had lived in my own internal vision. My eyes instantly fell upon his left hand. It was gloved, and I prayed that he would not remove the glove to reveal the bones and tendons, stripped of their flesh, just as I had described the result of the archaeologist's merest touch of the hungry black stonework of the occultist's sarcophagus. I thought that no horror could be worse than this, but when he began to talk, and talk in a voice that I had heard vividly in my head as I had written his story, I found that I was wrong. For he told me where my version had got the details wrong, and of what was really to be found in that tomb, until I finally had to beg with him to stop.*

Now comes the task of completing the story that is demanded of me. It is short and it is ill-written but my hand is restricted in certain matters, and there is a certain form that it is forced to take. This is the only way that I can discern of honouring that contract, which I now see is binding in more than any legal sense. The true meaning of what was passed to me across my desk was obscured at the time, even though my initial reading of that particular choice of wording should have revealed its depths, for it is there, hidden in plain sight, and I must follow the directions 'to the letter' in constructing these paragraphs. The revisions have been made to those stories which I once thought complete. The task has been less onerous than I had anticipated; in many cases dreams have furnished suggestions, although I must admit that sleep is no longer as inviting as once it was. The emissary tells me that his employer is appreciative of the results. I comfort myself with the thought that if the audience for these tales is truly made up of associates of my patron, the effect provoked by what may be found contained herein may not be undeserved, and I can feel little guilt should this be the case. If I fail in this, I believe that I know more than any man could of what is to follow. I have written of such things. And if as innocuous and only fleetingly described a character as Mr. Tarrant could be plucked in his entirety from the recesses of my mind, what of those whose descriptions have tended to be more vivid? I fear that the next such visitation will come from those ranks of the not-so-innocuous that my pen has unleashed.

Given my earlier assertion that my stories had been in no way based upon my experience or that of others, I feel an addendum must now be made. There is now one ghost story that is entirely based upon my experiences. This you have just read. As to the experience of others, I fear that once the companion pieces to this account are read, that latter claim can no longer be taken as truthful.

"A stunt," declared Endicott, firmly closing the book. Then, with an attempt at more conviction, "A macabre practical joke, designed to appeal to his patron's vanity. He even admits to it being a story. It may have been inspired by a genuine event, but it's a story still. And not a particularly good one at that. It's badly structured, inconsequential, inconclusive and..." Here his attempts to hold back the shudder that had long threatened to convulse him failed. It seemed to him to be almost by design that he hadn't discovered the story until after he'd read the rest of the book. Had the ink seemed somehow fresher, even wetter upon those pages? It was now quite dry, but even so... With so many of those other tales being about stories or books and things found hidden in books, it struck him that he was being given gloating hints all along. This thirteenth story may have been a joke, it even had the feeling of a riddle, but if it were true, and if there was indeed something woven into the text... The implications for anyone unlucky enough to find themselves in possession of that unnamed patron's gift were far from healthy. Another story within the book's pages had made this much clear; to be freed from the power of a malediction that has been passed on, it must itself be passed on to another. In this instance, had the construction of that peculiar story allowed something to be passed on thirteen-fold? That being the case, if he were to have any hope of unravelling the truth of it—and hope now looked to him to be a commodity in which he was in drastically short supply—there was only one person left that he could possibly ask.

Next morning saw telegrams dispatched to a number of academic institutes. The message in each was a simple query as to whether a Dr. H.S. Grace was known to them. Endicott was certain that he'd heard somewhere that the good doctor, when not pursuing his literary career, was a respected scholar, and those examples of fictitious documentation and authentic sounding folklore scattered throughout his stories tended to bear this out. An anxious wait followed until the reply was received; the sender informing him that Dr. Grace was not employed at that particular institute but he was certainly known, as he was throughout academic circles, before directing his enquiries toward the correct venerable seat of learning.

Despite his best efforts to do otherwise, Endicott spent the train journey hunched over Grace's book, poring over that account of the volume's origins until the words lost all meaning and became simply a jumble of disconnected letters. Or were they quite so disconnected as all that? His attempts to force the emergence of some order saw those glimmerings of understanding that had begun to amass being thrown apart once more. He had to be patient, to stop trying so hard, and to let his eyes drift over the pages. As the words swam, they might hopefully resolve themselves. There, a word had formed, then another... It was coming, but the sense of elated dread gripped him so strongly that he lost them once more. The text of the story jumped sharply back into focus, before dissolving again, although this was now caused by the frustrated tears that sprang to his eyes.

"I'm afraid Dr. Grace isn't here, Mr. Endicott," was the dismaying report which he received when he'd finally located the correct building within the ancient precincts and had made himself known at the Porter's Lodge. "If you'd just waited until you'd received that telegram as I was charged with sending you, you might've saved yourself a journey. Are you a friend of his? No, I see. A professional call. Well, I wish I could venture as to when he'd be back, but he's on a sabbatical leave, and has been so for some months. Sometimes it's the way with our learned gentlemen, sir. Too many dusty, old books in one confined place, well, it can't be conducive to health, can it? And Dr. Grace shared my view, I believe. He had me and my friend, Albert, pack all his books away for storage; that's a pretty corner of the stores quite taken up, what with his habit, so I'm as keen as any to see his return so I can clear that area. Very partial to his books, and forever haunting the library, he was. Leastways up until just before he took off. As if he'd took some objection to books, the way he went pale when I asked him when his next one was due. You did know, didn't you, that he's written himself, and been published too? Proper books, mind, that you or I might read, and not like some where you might find yourself lost without hope after the first letter of the first word... Where might he be found? Well, I couldn't swear on it, but not anywhere nearby. He's fond of the continent as a destination, and it wouldn't surprise me if that wasn't where he got himself half the notions for his stories..." But before the porter could get much further in his discourse on the ways of their European neighbours, Endicott pleaded an imminent train and took his leave.

There were boarding houses and hotels aplenty nearby, and Endicott considered that it might be less oppressive to spend a night away from a home which he'd grown to feel had been invaded. But, given the nature of his fears, geographical distance looked unlikely to prove of any effect, just as little he could think of offered any hope in that direction. Probably it was sheer habit that brought him to the railway station. He numbly bypassed the ticket booth and that station employee within who beckoned with a multitude of limbs through the stained glass panel that kept him mercifully separate from the passengers. Hours passed—how many Endicott neither knew nor cared—as he sat on the hard wooden bench and ignored the carved heads in the armrests that uttered terrible things. Trains came and went, arriving out of and disappearing into the eternal darkness that lay in either direction down the tracks. Their whistles shrilled out a mournful lament, one that drew a stick thin and ragged figure ever closer through the fields in the distance.

"Is everything all right, guv'nor?" enquired the station master. "Only you've been here all the day long, and the last train's going to be through here shortly. And you really wouldn't want to miss your chance, now would you?" Endicott looked up only once, unconvinced by the attempt at concern showing on that pink, waxy face, and the station master left him alone on the empty platform. He was once again reviewing those stories, one by one, then as a whole. It was too dark for reading, but by now he no longer needed the book to be open in front of him to see the printed text. His mind was turning the accounts over, allowing characters and incidents from one story to spill into the next; the library labyrinth with its shelves crammed full of identical bestiaries, all ready to burst their bindings and spill forth their inhabitants at the shrill summoning of a desolate tune; the hapless victims awaiting their revised fates; Simon Eaves in the grip of the mannequin; the traveller, Nesbitt, at the jaws and claws of devils; Mr. Dylan and the concealed occupant of the maze; Dr. Ibbotson's endless darkness; Carpenter and the inhabitant of the ruined house; the tragic Ordishes plunging through that window into madness; Tewkes and the gibbering thing that had come crawling out of a stain in the wallpaper to claim back the journal and its secrets; the archaeologist, Tarrant, his tale destined never to be told, yet still trapped in a hellish half-life in some awful service. Then there were those that gathered against them, Hugo and Osric, Bracemyre and the scarecrow, Glavering and those 'arachnidial' things, the Templar and, in the shadows, that unseen 'employer' who had so twisted their destinies. These characters were merging into one, the names fading together; *Eaves, Nesbitt, Dylan, Ibbotson, Carpenter, Ordish, Tewkes, Tarrant*—until he finally saw, with horrendous clarity, one name emerging, one victim revealed!

Something rustled behind him. He had a dim idea that it was the book, abandoned as he'd left the bench and stepped towards the edge of the platform, its pages turning in the wind. But there was no wind tonight. A memory flickered of something black that had scuttled and flapped through the night toward him, and out of the lightless emptiness that lurked along the tracks, that crippled umbrella gusted along, its broken frame scrabbling against the platform's edge, the thin fabric billowing out and revealing the nest of glittering eyes within their folds, before it was lost once more to the dark. In the distance, the station master was announcing to the vacant platform the imminent train and the various halts along the line, "Altingley, Glavering, Harewynd…" The names were obscurely familiar, but when his time came to depart, he hoped that he would never be compelled to visit any of them. With this wish in his mind, he took another step closer to the edge and waited for the oncoming train.

"Why me?" was the simple question that he heard himself mutter, talking aloud but expecting no response. He hadn't sought after hidden knowledge, hadn't delved too deeply into any best forgotten past, yet still his name was there amongst those of the ill-fated and the damned. Would his own fate bring him within reach of the horrors that had awaited these characters, and, if so, which one was it to be? Or, as he had read all of their destinies, had he perhaps absorbed them all, and was he even now awaiting thirteen-fold damnation? He could hear the far-off train, and in its approach lay his solitary chance of escape, if he could but rewrite his own ending and thwart whatever malign plan had brought him to these straits. But while he was still ensnared in this plot, the idea of some other audience, earthly or otherwise, following his sorry tale demanded that some exposition was still to be forthcoming. An ambiguous and unexplained conclusion seemed even more unthinkable than those dark entities into whose unreal world he had been manipulated. He repeated his question with more insistence, "Why me?"

His answer was delivered in a voice which he'd heard before. "This fate was never intended for you. You were never part of the right audience." Endicott turned his head in time to see something dark step onto the platform. The woman raised a beckoning hand, inviting him to step back and away from the platform's edge. Around the pale skin of her extended wrist, did some shadowy thing shift? A whistle sounded, closer now. "What you purchased, and what I was thwarted from claiming, should be the last of its kind. If the originator of this situation can be said to enjoy such sentiments as amusement, it amuses him to bestow such gifts, in various forms, upon those who have, unwittingly or not, laboured in his service. The other gifts found their rightful recipients; the menagerist who walked willingly into the cage to be rent apart by those beasts which he had so mistreated; the aesthete who collected innocents of untainted beauty only to spoil and then discard them, driven to his end after having his sight robbed from him; the musician whose hands could coax his instruments to life with such delicacy, yet wreak such savagery on human flesh, haunted to madness by the melody which he could not shake off, yet could never replicate; these and all the others. But the bibliophile, he who cheated, stole and murdered to acquire his library of forbidden lore, and who was the intended possessor of this gift? His own debaucheries ended his sordid career before he had even once opened the pages of that book. This should have been an end to it, but there are some things that, once unleashed, cannot be recalled until they have been satisfied. It was not supposed to come to you, but it is hungry and an innocent soul is far more nourishing than a withered one, so it is rewriting the original enchantment to include you in the design. It can do such a thing because it lives in those words and on those pages. If you are to be free of it, you must pass it on, Mr. Endicott. You must pick up that book and pass it on to me."

It was madness, of course! Since this woman knew of the horrors that the ownership of the book brought with it, she surely couldn't wish to accept them on herself? And if not madness, then a trap. From the very outset hadn't he thought her unnatural in some way? Yet even as he now faced her, those previously unattainable features had grown more defined, almost as if lines of delineation were drawing themselves around her, lending her the aura of a nearly lifelike illustration become real, or of a figure stepped out of an illuminated manuscript. The woman's hand was still held out, as if to draw him to her that he might hand his burden over to her. He had an intense desire to rush to the bench and snatch the book up, but even as this burned in his mind, the book tumbled to the ground as if of its own volition.

Some power seemed to propel the book across the concrete, flapping and sliding, and Endicott watched in dismay as the pages worked themselves loose. Most were whipped up into the air where they fluttered in lazy circles, but he was able to stoop and retrieve a handful that scampered across the ground to where he stood. Single words and phrases on torn edges caught his eye, *'desperation,' 'isolated,' 'of little consequence,' 'cursed,' 'eternal,' 'self-slaughter,' 'hopelessly imminent.'* The pages were a storm of motion yet these words remained painfully visible, as their type thickened and grew bolder while the other words flowed into them, feeding their blackness until they overflowed the edges of the paper. Droplets of ink became a torrent that coalesced into something gaunt. The fading of the typography had left the pages blank and unmarked, and they flocked and fluttered toward one another before clinging together. Here they curled and crumpled, folding in on themselves and taking on a more solid shape. The face that formed itself from that crushed paper might have been that of some hideously aged hag, for here was the witch of childhood nightmares, with that straggling, liquid body that supported it, and those wrinkled, leathery hands.

Perhaps it was the sight of those brown claws clutching at the air as the creature prowled, as if seeking its prey, that spurred Endicott into motion. More likely it was the dry whispering from those papery lips as they moved constantly, murmuring dreadfully, alternately goading or threatening. The woman was calling something to him, but he heard nothing of what she spoke over that incessant, urging whisper. The voice was chillingly familiar, though he'd never heard it aloud. For he was instantly conscious that here was the voice that had guided his dreams, that had narrated his terrors, and that this frightful thing had been his constant companion wherever he had travelled these past few days. It had sat by his side by day, had followed in his steps, and it had crouched over him as he slept, its words pouring from that torn mouth into his ear and into his thoughts. Would it be with him always? Such a thought, to be alone with this abomination throughout his remaining days, was unbearable. Yet he was not alone, and as his eyes turned upon the woman, he saw that she too was whispering, while her hand and her eyes reached out to him. He moved then, a single step.

Even as he took that first step, he heard another sound that drowned out the babble of voices. It was the rattling roar of the locomotive as it made its final approach. In this instant Endicott had his first conscious realisation of what he had been contemplating as he'd stood there on the brink, and he was wracked by a terrible shuddering. When this abated he saw those two mysterious figures before him—the one biding its time with an awful patience, which the words that crackled from the brittle mouth told him was infinite—the other gradually shifting to interpose herself between the dark whisperer and Endicott, her voice fully engaged in speaking her unfamiliar words, but her intense eyes imploring him. "I can't just pass this thing onto you," he pleaded. "What will happen to you if I do? How can you fight that thing?" But her gaze was determined, resolute, and he ran to thrust those few snatched up pages into her grasp.

Reaction from that awful thing was instantaneous. The whispering mouth widened into a shriek of piercing intensity, the maw gaping so massively that the parchment face ripped and split around its edges. It moved across the platform, its fluid body spattering inky beads in its flight, and leathery hands closed upon the woman's wrists. The marks on her skin were then exposed. They weren't faded like old tattoos. The words were black and clear, even if their meaning wasn't. Then she too let her grasp close upon the thing from the book—the thing *of* the book! As she did so, her fingers slid under the inky surface of the spindly arms, and the screech which the entity let fly nearly saw the upper half of the dreadful head tear loose from the lower jaw. It looked to Endicott like some ghastly dance, as the two dark figures whirled and spun backwards, teetered for an instant, and disappeared over the edge. And even still that shriek blasted out its shrill whistle that proved not to be a scream after all as the massive bulk of the locomotive thundered through, sending up an explosion of white scraps as it passed across Endicott's horror-stricken view, before slowing to a halt.

It was the station master who helped a shaken and obviously distressed Endicott to the bench. Having come from his office to greet the train, he had been met with the sight of a single, pale-faced traveller gawping at something on the tracks below the carriages. Eventually he'd been able to say something to the effect that there had been an accident. Such things are every railway employee's dread, and after a moment's consultation with the engine crew, torches had been put to use, while the driver and engineer warily inspected the front and underside of the great engine. But there was no trace of any tragedy. The only thing found to be amiss was that the tracks were littered with a mass of papers. The station master plucked a few from where they'd been caught around the wheels. But Endicott showed no indication of wishing to see them, even those the engineer declared weren't entirely blank, as with all of the others, but looked to be in Latin or some such elderly tongue, and might well have been prayers. His thoughts then were of home and a future that would no longer be spent in such solitary travels. In these respects, happy to relate, Mr. Endicott succeeded and his tale has what might be regarded as a happy ending.

Nothing more was to be discovered of the woman's identity—Endicott's decision being that further investigation was undesirable—and it was some considerable period later that a researcher with a scholarly interest in the, by then, late Dr. Grace's ghost stories discovered, by happy chance while she was supposed to be investigating one of his academic works, a few pages of an unrelated manuscript. These had somehow found themselves concealed amongst the sheets transcribing a mediaeval ritual in Latin for holding 'the Evil One' at bay, and it was evidently this that had shielded them from discovery for so long. The handwriting, illegible as it was, was unmistakably the late doctor's, its very unintelligibility being the giveaway. This find was exciting enough for Miss Allen, but when a headache-inducing closer look revealed it to be the draft of a story, and one not amongst those included in the pages of those three slim collections of ghost stories that he had released, this made it of considerable interest. Dr. Grace's career as a writer had been all too brief, and in his latter years he had refused any inducement to take up his pen again. Yet the date which was scribbled at the top of a page suggested that this latest find had been drafted around that time when he had sworn off the writing of supernatural fiction, and might even prove to contain his last words on the topic. Even this wasn't the most unusual aspect of this unearthed tale. That was reserved for the nature of the central character. The author had never been noted for his overuse of female characters, having looked at the worst being produced by his peers and rejecting the notion of *'going to the trouble of developing a character, simply to induce a fit of the vapours into them the instant our ghastly thing rears its head.'* Such quotations were often used, or misused, in attempts by latter day critics to fashion hearsay evidence of misogyny. Therefore it was an unexpected pleasure to discover that— from what could be gleaned without stronger light, a week of close scrutiny, and a ready supply of headache pills—the central force for good was *'a tall and somewhat striking woman'* with *'a very confirmed countenance, the expression intent and the eyes shining,'* and the account concerned itself with her dealings with and ultimate defeat of some fiend. Evidently the draft had been completed in a hurry, as there was some confusion in the details: references to a veil were scored through in places, left intact in others, the woman's name was left throughout as a blank, her age varied from page to page. Whatever the case, this would require closer examination, and the only hope was that it was complete.

Glancing at the first and last sheets revealed that at very least the commencement and conclusion were present. With interest, the researcher noted that the latter was closed out with what appeared to be a dedication of sorts; *'For the benefit— so to style it—of somebody else, for whom a certain type of story was not intended, and in whom the perusal of such a narrative may have incurred undue discomfort and displeasing terrors—in particular should their initial reading suggest to them a hidden malevolence that, from the first letter and through subsequent paragraphs, is at play—in the hope that they might gain by the actions depicted herein; although I regret to report that, should this description apply in more than a single case, the cure may only be effective the one time.'*

A Ravelled Tress

"I think it's rather beautiful. Wherever did you find it?" Alice Wynngrave asked finally.

"Beautiful?" retorted Geoffrey. "I'd say it was altogether the ugliest thing I've ever seen." But there was a definite hint of admiration to his comment. Geoffrey Wynngrave had always had an eye for the grotesque; indeed some had been heard unkindly to remark that this explained his taste in both neckties and female company. "What on earth possessed you to hang it in here?"

"We thought it might look decorative," Elspeth said, and Roger nodded in silent agreement with his wife.

"Well, I can't think of any other use for it besides decoration," drawled Sir Nigel Fenwick, "though it's certainly eye-catching enough. And I've never seen anything quite like it in someone's drawing room before."

"I think it's what they call a conversation piece, Sir Nigel," Geoffrey pointed out. He had a way of pointing things out that always seemed to verge on the scornful.

Alice, who often wished that she was oblivious to her brother's less agreeable mannerisms, concluded, "Then it's done its job, hasn't it? Because here we all are, talking about it."

The object under scrutiny was a thick tress of black hair, pleated throughout its length, the pleats held in place by the red ribbons tied at either end. It was, at that moment, sus-

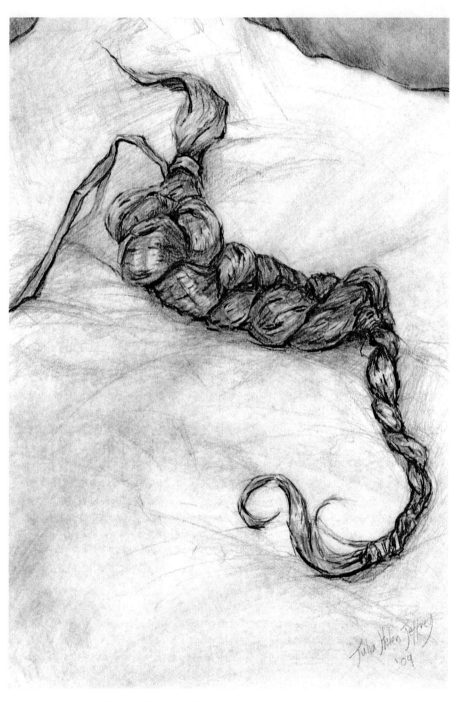

*...Roger had to fight the urge to unravel the pleats,
rend them apart, and toss them to the winds.*

pended from a picture hook snagged into one of those ribbons, above the blazing fire that had greeted Roger and Elspeth Morgan's guests when they had moved through to the drawing room after dinner.

The meal had been a tremendous success, much to Elspeth's evident, and Roger's more internalised, delight. These were the first visitors, apart from the thankfully now departed workmen, since the Morgans had taken over Nightmane Lodge. Roger, who was more sensitive to the moods of others than his outward jocularity usually betrayed, was very much aware of his wife's anxiety that everything should go swimmingly. Even as small a gathering as this had to be meticulously catered for. Days of planning had passed, during which time Roger had felt he would be better employed in doing something practical to avoid being underfoot. The Lodge, though by no means approaching a great country manor like the ancestral Fenwick home some miles away, nevertheless had more than enough rooms, and in each of these rooms there was something that demanded attention. "May as well start at the bottom and work my way up," was something of a saying with Roger—he was given to sayings, sometimes to his wife's feigned annoyance—so he'd exchanged his city clothes for overalls and, torch in hand, descended into the cellar.

"The workmen had done just about anything that was urgently crying out to be done," Roger explained. "You'll remember I told you what a state of disrepair the house was in when we first chanced upon it. Inevitable, I suppose, after being empty for so long. And it helped us no end on the price. But I told you all of this over dinner.

"No, the problem in the cellar wasn't in the pipes or with damp. It was just the mess. You know how people, when they move from one house to another, often leave things behind?"

"Quite," Geoffrey nodded, before dryly commenting, "I left a wife behind in each of the last three houses I vacated." This brought a chuckle from Roger—with whom Geoffrey had boarded during their college days—a grunt from Sir Nigel, and a sharp nudge from his sister. Geoffrey, who had only invited Alice to accompany him because it had seemed a safer option than inviting any of the unattached females he knew—and subsequently running the risk of a fourth unhappy union—ignored the application of elbow to rib, concluding, "No-one ever seems to leave anything very useful behind, do they?"

"I don't know," murmured Sir Nigel between puffs on his cigar. "One reads about these people who find they've got themselves an Old Master that's been gathering dust in a spare room, or patching up a hole in their outhouse roof for years." To Elspeth, the old man's tone suggested that he wouldn't be adverse to such a windfall himself. She was aware that, like many born into a title and property, his responsibilities outweighed his means, and even the selling off of heirlooms would no longer be an option soon. Pride meant that he never complained about it, not even after Geoffrey's blunt comments on the lessening quality of his cigars earlier in the evening. Nor would he have heard of accepting charity, yet this was one of the reasons behind Elspeth's invitation to join them that weekend. She didn't much care for the thought that on Christmas Day, only a week away, the man who had been her father's closest friend from boyhood until the day he died, would be dining alone in an increasingly unfurnished and unheated house.

Roger, who didn't like beating about the bush, continued his story before anyone else could interrupt. "When I first saw it, if I hadn't known better, I'd have said that whoever built the Lodge had found a municipal dumping ground, then put the old pile up on top of it without bothering to clear the area first. There were heaps of the stuff. But, curiously, not much of it junk. Some of it was really of rather good quality. You see that decorative little table by the window? And you commented on those high-backed chairs and the bureaux in the parlour, Geoffrey."

Geoffrey shrugged. "They might make a bob or two at auction, I'd say. You know how in vogue this stuff from the last century is just now. Can't see what's wrong with new, myself." This last comment might have been specifically intended to irk Alice, and it lead to a discussion pitting the relative merits of decorative against purely functional crafts-manship, and the overly romantic streak inherent in the sister against the philistine beastliness of the brother.

"Well, to cut a long story short," persisted Roger, "there was a great teetering stack of this rather nice furniture. Some boards, too. I think they were from the bookshelves in the study, but the worm had gone into the frames, so we replaced them and I never had the chance to check if they matched. But I reckon they were, because the books were there too. Rather dreary looking ones, I'd have to say, from the glance I had at one or two. All very dry, and not a decent potboiler amongst them. But there they were, in the heap."

"You know what that sounds like you had there?" puffed Sir Nigel. "The makings of a pretty good bonfire."

"In a cellar?" smirked Geoffrey. "Sounds a pretty severe way to deal with the rising damp, old fellow."

"Anyway," interjected Roger, still set in his stated pur-pose of cutting a long story short, despite the increasing dif-ficulty in doing so, "I sifted through the pile, and I'd started to put things in order, when I found this," he indicated the hanging tress, "right at the heart of it. It was in this small wooden casket... Where did I put the casket, darling?"

Elspeth went to the sideboard, itself another souvenir of her husband's find; "Right beneath our feet," as he'd described it, before laughing when he realised the inadver-tent literalness of the expression. What she brought out was an oblong box, some twelve inches long, and of some darkish wood. And, when she opened it for the inspection of her guests, it appeared to emit a dazzling glow from within—the result of the chandelier being reflected back from the mirrors that lined the hinged lid and interior of the box.

"That's really very pretty, too," said an entranced Alice Wynngrave.

"Everything's pretty to you, my dear," muttered her brother.

"Not quite everything," was her retort, "or everyone. But see how it reflects the light back and forward from surface to surface, until it almost looks like it's full of jewels."

"You have an artist's eye," smiled Sir Nigel.

"And a street brawler's elbow," added Geoffrey, his ribs having been dealt another, sharper nudge.

Roger, realising the end of his account was mercifully in sight, pressed gamely on. "I thought it was rather unusual. And, when I saw what was inside it, it just became all the more unusual. So I brought it upstairs and asked Elspeth to give it the once over."

"And I nearly dropped our best china tureen," his wife said reproachfully. "When I first saw it coiled up in there, I thought it was a dead rat."

"In its own coffin?" Geoffrey observed. "How sentimental these country rodents must be."

"But I'm with Alice on this," Elspeth insisted. "Now that I've seen it properly, I think it's quite lovely."

In response, Geoffrey considered mentioning the name of a girl he'd spotted in the chorus line of a certain variety theatre who he thought quite lovely, but who he wouldn't want to hang over the fireplace. However one glance at his sister's sharp elbow suggested that it might be a thought best kept to himself. Instead, he had a suggestion. "I'll tell you what, Allie, lend me that brooch, would you? We'll attach it to that thing and have a round of pin the tail on the donkey."

"We don't have a donkey," Elspeth pointed out.

"No, just an ass!" Alice flashed her brother a nasty grin. "But you could always have the hair turned into a wig. I'd say it was, what, at least three feet in length if you were just to unravel it."

Roger patted his wife's head in a manner intended as reassuring, though no reassurance was strictly necessary. Still, his fingers caressed her sleek locks. "We won't be needing that, will we? As the saying goes, I wouldn't change a single hair on her head. Besides, give me a flaming red-head over a dark temptress any day."

Shortly afterwards, while they had gone to fetch the last coffees of the evening, Alice remarked to Elspeth on her husband's sweetness, a far cry from that brute sibling of hers, and how the method by which the two men had ever become friends was still a mystery to her.

"Yes," Elspeth had to agree, "Roger is very sweet. He knew just how worried I was that tonight would be a success. Only last night, even though he was worn out himself after clearing out the cellar, he sat in the dark and stroked my hair, ever so gently, until I fell asleep. But, I fancy he must have been drifting off himself, as he got rather clumsy and gave it the most fearful tug. I yelped a bit, and he woke up, all full of apologies, even though he couldn't remember a thing about it."

A further enjoyable hour or so was spent over coffee and further chat, mostly concerned with the sterling work that had been done around the Lodge, before the relaxed group made their way to their rooms. It must have been some three or four hours afterwards that Alice Wynngrave was awakened by an unexpected sound issuing from somewhere in the darkness. As she strained to make it out, it became clear that what had roused her was a ragged breathing, somewhat choked, coming through the wall. Her room was next to that of her hosts, and she listened anxiously for some minutes, before slipping into her dressing gown and out into the darkened hallway.

Her knock on the bedroom door was a little timid to begin with but, when the painful sounds from within did not abate, she rapped more loudly and called out to ask if some assistance was required.

It was this beating upon the door that finally roused Roger Morgan from a very deep and dream-filled sleep, though the content of the dream fled when he found his wife, asleep still, writhing and choking at his side. When his efforts to shake her into wakefulness failed, he leapt from the bed and rushed to her side. Lifting her into a sitting position, he brushed her hair away from her face, which was damp from her slumbering exertions. Fearing that she was undergoing some form of seizure, he cried out for someone to, for pity's sake, help him.

When Alice entered and switched on the newly installed electric light, she was momentarily frozen by the sight of the ghastly purple tinge to Elspeth's face as she struggled to wake up. Regaining herself, Alice hurried to the bathroom, fumbling for the cold tap in the darkness. As she released the water, holding the glass underneath, she almost let it shatter when she became aware of something dry and wispy, like a cobweb, brushing against the back of her hand, before the water caught hold and washed it away.

By the time Elspeth had taken a few sips, and her cheeks had resumed a more healthy colouring, the entire house was awake, and even Geoffrey's comments were reserved for questions of concerned interest. "I'm honestly quite alright, thank you, all of you," Elspeth insisted, the reddening of her cheeks now being caused by embarrassment over the fuss and the distress to her guests, and not through some reoccurrence of whatever had attacked her during her sleep.

But when the others had returned to their rooms, and peace had finally settled once more, her assurances to one and all were replaced by concern over whether she had contracted some infection, and should they suggest their guests leave before it had a chance to contaminate them? Roger's own natural concern over his wife's well-being was doubled by feelings of guilt that he had slept on, unaware of her plight, and trebled by some vague unease about the dream that had kept him in its grip, and whose details he still could not recall. His fingers strayed to his cheek and to his throat, before he took Elspeth's own trembling hand in his and suggested they wait until the morning before making any decisions.

That morning was crisp and cold, with the snow lying thick across the fields and in the branches of the trees. The briskness of the air served to revive the otherwise sleep-deprived inhabitants of the Lodge. And, with no further symptoms of any supposed illness being displayed by their hostess, all notions of breaking up the gathering were dismissed. Instead, they passed the most pleasant of days. It began with a hearty breakfast, after which the men selected and gathered an attractive tree from the adjoining woods, and they all joined together in hanging it with paper and foil decorations in front of the drawing room fire, before another excellent meal was enjoyed.

Almost all thoughts of Elspeth's misadventure of the previous night were put out of mind as it came time for those merry companions to retire for the night. Almost, but not all, for Roger's disquiet over his ineffectual presence when his wife had most required his assistance made sleep an unlikely prospect. Thus, several hours of lying awake and gazing into the darkness passed before a drowsiness began to creep over him, slowly and stealthily, practically caressing him into sleep.

On this night, Alice did not wait in the corridor after Elspeth's gasps once again disturbed her own dreams. She burst into the room to find both Roger and Elspeth sleeping, he wearing a look of vacant contentment, she thrashing in useless efforts to catch her breath. When Roger snapped awake, startled, his hand shot to his throat, as if feeling some icy sensation there, before his other senses returned and he joined in the efforts to rouse his wife.

Geoffrey, of course, had the latest motor car, and it wasn't many minutes later that they were making full speed to the nearest cottage hospital. Throughout that journey, a flustered Roger divided his time between asking Elspeth how she was feeling—if she was able to breathe, if she felt any pain—and gently trying to shush her into silence whenever she tried to reply.

A fretful half hour or more, during which a number of cigarettes were lit and then discarded half-smoked, proved to them how apt the designation 'waiting room' was. And, when the doctor and his nurse, at last, came through to inform them that they could see Elspeth and take her back home, their frankly hostile and suspicious looks puzzled the already bewildered Roger immensely. But when he saw the livid bruises around his wife's throat, he understood entirely the cause of their suspicion.

"I told them, I must have been tangled up in the sheets as I slept," Elspeth told them once more, as they gathered before the drawing room fire with warm milk or brandy to take off the chill of their journey. Her focus for this comment was her husband, whose look of shame-faced disbelief was heartrending for her to see. "I told them, no, I insisted, that you would never, not ever, do anything to harm me."

"Quite right," barked Sir Nigel, giving Roger's shoulder a clap. "You're not that sort of wretched creature, lad. Not that sort at all. We all know it, so don't give it another moment's thought."

But Elspeth Morgan's remaining few hours' sleep, before the house party were due to arise for that day's church service, had one further disturbance. This came when she awoke to the sound of her husband weeping in the bathroom.

That Sunday, the last day on which the group was due to be together, was a distinctly gloomy one. Even Geoffrey, who was never noted for his sense of good taste or discretion, judged that gallows humour might be amiss. Sadly his attempts at pleasant small talk, be it about the gardens or the décor, sounded so out of character that he ceased altogether and got morosely more drunk. While Sir Nigel, sensing that he was, despite their protests to the contrary, an added burden on his young friends, insisted on travelling back to Fenwick Hall that day, and early enough that young Wynngrave could drive him to the station while he was still capable of avoiding an accident. So he departed, telling them to call upon him at any point, should anything be required, leaving only three in the Lodge.

Of those three, Roger was still exceedingly downcast, and Elspeth took the opportunity, while they prepared an uncomplicated dinner, to confide her worries to Alice.

"You said yourself," Alice reassured her, "that it must have been the sheets. You must have wound them tighter round your neck as you struggled. What other explanation is there?"

Elspeth agreed that this was the only likely cause. "I'm normally such a still sleeper, though. Maybe it's this house, and trying to settle in a new environment. Could it really be that I miss the noise and bustle of the city? But I still find what happened last night so very strange." And here, something else struck her that she felt she ought to share. "And that's not the only strange thing. You see, after we came back last night, and I was getting into bed. I found...well, I don't know how they could have got there, but I found some hairs on my pillow. No, I know that doesn't sounds like anything very unusual. But, the thing is, they weren't my hairs. They were black, and they were very, very long."

That night, there was no outcry to raise the household from their beds. But it was a night that brought little rest for anyone; anyone with the exception of Geoffrey, that is, whose consumption of brandy had forced him to retire early. Alice lay in her room, half in a doze, but also listening. Elspeth, thankfully, slept, even if only fitfully, having taken a few tablets to ease the ache in her neck muscles. And Roger, unable to face the prospect of another awful night like the one he had just endured, sat in a chair facing the bed, watching for any sign of discomfort from his wife. Only once did he feel his eyelids begin to droop, but this moment passed when he jerked violently awake, convinced that he'd felt something cold brush across his face.

The next morning, Geoffrey, looking almost as seedy as his exhausted friend felt, had to return to the city. But his sister, whose friendship Elspeth privately regarded as one of the few positives about her husband's continued acquaintance with his college mate, found herself at a loose end—the school where she taught piano and flute being closed for the festivities. It had been decided in advance that she should stay and keep Elspeth company, allowing Roger to attend to those last few jobs that are always found to be remaining just when one is congratulating oneself on the completion of a long task. Instead, she proved a much-needed companion while Roger slept on into the afternoons that followed each nightly vigil.

And it was during this week that what began as a nodding acquaintance with young Mr. Townes, the village chemist to whom she went to collect more tablets for Elspeth's raw throat, moved from mere nodding to exchanged helloes, to a more intimate friendship. So famously were they getting on in Elspeth's eyes—and hers were eyes that rarely deceived—that, after some gentle coaxing, a blushing Alice Wynngrave asked if Mr. Townes would care to join them at the Lodge on Christmas Eve, and a blushing Mr. Townes accepted.

Elspeth's bruises faded as the week progressed and, with them, the horror of that near-fatal night. Even Roger was approaching his old self, something that was aided by the return of his college friend early on the morning before Christmas. After the usual pleasantries—"You look awful," "And the same to you"—they found themselves seated before a blaze in the drawing room as the afternoon lengthened. Here, Geoffrey gave a peculiarly concentrated look toward that unusual decoration hanging above the fire, and said, "I've been looking into the history of your house. Why? I thought I might find a nice ghost or two in the old place's past to spin you a yarn about on Christmas Eve." As has been stated, Geoffrey had an eye for the grotesque.

"And did you find one?"

"No," he admitted. "And thoroughly disappointed I was, too. I even went to an expert. Well, I had some business that took me back near the old college, and I thought, 'I wonder if that antiquities fellow is still there?' You remember? He always had a tale or two, as rumour had it. Well, yes, he was there, and, no, he couldn't give me a ghost."

"How utterly dismal for you," Roger commiserated.

"Quite. At least it was dismal, till he found me a murder instead."

"A murder?" Roger echoed, after he had first ensured that the women were elsewhere and the door was closed.

Geoffrey nodded. "And quite a peculiar one at that. The Lodge was built, round about the turn of the last century, by a certain Gabriel Lockhart, a merchant of some description. His business often took him to the continent, all over, really, and he returned from one of these voyages with a bride. So this place was built by him as a marital home. His new, young wife, Luciana, was apparently a great beauty, much admired for her dark eyes and her long, jet black hair. I believe lustrous is the word I'm looking for. That's how the house got that odd name it's saddled with. Nightmane Lodge? Rather too close to Nightmare, I'd say. Still, it's reported that the exotic creature he'd brought to this quiet little place was considered one of the great beauties of the day. And, it would seem, no-one considered this to be the case more than she did, herself. She was quite the wild one, with something fiery and untameable in her blood. She might have loved her husband, but she loved attention more, and was quite adept at turning men's heads. If the gossip of the time was true, she'd apparently claimed she could tempt any man, be they young, old, married or not."

"She sounds just your type, old boy," beamed Roger, pointedly.

"No, thank you, very much," retorted Geoffrey, not returning the grin. "Now Lockhart was besotted with his bride, and was either blinded by her beauty, or simply so unable to believe his own luck in gaining such a prize, that he put up no objection to her ways. And it appears that she was never actually unfaithful, though she merrily disrupted a fair few marriages just for her own sport. No matter what she may have felt for the merchant, he was only ever going to be a poor second in her affections to her own beauty. Even so, the marriage seemed to work, in its way. Then her cousin made the sea journey to join the household, and things changed.

"The strain of dark beauty must have been strong in that family, because the cousin was quite, quite lovely. And the local menfolk, already only too aware of Luciana's habits, transferred their attentions quickly. The cousin was unattached, you see, and of a wholly different temperament. After some time there was talk of her marrying one of the village lads. But it wasn't to be. She was found in her bed, dead of asphyxiation. No-one could find the cause, an unfortunate accident was diagnosed, no further explanation was forthcoming, and a few years passed.

"It was only when a second tragedy came close to striking, this time with Luciana's own sister, that the truth of Lockhart's bride's madness came out. The sister, only a child at the time of Luciana's marriage, had grown to match and, quite possibly, excel her in beauty. And Luciana's vanity simply wouldn't stand for such an affront."

Roger, who had grown in his unease during this account, nevertheless shrugged. "A murder spurred on by jealousy. What's so peculiar about that?"

"What was so peculiar," Geoffrey said, his eyes fixing once more on that pleated tress above the fireplace, "was what she used as a murder weapon."

It took a few seconds for the implication to sink in. "Her hair?"

"Their own hair," Geoffrey corrected. "She was caught winding her sister's hair around her throat while the girl was still sleeping." With this, Geoffrey concluded his recital, and the look on his old friend's face made him wish he had never begun it. "Don't dwell on it, old boy. It's in the past, and what's long gone can't touch us now." But Roger merely sat, deep in thought, his fingers idly brushing at his neck. Clearly a change of tack was needed, and Geoffrey declared how eagerly he looked forward to being unable to move after another of Elspeth's splendid dinners, "And, if I'm not mistaken, I spy my sister's new amore coming up the path. He must've been raiding his own supply cupboard to be deluded enough to lumber himself with a dreadful bore like Allie. Come, let's warn him off before he gets too embroiled."

But, of course, he did no such thing, and there were once more five seated for a congenial meal. It gladdened Elspeth to see Roger striving, and succeeding in the attempt, to enter into the spirit of the season. Mr. Townes—Herbert, as they came to know him—was agreeable and affable company. And when it came time for the young chemist to leave for home, he and Alice spent some time together on the porch—Elspeth shooing Geoffrey away from the prime eavesdropping spot at the drawing room window. That what was said by the young man was of a highly pleasing and complimentary nature was evident from the glow in Alice's cheeks upon her return, and it was with happy expectations of a bright Christmas that they made their way to their beds that night.

What happened after darkness and silence had stolen over the house that night had the quality of a particularly disturbing dream that the dreamer finds it impossible to awaken from. Indeed, after some time had intervened, those that had been present at the Lodge in the early hours of that Christmas morning found it difficult to recall if it had been a dream at all. If so, none could tell if it was a dream that was shared, or one that had been described so vividly by the one who had dreamt it that it had taken root in all of their minds, as if experienced at first-hand.

It begins with the sensation of waking to find that there is some other presence in the room—one that had not been there before sleep was commenced—and with this comes the awareness that, if wakefulness hadn't come at that precise instant, something would have reached out and brushed against the sleeper. A bedside lamp is quickly lit, but its glare reveals nothing standing soundless and still in the room. Yet it is still a faltering hand that reaches for the switch that will plunge the room into darkness yet again.

Instead, a dry throat necessitates a trip to the basin. But when the tap is turned on, the water that emerges looks to be murky and full of some dark substance, and the hand that reaches under the flow is snatched away as black tendrils begin to creep and coil around it.

From somewhere below, there is a noise. It is a soft, insistent *shshsh*-ing sound, as of something brushing back and forth across the floor. The thought of long, black strands comes to mind.

The staircase is dark, but there is light from one of the downstairs rooms: the warm, yellowy glow of the drawing room fire. But there is no warmth in the approach to this room, from where that sibilant noise is now evidently coming.

A monstrous and lurking shape at the window proves to be the Christmas tree, although it seems altogether darker and less festive than it had appeared beforehand. Why this should be is forgotten, as the *shshsh* resumes and the firelight is blotted out by what it is that steps out to stand before it.

The expectation of long masses of black hair that fall down to brush the floorboards at the thing's feet is quashed by that which can be glimpsed above the hand-mirror that is clasped in what remains of a hand. It is the tatters of the ancient dress, hanging loosely on the emaciated frame that can no longer hope to fill it, that sweep across the floor, *shshsh-shshsh*, as it turns and turns, as if dancing and preening by the glow of the flames.

No, there is no hair there. Instead, the dome of the head is grey and mottled, and flecked with stubble. At least this is so on what little flesh there is still adhering to it that isn't scarred and blackened. As this realisation dawns in the mind of the observer, it appears to transfer itself across the room to the ragged dancer, for it raises a questing finger to its scalp, before reaching skinny arm out to gently stroke the length of hair dangling from the hook in the wall.

The mirror drops, the head snaps upwards, and there is the shock of seeing that, glaring out of that skull, there are dark, green eyes, the eyelashes still intact, though what surrounds them is crumbling and scorched.

The full vision of this skeleton in its shredded finery creates the urgent desire for escape, but the door now seems so far away that it surely must be unreachable. And even if it could be reached, it has the appearance now of being thoroughly webbed over with a black and quivering mesh. The thought of having to grasp and tear through this barrier is loathsome, yet the urge to flee remains. But the windows, too, are concealed behind that same network of crisscrossing strands. Thus the observer, to their profound horror, knows then that they are trapped with the corpse.

And as it rushes swiftly forward, the thought of a chill kiss from those seared, wriggling, grave-worm lips as they fasten upon an exposed throat causes a recoiling step. It is a step that brings contact with something that is coated in hair. The paper and foil decorations are lost. The Christmas tree is swathed in more of those black strands, which brush across fingers, creep up wrists, knot and entangle, ravelling and travelling upwards, moving relentlessly towards the neck.

A horrified backwards look from this crawling nest of dark locks shows that the doorway is unbarred. The creature is gone. So, too, is that hanging tress, though where they have gone, and with what purpose, will not be known until waking comes. And when it comes, it comes quickly. But the escape from one nightmare leads only to a headlong plunge into another!

Alice's cries brought bleary-eyed progress from both directions, and she was found in much the same straits as her hostess on those long nights of the prior weekend. The difference was that she had managed to claw her own hair back from her face and throat, and her rescuers could clearly make out the noose of black pleats that was drawn tightly round her windpipe, even if the hands that held it were unseen.

It was Geoffrey who moved to snatch the grisly thing away, but he met with resistance. The tress was coiled so tightly that it bit into the skin of Alice's throat. Terror that his own attempts to find purchase would only cause more harm to his sister had to be disregarded, since it was plain to all that if he failed she would soon be beyond either harm or salvation. Whatever he struggled against remained unseen, but as he dragged at the black cord there was, just before it gave, a sound like the brittle snapping of slender bones. With a grunt of disgust, he pulled the suddenly limp band free and tossed it into a far corner. Then he threw his arms around his sister, and remained there, holding her while she regained her breath.

Needless to say, they did not stay on at the Lodge throughout that night, and thus Sir Nigel Fenwick did not spend that Christmas alone after all. As they sat before the hastily banked-up blaze in the library grate, Sir Nigel, who had not spent an entirely uneventful life, had views when the proceedings had been fully detailed. His first remark was to Geoffrey. "Normally it's a task to get you to hold your tongue for a minute, but there's more to that yarn of yours than you told Roger, isn't there?"

A stiff drink was handed across, and Geoffrey, with none of the glee with which he had earlier begun the tale, finished recounting what had been described to him in a distant college study. "After Luciana was caught out in her attempt on her sister's life, the method of the cousin's death was instantly clear to all. There was a trial, but prison wasn't the fate decreed for her. Instead, she was sent to Bethlem Royal Hospital. You might be more familiar with its common name... Bedlam! When they cut off her hair—lice being a constant problem among the inmates—she started to scream, and she never stopped till the day she died."

Roger shivered at the memory of the length of raven hair above his fireplace. "Then how did her hair find its way home?"

"The husband, of course. And what a keepsake! Gabriel never quite allowed himself to believe her capable of such an act. He would visit her, but I gather her ravings were too much for him, and when she at last died it may have been a relief. How did she die? In a fire in one of the wards. Since many of the locals were convinced that she'd had something of the witch about her, this was seen as a fitting end. Lockhart's grieving was long, but life is resilient, and he eventually remarried. The marriage wasn't long lasting, though it isn't clear if she died or if she left him. Perhaps now we might suppose that there were too many memories of the mad, jealous first wife held alive in the place, and she fled? If she was given the chance to flee..."

"I think there you have the key to why this creature turned her spiteful attentions from Elspeth to your sister," mused Sir Nigel. "Roger, your guilt over no action of your own has meant you've barely been able to look at, let alone touch your wife over these past few days. There was nothing to feed the envious rage. But if Miss Wynngrave's young chemist had been offered a room at the Lodge tonight, he may well have felt some cold thing laying its lips upon his throat." And Roger once again felt his fingers drift to skin that even now crawled with gooseflesh.

This concluded the talk of what had occurred. It was what was to happen next that now concerned the friends. Sir Nigel, after a deal of thought, turned to Roger. "Tell me, when you found that stack of furniture, did you find anything nearby in the nature of oil or paraffin?"

Roger thought a moment, before affirming, "There was a jug that smelled as if it might have held something of the kind at one point. But the lid had been left uncapped, and it had evaporated."

"Then I'd say someone had been interrupted before he could finish his task. Now you have no option but to complete the job."

"But the house..?" Roger began, until his wife silenced his protest.

"I think she rather pervades the house. How did you put it, Geoffrey—'Her jealous, mad memory held alive there'? He must have realised it, the merchant."

"You have insurance of course?" offered Sir Nigel. "Well,

no matter if you don't. I'm still on the board of one or two reasonable city firms, purely on an informal advisory basis. But you would be amazed how easily the wrong commencement date can be written on a policy against fire or flood."

It was unanimously decided that the remainder of Christmas Day should be observed as normally as was possible under these far from normal circumstances. So it was on Boxing Day that Geoffrey drove Roger and Sir Nigel back to Nightmane Lodge. Once they had recovered that item whose discovery had caused so much grief, Roger had to fight the urge to unravel the pleats, rend them apart, and toss them to the winds. But on Sir Nigel's reckoning that it was better that no single strand should escape, they sealed it intact in its casket, and trooped down into the cellar, taking as much lumber as they could carry, as well as the spare petrol canister from Geoffrey's motor car.

They remained only long enough to ensure that the blaze caught hold properly. As for the dark and writhing shape that appeared to rise up, shrieking, from the flames; as Roger would later recollect, it must have been the same spectacle that greeted those who once gathered round to gawp at the burning of suspected witches.

These events were some years ago, now. Roger and Elspeth Morgan's stay at Fenwick Hall became a permanent one, with Roger eventually bringing some order to Sir Nigel's erratic bookkeeping, and even some profit to the estate. Their children—the first of whom arrived a year or so after they began their residency there—find much to amuse them in the many rooms of that great house, and in 'Grandpa Nigel's' many stories. They are often joined in their play by Alice and Herbert Townes' young family, and by Uncle Geoffrey, whose sister regularly declares him to be the biggest infant of the whole unruly pack.

There have been no more disturbances of the kind that so marred their time at Nightmane Lodge, and these events are seldom discussed. But each Christmas sees extra, silent prayers being said, and, it might be added that still, to this day, both women wear their hair cropped short.

'And Still Those Screams Resound...'

In the past I have spoken of my friend, Dr. Lawrence, and some of the accounts of the supernatural that have, in his duties as an antiquarian, been presented to him. In each case Lawrence has acted, much as you yourself do, as little more than an audience for some peculiar narrative. But his particular interest in that field of study has seen him record the details of these accounts, and this has led to many a long evening's discussion with friends as to the significance of the events to which he had been made privy.

As one of that group of friends, I regard myself as privileged to have been consulted by Lawrence, even if it was in no more exalted a position than a sounding board. For, although I can claim no real knowledge of folklore, and while I prefer to maintain a neutral stance on the existence or otherwise of ghosts and their ilk, it was certainly an experience to witness my friend as he regaled his company with whichever tale had been freshly brought to his notice. He would not only narrate each account in precisely recalled detail, blessed, or perhaps cursed, as he was with a remarkable memory, he would literally reenact it: impressing the tales upon all who heard them so that even those of us not equipped with Lawrence's agile memory found them impossible to forget.

I can picture him now, prowling the floor of his study, assuming the mannerisms and vocal intonations of whom-

When I looked back to the apparition, with a jolt I saw that,
through tear-rimmed eyes, she was looking directly at us.

soever had imparted their story to him. During the course of a single evening, I saw him alternately hoist himself up to seemingly beyond his own full height and assume the bellowing tones of the retired military man who had cornered him in a clubroom to confide an unpleasant incident in the Indies, and shrink in on himself, dropping his voice to the tremulous whisper of the spinster that he had shared a train compartment with, and who had, rather brazenly, told him of the suitor who was still as ardently attentive to her as he had been before his death, five decades earlier.

So convincing were the doctor's displays of mimicry, and so compelling were his accounts, that even the most avowed sceptics would find themselves startled to realise that the night had deepened perceptibly while they sat entranced, and that the chills they felt creeping at their spines had little to do with the dying down of the fire in the study's grate.

There were, though, those occasions when these reports merely left his audience hungry for more, and Lawrence would find himself pressed to provide a more personal account, one taken from his own first-hand experience. In one such instance, he was persuaded to recount his experience with a haunted phonograph, wherein he discovered that a portion of the wax utilised in the manufacture of the recording cylinders had been recovered from the remains of certain black candles involved in a particularly grotesque occult experiment. On another memorable night, I heard the grim chronicle of the travelling mausoleum, and its awful, grinning proprietors, and to this day I cannot pass a cemetery by moonlight without feeling a shudder coursing through me.

It was on a night such as this that my friend was faced with the question, "What would you consider the most evil being your investigations have brought you into contact with?"

"There is, I would say, an evil presence that I have felt my work has brought me into close proximity with. Yet it remains vague, unformed and insubstantial, hovering only on the edges of my awareness." With that, Lawrence would have been happy to let the matter rest. But his interrogator was not to be put off with hints of shadowy, amorphous presences.

"Are you saying that you have never come into contact with genuine, corporeal evil?"

A troubled look clouded the scholar's eyes, something that this interrogator seized on as an affirmative response, and one that demanded elaboration. As it became apparent that he could not escape this line of questioning without providing satisfaction, the usually animated Lawrence seemed overtaken by a sudden heaviness of spirit and of limb, and he dropped into a seat and seemed reluctant to meet the gaze of his company. When he finally raised his head, the face he presented was nearly as white as that hair of his that so belied his relative youth, and when he spoke, it was in a quiet and almost emotionless voice.

《《——》》

Yes, I have encountered what I can only describe as evil. An absolute lack of what most humans would consider goodness.

I should, I suppose, begin by admitting to you that my interest in what may be described as unearthly matters began with the influence of one man: my old History tutor at St. James's, Professor Lucius Shadwell. It was he who first opened my eyes and my mind to the possibilities of forces beyond that which may normally be perceived. Not just mine, I would add, but all of those under his tutelage, as he was given to proffering his theories at any moment, often wandering away from his intended topic of this particular battle or that particular medieval reform. In some of us boys he found a rapt audience, but from most, I recall, he received only bemusement or scorn as he eagerly detailed legends of wailing nuns sealed in abbey walls, or of ancient bloodstains that resolutely declined to dry. Even so, he appeared to accept the unkind laughter and whispered comments in good stead, his own delight in the topic and the attention of those few of us with a less sceptical response evidently outweighing the criticism.

But, for the professor, the uncanny was more than a mere interest. More than a passion, even, and before long even my open-minded fellows grew weary of his regular digressions from our studies. I, however, remained an exception, and in me he saw a fellow enthusiast. He would return my essays with additional notes in his markings to suggest I seek out a particular book with an intriguing entry or a specific history with a pleasingly terrible legend attached. It became increasingly more common for me to stay on after his classes had concluded to chat about such matters, or for him to send word that I was required urgently in his study whenever he was to happen upon some fresh piece of lore.

Of course, this had not gone unnoticed amongst my peers, and their mockery of our eccentric master was soon directed in equal measure at me. But the subject was of such overwhelming fascination to me that I shrugged off their remarks and they, seeing the lack of effect they were achieving, gradually transferred their attentions to other targets.

Despite our relative status, the professor was only ten years or so older than me, and he felt more akin to an older brother than a teacher. Therefore it seemed only natural that I was soon a regular guest in his home. There, I would dine with him and his young family, before joining him in his well-stocked library to pore over books and manuscripts. Often we would talk at such length, dissecting that which we read, that I would find myself running after dark across the playing fields that separated the married staffs' residences from the main school building, in order to make it back to the dorms before lights out.

Shadwell's wife, Meredith, was as welcoming as he, though I believe I detected a trace of weary indulgence in her smile whenever his excitement would begin to grow as he propounded on his favourite theme. But I think she was happy that her husband, to whom she was so obviously devoted, had found an ally of sorts. And, over those months, I began to feel almost part of their family, occasionally joining them for church services or for Sunday strolls, where their infant daughter would delight us all with her wide-eyed, innocent reactions to the sights and sounds of the park.

But it was within that book-lined inner sanctum of his that, after months of companionable friendship, Lucius Shadwell let slip his mask of contentment to reveal a private sorrow. "Lawrence," said he, putting a volume of translated French ghost stories to one side and lighting a contemplative cigarette, "I fear the situation is becoming all too unbearable."

What was this? Had he grown weary of my company? Did I impose myself too freely on his domestic affairs? Or had I somehow caused him some offence?

He waved these concerns away, with earnest reassurances that such was far from the case and that my kinship was a relief to him. "You and I, we are not blinkered. We accept that the supernatural is not only a possibility, it is the only sane probability in such an as yet unfathomed universe. I have always accepted it, welcomed it, sought it, but my frustration lies in the simple fact that it has not welcomed or accepted me!

"You see how I surround myself—how I have immersed myself. You might think it enough to have such a treasure trove of stories to hand at all times. But what I desire most of all is to experience these things I have studied so zealously for myself. To examine the evidence at close quarters, and to see the truth revealed before my own eyes! And it's not as if I haven't tried!"

And he told me then of what he referred to as his 'pilgrimage' around as many of the reputedly haunted sites this country has to offer that his post and his salary would permit. He told of damp nights encamped in monastery ruins, or under canvas on ancient battlefields, of being turned back at the doors of Scottish castles, and of a near-arrest upon trying to gain entry to a notorious house in a London square where several alarming deaths had occurred. And all his efforts to no avail.

Sharing this revelation had, however, a positive effect, and he crushed out yet another cigarette, declaring, "No avail thus far, perhaps? But I have no intention of giving up, young Lawrence, you just mark me! I'll continue to seek out these places until I succeed, no matter how long it takes.

Indeed, I may yet end up as a restless spirit myself, haunting one of these gloomy spots. Hah, now wouldn't that be an irony, m'boy?"

From then, our friendship resumed its regular course. But time must pass, and boy and master must, of course, part company. Yet, still, I was aware of him, watching my course through life from afar with interest and, I'd liked to believe, approval. And once or twice a year I'd receive a message, with the familiar St. James's coat of arms upon the envelope, that I knew would point me to some new and exciting find. And each new missive would remind me of that long past confession, and I would wonder to myself if he had ever come closer to achieving his goal.

Which is why, when I received the telegram reading simply, 'It has happened... Shadwell,' I knew instantly to what it referred. The message's arrival at my rooms in college had come as a surprise, it having been a period of some years since our correspondence had slowed and then stopped. The lack of James's stationery had me double-checking for an address, and there it was—'Wraithvale'!

A suitably portentous name, I'm sure you will agree. Indeed, it was no difficult task in surmising why such a place would have drawn Lucius Shadwell. And I did not have to reach for a gazetteer to establish its location. The name was already familiar to me, as my old tutor was surely aware.

Wraithvale Priory, situated in the border country, has a reputation that has preceded it like a particularly long and crooked shadow; from the disappearance of its original architect upon the building's completion, to that more recent scandal of the church minister found hanging in the family chapel, with his own family, what was found of them, propped up like a mouldering congregation. If there was any one place in the land where my old friend's goal to encounter a ghost had a better than average chance of succeeding, I thought, it was in that house known as Wraithvale.

Before the day was out, I was on a Northbound train. Although the telegram didn't say as much, it was clearly an invitation, and it was not one which long-standing loyalty left me capable of declining. And, I may as well own up to the fact, I had long harboured a desire to visit the notorious Priory myself, though my previous visits to that part of the country had afforded me little opportunity.

I had left so quickly on receipt of Shadwell's message that I'd had no time to send word of my imminent arrival. Therefore, as I stepped from my compartment several hours later, I was somewhat surprised to perceive the familiar figure of my tutor striding toward me down that lonely platform. I should not have been so taken aback for, after allowing himself a moment's mirth at my expression, he explained, "Unless my young friend Lawrence had grown into an entirely different man, I knew he would be unable to resist immediate action regarding my summons. And as this spot is scarcely well-served by trains, I could fairly accurately predict the hour of your arrival. You've packed for a few days, I see. Splendid, then let us have your baggage on the cart and be off. I'm sure you're very keen to see my infamous house!"

It was a grey, chill evening as we drove, he at the reins and I beside him, through the twisting streets of the drab little town, then out into the open countryside that separated the town from the house. I couldn't help but wonder if the inhabitants of that place were not happy for that distance between themselves and the Priory, with its attendant reputation. As we rode, Shadwell answered my questions as to his activities in the years that had intervened since last we had communicated. He was, he admitted, no longer at St. James's, no, nor at the nearby university, nor indeed at any educational post. His interests had apparently proved of such embarrassment to James's ruling cabal, they had felt compelled to offer him a more than generous settlement to go without a fuss.

"Generous enough to net you a country estate?" I laughed, incredulous.

Shadwell joined me in my laughter. "You would be surprised how a notoriety such as the one Wraithvale has nurtured can adversely affect the price its owners may seek. I think my taking it off their hands may count as an act of charity."

We were by now approaching the edges of the woods beyond which, in a narrow valley, the Priory awaited us. "And Mrs. Shadwell," I enquired, "How is she taking to being the lady of the manor? I look forward to seeing her again."

"Meredith?" His voice was oddly flat as he said her name. "She has not been at all well of late. There is a weakness there, a physical one, and it has an effect on her moods. If she is strong enough, of course she will be thrilled to see our old friend once more. I fear she misses her previous existence, with the young people close by, so full of life. And Sarah, naturally."

I was suddenly aware of the passage of years. That happy infant of my memories would now be a young woman, quite beautiful and charming if she had inherited her mother's looks and manner. She might possibly even be married and with a family of her own. I felt an overwhelming sadness that it had taken so long for my friend to have fulfilled his cherished ambition, though it was driven away by a sense of admiration at his determination over a period that would have seen weaker wills surrender to defeat.

But these thoughts were sharply interrupted when Shadwell, after taking his watch out and squinting at it in the gloom, let out an oath and spurred the horse on into an unexpected burst of speed. I merely gaped at him, and he once more let out a braying laugh at my surprise, yelling above the clatter of hooves and wheels on the rutted road, "We don't want to miss it, do we?"

We were passing now through the gates in a high, forbidding wall, now along a curving carriage drive through yet more trees, and I was holding on for dear life as I yelled back, "Miss it? Miss what?"

"Why, what you came all this way to see, m'boy," he grinned. "My ghost, of course!"

When we were through the trees, I had my first view of Wraithvale itself. How did it look, you no doubt wish to know? It looked, as best I can tell you, how you would imagine a haunted house to look—turreted, stark, grey, and shadowed by the hills that surrounded it and in whose shade the trees, deprived of light, had grown twisted and stunted. Looking away from the house, across the lawn I saw what I first took to be a cemetery, though a backwards glance revealed the gravestones to be statues, bone white and crumbling with age.

Though the evening had grown cold, I felt no sense of imminent comfort as we drew nearer the Priory. I tried to tell myself that it was only what I'd already heard of that place's history that made me think so irrationally. But I could not dismiss the feeling that here was a house that had never offered warmth, or comfort, or had rang with the sounds of life or laughter.

I waited with my cases on the shallow steps leading to the heavy doors, and Shadwell deposited our transport in a small stable block, before returning to escort me over the threshold and into the house beyond. Had the interior been thick with gloom, bedecked with cobwebs, and coated with a century's worth of dust, I would have been less surprised than I was to find myself in a warm, brightly lit and spacious hallway. True, the stained glass window that towered above the staircase appeared a little too grotesque, from what I could see of the battling angels and demons against the night sky beyond, but my notice was drawn to my host, and my mind returned to my previous thoughts on time and its passage.

Under the dim glow of the railway platform's lighting, my former professor had appeared quite unchanged, and our twilit journey had shown me little to dispel that belief. But here, in the light of the great chandelier, I saw more clearly that time had not quite stood still for him. His blond hair, always rather fine and wispy, was even finer and more scant around the temples. It was now evident that it had whitened, and that its yellow tint owed more to nicotine than any vestige of youth. Then there was that hollowness to the cheeks and eyes and, as he hung his overcoat, I saw that his figure, though slender before, was now positively skeletal. Thankfully he seemed unaware of my scrutiny, looking once more at his watch and smiling before saying, "It is beginning."

I was about to enquire as to what was beginning when he waved for hush, glancing between his watch and something, I could not yet tell what, at the top of the vast staircase.

Thus it was that I heard it before I saw anything. A thin, high-pitched whine, the source of which I had to strain to perceive. It wavered, then dropped, then rose again, resuming with more strident force, before falling silent once more. Whatever it was, it was issuing from somewhere in the darkness at the top of the stairs. And when it rose again, it was unmistakably a shriek of absolute, abject terror.

I turned to Shadwell, a whisper of, "What on earth is it?" barely escaping from my lips, for he was already on the stairs, racing up two at a time, giving me no option but to follow, else be left alone with that hideous shriek ringing around me. "What is it?" I demanded once more, following in his wake.

But his only response was, "Come, there is little time!"

A long and ill-lit corridor led to yet more stairs and, as we moved further from that unexpectedly inviting entrance hall, the house reverted more to the image I'd held of it as I'd waited outside. Dusty panelling of some dark wood added to the dimness, before giving way to the bare stone walls of the staircase as it wound its way upwards. Despite his gaunt appearance, the professor was as sprightly as in his youth and clearly energised, while I struggled to keep him in sight as he rounded each turn. Our destination, I realised then, was in one of those looming turrets I had observed, and at last, just on the point where I feared my stamina would give out, the door to the upper chamber came into view.

The door was sturdy and studded with iron, and it creaked most appallingly on its hinges as Shadwell wrenched it fully open. That screech of metal, though, was as nothing in comparison with that other screech that blasted out of the chamber and down the spiral staircase. It buffeted around me like a gusting wind. As I instinctively clasped my hands to my ears, I lost my footing and feared that I was to be swept back down those perilous stairs by the sheer anguished force of the cry. But a bony hand gripped my arm, dragging me on and upwards, before slamming the door shut at our backs. Shadwell had sealed us both in that chamber with whatever it was that shrieked there.

We were in darkness. The only sensations I was aware of were the ringing that persisted in my ears after the scream had died away, and the pounding in my chest as I strove to regain my breath. Little by little I registered that there was light, even if it was just a dull shaft from a feeble moon, struggling through more stained glass mounted high in the opposite wall. I could see no lamp near to hand, in fact saw little of my surroundings. So little that, when I insisted my companion tell me what I had just experienced, his reply of, "Wait and see," left me perplexed.

"At first there was only the sound," and the excitement was evident in his voice, even if I could not see his expression. "To begin with, a merest whisper of a sound. Always at the same precise time, every evening without fail. Every evening for the past six weeks. And every evening it has grown stronger, louder, more...vibrant. But it has only been in this past week that the manifestation has altered, from purely audible phenomena to actual apparition. You see?"

And I did see. For while he had been speaking, the light in that turret chamber had changed. A circle of pale yellow illumination had formed on the floor in front of us, though the moon beyond the narrow window was still sickly and pallid. In this eerie half-light I could now see that the chamber was as narrow and cramped as it was tall. The claustrophobic lack of space, coupled with the bare, black stonework and that solid door put me at once in mind of a cell or dungeon. My attention was drawn from the starkness of my surroundings as, there in the centre of the uncarpeted wooden floor, I saw first the ring hazily ripple and form, then the flickering of unseen candles that seemed to surround it and fill it with its unnatural luminescence.

Once the image had grown more defined, the ring was shown to be more than a column of projected light. It was clearly outlined by a perfect circle that looked to be traced in white powder. Instantly I thought of the ritual protection afforded by a circle of salt. At this point, my inherent curiosity must have overtaken me, as Shadwell had to nudge my hand back even as I attempted to pluck up a sample of those white grains. "You can't disturb it," he insisted. "You must...you can only let it act itself out!"

As I drew my hand away, those awful sounds began again, though there was something more than the shrieking now that whatever we were to witness had begun in earnest. I heard the ragged breathing, the painful gasps, practically sobs, still emanating out of thin air—a voice without a mouth. But the mouth would come. That gaping, clamouring pit of a mouth would come soon enough.

The first movement was of something white at the heart of the fluttering glow within the circle. It might have been a maggot that had writhed its way out of the floorboards. Only, within seconds, it had grown larger than any maggot; longer, thicker, yet still with that same shimmering whiteness to it as it continued to twist and to wriggle and to swell. And the worst of it was that darkness at one end of it that also grew, splitting apart in time to let out that all too familiar shrill of horror.

As the mouth let loose its piteous yell, the distended body twisted in on itself, and folds of some white matter flowed out from it. Then the limbs took shape that filled out these folds like some shroud. The pallid flesh that formed itself around that dark mouth was now fringed with hair that sprouted and then cascaded down to frame the oval of a face. Even though the features were blurred, more a suggestion than anything solid, the eyes that opened and stared out of that recently formed head pleaded with just as much intensity as the voice that once more sobbed.

"This is the most complete manifestation yet," whispered Lucius Shadwell.

I struggled to find my voice. "Who is she?"

When I dragged my eyes away from that newly gestated thing with the appearance of a young girl, I saw that my tutor's watch was once more in his hand. "A whole minute longer than last night," he noted, more to himself, I thought, than me.

When I looked back to the apparition, with a jolt I saw that, through tear-rimmed eyes, she was looking directly at us. Had she somehow heard our talk? Was she aware of some other presence there? But her gaze then shifted, never blinking, seeming to watch something unseen by either of us observers outside that now rapidly dimming ring of light.

She was gone in a matter of seconds, not coiling up again into that maggoty swirl of ectoplasm, but simply fading from sight, her silent cries still hanging on her lips. And, before the room was even fully dark once more, the professor brushed past me, opening the door onto the stairs beyond, declaring, "It is over. Come. We have much to talk about, I think."

But an hour or more was to pass before we had that chance to talk for, on opening the door to his ground-floor study, we were greeted by the insistent jangling of a bell-pull. Ushering me in and indicating where I could find both cigars and a stiff drink, he left, his only word of explanation being, "Meredith."

I sat alone in that study, its shelves full of well-remembered books, with a generous measure of brandy providing a deal more warmth than the fire's feeble efforts. What I had seen... What I had heard... It had shaken me. I thought, though, not of myself and how I had been affected, but of the professor's poor wife, uprooted from a life of routine normality and bedded down in this blighted plot. How must it have taken its toll on her health, to share a home with such a powerful disturbance? Particularly if, as her husband had divulged, there was already some deficiency in her health? I grew angry then, angrier than I had felt for many a year, angry at my old friend for subjecting his loving wife to such a strain simply to satisfy his single-minded, selfish obsession! Had he walked into the room at that moment, I felt sure I would have struck him. But I was alone there with my fury and, as minute by minute ticked past on the mantel clock, and the occurrence in that lofty cell crept inexorably back into my mind, my anger dimmed and curiosity flooded in again to take its place. Here I could sympathise once more with Shadwell, for I knew curiosity to be a powerful guiding force.

There was one more incident before my companion returned. As I sat musing upon the identity and plight of that apparition, with all her terrifying despair, from somewhere far off inside that old house came a cry, one which I immediately assumed was to lead to yet more unearthly clamour. However, only silence followed and, after a minute or two, the echo of a door closing somewhere overhead and, in time, footsteps on the staircase and approaching across the hall.

When Lucius Shadwell reentered, he displayed a guarded smile and offered an apology. "This is not one of her good nights, I'm afraid," he confided, the cigarette already lit and at his lips. "She'll sleep now, don't worry. But sometimes she needs someone to reassure her. She gets confused, you see. I wouldn't leave her alone here, don't ever think it. There is a nurse. Not a local woman; I don't think you need ask why. She's good at what is required of her, but she's practically deaf, and sometimes she doesn't hear..." He allowed himself a small chuckle. "Which is possibly a very good thing, considering, wouldn't you say?"

I had to laugh with him, and my bitter feelings were forgotten when he, after pouring us both a stiff measure of whisky, settled back and asked, "So, what do you make of her, then: my white lady, if I may borrow a somewhat clichéd and mundane term?"

"I've been asking myself that single question since we left the tower," I only half-lied. "So let me ask you, instead, who is she? Do you have any history of her? I thought I'd read all of the available reports on this house, but a lady in white or screaming maiden, or whatever you want to call her, I don't recall. There was something about a turreted chamber, but it involved a disfigured nobleman, as I remember..."

"Who skinned his victims and drank of their blood, believing himself to have been cursed by an Ursari gypsy to carry the taint of the 'Strigoi'," he interjected. "You forget, I've read all of the legends too. But, as I told you, this manifestation is new, though how long she has waited up there to make her presence known I couldn't say. That dress or gown she wears...she wore, it looked, would you say, seventeenth century?"

I had to admit that her mode of dress had not been foremost in my mind as she'd screamed and howled herself in and out of existence before me. "However, you also say that her materialisations are a nightly occurrence, and that her powers of apparition are growing stronger? Then more details may quickly make themselves apparent to us."

He let out a great roar of a laugh and clasped my hand warmly in his. "You'll stay, then, and help me record the sighting? I can think of no better man to have by my side, and your practical expertise will, I'm sure, prove invaluable. Come, don't look so abashed, m'boy. You think I don't know of your...pursuits? I may be merely a near-disgraced ex-tutor but I still do have some contacts in the educational establishments, and such outré achievements as yours don't go unremarked. You may also spy certain monographs with your signature to them taking up space on these shelves. You see, I've never lost interest in my young apprentice, yet now I fancy you are the master, and it is you who will be giving me the benefit of your experience. Though I thank you for not gloating about your exploits when we were in closer contact."

We talked that night through. Before long those shelves had been raided of their books, and it felt as if the preceding two decades had melted away and we were once more in my History tutor's house across the playing fields, man and boy, master and pupil, friend and friend, talking and arguing and laughing together.

It was the jangling of that bell, long after dawn had bleached the sky, that dragged us back to the present, and reminded me that everything was not as once it was. Unlike on the previous evening, however, the bell rang only once and my old friend was gone from me only for a matter of minutes, before returning with a smile across his weary face.

"All is well?"

"All is very well," he affirmed. "She has slept and is in a good frame of mind. Just this moment, she's taking some breakfast in her room. The nurse doubles as a cook, you know, though thankfully only charges a single wage. Yes, Meredith is quite hale, and she's asking to see her friend of fond memory." My face must have betrayed how unexpected this request was, for he continued, "Unless, of course, you're too tired and would like some rest yourself. What a host I am! I've kept you up chattering all night."

I bade him dismiss his concerns, as I was entirely uncertain if sleep would have come following the visitation of the night before. Indeed, I was anxious to see my hostess. Not merely to convince myself that her continued presence in the confines of Wraithvale was having no damaging effect on her, but because I too held her in fond regard.

Although the bed was screened by a thin curtain of gauze, I could see quite well enough that the woman within it was sitting, propped up on cushions, and the tray of empty breakfast plates showed that her appetite, at least, was healthy. "My dearest Master Lawrence," Meredith Shadwell laughed. "Or shouldn't that be Dr. Lawrence? How good it is to see you again. Lucius told me you were to visit, and I am delighted that you could make it. Please, sit awhile. I'll ring Paskins to bring you some tea... No, I think it had better be coffee, and strong, as I know my husband won't have given you a moment's rest."

With coffee duly served by the monolithic, monosyllabic nurse, and with Shadwell hovering ever attentive, I enquired gently as to Meredith's health.

"Yes, I must apologise for not greeting you last night. No, no, I insist, and also for dragging you up to this gloomy room." Here she indicated the heavy curtains that were only partially drawn, letting but dingy light into the bedroom. "I'm afraid I'm prone to the most infuriating headaches, and I find the darkness rather soothing."

"If you're feeling unwell," said I, rising, "I'll go and let you rest in some peace."

Her response astonished me. It may have been intended as a laugh, but it emerged as a cackle. "Rest in peace? In this house? You always were a funny little boy, Lawrence. Full marks! Top of the class!"

Shadwell shot me a terse smile as he strode across to his wife's bedside, striving for her hand through the filmy folds and clasping it gently. "Dr. Lawrence is, I think, a little tired, m'love."

The laughter from within the bed fell silent, and there was a pause before Meredith's voice returned, its usual bright tone restored. "Of course, Doctor. You should have said so. Or maybe you did say? I can get a little muddled at times. Wherever is Paskins with that coffee?"

But before she could reach for the bell-pull, her husband stayed her hand, holding it tenderly in his. "You know coffee stops you from resting properly. You need to sleep, m'dearest heart."

"But I've only just woken. Haven't I?" There was irritation in the voice, annoyance at her own uncertainty. "I will try, Lucius. Has Paskins left me my pills? Ah, I see them there. I'm sorry, Dr. Lawrence, but I'm a little tired. Would you please excuse me? So kind of you. Always a kind boy."

I left them then, the professor and his bewildered wife. I could see only too clearly that her confusion was causing her no little distress. And it was not only her confused state that was the cause, I deduced, as her words to her husband before I had fully closed the door were a pleading, "But what if, while I sleep, she comes back?" I had no need to wonder on who was meant by 'she.' "You will tell me, Lucius? You'll tell me if she comes back again?"

"Some houses, some places—places with something of the dark about them, you might describe them—can have a psychically damaging effect on both body and mind." I spoke these words to Lucius Shadwell over a cold luncheon some hours later.

He threw down his knife, and the face he turned on me was furious. "Don't presume to lecture me, Doctor!" He virtually spat the last word. "I know about these dark places! Or do you choose to forget he who opened the door to that knowledge you now parrot back at me? And I know my wife! What ails Meredith is both physical and psychological, but it is not psychical. She just gets a bit confounded in her thinking sometimes. But she's well looked after, she's protected, and she's damn well loved!" And he stalked off, pacing on the lawn for the time it took to smoke several cigarettes.

Upon his return there were apologies on both sides, and acceptances also, and we swiftly fell back into the discussion that had consumed so much of the night before, and which subsequently devoured the remainder of the afternoon and evening.

When the hour came around for the apparition to commence, we were already ensconced in that bleak turret cell and, as Shadwell had predicted, the shrieking began on cue. There, again, was that unnatural ring of glimmering light. There, again, was that white form that convulsed into being before us. There, again, was the horror in her eyes, when those eyes had finally formed. This time, on Shadwell's urging, I noted the dress. It was not, as I'd imagined it, a simple white smock. Perhaps more detail had come through on this night, as I could now make out the embroidered flowers and birds that covered every inch of it. I had seen similar, of course, my more regular career ensuring that I spent much of my time in museums. I believed my tutor to have been correct in dating the garment, and consequently the phantom it clothed, to early in the seventeenth century.

And there, again, was that moment when her eyes seemed to find us, before darting, terror-stricken, away. And since the materialisation lasted yet longer than on my first night in that room, I was now assured that those eyes were watching the progress of someone or something that prowled and circled where she stood. And wasn't that..? Could it have been..? Just before she dissolved away again, wasn't that the wavering edge of a shadow that fell into the circle? I couldn't be definite. If it was there, it was gone again in an instant, fading away with the rest of that ghastly projection. But if it had truly been there, what was it that could cast so monstrously alarming a shadow?

All these questions I would have put to my companion, were it not for what happened in the final second before the girl vanished entirely from our sight and faded from our hearing. It was a whisper, naught more, but in that whisper was a single, pitiful word. "Please..."

This fresh addition to Shadwell's spectre's repertoire led, as you may well imagine, to many more hours of pacing and talking between us. The identity of this poor unfortunate was as yet a mystery, but on one thing we seemed to reach some agreement.

"So many recorded instances of sightings have occurred on sites historically linked with great tragedy, suffering and anguish. I told you before of my uncomfortable night on that blood-soaked battlefield," Shadwell mused ruefully, "though I didn't hear so much as a single clash of sword on shield or a single note from a phantom piper. But others evidently have, and we know the thinking; the trauma of a death in particularly tragic or violent circumstances can leave its imprint. A psychic scar, if you will."

"Like a wound that refuses fully to heal," I furnished, "and continues to ache away over time. I find the conjecture entirely plausible. I think that this girl, whoever she was, died in an agony of terror. I think that something she saw in that room terrified her to death. And I also think, no, am convinced, that if we let this thing play out in its natural course, we will catch a glimpse of whatever caused her fatal distress."

My host gave this a moment's thoughtful consideration, before declaring, "Then we have little option but to watch, and to see what there is to be seen."

Over the following days, Shadwell and I slept by day when we could, while by night we would watch and confer. On some days, during our wakeful daylight hours, we would spend some brief time with his ailing wife in her room. During most of these visits she was quite how I remembered her, but on others she was a stranger to me. And on certain days I would not see her at all. On these bleak days the only other company I saw, besides the professor, was that large, and largely silent, nurse.

As I entered my second week at Wraithvale, a feeling of heavy, cloying depression had already taken me in its grip. I could not entirely lay the blame with the distressing nature of the apparition, nor with the worsening mental state of my hostess. No, there was more to it than that. I longed for sunlight, so scarce in that dreary valley. I also longed to be in my own familiar college rooms again, with their own particular sounds: the hiss as the fire died, the steady ticking of my own clock, the accustomed creak as the old timbers settled. I missed these comfortable things, for I was increasingly aware that my hours of attempted sleep were disturbed by vague sounds that seemed more than structural in origin, and that my every movement was followed by echoes that were not of my own making.

Meredith, too, evidently felt some inkling of my anxiety, though I naturally mentioned nothing of it to her. Yet, in her more strained moments, I overheard her tell of sounds, and of smells, "like the stench of rising decay," and yet again her concerned plea of, "What if she comes back?"

What I longed for above these others, however, was company from outside this troubled household. So strong was my desire to be with another soul, I began to think on that shade of a terrified girl as an ally—one that I would help if I could only find a way. Her face, as stricken with fear as it was, became a familiar, almost welcome sight. And when the realisation that this was the case hit home, I knew that I had to leave that place, before my senses were warped out of all natural proportion. I had to leave and I had, also, to persuade Lucius Shadwell to take himself and his wife from there, for her sanity's sake, if not his own. But how could I simply go and desert that pathetic girl before I could break through what I now thought of as a steadily more flimsy barrier to knowing her and understanding her plight?

My former tutor, too, seemingly sensed my growing mental unease. I had been obsessing about the shadowy form that had first caught my attention on that second night in the chamber. It had passed from my thoughts following the first whispered plea, but as each night saw the girl's torment lengthen in duration, so too did that other, yet more alarming shade make itself more evident. Or was it evident only to my eyes or, perhaps, in my mind? For my friend appeared oblivious to it, despite my repeated efforts to point it out to him as it skirted the edges of that protective circle of salt—apparently kept at bay while it, in turn, held the girl a captive within, her simple cry of, "Please...please...please..." repeated like a chant. "Some optical effect of the materialisation, perhaps," was the most he would concede. But it was as integral an element of the haunting to me as the girl, and whether it glided or stalked on legs, in my sight it prowled ever onwards with some frightful purpose to its movements.

At the end of that second week, concern for both his wife's well-being and, apparently, my own, saw Lucius Shadwell track me down to his library. Here I was engrossed in some urgent researches, when he announced, "I think it is time for us to cease our experiment. You've become a shadow of yourself, and it would be better that you leave, for a short time at least. I will notify you if there is any significant alteration in the manifestation."

"You intend to stay?" I cried, but my protest was quelled.

"Aye, but alone. Meredith will leave too. You were right, of course, Lawrence. This house is no place for a sensitive creature like her. Paskins has gone to make arrangements with an excellent private nursing home some miles South of here. When she returns tomorrow, she will take my wife and go."

"But you?" I insisted. "What will you do here, alone?"

He smiled a grim smile. "You forget, I am not alone. 'She' is still here. And I will do what I always set out to do. I will watch. I will observe. And I will record."

I could see that he was resolute in his intention, and I no longer possessed the energy to argue the point with him. "Then if Meredith is to go tomorrow, I will do likewise. And, for this one last night, you won't observe alone."

He accepted my offer as an inevitability, stating that he would have expected nothing less, before leaving me once more to my solitary studies. And, when the first cries rang out that night, we were in that tower room together.

Had my loyalty to an old friend not been so strong, I might never have known the grim secret of that dreadful room. I was not quite hardened to the shrieks and the pleas—I think no-one with a spark of humanity could be— but they had lost their ability to chill my soul, and I was as detached in my observing as I could possibly make myself. I watched, and I waited. I followed the pale figure's damp-eyed stare around the perimeter of the room, slowly circling back now to where I stood, turning full circle for the first time in my sight. And it was then that the vague shadow that circled in time with her gaze lurched suddenly forward and expanded until some thing appeared to move through the circle and, for a moment, swallow her entirely. Some 'thing' was as specific as I could be at that time, for I could not actually see it. Whatever it was, its image wasn't captured in this impossible lightshow. It registered only as a dead spot in the projection, a patch of emptiness that obscured the girl, and through which the present time, the bare boards of the floor and the stone walls, could be seen. From its silhouette only, what I was aware of was a form that loomed up, as thin as a corpse, its stick-like arms clawing and rending at the air. And as it did so, the cry that choked off from that poor girl was enough to break through my attempts at detachment and bring a sob issuing from my own lips.

Then it was gone, moving aside suddenly so that my view was once more unimpeded. And as the unbroken circle resolved itself before my eyes, in its centre lay the still figure in white, her eyes still gazing in horror at that which had rendered her lifeless.

My first thought, irrational since I knew already that this girl was long past any physical help, was to run to her. But the idea of stepping into that circle drove the notion from my mind. Possibly it was the thought of being trapped there, frozen in time, my last moments to be replayed constantly for the amusement or the horror of unseen spectators. Or was it the idea of encountering that lurking dead spot and perhaps seeing its face? Would I scream and beg, just as the girl did?

Lucius Shadwell stared at the prone figure, and it was long moments before she had dimmed and vanished. "I was too late," I heard myself mumbling. "Too late to help her." But he paid me no heed and, even if he had, I would not have been able to explain myself. My own shock had brought a jumble of thoughts crashing and reeling through my mind, and I struggled to snatch hold of any one of them. What kept repeating though was, "What was it she saw and why could we not see it?" If...oh, but if it was to materialise as a ghost...

Somewhere in the house below us, doors crashed and slammed, and we were shaken roughly from our reverie. There were yells and curses, and as I attempted to follow my host down the spiraling steps, his efforts to hold me back fell on deaf ears.

The creature that leapt on the professor at the foot of those stairs was a frenzied rush of thrashing, clawing arms, and wild hair flying, allowing only glimpses of the scarred dome of bare scalp. It was only when it ceased its banshee howl and shouted its damning, bitter reproaches at my fallen companion, that I realised it was Meredith Shadwell— that devoted, gentle, loving wife, now gone feral. "It's as I heard it before, on that night, that awful, awful night," she cried. "It's the same! It's how she sounded on that night!"

I struggled to wrench her back from her husband, and my hand nearly recoiled when I saw the swirls and knots of scarred flesh that traced their way up her arm, up her neck, and across half of her face and skull. A bundle dropped from her hand, and it too was burnt. I snatched it up, despite Shadwell's breathless protests to ignore her, to watch her, to be afraid of her. "Her mind's gone. It went months ago. She's dangerous! To you. To herself! You see what she did to herself? You see what her madness led her to?"

She seized the bundle from me before I could think to examine it. "In the furnace, it was! You tried to hide it from me!" Then she emptied the charred bag, so that vials of white substance rattled to the floor, before a white mass spilled out. It was blackened at the edges of the collar and sleeves but still instantly recognisable as a long white dress, quite new, but designed to give the illusion of antiquity. And still she raved. "You told me it was an accident. You told me it wasn't meant to happen, but I found this. You tried to burn it, but I saw. I saved it!

"You said she would come back, always. Tell me she hasn't gone, Lucius! Promise me this! Please..."

And as I watched that word form on her lips, I saw! Dear God, I finally saw it all! That familiar quality I'd imagined in the face of that pathetic spectre, I knew now wasn't imagination. It was a memory! The face was Meredith Shadwell's!

Not as that scarred and fractured creature now was. The face was that of the indulgent young wife, whose company and friendship I had enjoyed all those years before. The girl was the image of her mother!

And I at last understood Meredith's cries of, "What if she comes back?" They were not the words of protest against an unnatural and harrowing disturbance. They were desperate pleas for the return of her daughter!

"'It has happened!'" I said, coldly quoting the words of that man whom I had once counted as my greatest friend. "It happened because you made it happen. Your own daughter? Sarah?"

"Yes." There was no trace of shame as he gathered himself up to his full height, but it was a trembling hand that raised the cigarette to his lips and tried to light it.

I swatted it from his mouth. "Your own daughter! Growing up with you and your stories and your legends. You created another believer, just as you did with me."

"But, unlike you, unlike I, she did not embrace the unknown. She feared it. She believed and that belief frightened her. I realised, were it nurtured correctly, that I could use that fear, use that anguish, to perhaps re-open some of those psychic scars we talked so much about, you and I." Though I could scarcely credit it, his tone as he confessed to this was entirely the same as when he'd excitedly held forth on his theories to my younger self. This wasn't a confession. It was a lecture! "I imagined that I might use her terror to awaken something dormant in this house. And with such an opportunity, such an instrument at my disposal, why should I not use it...use her? Why should I be denied what I've sought so long?"

I scooped up the vial of white greasepaint that had rolled at my feet. The image came to mind of that thin thing, that positively skeletal thing. It had not shown up as part of the haunting because, if it was to materialise as a ghost...it would have to be dead first. And Lucius Shadwell was very much alive. "So you became what she feared most! You trapped her in that room, with its legends already in place and fresh in her mind. And you terrorised her! You scared that girl witless! You scared her to death!" My hands were on his collar now, dragging him closer so that any remorse in his eyes would be clear to me. But there was none to be found.

"It was an accident. Her heart wasn't strong enough to withstand the experiment. An inherited weakness from her mother. I didn't know!"

Possibly he believed it, but I did not think so then and I still do not now. He was not deluded. There was method here. "The circle of salt, from rituals you've studied in depth. It wasn't to keep something out. It was to keep her in! To bind her soul in that chamber, and force her to go through her final agonies again and again, while you watched, observed, recorded!" I thrust him back from me then, unable to bear being in such close proximity to his coldness. Had I the strength, I would have knocked him to the floor and continued to strike him till his cries matched those of his poor, lost daughter in intensity and pain.

However, all I felt then was that familiar heavy numbness that had dogged me throughout my stay. It took my legs from under me, and I dropped, sliding down the panelled wall, falling into a heap opposite Shadwell's wife, who crouched still, hugging that scorched dress to herself.

My head was filled with noise: a pounding that echoed as if from within the walls and floors of Wraithvale itself. A sour smell of cold, clogging earth, and whatever had once lain under it, assailed my nose and caught in my throat. Shadows, or what I at least thought to be shadows, filtered past my already closing eyes, and the vague thought of things long dormant that had gradually been awakened stirred in my mind. The scar had been opened, and who knew what was bleeding through?

The last thing that I was conscious of was the distant sound of urgent footsteps upon stone, becoming even more distant as they spiralled away from me. Then, after a silence that might have lasted a minute or an hour, there came from some chamber above a scream of utter, fatal fear and loathing. Then, mercifully, darkness descended on me.

The great grey figure that loomed into my view, when next these eyes of mine opened, extended a squat hand and hoisted me to my feet. Paskins would later explain how she had found us both, two crouching figures in that cold corridor, when she had returned that morning. Her first duty had been to her former patient, laying her out in her bed and arranging her so that she looked at peace, before returning to rouse me.

Of Lucius Shadwell, there was never a living trace found. Eventually there was the usual inquest, though the local constables seemed unwilling to pry too closely in that old, once more abandoned priory. What they did turn up were certain remains concealed in the long-cooled furnace. These were later established to be the bones of a young female, disposed of unlawfully. I heard all of this at the inquest where, naturally, I was summoned to testify with regard to my former tutor's, and recent host's, apparent state of mind before the death of his wife and his unaccounted for disappearance. I told them then that I considered him to have been entirely sane in those last hours. Whether this remains the case...

You have asked me to identify for you the most evil entity that ever I was in contact with. I have told you now. Not, as you no doubt were expecting, a ghost or some other revenant, but a living human being. But, as in life, so in death?

To provide a possible answer to my own question, I will inform you only that I spent one last evening at Wraithvale, and I spent it within that turret chamber. There I waited, fervently beseeching The Almighty that Sarah Shadwell, that screaming maiden of Wraithvale Priory, would cry into the night no more. And when the time came and passed, I thanked all that is good, and voiced a hope that mother and daughter were at last reunited.

But that was not quite an end to it. The shrieking may have been stilled, yet that flickering yellow radiance did still cast itself upon that cold floor. For a few long moments, that thin shadow made its habitual circuit around the edges of the light, until, with a lurch, it burst through into the circle, hands outstretched on bony arms to rend the air yet again. The figure was now as visible to my eye as the ring of salt, and as its dark robe brushed through this protective barrier, it obliterated a portion of the powdery trail. Upon realising this, the gaunt face, underneath the greasepaint pallor of its vampiric nobleman's masquerade, grew paler yet. Fearful eyes darted as more shadows began to stalk and slouch and crawl around the edges of the circle, drawing in slowly, but not too slowly, toward the gap in the defensive outline. I had the impression that some of the owners of those encroaching shadows might even have once been human.

It was not very much longer after this that a new voice screamed from that haunted turret chamber.

«« —— »»

Shortly afterwards, the others of our company left the doctor's study, numbering amongst them that individual who had coerced Lawrence into telling his tale, and whose expression on leaving suggested that he rather regretted it.

I, too, was ready to bid my farewell to my friend, as the sharing of his narrative had evidently worn him down. But he indicated a seat and poured me a generous measure of brandy, before taking his place before the embers in the fireplace.

"There is one last thing to be said, then the story is complete, and I will never tell it again. I didn't wish to share it with the others, but it cannot be left untold. It is not something of which I am proud, yet I cannot claim any great feeling of shame.

"You recall I made mention of some solitary researches in which I'd been employed as my last full day at Wraithvale came around? Well, there was a result to these studies. It took the form of an incantation, a variant form of the rite of exorcism. Whether such an attempt would have had any effect in that house, I could not hope to know, but it had been my intent to at least try to free that wretched spirit from her torment. As you heard, her tragedy played itself out before I had the chance to mount my attempted rescue.

"That next night, as I saw her tormentor find himself consigned to a fate that entirely paralleled that which he'd engineered for her, I became aware that the pages onto which I had inscribed those words of release were still secure in my pocket. Here I had the potential means to deliver my former friend from a possible eternity of terrors.

"Then, I heard only that girl's voice, and still those screams resound in my mind during unguarded moments. But, at that moment, her pleas became a cry for justice. The decision I made in that room that evening may not have been as others would make. You, yourself, may well have chosen differently. We all of us, after all, have our own individual ideas of justice.

"So I left the pages folded up in my pocket, and I closed the door on that chamber, closed the door on Wraithvale, and left Professor Lucius Shadwell to those ghosts he had so long sought."

An Unwise Purchase

by Dr. H.S. Grace

Herbert Sidney Grace (1863 – 1935) was, first and foremost, an academic. A graduate of St. Montague's, he subsequently became Master of Rhodes House College, before accepting the post of Head Master of St. James's School on the brink of the First World War. His scholarly pursuits encompassed a wide range of subjects: his expertise in the fields of archaeology, ecclesiastical studies and folklore leading to the publication of numerous articles in various college journals, and the reference works 'The Lost and Forgotten Buildings of Greymarsh,' 'The Witch in the Well and Other Mediaeval Tales Translated' and 'A Child's Book of Revelations'. He was also an author of ghost stories and was, for a brief period around the turn of the nineteenth century, quite prolific in his output. These supernatural tales, originally written to be read to friends as a Hallowe'en entertainment, appeared in a number of periodicals and were later compiled into three volumes; 'A Ghostly Study' (1905), 'Further Tales from a Ghostly Study' (1908), and 'Intangible Apparitions & Other More Substantial Terrors' (1910).

Rumours of a further privately published collection, containing revised versions of earlier tales and completed drafts of stories which today survive only as fragments, have never been substantiated. However, as enticing as this volume may sound, its existence would seem unlikely, given Dr. Grace's sudden decision to forego the writing of supernatural fiction

251

in order to concentrate on his more serious researches, which in his later years tended toward the pursuit of religious knowledge.

It may have been this refusal to return to that branch of writing in which he had begun to make his name that allowed his reputation to dwindle to the point where he is virtually unknown outside the ranks of ardent collectors or those who have been fortunate enough to stumble upon his work by sheer chance; my own first encounter with H.S. Grace occurred while browsing the shelves of an establishment not entirely dissimilar to the one described in the story that follows.

While the works of many of Dr. Grace's more celebrated contemporaries remain in print, either in collections of their own works or in the pages of anthologies of classic ghost stories, I am indebted to the Trustees of the Estate of H.S. Grace for allowing, in tribute to an author whose work has had such an effect on my own, the first reprinting in over a century of the closing story from 'Further Tales from a Ghostly Study' – 'An Unwise Purchase.'

On the corner of a certain road in the city's East End can be found a little curiosity shop. It is one which I have been known to frequent at irregular intervals for, although I would not care to possess many of the objects to be found within its dingy confines, there are things to be encountered there of such a sufficiently grotesque nature as to provide inspiration for a dozen or more tales of the type that give apparent entertainment to my readers. What is it, for example, that leaves me wary of peering too closely at the smudge of shadow within the doorway of that decaying manor house which is the subject of the framed daguerreotype that hangs in one of the alcoves? Or of listening to more than a few notes played upon the dusty harpsichord with those alarming red stains upon the ivories? What prevents me from sitting between the carved and grinning armrests of the scholar's chair, or from leafing too eagerly through the folio pages whose couplets I care not to translate? Some of these have already provoked my pen into action; others may yet spark off some fantastical tale. There may be some idea furnished by whatever those pallid things are that float murkily in their nameless fluids within the glass jars on that gloomy shelf at the back of the shop. Then again, perhaps not. There are some stories that would, if written, stray beyond the boundaries of legitimate horridness.

It was, in point of fact, just as I was recoiling from the sight of those hideous contents as they threatened to resolve themselves through the dark liquid, that I turned to see the three animal faces which gazed back at me. I say three gazed but, of course, one had its vision obscured by the paws that it clamped over its eyes; these being the Three Wise Monkeys, sculpted in the traditional poses that permit them in turn to see no evil, hear no evil, and speak no evil. It was rather a fine representation, carved in brass, and mounted upon a deep, lacquered plinth of some twelve inches in length by six inches in width and depth. The base may have given the impression of some Far Eastern origin, but the crouching figures struck me as being of European design. I could perceive no maker's mark or stamp as I turned it over in my hands, only a dark smear that might have been dust or soot ingrained into the lacquer. While I was making my examination, the shop's proprietor materialised at my side; or, at least, he gave the appearance of doing so, so soundless was his approach. Contrary to what you may imagine of the owner of such a gallery of macabre objects, he is no cadaverous creature or gnomish dwarf, given to looming out of dark corners to supply enigmatic comments as to the history of the items he sells. Rather, he is a rotund and cheerful fellow, with a smile that gleams as brightly as his balding dome under the lamplight. "You are surely not contemplating making an actual purchase?" he enquired, having long been aware of my status as a perennial browser. Yet there was no rancour in his query. Indeed we had, on several previous occasions, struck up amiable conversations, during which he had made no effort to push his wares upon me—a feat which one might wish to see mirrored amongst the employees of many an otherwise excellent establishment. "It is rather a nice piece, is it not? So said the last gentleman who bought it. Why, yes, it has passed through here before. I remember it quite clearly. And the chap who took it off my hands then was, after he had taken the time to examine it, very taken with it."

"Clearly not so taken with it after all," I ventured, "if he chose to return it."

"Ah, indeed, there you would have a point, were it in fact he who returned it. No, that was not the case. Well, this was only last week, so he could hardly have done so, could he?" And, after my assurances to you that the shop's proprietor is not of the type to make cryptic comments, he was, in this instance, intent on proving me wrong. "But I have said too much on the subject. I really ought to follow the example of that third little monkey. Discretion at all times, don't you agree, sir? Now, if you would just excuse me; the fellow in the muffler eyeing those continental art studies is the Earl of Dashshire, posing incognito in hope of keeping his hobby private and the price down. Never trust a collector, I say, especially one from the noble classes."

Alone once more with the brass carving, I could not avoid wondering at the proprietor's unwillingness to speak of the prior owner of the piece. Perhaps it was some cunning salesman's ploy to pique my curiosity, in which event it had proven successful. I was of a mind to await the conclusion of his business with his noble client, until I spied the open ledger book on his desk, in which I had many times observed him writing out the particulars of anyone making a purchase. It was the work of a minute to sidle into a position that would allow me to scan the pages, whilst ostensibly admiring a stuffed ocelot under the front counter. I quickly located the entry for *'Brass trilogy of monkeys'* and reading the name opposite this put any fleeting notion of buying the carving from my thoughts.

The case of the man whom I shall herein call Henry Hartwell had been prominent in many of the local newspapers, and was also the talk of the establishment which he had, until recently, served, and where I have a number of professional and personal acquaintances. I cannot profess to have all of the facts at my disposal, even though those transcripts that have made it onto the printed page have been quite thorough in cataloguing the bizarre aspects of the affair. However, with a degree of creative licence, I believe I am capable of presenting a version of what *may* have occurred following his visit to the establishment which I have already described.

《《——》》

"This really is a most popular design," remarked the proprietor, as he carefully handed the blue China plate to the tall man in the clerical garb.

The Reverend Dr. Henry Hartwell handed it back with less care, and with barely a glance at the pattern, commenting, "It would be just the thing, were I looking to decorate a Welsh dresser in the scullery, and not the shelves in my study. No, no, Mr. Barnabas, we must do better."

This brusque response brought forth a smirk from a large fellow browser nearby, and a pained expression to the habitually smiling face of Mr. Barnabas, who had so far shown Dr. Hartwell the greater proportion of the goods on display. However, never one to be easily beaten, he pressed ahead, directing his customer's attentions toward the unusual carving upon the next shelf. "Now here is a piece whose message must surely appeal to a man of the cloth like yourself, Dr. Hartwell, for is not the disdaining of evil thought, word and deed that which you preach?"

"I do not preach anything at all, Mr. Barnabas. My post is a scholarly one. But let me see what we have here. Yes, well, it is rather a crude representation, I must say."

"Crude, sir?" gasped the proprietor, returning the object to its shelf. "Most have commented on the unusually fine craftsmanship."

"Then let them buy it, if they are so easily impressed," retorted Dr. Hartwell, "for I think you take me for the monkey, if you expect me to match the tag you put on this basic hunk of brass."

The proprietor fought grimly to maintain his smile, saying, "If that is your feeling, Dr. Hartwell, perhaps I had better check in my storeroom to see if there is something amongst my latest shipment to match your requirements."

The doctor agreed that, yes, perhaps he had, and as the little shopkeeper bustled away to the private room in the shop's rear, he turned his attention once more to the wares on display. Candlesticks, bookends, figurines, incomplete sets of encyclopedias; these were all unlikely to meet with his approval, and he once again found himself back in the narrow passage where he had been when Mr. Barnabas had left him. From behind the door marked 'Private' he could hear the creaking and thudding of crates being opened and unpacked, and also the muttering of the proprietor, no doubt commenting on the tribulations of aiding over-fussy customers. Then there was another sound, whose origins were less easily ascertained. It was a slight, rhythmic pounding, not unlike the mechanism of a clock, and it was accompanied by a metallic squeaking. He looked around, his expectation being to find a cheap timepiece whose label passed it off as the work of some long-departed master craftsman, yet the only thing nearby was the brass statuette that he had so recently dismissed. Was it, in fact, the same one? Certainly something looked not quite identical about it, but his thoughts of examining it more closely were inter-rupted when that other customer rounded the corner and barged roughly into him.

The large fellow seized Dr. Hartwell by his lapels, righting him before he could crash into some carefully arranged glassware, before apologising profusely and, evidently embarrassed by his clumsiness, making for the exit. The shop bell gave its first faint jangle, when a shrill voice from behind the still shaken Henry Hartwell cried out, "Stop that man! He has taken your wallet! Thief! Villain!"

Dr. Hartwell's hand flew instinctively to his inner pocket. It was empty, obviously the work of those hands that had grasped him. Without a pause to thank whoever had issued the warning, he rushed to the doorway, where he gripped his assailant by a brawny forearm. A pig-skin wallet dropped from his surprised fingers, and a snarl burst loose from his startled lips. The man was a head taller and considerably broader than Dr. Hartwell, but the doctor had not obtained several medals in pugilism during his undergraduate days for nothing, and a very few jabs saw his opponent retreating as fast as his shaking legs could carry him down the busy street. In his haste to be gone from this unexpectedly hardy former victim, he lost his voluminous overcoat to Dr. Hartwell's grip. That it landed on the pavement with a metallic clatter was proof that the doctor had not been the only one robbed, and a number of items of silverware were found to be concealed inside the lining when Dr. Hartwell deposited it on the proprietor's desk.

Mr. Barnabas shuffled through from his storeroom as fast as his weight would allow, demanding to be told the cause of this undue commotion. Perplexed by the other's indignation, Dr. Hartwell began to protest, "But was it not you who alerted me to the theft?" before halting himself when he realised that it was impossible for the shopkeeper to have witnessed the crime from within the confines of that other room. Besides which, he then reflected, that had not been Mr. Barnabas's deep tenor that he had heard. The warning voice was sharper, with an almost metallic ring to it, and his eyes, searching in vain for another previously unnoticed customer amongst the bric-a-brac, fell upon the brass figures, just as the jaws of the third monkey appeared to him to disappear once more behind long fingers.

"On consideration, this really is rather a fine carving," Dr. Hartwell opined, once the matter of the attempted theft had been fully explained, and an inspection of his goods had satisfied the shopkeeper that he had not actually lost any of his stock. "I can picture it sitting quite well above my mantel."

"Then you must consider it yours, Dr. Hartwell," beamed the proprietor, "at a reduced rate, considering your part in the apprehension of that rogue. I cannot possibly give it to you for less than I paid for it myself. Mind, nothing would make me happier than to present it to you gratis, but these are lean times, I'm afraid." And, as he squeezed his hefty frame past, in order to seek out a box in which to place the item, he concluded, "Shall we say twelve guineas?"

That high-pitched voice once again rang out, startling Dr. Hartwell as it declared, "He lies. Only a quarter of that amount was paid." But as he turned sharply to where he believed the source of that voice lay, he could not be certain if he detected a hint of movement as fingers curled around ears and across a mouth.

"I believe the figure agreed upon was twelve," blustered Mr. Barnabas, when a heavy box was exchanged for three coins.

"And I believe the figure agreed was what you yourself paid," insisted Dr. Hartwell. "Shall we consult your ledger, where I have little doubt that the true amount is recorded? I thought not. My thanks for your assistance, Mr. Barnabas, and I will bid you good day."

An hour or so later found Henry Hartwell seated in his study, eagerly turning his purchase over beneath the light of his desk lamp. The more that he had considered it on his journey home, the more convinced he had grown that he had, on three occasions, detected some alteration in the little figures. Though he could not swear to it, it had appeared to him that, just before that ruffian had accosted him, the hands of the first monkey had not been clamped over its eyes. Instead, they had been angled out from the prominent brow, as if to shield the beast's vision from the unaccustomed glare of even the shop's dim lamplight. Then there had been those following glimpses of ears and mouths being hastily concealed. Unless he had received an undetected blow to the head during his tussle with the robber, Dr. Hartwell had not imagined these, and he was keen to determine how the trick was done. In his reading, he had encountered stories of various cleverly conceived automatons; was one of these not also in the shape of a monkey, one that had played chess with surprising adeptness? Possibly what he now held in his hands was some ingenious clockwork device. The base did not appear too shallow to allow for the concealment of such a mechanism.

With this suspicion in mind, within moments Dr. Hartwell had the tip of his letter-opener applied to a groove around the outer edge of the base's underside. And, within a few moments more, he was standing with one hand below a cold tap to stem the blood, the other hand still clutching the letter-opener's handle and the quarter of the blade which was still attached to it. The chiming of the kitchen clock told him that his investigation of the workings of his strange acquisition would have to wait, for, after applying a bandage, he would have to prepare for the dinner guests who were expected to arrive within the hour.

The importance of that dinner party cannot be underestimated, since the guests were officials, plus a brace of wives thereof, of that institute of learning on whose staff Dr. Henry Hartwell loyally served, and within whose precincts talk had so recently begun to circulate of an impending vacancy in a senior post. That Dr. Hartwell wished to be considered a candidate, should such an opening arise, may be judged from the way in which his habitually monastic existence had allowed itself to be disrupted for this gathering.

Some hours having passed, Dr. Hartwell considered that, in the end, the experience had not proved too gruelling—which was as well considering that, if the post were to be presented to him, such evenings would have to be endured on a far more regular basis. But, by and large, he judged the evening to have been a success. Over dinner, Mr. and Mrs. Dean had both made highly flattering remarks: she on his domestic arrangements and the excellence of the meal provided by such a small staff—which Mrs. Senior Fellow perceived to be a necessary frugality under his current position – and he on the thorough and exacting research that was their host's stock in trade, and which could only bring credit to the university—something on which both Mr. Senior Fellow and Mr. Bursar heartily agreed. More such praise had followed after dinner, although Dr. Hartwell, having no wife, was forced to divide his attentions during this part of the evening between the cigar smoking and brandy imbibing in his study, and ensuring that the wives were being well-tended to in the drawing room.

Now, with his guests gone, Henry Hartwell surveyed his study, reflecting that, if he had divined the mood of the evening correctly, he might soon be exchanging it for a far grander room within the chambers that came as part and parcel of the advanced post. Here he occasioned to glance at the mantelpiece and the new ornament atop it, and the words of Mr. Senior Fellow shortly before his departure came back to mind. "I was just remarking, Hartwell, on what a handsome piece this is. We must be paying you well if you can afford such trinkets. Ah? I see. Well, that is rather a bargain, though perhaps it is to be expected, since there is a defect in the design. Well, look here. This middle chappie should be covering his ears completely, not cupping a paw to them as if to hear more clearly. Now, that would be a rum thing—to see all evil, hear all evil, and speak... What was that? Oh, now, you are quite right, he does have his ears closed off. I rather think I must have sampled too much of your brandy. I had better lay off it before we rejoin the ladies, or I might be hearing all evil from my good lady before the night is out."

Dr. Hartwell had considered explaining his suspicion that some hidden spring or cog caused motion in the monkeys, but he was reluctant to do so until he had discovered for himself just how it was triggered. Yet his current examination seemed to go against that theory, for he could discern no seams or joins in the brass limbs to allow for movement. "Unless the joins are incredibly fine," he mused, tracing a searching finger around the three forms. No, they seemed to be entirely solid. More than ever before, he found himself marvelling at the intricacy of detail, to the point where he became convinced that the fur would bristle under his fingertips, and he hastily withdrew his hand. His sudden alarm startled him, and he considered that, quite possibly, Mr. Senior Fellow had not been alone in his overindulgence that night, and that it was time to retire for the evening.

It was while he was in the process of extinguishing the study lamps that a noise in the gloom caused him to pause, listening. Was the clock in the corner running down? Not so, for he had watched as the maid had wound it only that morning. So what could be the source of that regular thudding tick, and that whirring and clinking that still chimed out? Before a lamp could be lit to allow for further investigation, Henry Hartwell found himself frozen, the match poised to strike, when a voice rang out in the dark.

"He really is as grim as I feared," it intoned.

A second voice joined it, and Dr. Hartwell had visions of a gang of burglars lurking somewhere in the room. Could that scoundrel from earlier have followed him home in order to extract revenge? "It has rather been a wasted evening. Let us face it, we all of us knew where our loyalties lay before accepting this absurd invitation."

This did not sound at all how he had imagined the talk of common criminals might, and, when a third voice piped up, Dr. Hartwell was suddenly aware that he knew exactly the tone and nature of this unseen discussion. "He is a diligent fellow, there can be little doubt about it, but he could hardly be described as our sort. Too fussy, too cut and dried. There simply is no flexibility there."

The voice was that of Mr. Dean. But it was his voice as if heard through some other medium. There was a metallic, echoing quality to it, rather as though it had been recorded and was now being amplified back through some brass horn.

"Brass?" thought Dr. Hartwell, the word striking an immediate chord, and he ignited that forgotten match to light the lamp, raising it up and directing its glow upon the mantelpiece. It was true, then. The figures were capable of motion. For that third monkey no longer had its hands fastened over its mouth. Instead, it cupped them around the open jaws, as if forming a makeshift speaking-trumpet in order that the words it repeated could be heard with greater clarity. And as Dr. Hartwell listened, he heard all too clearly a cataloguing of his own faults: that he lacked in humour, he lacked in charm, he had attended the wrong school, certainly not that institute attended by all three of his accusers, that he was too precise, that he was too keen, and that he was too honest.

Henry Hartwell had never regarded honesty as a fault, though he therefore had to be honest with himself in admitting that he could, perhaps, be brutal with the truth. However what he was to hear relayed to him next made it clear that his forthright opinions were not the issue.

"Could any of you imagine if honest Henry Hartwell were to discover the irregularities in the accounting over the new faculty building, or the 'donations' by those former students more endowed with cash than brains come examination time?" This in the voice of Mr. Bursar, followed seamlessly by the replicated tones of Mr. Senior Fellow, as he attempted to hush this line of talk lest their host return. Yet that first voice was not to be stilled, and Dr. Hartwell heard listed the names of several who had passed through the university and had achieved degrees that had come as a surprise to him in light of their academic records during their time in attendance.

The three voices that issued from that single mouth seemed in agreement that Dr. Hartwell's chief rival for the post was the man best suited. Furious, despite his incomprehension over just how this information had been brought to him, he grasped the carving, as if attempting to quieten the monkey by force. As he did so, there was a resumption of that grating squeak, and he watched in wonder while the first monkey lifted its hands from its eyes and gazed out into the room.

A dim yellow glow sprang forth, seemingly from those staring eyes, and it filled the centre of the study. Three figures were caught in the glow. These were little more than blurred shadows, yet each was recognisable to him: the short and corpulent Mr. Bursar, the equally short but far more skinny Mr. Senior Fellow, and the tall and stooping Mr. Dean—the three men who had shared his table and his hospitality. This strange spectacle had commenced just at the moment when they had converged to shake hands upon an agreement; one that was made plain by the voices still issuing from the monkey's maw. Then, suddenly, the three shades broke apart, as a fourth figure entered the scene and the glow faded. Just as the light was extinguished, Dr. Hartwell recognised this indistinct newcomer—a tray of glasses and a decanter in its hands, interrupting the cosy conspirators—as his own self, just as he had been not one hour before!

Had this betrayal truly taken place within his own home that very night? Had he almost caught the schemers in the very act of stabbing him in the back? A few seconds earlier and he would have heard enough to arouse his suspicions. But, had he not just heard all of what had earlier been missed? His fingers tightened around the cool brass, feeling a faint vibration running through the figures that might have been his own angry pulse, and he thought again of his treacherous guest's comment—that this purchase of his could see, hear, and speak all evil.

Recording devices and hidden lenses were considered, but even the limited knowledge he had of the bulky cameras and phonographs owned by some of his younger colleagues was sufficient to dismiss these theories. Clearly there had to be some mechanical element to it, but the smarting of his bandaged hand dissuaded him from any further attempt at revealing the mysteries within, and a sudden tiredness following all of the day's events swiftly convinced him that such matters were better left to a new day and a clearer mind, before strange fancies began to take hold.

The coupling of that new day and clearer mind conspired in persuading Henry Hartwell that the experience had been nothing more than a vivid and troubling dream. However, as he sat before the freshly made up fire in his study, the realisation came that he had not recalled a single dream after waking since his seventh year, when a particularly unpleasant nightmare—one in which spiders made of tin had swarmed over the ceiling above his bed on cold, sharp legs—had brought him screaming awake. That had been three decades before, so the prospect that he was now debating the reality of a dream struck him as extraordinary, despite it being the only answer that was tolerable to him. And, as he rang for the maid to bring him his morning tea and toast, he endeavoured to tell himself that, extraordinary or not, this was the case.

The next extraordinary occurrence of that day concluded with the maid's tearful departure with her few belongings crammed swiftly into a suitcase. It had begun, for her, as she had brought her employer his second round of toast to be eaten at his desk, as was his habit; and how was a soul supposed to digest his breakfast properly when their minds were on books and old papers, and who would it be who was expected to clear away the crumbs while not disturbing his prized volumes or interfering with his precious type-writer? Not that she would have to worry about that after this morning, when, out of the blue, Dr. Hartwell had accused her of not only helping herself to his brandy while he had slept, but also of stealing some coins and notes from the small wooden box which he kept in a drawer of the bureau. Her denials had been a little too forced, and entirely too late, after her initial amazement at having been so swiftly caught out had left her blurting an apology. How he could have known when he had been above, snoring loud enough to be heard throughout the house, she could not fathom. Though her subsequent tears and pleas for forgiveness from the man of the cloth had failed to retain her job for her, they had, at least, prevented him from summoning the police, but only on condition that she leave his house immediately. Even as the sobbing girl had departed to pack up what was hers, Henry Hartwell had looked long and hard at his purchase, and had wondered if his brass informant was grinning behind its paw.

The maid's confession did more than confirm that he had neither imagined nor dreamed the shadowy conversation of the previous night. It also resolved Dr. Hartwell's decision to show his accusers that he did not, after all, lack in flexibility; indeed it would be they who would have to bend or be snapped. Upon his arrival at the university, his request to inspect certain accounts and documentation pertaining to the recent construction work, "In order to give a thorough grounding to certain researches into the changing face of this great seat of learning," prompted a summons to the Dean's office. And here, a casual remark on his intention of composing letters of thanks to certain recently departed graduates over their generosity to their former university lead to a rather urgent conference between three senior staff members, to which Dr. Hartwell was not made privy, but which was concluded by the verbal assurance that the impending position which they had been so recently striving to fill would his for the taking, once its current incumbent had finally settled upon a date on which to vacate his tenure.

Thus began the remarkable and rapid ascendancy of Dr. Henry Hartwell. Even as he awaited the arrival of the day when he could take up residence in the more well-appointed quarters that would be afforded him by the imminent appointment to his new post, his previous, almost reclusive, existence was put behind him, and colleagues found themselves ever more frequently in receipt of invitations to share a convivial cigar and a chat in his study. That these same colleagues—many of whom had accepted the offer out of sheer curiosity at this change in the doctor's nature—afterwards had a tendency to look somewhat strained when his name was mentioned was apparently inexplicable, as few would be heard to utter any word of complaint about their host. Indeed, he appeared to inspire a form of peculiar loyalty, for all seemed keen to assist with any request he might then make upon their time and resources. The same was true with his students, who had found themselves undertaking the larger portion of their tutorials within the doctor's study, and whose productivity increased dramatically due to his almost uncanny ability to spot a cheat, a malingerer or an idler in their midst.

Throughout this time, Dr. Hartwell made no further attempt to prise the secret of the monkeys' workings from them. This, however, owed less to any lack of curiosity on his part, and was more through a wariness that his attempts to expose the mechanics within might damage the remarkable gift that fortune had bestowed upon him. Truthfully, with each instance of the brass creatures springing into duty, he had grown stronger in his belief that whatever it was that thudded and vibrated within the base was not the work of any mere technician, no matter how skilled. Yet curious as he may have been, Dr. Hartwell's ecclesiastical training had long ago taught him to accept that some mysteries simply *are!*

What was less easily ignored was the baffling prospect of someone in possession of such a valuable instrument—one which detected enemies before their schemes could reach fruition, and granted a certain degree of power over weaker individuals—should have surrendered it for a mere pittance. He, himself, could see no negative connotations in its use. In fact, what he saw was only justice, that the guilty should face threat of punishment and exposure in order that a righteous man might prevail and prosper. But there still remained the desire to know just how it had been allowed to come into his custody. Could it be that the previous owner had not known of the power he or she was surrendering? Was it possible that the statuette's abilities worked only for him?

On his return visit to the curiosity shop, Dr. Hartwell carried with him the heavy satchel that it had become his custom to sport—useful when there were some who could not be prevailed upon to open themselves up to scrutiny in his home. Mr. Barnabas, on seeing the familiar brass figures, assured him that there had been entirely no need to bring his purchase with him, as he did not need to view it again to recall it precisely. Dr. Hartwell might, at this point, have privately mused that it was not the plump, little shopkeeper he wished to inspect the three monkeys, rather the opposite. Yet he met with little of the expected resistance to his queries concerning the item's provenance. Evidently it was not simply the carving that Mr. Barnabas remembered only too well, but the hour or more of the customer's relentless stubbornness that had preceded the sale, and, not relishing the prospect of another such drain on his time and his patience, he supplied the following information, "The owner was a sailor. His name, I do not know, as you see he signed my ledger with the 'X' of the uneducated. Mine are the additional brackets and appending legend, 'A Sailor – Merchant.' And the date of purchase, you see for yourself, was August 15th, so there was only the two month period where they sat in my display before you offered the little fellows a new home. What I recall of him was that he looked to be greatly distracted, as if he wished to be away quickly. He took the first sum I offered, and he seemed quite grateful for it, for it would buy him a ticket, he said—by train rather than boat was my impression. Would I say that he appeared anxious to be rid of the thing? He seemed more anxious to be rid of himself, for no sooner had I placed the twelve...no, quite right, the three guineas in his hand, than he was off on his heels. No, I had no reason to suspect that it had been stolen, for he told me that he had made the thing by his own hands, with the exception of the base which he had acquired on his recent travels in Japan. I recognised it as a jewellery box, though one with a hidden catch for opening it. Certainly I never found it. I believed him, for, though he might have had a brawler's face, with bruises to match, those were craftsman's hands. He had further proof with him, too, in his kit bag: further carvings in brass and wood, some unfinished. I would have offered to pay a similar price for those, but his departure was, as I say, swift."

As had been the gist of the few words of genuine praise during that fateful dinner party, Dr. Hartwell was diligent and dogged in his researches, and these attributes were to be put to the test as he set about using what little information he had gleaned and, by careful investigation, to reveal more of this sailor whose handiwork was now in his ownership. Armed with the date, he consulted shipping records to ascertain which merchant ships had docked nearby that day, narrowing his search to those that had come from a Japanese port. There was but one, and he made note of the name—'The Victoria Jack.' Perhaps recent experience had caused the doctor to suspect everyone of some ill—certainly he would not trust his newly employed maid to live in, and she had to travel several miles to and from her duties each day—but considering the sailor's apparent desperation to escape to new surroundings, he thought to cross reference the name of the ship with the newspapers of the days following August the 15th, and his suspicions were to be rewarded. One Jonas Drewe, missing from the crew of The Victoria Jack, was sought following his unauthorised departure from the vessel. The public were warned that Drewe was to be considered dangerous, and that the local constabulary was acting on information received from the Japanese naval authorities. This seemed to be the man that Mr. Barnabas had described, but there was little more to be gathered from the report. However, had he persevered in searching through the pages of the following week's editions, he might have learned of Jonas Drewe's apprehension and trial, and he might also have been disturbed by the details of the crime with which he had stood accused. But he had another matter pressing, and he returned the newspapers to the archivist at the university library with his inquisitive urge only partially sated.

That other pressing matter was an audience with one of those three men who had found reason to regret maligning him in his home. That Mr. Bursar would answer the summons was in no doubt. A climate of fear had grown up of late—the dread of incurring Dr. Hartwell's displeasure—so that, distasteful as it was for him to visit the doctor in his lair, the Bursar was prompt in knocking upon his door at the appointed hour.

"The truth of the matter is this," Dr. Hartwell told his guest, who sat ill at ease while his host paced, "I have grown bored of my parochial researches in dim and dingy corners. There are very few challenges to be found hereabouts. No, my tastes have begun to develop along much more interesting lines, and I incline more toward the exotic—such as my three good friends here." And here he laid his hand upon the brass heads and felt a certain emboldening of spirit as that familiar pulse built up under his fingers. Evidently something to add leverage to his proposition would soon be revealed to him, and he pressed on. "Once my new appointment has begun—and do not think I am ungrateful for your persuasive urging of my soon-to-be predecessor to end his dithering and, well, predecease me—it should be a simple matter for a man of your...imaginative bookkeeping skills to find the funding that will allow me to make my researches in the appropriate places, no matter how far-flung they may be, or what expenses may be incurred. Come, come! There surely is no need to bridle so? Pray, take a moment to walk in the gardens, and compose yourself, before making what I am certain will be the wise decision."

Having momentarily rid himself of his audience, Dr. Hartwell tightened his grip upon his instrument of extortion. With a shrill of metal upon metal, the arms of each miniature form adopted the appearance of life, uncovering eyes and ears and a mouth. What were they to reveal of Dr. Hartwell's unwilling yet unwitting guest? Some private vice, or hidden infidelity? The answer, one single word, was entirely, shockingly unexpected.

"Murderer!"

A flood of horror overwhelmed Henry Hartwell, as his eyes fixed upon the shadow play that was conjured up for him. There a short but bulky form rounded on a dreadfully familiar figure, pursuing him as he backed away, raising a thin, sharp object in a large fist as if to strike out. Such was Dr. Hartwell's shock at the vision of his own shade under threat that he threw his arms up to cover his own face, releasing his grip on the brass in doing so. The instant that his hand broke contact, the frightful scene of violence faded. Even so, he still heard the opening echoes of a mortal cry of agony and terror, before the long, bony fingers once more sealed the monkey's lips.

There was no time granted to allow for the processing of this alarming revelation, nor to reflect upon the fact that his purchase had gained the ability to not simply capture guilt over past misdeeds, but also, under extreme circumstances, to prophesise future wrongs. That moment of reflection was snatched from him by the Bursar's return, fury burning in his eyes as he stormed across to his would-be blackmailer, his voice the roar of a man driven to edge of reason and control, as he waved his host's new letter opener in an accusatory fashion and defamed him as a craven, cowardly abuser of people. Dr. Hartwell made no attempt to answer to these charges, fear having denied him his voice, and this silence only succeeded in magnifying the other's rage, until he raised his hand to deliver a blow that would release months of pent up wrath. But this blow never fell. That Dr. Hartwell's grip had found the heavy type-writer as he'd backed into the desk came as a surprise, both to him and to his accuser, and the cry of astonished pain from the Bursar, as he dropped to the floor under the impact of the swinging blow to his skull, drove all thought from the doctor's mind. Then the man slumped forward, his bulk driving the blade of the letter-opener he still gripped into his own chest, and the cry died with him. But worse even than that final death yell was the echoing chatter of the harsh voice that repeated over and over the cry of, "Murderer! Murderer! Murderer!"

What was to be done with the body? He could scarcely leave it staining his study rug, just awaiting the maid to find it. Might he drag it outside and leave it somewhere, possibly in the bushes, to be discovered and thought of as a random tragedy? The Bursar had been a heavy man, and progress in dragging him across toward the study door was by no means swift. Even if Dr. Hartwell were capable of pulling and jostling him down the several flights of winding stairs outside his quarters, then out through the gardens, he was sure to be seen. At least, he would be if the Bursar was still in his present, unwieldy state. No, the thought was too gruesome. There had to be another way, but his thought processes were not aided by that persistent accusatory animal shrieking. Someone was bound to hear, so he had to silence the cries one way or another.

The pounding thud from within the statuette was of such intensity that it seemed set to split the lacquered base, while the whole thing appeared to rock and sway atop the mantel. Had the three figures somehow grown larger? Certainly this looked to be the case as he grasped the lacquered sides, his fingers wary of snapping jaws and thin, grasping fingers and toes, before consigning the accursed thing to the fire below. At what temperature did brass melt? He had no idea, and he was not soon to find out. For the ghastly shriek of bestial pain and fury that was released was of such a pitch that he was convinced that it would carry up the chimney and into the evening air, and be heard across the streets and gardens for miles around. Fumbling with the coal tongs, he knocked the statuette from the flames. It was undamaged, apart from a little blackening to the base, yet it was hot to the touch as he juggled it across the room before fumbling open a deep drawer in his desk and dropping it there. A thick cushion was then seized from the couch and thrust in on top of the screeching object, and this and the slamming of the drawer dampened the noise sufficiently so that he could think. And, within seconds, his thoughts were once more directed toward a more weighty matter, and he dashed from the room to find something more substantial than his letter-opener in order to cut the problem down to size, so to speak.

The grisly work took longer than he had anticipated, and it was by no means complete when Henry Hartwell sunk onto his couch, exhausted by his exertions. The room was thankfully still and quiet—it had been so since he had returned with the kitchen cleaver—and he needed only to regain his strength before venturing out to dispose of the evidence of the evening's madness; something which, judging from the number of bags and pillow cases he had filled, would require several trips.

He had not intended to doze off quite so suddenly, but this was, indeed, what had happened. As to what roused him, he could not at first be certain, until he saw the shadows cast by the red and flickering glow of the firelight, and heard the sounds of destruction from all around him. He had not lit the lamps, except the one upon his desk, before he had been overtaken with events, and he had been thankful of the obscuring gloom as he had performed that loathsome task, so the room was hazy and dim. Even so, he felt instantly aware that the hunched and spindly shapes thrown against the wall were those of very real, very tangible beings. That tangibility was swiftly confirmed, when his dangling hand brushed against coarse and bristling hair that sprouted between rough and raw patches of hot skin, as something darted across the floor below the couch. His twitching nostrils detected an animal scent, one that mingled with the stench of scorched meat and fur. He heard the fabric of the curtains tear, as something scrabbled up them, the crash of books as they were torn from high shelves, and, worse, the sound of bags and cotton being ripped asunder, the wet slopping of what spilled out, and the horribly unmistakable sounds of feeding, before three shadows once again raised themselves up. It was with merciful difficulty that he made out the rounded heads upon twisted, bony bodies, before the long fingers closed themselves over his eyes to blot out the sight, over his ears to close off the excited jabbering, and over his mouth before he could open it to scream.

As has been stated, Henry Hartwell was not an individual prone to lucid or memorable dreams. Therefore the hideous memory that presented itself to him within seconds of his waking that next morning caused him to leap stiffly from that crouching position in which he had slept, and survey the room in alarm. The great bells of the nearby churches of St. Mary and St. Emily were tolling the hour of seven, and the maid would be arriving soon to make up the fire and prepare his breakfast. He had little time and little hope of disposing of... Disposing of what? There was no heap of savaged bags or grisly stains to be seen when he could finally force his eyes to look to the floor below his desk. And there, atop that same desk, were the weapons that had dealt the killing strokes: the type-writer, a fresh sheet of paper nestling in its hold, and, next to it, the letter opener, its blade gleamingly clean, just as it had been before the previous night's appointment had gone so unexpectedly awry. The loud pealing outside faded in his ears to a distant, brass chime. He stood dumbly at the desk, staring at the blade without actually seeing it. Then, as his senses returned, he dropped to his haunches, dragging open the desk drawer, ready to drag out the muffled bundle that should have been within, yet which was not there when he gazed into the wooden recess.

Dr. Hartwell rose and turned, startled, the sudden sensation of being observed upon him. He expected to find the maid at the door, gawping at her master's dishevelled clothing and haunted expression. Instead, his eyes fell upon those monkeys, squatting in their habitual spot above the now cold fireplace. He raced across to them, intent on grabbing hold of the tiny figures, as if touching them might be the only way to prove that they were actually there. Yet he drew his hand back before his fingers could come into contact with the cool brass, fearful that those simian limbs might again shift into motion, and that what he feared had occurred within that room would be confirmed by having the long moments of lunacy played out before him once more.

No, he had to be prepared to believe what it was his eyes were telling him. The room was unaltered; everything was as it had been before the Bursar's arrival. If this was so, had that confrontation even taken place outside of his own mind? The memory of tin spiders surfaced, and had he not dimly observed something that had scuttled across the ceiling above him during his night terrors—something that united the scurrying rapidity of an animal with a metallic hollowness in its every movement? Two nightmares within the span of thirty years did not strike Dr. Hartwell as excessive, or as evidence that he was losing his mind. The fact of it was, the very rarity of the occurrence would almost certainly account for the unaccustomed sensation of lingering dread that wakefulness had done little to dispel. Such a disturbed and restless night could all too easily be an indication of an oncoming malady. Yes, plainly he was unwell, and not merely with regards to this uncommon tension, for he could feel the physical signs. There was a tightness to his scalp and across his brow and forehead, a weight pressing upon his shoulders and backbone, and a painful constriction to his throat.

The maid was turned away on arrival, much to her irritation following her early morning rise and walk, and a notice was pinned to his door advising his students that tutorials were suspended for the day and would, upon their resumption, be held in the more formal surroundings of the faculty building. But, in spite of his conviction that he was ill and suited only for bed-rest, Dr. Hartwell was seen entering the main university building. Here he hastened to the office of his recent guest, determining that it was better to hear the worst rather than face the dreadful wait for the heavy knock of officialdom on his door.

"I am afraid the answer is no, Dr. Hartwell," replied the young man who assisted the Bursar in his duties, and who had seemed alarmingly perturbed on his entrance, upon hearing his urgent request to granted an audience. "You cannot see the Bursar. No, he is not at his desk today, since you ask. Are you quite all right, sir? You are rather peaky looking. No, I cannot tell you when he might be back, as I do not know that myself. No, sir, why should there be anything amiss? Quite simply, he has gone on holiday. Yes, in the middle of the term. Of course, I am quite certain of it. Perhaps it has been rather sudden, but the Bursar is, as you know, a very busy man, and he clearly felt that he needed to absent himself in order to seek temporary relief from the burden of his work. Yes, Dr. Hartwell, as I said, a holiday. Oh, there is entirely no need to thank me so effusively, sir. I am simply doing my duty. And a very good day to you too, Doctor."

And as Dr. Hartwell departed, looking to be in infinitely higher spirits than he had been on his arrival, the assistant was forced to wonder if there was some ailment amongst the staff that was making them act so oddly. For, although loyalty to his immediate superior had made it unthinkable for him to say so aloud, there was certainly something strange in the Bursar's sudden abandonment of his duties. Normally fastidious in his arrangements, it was entirely uncharacteristic of him to have given no notice of his departure. Yet there, on his desk awaiting him when he had arrived that morning, had been the note that had made the official's feelings exceptionally plain—declaring him to be *'entirely cut up about the pressures of work, so much so that I feel myself quite buried, and to have no life left to me,'* and insisting that, *'now I am packed, and I am ready for my long-awaited rest.'* Perhaps it was for the best, mused the assistant, as the man was clearly becoming careless in his actions, since, after typing out his missive the previous night, he had forgotten to close the office window, and anyone might have entered unseen intent on mischief.

Even as that young man put aside his musings to focus on the unforeseen extra duties that lay ahead, Henry Hartwell was proceeding homewards in rather a cheerful frame of mind for one with good reason to believe that they were now prone to disturbing hallucinations. However, his good cheer was to desert him as he wended his way through the busy streets, as a result of a number of incidents which could, if taken individually, have been regarded as coincidences, yet whose cumulative effect was to persuade him that his private inner thoughts were being intruded upon. The first of these came as a voice reached his ear amidst the hubbub of passersby.

"I could murder him, I sometimes feel that I really could." Naturally it was the word 'murder' that drew his attention so forcibly. What he saw, on the pavement opposite, was a couple, presumably married, of advanced years: he in the process of looking intently at the various fishing rods and rifles within a shop window, she waiting with little patience, her face the vision of disgruntlement. The old man stood, oblivious to his wife's words, despite the bitter strength to them that had caused them to ring out so clearly above the din of traffic and people. Perhaps the fellow had grown deaf, or it might have been that, after so many years together, his spouse's complaints no longer affected him. There was nothing here that need trouble Dr. Hartwell, and he moved swiftly onwards.

Throughout his brief walk home—and he was to curse himself for not taking the more direct route through the university grounds—fragmentary bursts of chatter assailed his hearing, all of them seemingly unsavoury, though he hoped that it was merely the lack of context that made them so: "Strike him down, I ought to...", "...but not a soul must ever know...", "...if I am discovered, my end is inescapable...", "...worth killing for, I would wager...", "...cut him down to size, I did...", and so much more that it was a trial not to cover his ears and charge pell-mell through the remaining streets to the safety of home. As it was, he was aware that his brisk step and his distracted manner were drawing curious glances from those he passed, and that, even as this spurred his progress to hasten himself with yet more urgency, those glances had developed into hostile or suspicious glares.

Henry Hartwell had never before had occasion to consider his conscience to be pricking him. Yet it seemed obvious to him that this was now so, even if he was uncertain as to why he should experience such guilt over an incident which had never taken place in reality. That it had felt so genuine gave him cause to consider that what he had undergone had been no dream, but was shown to him by some power that those primate figures had not previously displayed. Was he to consider it a warning of a potential path to which his actions, in allowing himself to be guided by forces beyond his understanding, might lead? Whatever the case, in the days that lay ahead, he was to find the thought of spending any great length of time in his study unbearable. He could barely bring himself to sit at his desk, he certainly did not relish working at his type-writer, and he avoided looking at those monkeys lest his gaze be returned. Might he not dispose of them? The idea of touching their brass hides repelled him, and to ask the maid to remove them was likely to lead to questions that he did not wish to face, thus they remained put. There were other reasons behind his desire to be free of that dismal room. He had not noticed before quite how shabby the study had become. There were faint stains on the rug, and he now noticed a distinct tear in one of the curtains. He was thankful that, within a very few days, he would be able to leave the place behind. And, as he did so, he would leave a parting gift upon the mantel for the room's next occupant.

The reversion to Dr. Hartwell's more secluded habits had gone unremarked, though there may have been some unvoiced relief amongst his fellows when each day went by without receipt of a summons to visit him at his home. But the truth of it was this; no matter how fervently Dr. Hartwell longed to escape from those quarters of his, the prospect of spending his time amongst others—to be under their gaze and within their hearing—was even more troubling. His students continued to work industriously regardless of whether he absented himself on other, more pressing business, as if they feared that even unmonitored laxity would be detected and punished. In this way, the week progressed until, with no calamity having befallen him, Dr. Hartwell began to relax. And, since to go out before the public he must, there being the formalities of the investiture service to be undergone, this lessening of his dread might have been seen as a good thing.

On the ceremonial day, the great university hall was filled, as tradition demanded, with staff and students alike. This, however, was a restive audience, not entirely con-

sisting of those had chosen to celebrate Dr. Hartwell's eleva-
tion of their own volition. The doctor, robed in scarlet, took
to the stage with confidence. He had, in the days leading up
to this moment, rallied considerably—the result of his
repeatedly telling himself that this day marked a new beginning, one that would allow him to shake off the vestiges of
the preceding weeks. He seated himself, looking along the
line of his colleagues: his outgoing predecessor, the Dean
and the Senior Fellow, the Chaplain. The spectacle of the
empty chair between the Senior Fellow and the Chaplain
caused him to shiver, and he drew the fur-trimmed collar of
his gown tighter around himself.

The oration that followed—first in praise of his illus-
trious forebear, next listing his own achievements—eased
his mind greatly. He was almost capable of forgetting the
day's earlier irritation, when he could find no trace of his
best white shirt when preparing for the ceremony. It was not
the first item to have been misplaced, since his attempts to
ready himself for the decanting of his property to his new
quarters had hit an obstruction when he could find none of
the bags, not even his satchel, that he had intended to fill.
To add to his annoyance, that less than helpful maid of his
had greeted his complaints with those of her own, over certain linen items that had gone astray from their closet.

Now the elderly relic whose post he would so shortly
assume was talking, and, putting domestic trivialities aside, he
attempted concentration—no easy feat considering the rambling nature of the discourse. His efforts were in no way
assisted by the persistent murmur from somewhere in the
auditorium. Scanning the impassive figures grouped before
him, he detected a great deal of fidgeting. Something glimmered
on the edge of his vision, and he glimpsed some oaf obsessively
wiping something long and shining on the hem of his shirt.
Such unrest was understandable during this ramshackle
address, but Dr. Hartwell was confident that, when his time
came around, he would hold their attention. And, when he had
ascended to the lectern with his handwritten speech in his grip,
sure enough, the muttering ceased, and several hundred eyes
and several hundred ears were focused upon him.

To begin with, he thanked the Dean for his generous introductory words, and he thanked his predecessor for his sterling work, which, he vowed, he would strive to continue. He did not thank whoever it was—a porter or messenger—who had chosen this moment to transport some heavy baggage across the back of the hall, dragging it noisily, and with great effort, in his wake. He could not clearly distinguish this unwarranted interloper, but he was now given the impression that it was one of the grounds-men, for who else would be carrying a shovel over his shoulder?

Striving to ignore the fellow, Dr. Hartwell returned to his speech. Yet he had achieved little more than a hasty repetition of his opening thanks when he became conscious that the murmuring had resumed, and it had grown more persistent and widely spread. A hot wave of anger boiled within him at this insolence, and he could feel the fur collar prickling at his neck until he shrugged it off. What was being whispered amongst the crowd he could not ascertain, nor could he pinpoint the culprits. It sounded to his ears to be emanating from numerous points throughout the room. In some places there were hints of desolation, in others a mocking tone. Here was sorrow, there anger, elsewhere proud defiance.

Someone had smuggled drink in with them, he observed, for now there was a figure crouching in the aisle, mopping away at some dark liquid that had spilled there, soaking it up with what appeared to be a white shirt. As one, the audience followed the now silent Dr. Hartwell's furious gaze to the sight of this affront, which merely added to his fury. The slam of his open palm on the lectern echoed like the thud of some heavy body dropping suddenly, and a mass of faces turned toward him. Curious, bestial eyes stared at him from below protruding brows. Coarse paws cupped ears, the throng attempting to hear the words that stuttered at his lips, even as their own jabbering drowned out his very thoughts. Beside him on the stage, gowned apes glared at him with a malevolence that was almost, but not quite, human, before they too shrieked their own guilt at him.

As Dr. Hartwell attempted to turn from the sight of this grotesquely altered audience, he felt the fur of his collar constraining his throat, and he raised a hand to claw it away, before he saw that discarded gown crumpled at his feet. The three ugly, skinny forms that were now visible, clinging to him—that he was now aware had clung tightly to him since his night of madness—gripped his head in their long fingers and directed it toward the horde, not permitting him to turn from their screeched confessions. Yet still he thrust his hands over his ears and splayed his fingers to hide his eyes. But in doing so, he had left his mouth unguarded, and when it opened it could not be closed. And so it talked and it talked, and it told of the early morning digging in the shadows of the bushes at the rear of the gardens behind his quarters: of the forged note with its unsubtly concealed admission of the crime, typed upon the very instrument that had robbed its supposed author of his life, and of the white shirt turned scarlet that had been burned in his study grate after mopping down the mess that had been smeared and sprayed across the floor and walls, and even the ceiling.

The scene which the police arrived to was one of chaos. The wild figure that clung to the stage curtains, where, after emitting a piercing, jabbering yell, he had clambered out of their reach, would not be calmed. Instead, he pointed and howled, gibbered and accused, declaring to the shocked gathering that looked up in horror which of them had been dishonest and which were frauds, that this professor had entirely invented the very thing he claimed to research, that that tutor had consistently failed an exemplary student's work out of sheer jealousy, that there were liars and deceivers and crooks and swindlers amongst them. These claims were met with howls of protest, though many denials were accompanied by expressions which suggested that there may have been an element of truth to what had been revealed. And the more these revelations were allowed to spill forth, the less gentile and learned these gathered scholars appeared, as savage, primal anger released itself from hidden reserves.

It was judged remarkable that Dr. Hartwell escaped alive from the mob that thronged around him following his accusations, even more astonishing that his escape from the promised reprisals was achieved by leaping over their heads onto a high gantry above the stage without falling to his doom. Here his declaiming of crimes and misdeeds continued undeterred—the Dean's and Senior Fellow's embezzlement of the building funds, and the Chaplain's less than pious thoughts being unveiled—until he was overpowered by a good half-dozen officers, while treble that number held back the crowds to allow him to be led in chains to the waiting wagon.

It can be supposed that considerably more constables would have been required to keep those angry spectators at bay had they known of the grim excavation that was shortly to be undertaken behind the bushes in Dr. Hartwell's garden. The search of the grounds was to be a lengthy one, yet no more was uncovered beyond the original find of bags and bundles of linen. This was a cause of some perplexity to the county coroner as, no matter in which combination he attempted to assemble those ghastly contents, he was still unable to reconstitute an entire Bursar.

At the trial that was to follow, much of what has preceded came out in Dr. Hartwell's testimony, as did several other claims concerning the judge, the county coroner, a fair number of jury members, and those in the public gallery, all of which were decreed contemptible. Such was the unending stream of confession and accusation that poured out from the defendant, that the inevitable conclusion reached was that he was insane, and he was committed to the institute on Gibbet-Peak. His effects were since sold on, in part to be put against the costs of his incarceration. Where most of his possessions ended up need not concern us, and we already know that a certain ornamental item made its way back to the place where he had first found it.

My understanding of Henry Hartwell's current situation is that he is held in a form of solitary confinement. This, it seems, is judged necessary for his own protection, as his indiscriminate speech had such a disturbing effect on his fellow inmates that an unknown assailant, armed with a knife purloined from the kitchens, saw fit to relieve him of his tongue. That his mouth still works, unceasingly attempting to form words that will never be given voice, might suggest that it would have been a mercy if his attacker had deprived him also of his hearing and his eyesight.

«« —— »»

There is one more matter to relate in the case of Henry Hartwell—rather in the case of that item, the possession of which might be considered the catalyst for his descent into madness—and it is one to which I have earlier alluded. Following my encounter with that brass carving in the gloomy precincts of that shop, my own curiosity led me to revisit the accounts of the case of Jonas Drewe, including those that the unfortunate Hartwell had missed. Amongst the reports of the trial could be found testimony from his crewmates that the sailor had, on the journey home, become a different soul from that who had sailed out with them, having become suspicious and distrustful of his fellows, his allegations leading to many brawls. The fact that he had assaulted an officer, merely for attempting to examine a trinket box that Drewe had bought in a Japanese port and had carried out some fancy work on, would have led to his incarceration upon reaching his home shores, had he not absconded.

It is possible that the reason for his change in temperament was to be found in the request from the Japanese authorities for the apprehension of an English sailor who had married, in secret, a young woman native to that country. This young bride had been discovered, in the days following The Victoria Jack's departure, with a person who was later identified as her lover, both of them violently murdered in a most grotesque manner. The accused, Jonas Drewe, clearly a man in the grip of strong emotions, confessed to his responsibility in this matter, and pleaded to either be hung on his own soil, or taken back to face foreign justice, rather than let him live under his current guilt. The only issue on which he would not, or could not, assist was related to the manner of death visited upon his victims. It seems that the hearts of both had been removed.

The whereabouts of those missing organs were never discovered, therefore it would only be supposition to propose that, had Henry Hartwell succeeded in opening the base of that peculiar ornament, what he would have found pulsing within would not be any skillfully contrived mechanism of springs and coils, but something of infinitely more complex and vital design. Personally, I have resisted the temptation to find out the truth of the matter. There are certain things it is best not to see, nor even to hear about, and perhaps my suspicions would have been better left unspoken. And I have not cared to browse in that curiosity shop, or even to glance within its darkened windows as I pass, since that day.

The Unmasking

'An Evening of Revels and Revelations'

D r. Lawrence has never been one for official college func-
tions, his antipathy in particular being reserved for
those formal occasions which attempt to hide themselves
under a guise of informality. This is common knowledge
amongst staff and students alike. Therefore, when rumours
first began to make the rounds that some sort of masked
ball was in the offing, the Dean's summons came swiftly. So
swiftly, that Lawrence hadn't even begun to make his decision over which piece of newly uncovered lore it was vitally
important he chase up in whichever location made it the
most inconvenient or, preferably, utterly impossible for him
to attend.

The porter—who had so unhelpfully refused to acknowledge numerous hints of financial inducement to report back
that the antiquarian had not been found on delivery of this
summons—was more forthcoming with the information that
Lawrence was expected to treat the matter with every
urgency. "You're to drop everything. Professor Burwell
stressed this instruction to me, personal, and you're to
make all haste. So, if you would oblige, Dr. Lawrence, in just
stepping lively..."

Lawrence didn't drop anything, but he had to resist the
petty urge to throw a rare volume or two at the wall upon
hearing of this unwelcome diversion. However he felt just
such an action would be entirely justified, as he pointed out,

*…what he saw was something long and sinewy and encrusted
with coarse, dark grey fur, that curled its many-jointed
length out of the darkness behind that socket…*

"If the Dean is going to insist on dragging me into his office like an unruly prep school boy before the headmaster..."

"Professor Burwell isn't in his office at the moment," the porter informed him, and, when he had told Lawrence where this audience was to be held, the notion of that childish indignity seemed not quite as unappealing.

The Zoological Department is housed alongside Botany in a series of long conservatories—the hothouse atmosphere provided by these structures necessary to ensure the survival of those numerous examples of flora and fauna which provide the raw materials for study. "A perfect place for reptiles," Lawrence mused as he marched irritably across the lawn, "though Burwell must have other reasons for being there, surely?"

In fact, he was aware already of one of those reasons, having prised from the porter what information he had—not the most difficult of tasks, since the man regarded every piece of intelligence told to him by any official as a confidentiality, and took great pride in letting it be widely known just how much trust was placed in him. So the doctor knew that the Dean was making urgent inspections of various faculties, even if the reason for this action had not yet been divulged—at least not to the porter.

With any luck, by now Burwell would be with Ferguson, the Head of Botany, amongst his ferns and lichens, and not with Usborne and those ghastly specimens he'd insisted on bringing back from his expedition to the Americas. The insects and the snakes, Lawrence could take, but not those other awful brutes with their long, hairy legs, skulking in webs large enough to trap birds and mammals let alone flies. He almost turned tail and ran before he was actually inside the glass house, the arachnophobe in him recoiling at the prospect of the merest glimpse, even safely in their cases and under a layer of glass, of one of those crawling creatures.

Luck, of sorts, was with the doctor, as he spied the door to the botanist's glass-partitioned office slamming shut, and the big, bluff Scotsman stalking back to his desk. This was typical of the sort of reaction the Dean was wont to provoke among even the most placid of the university's Fellows and, sure enough, he now perceived Professor Burwell proceeding in his direction through the transplanted foliage. What he hadn't expected was that the Chaplain would be at his heels, nasally pontificating about something or other.

"Lawrence, what kept you?" boomed the Dean, cutting Mr. Pargetter off in mid-flow—a feat seldom achieved by others unfortunate enough to be on the receiving end of the Chaplain's dogged attentions. "Never mind, never mind, you're here now. Not planning on leaving us on one of your...field trips over the next week or so, I trust? No, the Bursar tells me you haven't filed any applications."

"That's for the good, hmm?" simpered Pargetter. It was no secret that the Chaplain did not entirely approve of some of the areas it was rumoured that Lawrence's researches had led him. But, given that he was of a character never to employ a sentence when a paragraph could be found in its stead, it was a matter which the antiquary had vowed never to allow himself to enter into debate over.

"Come, Doctor. I have to see the Head of Mathematics, so we must talk as we walk," Burwell decreed, sweeping past Lawrence and out across the lawn. It was with a mixture of relief to be leaving the lurking horrors of that unnatural tropical outpost and growing annoyance at his superior's brusqueness that Lawrence followed the Dean and Chaplain, the pair of them resembling a pair of overstuffed carrion birds as they swooped toward their next victim.

"About this costume ball," Lawrence began, deciding to take the bull by the horns and terminate this gathering earlier rather than later.

Professor Burwell turned a pale and piercing blue eye on Lawrence, clearly impressed by his forthrightness, but spoke as if he hadn't heard what had been said. "You haven't published much of late, have you, Lawrence?"

The doctor hadn't expected threats quite so early on, but the tone made it clear that this was precisely what was being directed at him. It wasn't a point he could argue so readily, without admitting that most of his recent studies would prove impossible to publish without attracting a certain amount of speculation as to the balance of his mind. Evidently the Chaplain picked up on this unvoiced thought, as he nodded with a smirk unbecoming of a man of the cloth.

"We do expect the Fellows to, in some small way, earn their keep," Burwell continued, "particularly where there are field studies and, I think the term would be 'private projects,' involved."

"Any of my private projects are also privately funded," Lawrence pointed out, his knowledge of certain areas that are not commonly studied having occasionally proved of service to some notable and moneyed individuals, in particular those whose inheritances had the misfortune to include less corporeal legacies than simple wealth and property.

"That's as may be, Lawrence, but there is still an expectation that the results of these studies are made known. It reflects on the university, as you know. Although, perhaps all that has to be said on your own subject has been said already? After all, in the interests of progress in this still-young century, should we not be looking toward the future, the sciences and the technologies, instead of raking up the dead past?"

The effect of the Dean's words was that Lawrence was left dumbstruck a few paces behind. Had the man taken leave of whichever senses he had ever possessed? "Already said? Professor, the areas of past knowledge that are still to be explored—that might yet hold the forgotten steps toward newer learning... Already said?"

"You said that already," grinned the Chaplain.

"Mr. Pargetter, the reems of biblical studies and apocrypha..."

"Yes, well," sighed Pargetter, "I think the messages in the Good Book are already clear, don't you, hmm? What further exploration may be required can be found in more progressive texts, tailored to our rapidly changing times." Such sentiments were now so commonplace from the Chaplain that Lawrence had once formulated the theory that Pargetter's father had been a man of the cloth, his son had been too timid to protest against the path chosen for him, and only now was he attempting some belated form of rebellion.

"Of course," the Dean observed, "no hasty or rash decisions have been made over the fate of any department; I
would not wish for you to take the wrong impression away
from our little chat, dear me, no. And, should the type of
patron it is this administration's objective to attract favour
the continued presence of an Antiquities Faculty, then such
would obviously have to be taken into consideration. Now,
about this costume ball... You can attend? Splendid! I knew
I could rely on your co-operation. It's in all of our interests
to present a united front, Lawrence. Let us keep our inner
squabbles to ourselves and show a contented face. And I'm
sure those potential patrons would be fascinated to meet
you. You might amuse them with some of your diverting stories. After all, they won't have read about them anywhere
else, will they?"

Lawrence co-operated with the Dean's wishes that he be
present that following Friday, but it was a far from willing
collaboration. Unlike certain of his similarly blackmailed
colleagues, he hadn't immediately scampered out to some
costumier's to seek out an eye-catching guise in order to
impress whichever wealthy former students or local busi-
nessmen were being persuaded to part with their money.
Instead, he chose to wait till the last possible moment so
that he could truthfully claim that no costume in his size
was to be found. Hence the white tie and black tails. But,
after a few moments, even the simple elegance of this outfit
looked outlandish amidst the harlequins and gondoliers,
Punchinellos, and all manner of humanised beasts that
processed through the quadrangle. The splendour of some
Venetian festival was almost brought to mind but, this being
England and October, there was no open-air plaza with
flaming torches to light the sky, and the larger function
room in the main reception building had to suffice.

The liveried footmen standing guard on each door tran-
spired, on closer inspection, to be members of the porters'
staff, their blue serge and peaked caps replaced by velvet
and periwigs. And there was no little satisfaction when
Lawrence sighted that particular unhelpful chap of recent
memory shifting self-consciously in his knickerbockers, as

he held the door wide into the venue for the night's revels. This room had seen much ceremony and many gowned costumes before, it being the hall where graduations traditionally took place. And while Lawrence, who had received his own doctorate in this very room, was always happy to attend on such occasions and celebrate the achievements of those who had survived the rigours of university life, this was an altogether different gathering.

The throng might have been the result of some catastrophic collision between a travelling circus and a zoo. Here were clowns and monkeys, lions and conjurers. Even those dressed in human guises wore enough feathers to denude the peacock population of every stately home in Britain. Exactly who was under each wig and tri-corn and mask it was initially difficult to ascertain, and Lawrence pondered over how these prospective patrons would be distinguished from the faculty members. But, after only a few moments, mannerisms and characteristics began to make their owners' identities clear. That grand, golden-beaked eagle with the gilded wings, yet with the waddling gait of a penguin, could only be the plump little Mathematics tutor. It was telling that the most staid and tweedy of his colleagues had gone to the most elaborate lengths for the night. Over by the punch bowl, that gleaming-scaled lizard was a Geography Fellow, and, in the archway to the left of the stage...was that the great god Pan or a hobgoblin? Lawrence shivered, an unpleasant association of images coming unbidden to his mind. When he glanced back, the horned figure was gone. Most likely it had been the Bursar, now sharing a joke with the Geography lizard, complete with bell and tether, literally acting the goat.

So many had now filled out the hall, most whose identities might never be known to him, that Lawrence seized upon the idea of escape. For all Professor Burwell would later be aware, the antiquary might have been in attendance all evening long and simply never been seen through his disguise. Had the plan come to him a mere moment before, Lawrence may well have spent the evening he craved, in his study with a glass of port, his pipe and a favourite book. But, through the crowd, an unmistakable figure was approaching, for the Chaplain, like Lawrence, wore no mask.

"Won't your chum, Burwell, be a little put out that you've come casually dressed?" enquired Lawrence, indicating the black vestments. "I mean, he expects such flouting of his wishes from me, and I did at least try."

"As the Dean is fully aware," Pargetter retorted, "my duties have made it difficult for me to find time to deal with such matters. Besides which..."

"Besides which," interrupted the Dean, a disagreeably pleased look plastered across his similarly unadorned features as he bustled toward them, "it seemed altogether too likely that some guests would...have difficulty in obtaining a suitable costume. But not to worry, preparations have been made. Come along, Lawrence. The sooner we cover up that scowl of yours the better, wouldn't you say?"

Within that archway by the stage was a curtained antechamber. The functionary who moved stiffly back to hold the curtain aside with a loud rustling was, Lawrence presumed, yet another porter earning some overtime. This one, though, had been fortunate enough to escape the velvet livery, and was dressed in sombre black. Even the mask he wore was black, a bland oval that gave one the disconcerting impression of peering into the empty recesses of the servant's skull.

"Gentlemen," the voice that issued from that dark-clad figure was as blank as the face he wore, "three masks yet remain. Would you care to select that which you find most appropriate?"

The disembodied heads of a devil, a tragedian and an ape gazed back at them from atop a green baize table. Lawrence had little time to decide on which would make him feel the least ridiculous before the Chaplain strode briskly forward and lifted the red mask of the demon to his face.

"Isn't that a little risqué for a man of your position?" Lawrence couldn't resist goading.

"Not at all," the reply came from between the grinning scarlet lips. "In this day and age we're sophisticated enough to realise that such a figure is purely a symbolic representation. It's merely a hold-over from more unenlightened times. And symbols have no power over us." The mental image of the senior Pargetter revolving in his grave sprang to Lawrence's mind, but he thought better of indicating the symbolism of the crucified figure that hung at the throat beneath the devil's face. "And even if there is some residual power still in them, surely mockery is the best method of defeating that, hmm?"

"I wonder what this could symbolise," murmured Burwell, having selected the mask of tragedy, his ginger whiskers still visible through the downward crescent of the mouth.

"Perhaps your never-ending trials in maintaining this establishment, Dean," suggested Pargetter, and Lawrence thought it a pity that a more apt choice of a toad mask hadn't been available.

With a sigh, the doctor held up that remaining simian visage. It seemed entirely fitting, given that he felt very much the performing monkey, dancing to the Dean's tune. The heavy browed features, flared nostrils and imbecilic animal grin were sculpted with surprising delicacy. This was no cheap costume shop novelty. The hatching of tiny cracks in the golden patina suggested it was of considerable age, and he idly wondered if with age there came a history. Such thoughts were a facet of Lawrence's nature as ingrained as the cracks in the mask, and they occupied no more than seconds before he reluctantly pushed them aside and donned the guise.

The mask fitted snugly over his own face, and he looped the ribbons around his ears. The china was cool against his skin. Something appeared to shift as he adjusted the sockets around his eyes. The light seemed momentarily dimmer, the walls of the cramped alcove further away. But the effect was momentary and forgotten when the leering devil barked out a laugh, saying something muffled about fetching Lawrence a banana. And, as the servant rustled back the curtains, the newly masked trio rejoined the others in the main hall.

At one end of the room, a refectory table was wearing its own disguise as a banqueting table, so laden was it with fruits and cold cuts and various beverages. Here, Lawrence mingled with a gallery of the grotesque and the fantastical, amongst them, a bear who complained loudly in a Scottish accent about being put on parade simply to line the Dean's coffers. Recognising the Head of Botany, and also a kindred spirit, Lawrence enquired if the guests of honour had been seen. "Guest of honour, y'mean?" growled the bear. "There's only the one, as far as I can make out. The big lad over yonder with the devil at his shoulder."

The 'big lad' that Dr. Ferguson had raised a paw to indicate was a tall individual dressed, not in some fanciful gown or faux animal skin, but wearing a black frock coat, a rich red waistcoat and a neutral, emotionless expression. Rather, the mask he wore, bone white and gleaming, displayed an expression devoid of emotion in its classical featured simplicity, as if a Renaissance sculptor's work had sprung to life and viewed the world it found with detached indifference. Such a false face would have been of great use to anyone cornered by the Chaplain, whose incessant droning could, in the main, be made out even from this distance. What could he be finding to bore this fellow with?

"Seems," and here it suddenly became clear to Lawrence why Pargetter had been on the Dean's gown-tails the previous week, "he's looking for the funding to publish a progressive tract or two that are going to... Now, how did he modestly put it? Oh, aye, 'that are going to, hmm, revolutionise our thinking on how we should perceive, hmm, sacred rituals in our modern day and age,' no less." From which news the doctor couldn't help but imagine the yawning that was no doubt taking place behind that impassive white visage.

"If one were to strip away some of the more fanciful, rather fantastical elements of the teachings, and remove certain of the more willfully esoteric ritualistic trappings that divide the preacher from the preached to, might this not humanise the whole process of belief, hmm?" Pargetter paused, awaiting the agreement that must come to what he clearly felt was a most sensible and well argued case. But the expectant tilt of his head swiftly righted itself under that unreadable, expressionless gaze.

The answer, when it came, was spoken in a low, unassuming tone that nevertheless commanded the attention of those revellers within close proximity. "Evidently you have put your heart and soul into pursuing this train of thought, Mr. Pargetter. Forgive me, I hope that 'the soul' is not too fantastical a notion for you? No? But surely those who attend that church of which you are a servant, in fact they that gather in all the diverse churches this world over, welcome the comfort that ritual provides? Is it not infinitely more reassuring to maintain the belief that greater powers yet still play their parts, rather than being left to the mercies of the sometimes well-intentioned, oft-times malicious, and all too frequently blundering machinations of man." It was the prospective patron's turn to adopt that expectant tilt of the head, his whole demeanour reminiscent of a patient nursemaid talking to a precocious charge. And, for once, Lawrence keenly waited to hear what the Chaplain had to say next.

What that was a rather desperate, "Yes, I see this, naturally, but understanding these mysteries..."

"Renders them no longer mysterious," the antiquary could not resist throwing in. Panic-stricken eyes narrowed in his direction from behind the devil mask. From the dark sockets of the guest's mask he could see no flicker, but there was a discreet nod of agreement.

"Precisely. And is the mysterious not a cornerstone of faith? 'I believe even though I do not see,' rather than, 'I believe because the inner workings have been laid bare before my eyes and labelled clearly for me'? Should thoughts, ideals and beliefs that have endured throughout centuries be reduced to the equivalent of a technical diagram on the galvanic principle?"

For the first time since the invitation had been forced upon him, Lawrence found himself happy to be in attendance, simply for the pleasure of witnessing the odious Pargetter's slump of defeat, as his dreams of literary immortality looked to have flown. No-one, with the exception of the Dean, had displayed such an ability to silence the man. Yet this stranger in their midst had managed to offer a reasoned response that had evidently been heard over the sound of the Chaplain's no-doubt relentless inner voice. Perhaps the outsider felt some sympathy, though, as he continued with, "If, however, I made it my habit only to cultivate and encourage the work of authors with whose every word and sentiment I was in total agreement, mine would be an impossible task. While I freely admit that, on rare occasions, I have been compelled to impose my own impress on a particular work, my inclination is more to let an artiste find within themselves an essential truth. So, if a suggestion would not be deemed unwarranted," a fervent shaking of the head from Pargetter suggested otherwise, "by all means proceed in your attempts to add illumination to that which is preached. But approach it in a manner whereby the full glare of your beam does not cause that which you explore to wither and crumble to cinders. And be aware, always, that if the darkness surrounding these areas of light is made to seem all the darker in contrast, then in these areas may yet be found further mysteries to ponder and perpetuate."

The Chaplain stood nodding dumbly, as if he didn't know whether to regard himself as rejected, commissioned, or edited out of existence, when the man in the white mask left him with the parting words, "You will find what you seek, Chaplain. Have faith." Indeed the demon-masked figure appeared slightly dazed as he raised a hand to a horned forehead and gave a tottering sway, before thrusting out a faltering hand to grasp the table's edge for support. His companion of only a few seconds before gave no indication of noticing, and Lawrence feared he might be given no option but to go to Pargetter's aid himself. But his own reluctant actions were halted when he noticed the lights dimming sharply throughout the hall, the gas dropping so low that the jets flickered like candle flames on the edges of his vision.

When the lighting returned to normal, a huge, furred paw was supporting Lawrence's elbow. "Looks rather like old Burwell's put the funds due to the gas company to other uses," he told the botanist as he recovered his footing.

A mystified grunt issued from the mouth of the bear costume, followed by an admonition that Lawrence had had too much to drink, "Or not nearly enough," and a glass of brandy was thrust upon him.

The babble around him continued uninterrupted, and Lawrence considered the possibility that the unaccustomed pressure of the mask was affecting his vision. Everyone else seemed utterly unfazed by dimming lights—rather almost everyone, as he then caught sight of the Dean waving an irritable hand in the direction of the gas lanterns.

Inevitably Burwell had wasted little time in attaching himself to the evening's guest of honour. "Surely he's not after the money to publish his own book?" Dr. Ferguson muttered. "I reckoned the only reading he ever enjoyed was going over the ledgers every night as he curled up with his cocoa, like the jumped up wee auditor he is."

But the Dean was pursuing other, less high-flown goals. "Of course, we would envisage a complete overhaul of facilities, including the introduction of electrical lighting throughout the various buildings. Naturally this would not be without its cost, but such must be considered an investment in a brighter future... Rather apt, wouldn't you say? A brighter future with electrical lighting?" The attempt at flippancy sank leadenly. "And were the funding to come available..." He left the sentence hanging: his idea of tact in the wake of so blatant an approach. But the man in the white mask gave no response, and the awkward silence demanded filling. This was not a problem for the Dean, for whom it was a rare occasion to find himself lost for words. "Most of the buildings are deserving of modernisation. These old structures have their charm, but charm and practicality don't always sit hand in hand, do they?"

"Then you are one who does not believe that the history of a place becomes ingrained in its fabric over time?" Between the grimacing lips of the tragedian's mask, the Dean's own lips pursed, reigning in his response to this unexpected query, this being one of those rare occasions: obsequious greed overcoming his usual overbearing bluntness.

The guest continued, "Should the physical façade concern us more, or what goes on inside, Professor? So many minds, some of them brilliant, engaged in so much activity over so many years within these walls and the walls of the other great buildings that comprise this institution. Would it not be a great shame to believe that they have left no sympathetic vibration?" Here was a man Lawrence could agree with. He knew only too well of just such places: ones that, even many years after entering, still intruded on his thoughts. And suddenly the conversation between 'jumped up auditor' and impresario, or businessman, or whatever he was, held great interest for him.

The Dean seemed to be looking round rather desperately, as if hoping to spot one of these sympathetic vibrations at work. In the few years since his appointment, he'd made no secret of the fact that he'd happily tear down some of the ancient buildings and fashion the university anew to his own design, functional and stark, though few doubted that he would find room for a statue of himself as the father of this modern rebirth. "It's rather a romantic notion," he finally ventured.

"Romantic? Perhaps. But in my experience, I have found that, just as the character of the architect can shape the building, buildings themselves have characters that can shape those who inhabit them."

As these words were being spoken, Burwell continued his survey of the room. His eyes were therefore not on the man before him when something shifted across the lustrous surface of the porcelain face. But Lawrence's eyes were, and what he saw emerging from the eye socket of that white mask practically caused him to turn and flee into the night. It happened with such rapidity that he might have, indeed frantically endeavoured to, put it down to his imagination, or perhaps that impairment of eyesight that had plagued him throughout the evening. For what he saw was something long and sinewy and encrusted with coarse, dark grey fur, that curled its many-jointed length out of the darkness behind that socket, before rapidly folding back in on itself as it darted from sight.

Was it horror that rooted him to the spot? Was this what prevented him either from fleeing, or from dashing the mask from this stranger to expose the face that lay beneath—if indeed there was any face to be found there at all, and not some gaping maw that would disgorge wave after filthy wave of cloying, clinging webs while the things that nested within the hollows there laughed in voices alien to human ears? Yes, there was horror, but even as his inner voice urged him toward the belief that an old nightmare had not been made incarnate to stand before him, there was something more that left him motionless and staring.

Anyone who, like Lawrence, has spent much of their life in the time-consuming business of studying books and manuscripts will be familiar with the loss of sensation in a limb after hours hunched over the object of their attentions. Such a loss is gradual and creeping and can, of course, be remedied with movement. In this instance, the cessation of feeling was instantaneous and affected more than a single limb. It was as if his entire body had fallen into a sudden, deep sleep, leaving only his eyes awake. And try as he might, strain as he did, he couldn't even attempt that well-known remedy to reawaken his afflicted form, for he was utterly incapable of movement. At least, incapable of movement by his own will.

His head turned, the motion quite involuntary, as the lights dimmed once more. But there was more than a fading in illumination here. The music had grown fainter, and the chatter had died away to whispers and murmurs, before both ceased altogether. That flickering, he now saw, was candlelight after all, flaring away in elaborate sconces that ringed the room. Any lingering suspicion that this was an affliction of his ocular nerves was quashed. Those black, fatty cylinders burning there were real and defined, as clear in his sight as...as the leg or feeler of some abominable spider extending itself from the skull of a visiting bene-factor? If, indeed, benefactor was entirely the right term? Who exactly was this man, and on whose authority was it clear that he was in any way benign? The impression that was given, from the talk of his works in publishing and architecture, was that he was a patron of the arts. However Lawrence had thus far heard no name spoken and had, of course, not yet seen his face. But he knew, beyond mere suspicion, that with this individual lay the source of the mystery that seemed set to unfold around him.

For the moment, his concerted efforts were in the act of focusing—not just his eyes but his mind also—on what might be perceived of his surroundings through the limited field afforded him by the ape's eye-slits. Here were none of the wood panelled walls or portraits, either stern or benign, of long departed Deans and Provosts. Here were arches, framed by greenish grey stone pillars, the darkened recesses within leading he knew not where.

When his eyes were once more permitted to turn in the direction of the man in the white mask, he had gone. So too had most of the revellers, yet the paralysis that held him would allow no opportunity to seek out where they might have departed to. And even had he been able to part his lips to call out to them, he wasn't entirely certain any voice would be heard or, if it were, whether it would be his own voice.

Of the hundreds of guests present moments before, he now discerned only five. A minute or so later, possibly twice that number, as he was once again granted motion to allow, rather to insist, on the turning of his head as some other will compelled him. These wore elaborate masks, as might have been expected, but the gowns beneath them had a sombreness to them that spoke not of celebration but of worship—dark and cowled, with no adornments other than the cords and clasps that bound them at the waist and throat. Here still were animal visages—the shimmering silver of a fish, the black beak of a raven—and other, less easily defined guises. In one he observed a similarity to the baleful face of a chalk giant he had seen carved into a Southern hillside. Others seemed neither man nor beast, but a peculiar hybrid of two or more creatures—a wolf with antlers, a maiden with golden tusks, something with fins and spines that might have crawled from a fever dream of Usborne of Zoology. None of these had he spotted previously that evening, and you may be sure that any one of them would have attracted his attention and been remembered. Then, not one but two faces that he most definitely had seen at close quarters swung into his view, a lachrymose tragedy mask and a laughing devil in scarlet.

Lawrence's earlier musings on a history to that mask he now found himself powerless to remove came forcibly once more to mind. It was plain to one with experience of phenomena outside the norm that what he was now witnessing was an incident from that long history; an incident that had left an impression of itself within the very object. If this were the case, it struck him as equally likely that the wearers of those other two masks were undergoing a similar experience. What followed, then, had three witnesses, from whom the testimony of one we may count as reliable. The testimony of the second is less easy to defend, given the mental state of the witness at the time it was given, though in the main it corroborates the views of the first. And the third? If we accept the accounts of the first and second, we may allow some conjecture as to the experience of the third, for there is no third testimony...

But for the lack of windows and light, the room might have been a church. In those arches lay only darkness. And if this was no church, then the huge oblong mass of stone that lay at the centre of the chamber was no altar. Instead, to Lawrence, who had found occasion to visit many such gloomy locations throughout his years of research, and to Pargetter, whose own line of employment must surely have brought him into such surroundings, it was clear that this was a crypt. And if this was so, in the darkness of those archways, behind shrouds of cobwebs and layers of dust, lay more shrouds and more dust, and the darkness was eternal. While before those gathered, judging from its sheer size, was the sarcophagus of someone of power and importance. Yes, he could see now the profile of the recumbent figure that lay atop it, carved from that same dark stone as the panels adorning the sides of the tomb.

We might imagine the agony Lawrence found in not being able to examine the carvings in those panels, his eyes constrained by the vision of whoever had originally witnessed this scene days, years or centuries before. We might also imagine the terror of the Dean and Chaplain, with none of

Lawrence's prior contact with the otherworldly, to find their movements held fast to the movements of those who had once trodden in this place.

"Come forward, gather near!" The voice that emanated from between the devil's lips was strong, vibrant, and entirely unlike the clogged whine of the Chaplain. Lawrence and the Dean were compelled to gaze upon the scarlet-faced form as he surmounted the shallow steps leading to the sarcophagus. "Are we as one?"

"We are as one." Lawrence experienced a wave of nauseating disorientation as he took an unexpected and uncontrollable step forward. A voice, feminine but as brittle as ice, echoed out from the air around him—close but directionless—speaking in unison with the other voices that filled the air of the mausoleum. It took him a few seconds to establish that the source of this voice was the mouthpiece of the mask he wore, though his own lips had remained set and still. As his vision swivelled from right to left, then back once more, he counted twelve others present—thirteen when he included the original occupier of the place he now apparently stood. Whoever had once worn the ape guise now knelt—the mossy flagstones rushing sharply into the doctor's view—as did the rest of the coven, and joined in the chant in a language that, only after a few moments had passed, Lawrence realised was not his own.

To the Chaplain, a kneeling congregation could have been no unfamiliar sight, and to the Dean, ceremonial duties were a necessary endurance. But Pargetter could never have presided over such a gathering, and Burwell had never knelt in praise of such an unknown, unknowable deity. The incantations were in a mix of tongues, Latin and Ancient Greek being the most instantly recognisable, some Germanic tongue, a few arcane Saxon and Celtic terms. There were even moments of silence, where symbols were described in the air, to Lawrence's eye reminiscent of runes. Logic, what logic could be grasped in such a situation, suggested to the scholar that this had been devised as a code to keep the blasphemies spoken a secret from the uninitiated. But darker thoughts spoke to him of a more alarming reason: an author who had wandered in many lands, who had sought out the very worst as he had explored those cultures at first hand, even those that had declined and died out millennia before. Such was the impression gathered from those words, which were directed toward that monstrous block of the tomb, with its panelling proudly displaying a crest of some description. Even in the weak light, Lawrence had an idea of what was depicted in that crest, for it was something he had already encountered in an unsought mental image that night—the archway and what was framed within it.

For Lawrence, that bestial form that walked in a parody of man, carved in the crumbling stone, had every significance. Here was a connection with an ancient corruption whose influence he had on several occasions witnessed. The name he had always taken as some macabre joke. The old English term for the Devil coupled with a corruption of the word gait—the Devil that walks amongst us. But now, as his eyes were forced to gaze more closely, did he finally detect a significance too in that archway? If the second part of that name had a different meaning... His detached mind swam with the horror of it. But for the other two unwilling participants in this relived desecration, surely there was more horror in what could be glimpsed peering out through the fissure that split one of those panels. The eyes had long since filmed over and shrivelled to dust, but still it appeared to gaze out, skulking, scarred and malign; all the more appalling for those vestiges of long abandoned humanity that still clung to it, even after the passage of time had wrought its ravages, and those other forms of life that clung and crawled there too.

So death had claimed the man who had been known as Sir Nicholas Hobsgate? Lawrence had long pondered the possibility that the ancient diabolist's fearful experiments had actually granted him the secret to immortality after all. Nothing in the scholar's time remained to prove that Hobsgate had died as mortals must: no tomb or marker to his passing. For, even if that was truly he whose remains festered before them, his name had lived on, as had his deeds, in the actions of those who followed him. This was why, a century after the depraved nobleman's death had been reported, the castle that had once been his earthly domain had been razed to the ground, and the crypt smashed up, in an attempt to obliterate his memory.

It was only after a long period had been allowed to pass after the night herein described that Lawrence admitted to entertaining even the most fleeting of thoughts that, under any other circumstances, to have the means to see the centuries peeled back, and to stand regarding times and places of which he had only read, might have a certain appeal. But the sequence that would soon be played out before eyes he could not turn away would do much to diminish that appeal.

One by one, following in the wake of the devil-faced priest, the cowled disciples knelt before the mouldering founder of their cult. Lawrence, when his turn came round, automatically stepped up to the tomb and to the slab atop it that served as an altar.

The slab was black and, like those panels around the sarcophagus, intricately carved. Lawrence looked down upon a man's face, seemingly asleep, while the hair swept out, radiating around the face in waves that twisted between the other, tiny figures carved around it. These figures writhed and curled, caught up in the waves, and the shifting candlelight made them appear almost to be moving— grasping and clawing at one another in a bid to escape those coils.

The carved mouth looked to be smiling. There were touches of green mould in the lines of his pointed beard, the same mossy growth streaking the hair at the temples, and in the widow's peak over the high forehead that curved back into what might have been horns. Just as the name the tomb's occupant had chosen had always struck Lawrence as deliberate, so too the features preserved here appeared by design to be Mephisophelean.

The doctor's eyes were shifted from the stone form as he clasped the symbols of the dark faith. He watched those slender hands lift the dagger with its obscenely carved hilt,

the chalice crusted with hideous smears of long past ceremonies, and the inscribed mirror that reflected back the primate face and those unfamiliar eyes that glimmered there
with a zealous fanaticism. Then, with reverence, each was
returned to the altar.

The ritual was the same for all until that final figure
strode up, the pale lips trembling behind the mournful
mask's contorted scowl. As the tragic figure took the profane
items in turn, instead of returning them to the slab, these
were taken up by his fellows; the cup by the raven, the
mirror by a frog-like thing, and the dagger by the presiding
devil.

It seemed that this may have been some form of initia-
tion, a novice being brought into the fold. But Lawrence had
no time to think more on this, as he then glimpsed, in the
darkness of an archway beyond the tomb, the skull that
observed all. It looked to his borrowed eyes not quite substantial, as if it hung weightlessly, suspended amidst thin
white strands. It occurred to him that long, spiny legs might
uncoil around it, and the whole thing might clamber up and
away into the vaulted heights above. Then he saw more distinctly that it was not after all a skull, but a mask, glimmering and white and classically featured, yet still vaguely
transparent. His sudden intuition was that if he could but
return his gaze to the crumbling sarcophagus, there would
be only lingering traces left of those remains that had spied
upon the living. But this thought was swiftly superseded by
the realisation that arrival of this masked observer meant
that there were fourteen present at the ritual—one too many
for a true coven. Unless one of those already gathered was
not there to worship but served a different purpose. After
all, did a ritual of this nature not require an offering?

The struggle that followed was brief, yet to those powerless to follow their own instincts the moments stretched out
limitlessly. Clearly the sacrifice saw his fate before it was
administered, because his attempted escape was frantic,
stumbling, and sighted before it could even begin.

"Stop him!" The voice shrieked through Lawrence and
around him, pouring out from the lips that had once moved

where his remained frozen. As his vision lurched forward in pursuit of the victim, he saw only a blur of motion—that female hand clawing at a wrist, others rushing forward, the sacrifice restrained—before a desperate, scrabbling hand smashed him across the face. He felt nothing of the impact, but still he fell to his knees as the china mask flew free of his own face to shatter on the floorboards at the feet of those startled revellers around him.

As the music and the laughter burst once more in his ears, the last fleeting image the doctor saw through those eyeholes as they tumbled away was the blade in the devil priest's hand as he lunged toward the sacrifice. Then there was only blackness. And as he removed the hands that he had clasped to his own eyes, he found himself squatting on the floor, rocking on his haunches, too horrified to be concerned by how ridiculous he must look.

What of the Dean and the Chaplain? From where he knelt, he located first one then the other. They were both some distance away and some distance apart, yet he knew that what was happening in this hall here and now mattered little, it was the tragedy that was surely still playing out to both those motionless men through the masks they still wore. Even as he dragged himself to his feet, ready to run to one of them, to tear the mask away and hopefully shatter the illusion for both, he saw the Dean slowly, almost primly, sink to the his knees, before sprawling noiselessly amongst the partygoers.

He was not the sole witness to this occurrence, as a murmur went around that spread in ripples till even the musicians were stilled. Finally a knight in armour pushed his way to the fore, announcing his true identity as a medical doctor, before kneeling to remove the mask. Those who saw the face of the late Professor Burwell later commented that it had apparently taken some effort to prise his fingers from his throat. Yet there were no marks to be seen, no signs of asphyxiation, and the only expression he wore was one that looked, for all the world, like surprise. Which, in hindsight, seems entirely an appropriate response should one's heart suddenly cease in its function for no discernible reason. None could have known the horror that must have stilled his heart: the sight of the dagger looming unerringly closer while knowing that the power to escape had been stolen from him.

Naturally the Dean's plight was the centre of focus for most in the hall, so it may only have been Lawrence who saw the great shudder that passed through the Chaplain before trembling hands wrenched away the grinning red mask. Through eyes that seemed unwilling to focus, Pargetter was examining those hands, as if expecting to find them coated in something unbearable. Forcing his way through the unheeding crowd, Lawrence gently drew the violently shaking Chaplain out of the reception hall and into a corridor, where he opened a window to allow the cool October air in.

His calm assurances that he knew what the man had seen and would believe anything that he may wish to tell him seemed first to steady Pargetter's nerves, before the implications of these words struck home. Lawrence would later admit to some feelings of ruthlessness in pressing the man for answers after what he had just been put through. But he was also certain that any opportunity to discover just how much of the experience had been shared would soon be overtaken by the events unfolding in the main hall, and that either a desperate attempt to rationalise the happening away, or other more severe reasons, would seal the Chaplain's lips.

"There were candles, but I could smell no smoke or feel no heat. No smells, no sensations of hot or cold. No touch. Only the sights and the sounds. I didn't even feel the dagger in my hand, though in my mind its hilt felt cold. I wonder, did he feel it so cold when it went in? Do you think he felt it, hmm? He stopped struggling then... Oh, but then there was something else! It was after he'd stopped twitching. We filled up the cup, like some obscene perversion of the sacrament, then poured the...the contents onto the slab. It was as though the stone was thirsty. Then such a noise, and an eruption of dust and grey strands. The slab of the tomb had split, and inside it, before it crumbled away... Perhaps once it had been a man? Perhaps it was only the unstoppable forces of decay over years that had left the limbs so twisted and misshapen and disjointed?

"One of them, those fanatics, had the mirror with those awful things carved into the frame. It was the woman, the one who had lost her mask, the one who had held him there while the knife did its work. We had to hold the...the body upright, while this creature held the glass before the dead face. Doctors do that, don't they? I've seen them do it, to check for a whisper of breath. Only this was no doctor, and how could he be breathing with that cold thing in his throat? But there was something else then, the smell, so foul and decayed, and it came when they pulled away the mask. Underneath it was a mere lad, young, utterly bewildered looking, and quite dead. But in the mirror, his face was that of something dead for a long, long time. It was that same face we'd seen before it went to dust."

The Chaplain reached out to Lawrence, gripping his wrist. He had more to tell, more that he must tell, more that couldn't be contained. "How is it that I could see these things? Hmm? How is it that I could see, not just through those other eyes, but I could feel in that other's mind? Old thoughts, dark thoughts. If he could have seen our world it would have terrified him, so much has changed. But his thoughts more than terrified me. It had been a game, you see. At the start of it, at least. That's what he'd told them, the other young people. But the ritual took hold. The dagger, the chalice, the masks and the mirror were all waiting down there in the dark. It was as if they had been prepared for them. And those words—even he didn't know where they came from. In the beginning he thought he was inventing them, but by the end he no longer cared that he wasn't! It wasn't a game any more. They'd entered the resting place of a bad man, playing at being wicked. But the bad man wasn't resting, and something of that place entered them. It whispered to them, and it drew them tighter to it. It drew me in as well, with its promises. Maybe if I'd fought it. Maybe if I had summoned my strength I could have held back the knife?"

"We were all of us powerless," urged Lawrence. "I saw what was to happen but couldn't cry out. Burwell saw the knife but couldn't break free. You could have done no different."

But his words held no reassurance. "But would I, even if I could have done? I hated him, you know, hmm? No, how could you have known? He never did! The idea would never have occurred to him. Maybe I wanted to plunge that blade into him. Maybe that's truly what I desired. For true desires were what were promised in those hideous whispers. And then something crawled out of the shadows, and its face was beautiful but as white as the bone, and still it whispered. Have you ever heard a spider laugh? It is the sound of madness and pain and grief and terrible, terrible pleasure!"

With a thrill of horrified anticipation Lawrence recalled that face, not from the crypt, but from within the very building where he now stood. He could not bear the idea that he had been so close to that being into whose shadow he had so frequently felt himself fall and might possibly have let him slip away unchallenged. Others were spilling out into the corridor as the masquerade broke up in disarray. Recognising the doctor who had performed the final diagnosis on the Dean, Lawrence gabbled something about the shock caused by the loss of a dear friend, then hurried off, leaving the Chaplain to his care.

Those still within the hall had removed their masks and all were familiar to him, even if the dazed expressions they still wore were not. Of the tall, dark man in the white mask there was no sign. A ring of porters, sombre yet ludicrous in their colourful garb, were gathered around the prone professor. As a mark of respect, someone had laid a cape across his face until proper arrangements could be made. There was no trace of the mask he had worn in his final moments, nor indeed of the shattered ape face or the discarded devil.

His eyes and his thoughts flew to the alcove by the stage, wherein those bewitched masks had awaited their wearers. The black-clad functionary was not amongst the porters, and Lawrence felt an instinctive certainty that he would not be found amongst the college staff—that he was the servant to quite another master. But still he pulled back the curtain.

In the near-tangible gloom which lay inside that room within the archway, a pale face gazed back into his own. He could see no eyes beyond the slitted sockets, only the darkness peering through from beyond. Perhaps it was an effect of the weak light from the main hall as it struck the polished surface, but the rigid visage looked to him to be smiling. The voice, when it came, betrayed similar traces of amusement. "Shall you see my face, scholar?"

Lawrence faltered. Perhaps his hand would raise and seize the mask and tear it away to reveal the countenance preserved in the stone of that tomb, the saturnine, haughty features framed by the dark swept-back hair and the pointed beard. His hand remained still.

"I know your face. At least, I know the face you would have us believe to be your own."

"Believe?" the voice brayed. "I could canter through this city and caper over the rooftops on burning hooves, and still so few would believe."

Would tearing the mask of the diabolist away reveal the face of superstition, the horns that crowned those animal features that merged with the features of man?

"And why should they believe? That's not your face? Sir Nicholas Hobsgate was a man. That other is the deity he worshipped. You may once have been one or both of these things, but now you are neither. What is a gate but a form of entrance? A portal? Hobsgate was nothing in himself but a conduit for whatever darkness he served. You are an impostor, an interloper, using the names and symbols of another in an attempt to find a foothold. Behind your masks are only other masks."

"And that mask you wear, scholar? The masks that every one of your kind wears? Perhaps all of you need to don guises of some sort to allow your actual personas to truly break through. All those dark little shames you think to keep hidden. The holy man's true colours were revealed only after donning a face not his own. Still, what use to this world is a rationalist priest? And the bullying tyrant would have shrieked his lungs out if he'd had a voice. Of his kind there are more than enough, and he will not be missed. And the intrepid seeker who stares by day and by night into the darkest of recesses? When the mask came off, he hid his eyes and turned his face away. Fearful of nothing, you may hope to look, but I know what you dread."

Lawrence held his ground, aware that his bravado was having no effect, that his own face must have been as pale as the image that looked back at him, but unwilling to grant the mocking creature its victory. "You cling to and encourage ancient fears, but what is it that you're trying to hide?"

"We each present the most acceptable face we can contrive. But, if the Lord of the Flies does not please you, what of those things that devour flies?"

His hand would raise to seize the masks, the white porcelain, the grinning dead man, the Beast, and tear them all away to reveal the face of crawling horror made flesh... No, there was never much flesh on it when it visited his dreams. He would tear them away to reveal...

"What will you reveal if you choose to tear all the masks away? Nothing? Something? Yes, there is something here to be faced. When I had that form with the same needs and desires as any of your kind, what I sought then is what you seek still. Answers. Lost knowledge! The travels I undertook, the studies I made, those amongst whom I walked and with whom I sat and communed... You understand this, Dr. Lawrence. You have felt it. It drives you. It obsesses you. And, eventually, it consumes you, even as you absorb it. I am knowledge made animate. In me flows the wisdom of antiquity. Would you not look upon this? No, for you are afraid, still. You fear that what you might see if you remove this mask is a mirror."

For the briefest of instants, Lawrence's thoughts went to the engraved mirror, the face of the sacrifice becoming that of a husk. But even as he thought this, the true meaning became clear. "No!" His hand shot out, a chill coursing through his fingertips before they could even brush the surface of that gloating porcelain face.

"No, my wisest of monkeys! Tonight you shall see no more evil!"

And, even as Lawrence lunged, the mask dropped suddenly, as if its wearer had instantly vacated it. The thick pall of gloom around it folded in on itself like a furling cloak, and he was alone in that small space under the glow of the gas. The white oval looked up at him with vacant eyes and, with a hesitant hand he lifted it from the green baize, revulsion overwhelming him when the coils of dusty web that coated the interior spilled out and clung to his fingertips. He let it drop to the floor, the better to grind it under his heel.

As he made his way through the hall, he avoided friends and colleagues, fearing that as one of them raised a hand to his face in an expression of grief, when he lowered it the face might come away like yet another mask, revealing a glistening redness, denuded of skin. His knees felt weak and dizziness threatened to topple him when more of the staring throng put their hands to their faces and the vision came of more mournful expressions crumpling like paper between their fingers, displaying bellowing crimson death-masks, white-faced creatures with jaws that distended in eternal screams, costume fronts ruined by scuttling forms that dribbled out from between bare bones.

On shaking legs he made it to the corridor. Here he found the doctor, wearily smoking a cigarette while the Chaplain crouched in a chair beside him, his lips moving rhythmically as if in prayer. The diagnosis was grief, the prognosis was for rest. "At least when he begins to recover, his faith should be a comfort to him."

But Lawrence had his doubts to that matter, in particular when he heard in those whispered words not an invocation to The Almighty, but a plea for protection, "In the names of the Spider, the Skull and the Unholy Goat…"

Throughout the long night that followed, the antiquary pored once more over those papers, gathered over the course of many years and from numerous and often unexpected locations, that now comprised a bulky package, which might have been considered evidence if the one whose deeds it enumerated was still subject to any earthly court of justice. Much that could have cast light on the subject had been deliberately destroyed, and in many cases only obscure hints of that dark influence survived. But all had been filed carefully in the hope that some connection or pattern might one day make itself known to Lawrence. Here he read again that account of the destructive action taken by the townspeople when, at last, they tired of living in the shade of Hobsgate's castle. The catalyst for this uprising was, in the words of the unknown author of that crumbling document, *'that fearful mania that did so afflict the young folk of Greymarsh, that brought dreams of the Evil One nightly to plague them, and that did account for the horrible and tragic murder of one of the town's favoured sons, and the madness that consumed both the son of the town's minister and the sister of he that was slain.'* The righteous people led, on the urging of that grief-stricken minister, by the local bishop, had put torch to both castle and crypt, while prayers were spoken and the exorcism rite performed. It may have been no more than an unfortunate coincidence, but both that minister and his bishop were dead and in their own tombs within the year. And from what Lawrence had that night observed, that cleansing ritual had been performed too late to have any effect.

Naturally the events of the night of the masked ball, those that could be comprehended by the majority, were to have wide-reaching implications for the university. The appointment of a new Dean was of the highest priority, and the Head of Botany found himself somewhat surprised to be filling the role of temporary replacement—publicly aggrieved at the extra duties, privately quite otherwise minded. It also swiftly became clear that Mr. Pargetter was unlikely to return to his duties, though word had filtered through that he had embraced the more traditional service and ritual afforded in the hospital chapel with a passionate intensity that surprised many who had been made privy to his previous views. In the words of that porter who freely spread the news, the former Chaplain had developed tastes that were 'very much of the Old Testament variety.'

The question of patronage afforded by the masquerade's sponsor was quietly forgotten in the disorganisation that followed. No-one could quite remember who the courted patron had been, or even having spoken directly to him. It appeared that he had walked through their company like nothing more than a phantom. Lawrence, who was the only one to show the remotest curiosity about the matter, knew that his enquiries would lead nowhere, and he quietly let the subject drop.

As it was, there were other matters still unresolved that more fully occupied his attention, and many more nights were to be passed without sleep, as he strove to interpret what he had been presented with that night. That the masks had chosen their wearers and not the other way around he felt certain. His role as witness and not as victim or murderer had been marked out by design—one which he was not yet capable of comprehending. Was he shown the scene in that long lost vault as a warning against delving too deeply into dark matters? Or, given that exchange whose occurrence now felt to him as dreamlike and distant as the view through the eyes of that mask, should he see it as an invitation? As he looked once more upon those accounts from many different lands, all of them seeming to tell of the same traveller on some black pilgrimage through places of fear and torment, a voice came to him. These weren't words that had been spoken during that encounter, but still they came in that calm, amused voice. *"In the past, I was you. In the future, might not you be me?"*

"No," he answered back to the shadows of his empty study. "No, that will not do!"

The enemy knew him all too well. Was it the case that what could be taken as a warning or an invitation, was, in reality, a challenge, goading him on to discover more in his endeavours to prove that he and his challenger were nothing alike? Could it be that his curiosity and his belief were perhaps feeding something and allowing it to survive on through future generations of humanity? And, if this proved to be true, could he don the mask of disbelief in the hope of starving it of sustenance?

Having now heard what Lawrence had witnessed, ask yourself, if your eyes had seen what his had seen, could you?

They That Dwell
in Dark Places

This is a ghost story about ghost stories. It tells a tale about the telling of tales, and of the need, the absolute necessity, for stories that strike fear into men's hearts—stories that delve into the unknown and the uncanny.

There is a tradition of reciting frightening stories around the fireside, huddled in the warmth and light, while the shadows dance, and the icy fingers of chill lurk just inches away. This was one such occasion where tradition was being more than fully observed. The evening had long since drifted into night and the talk in our corner of the club's smoking-room was as animated as it had been when we began, over an excellent meal in the supper-room. Our topic, unsurprising given that this was All Hallow's Eve, was that which might be deemed the supernatural. It had begun with a discussion of the various superstitions which once held sway in less enlightened times, and whose influences could even now be seen in such business as the lighting of lanterns to ward off evil spirits.

There had been an air of joviality about our chatter, almost an edge of contempt in our laughter, when we imagined the common man of the middle ages watching the flickering candlelight throwing grotesque shadows upon the walls and casting furtive glances into the dark, fearful of seeing some 'other' thing lurking there.

*The streetlamps were lit but, beyond the wall on the
opposite side of the street, a pool of darkness awaited.*

Naturally, as things often transpire under the effects of a heavy feed and a glass or two of brandy, our company had soon found itself in a form of competition, each fellow attempting to recall the most alarming and blood curdling ghost story he could remember. There was more laughter as familiar legends unfolded: of skeletal horses charging through the night under the whip of a headless coachman, or of foolish virgin brides being saved from a fate worse than death by the return of long lost first wives, interrupting the wedding ceremony to point a pale, accusing finger at their blackguard husbands and announcing, "That is the man who murdered me!"

This contest, with each storyteller trying to top the previous man's effort in grisly detail, had continued throughout dessert, and had followed us into the games-room, where, over billiards, Bayliss had finished off his tale of an ancient bell in a forbidden tower, which only rang to signify the death of a member of the local landowner's family. He spoke of the landowner's resolution to remove it from its tower. Of how the bell had tolled, even as he was unfastening it from its beam, and how both he and the bell had plunged to oblivion at the base of the tower. "And, despite the bell having been broken up, these many years, and melted down or lost," asserted Bayliss, "it is reckoned still to this day, that when one of that man's heirs is facing their last moments on this earth, there can still be heard a mournful chiming emanating from that empty tower."

Over a few more frames, we had savoured descriptions of monstrous scarecrows constructed of more than mere straw and sacking, and an account of a portrait that wept blood. Later, as we settled down for a hand of cards, Marston, losing heavily, regaled us with a pointed piece concerning a private gambling club, its meetings taking place in secret and ever-changing locations, to which entry was by select invitation only, and where to lose was to forfeit a far higher toll than mere money.

At some point, we had decanted to the Smoking Room, with its welcoming fire, the comforting creak of leather armchairs, and the familiar scent of pipe tobacco and old books.

Settled in such inviting surroundings, with the cold October gloom held at bay outside, our conversation proceeded pleasantly, though the tales had grown in their baroque grandeur. With each subsequent account adding yet one more graveyard apparition or night time visitant, one more curse or secret chamber or nameless thing that lurked and gibbered in dark corners, the stories had become so ridiculously overburdened with uncanny events that any inkling of dread which may have begun to gather had dissipated into a warm atmosphere of knowing grins and whispered ironies, while ghost upon ghoul upon spectre were heaped into the mixture for our enjoyment.

"My friends," said I, lighting a cigar on a hot coal plucked from the fire with a pair of tongs, "Your descriptions of these charnel house depredations have been so thorough, I feel as though I have been on a walking holiday around every churchyard and mausoleum in the country."

Marston, a sly glint in his eye, prodded my not inconsiderable stomach and announced, "A walking holiday? That is the most fanciful notion yet put forward tonight! Why, I've never known you to walk further than from the supper table to that sofa and back again!"

I took the jibe, and the laughter it provoked, in good spirit but added, in a mock serious tone, "Whereas you, my dear Marston, I have never yet seen able to walk after your usual intake of port."

Our merriment brought a few cold stares from some of the older members, seated at the far end of the room. But we were not to be put out. If they craved silence, there was a well stocked library on the next floor, where they could while away an eternity without so much as hearing a single word uttered.

As my attention returned from these frosty old troopers to my own group, I felt Anstruther nudge lightly at my arm, and he whispered to me, "I've just realised that one of our number is not joining in with our mirth. Nor indeed, I am suddenly aware, has he spoken one word since we left our places at the dining table."

The companion to whom he referred was a young man, younger than myself at any rate, named Ashbourne. A year or so previously when I had first joined the club, he had been introduced to me as a lawyer with a successful career ahead of him. But, all these months later, it appeared to one and all that his successful career must still be ahead of him somewhere, if it had not bypassed him utterly. Indeed, he had of late become so distracted in manner that I had grounds to suspect that the reasoned arguments of a successful trial might be almost entirely beyond his capabilities. Something, clearly, had been weighing on him, for, though he made no mention of any matter which might be pressing, he was growing more drawn and haggard, while his clothing was becoming increasingly threadbare.

Anstruther was not alone in spotting the quiet member of our party. "What say you, Ashbourne?" enquired Marston, in that booming voice of his that made everyone turn at once to look at our silent companion. "Or, more aptly, what don't say you, since you have been as quiet as the tomb all evening?"

"Again with tombs and graveyard terrors," asked Bayliss. Ever the diplomat, he had clearly sensed the unfortunate Ashbourne's unease at being brought centre stage, and was trying to draw attention from him once more. "Tell us again, that tale of the anatomist who began his grim work only to discover that the unlawfully procured cadaver he was carving was, in fact, his own beloved daughter."

But it was not Marston, who had previously told this yarn with hand-wringing glee, who answered, but Ashbourne, who had found his voice at last. "Why do you seek such horrors? Why is it only the morbid and the unnatural that brings you such pleasure? What joy is there to be found, dwelling in such dark places, and upon such dark matters?" His face was pale and livid, while his body seemed almost to be quivering with a quiet inner rage as he spoke the question. "And what do you know of horror, any of you?"

Our group was stilled for a moment or two, provoking a murmur of satisfaction from one of those elderly relics who had shown such dismay at our earlier jollity. It must be said that, among us, we numbered some very prominent men, most in comfortable middle age, some of us older, some younger. But these were responsible men with a degree of power. Therefore, it was a considerable shock to the system to be so upbraided by a man of Ashbourne's relatively junior years and position. I could sense that one or other of my fellows—the medical man, Harlstane, perhaps or, more likely, the hot tempered old soldier, Wickstaffe—was summoning up the rage to respond with an oath or a threat. Thus it was that I interjected myself, striving to add a trace of good humour which I believed might defuse the situation. "We certainly did not aim to offend or upset your sensibilities in any way, Ashbourne. In fact, the only persons with cause for outrage would be the authors of Penny Dreadfuls, over the wholesale plundering of their storylines."

"This is no joking matter," he told me, unnecessarily. One look into his eyes had been enough to make that point clear.

"In the name of the prophet," Wickstaffe thundered, his round face almost becoming as red as that shocking hair of his. "If the beggar doesn't care for the chatter, why doesn't he shoo away, eh? No-one's forcin' you to keep company with us, laddie!"

Ashbourne lowered his eyes before replying, "But I must keep some company. I cannot be alone. I am being..." Here, he stopped, clearly pulling himself up short, some final word or other being held back, either out of shame or fear. When he looked up once more, his tone had changed. "Gentlemen, I owe you all an apology, and an apology you shall have. I had entirely no right in speaking up against you so, and I ask for your forgiveness."

To their credit, each man nodded his assent, with mumbled entreaties to 'think no more on the matter,' assertions that 'such things are commonplace,' and insistences that it was 'all perfectly understandable.' Yet it was clear from their altered expressions as they regarded Ashbourne that they did not understand his outburst at all. But that understanding was soon to come.

"The lad has an interesting point, don't you think?" rumbled Wickstaffe, now fully calm. "All this talk of spooks and shades is a bit of a queer business, in my book."

I rose and wandered over to the tall window that looked out onto the park beyond. The streetlamps were lit but, beyond the wall on the opposite side of the street, a pool of darkness awaited. "That is what it's all about," I said. "Right from his beginnings, man has been at odds with the dark. His most primitive and underdeveloped ancestors knew for certain fact what modern man only feels as a crawling sensation, prickling at the back of his scalp. That hulking, uneducated brute knew that there are dangerous things lurking beyond the firelight—hidden predators that lie in wait, just beyond the edges of that which we can clearly see.

"The fear is instinctual. A man leading a life in a city like this, in this most civilised of nations, knows that there isn't some wild tiger waiting to pounce at him out of some unlit alleyway. Yet still he hastens his step, and curls his shoulders in on himself for protection as he passes."

"For fear of losing his wallet to some ne'er-do-well," Anstruther whispered to his neighbour, loudly enough for all to hear.

"Maybe so," I countered, "but how many cut-purses would you expect to find loitering in a cemetery at midnight? None. For any thief worthy of the name knows better than to mount an ambush where none shall pass. And yet, even with the knowledge that the graveyard path will be free of footpads, I daresay I will not be seeing any of you gentlemen taking that route home this night."

Marston shrugged, a rueful smile playing round his lips. "Not unless my losses at the card table leave me without my cab fare home, I'd say."

I was warming to my subject and, before one of the group might ask the question I knew to be forming in their minds, I continued, "The telling of ghostly tales is man striking back at the dark. It is a gesture of defiance at a primeval fear which has gripped the species since before the language even existed to express it. For, as we all must be aware, language, vocabulary, and the ability to express ideas are both wonderful tools and mighty weapons.

"By sharing such stories of what you may imagine might be haunting the unlit and unseen areas, you are staring out into the darkness and telling it that it holds no power and exerts no sway over you!"

As I spoke the words, I saw Ashbourne visibly blanch. "But," said he, gazing at the window pane, his eyes wide with wonder and fear, "what happens when you find that there's something in the darkness staring back in at you?"

The effect of this question on those around him was extraordinary. As one, they slowly allowed their gazes to drift toward the glass and the night outside. Just then, a carriage came speeding past on the cobbles below, the clatter shattering the silence like an unexpected thunderclap, startling several of my companions, and causing Marston to lose both his glass, which shattered, and his temper, which broke just as violently. "Somebody close those damn curtains. There's nothing to be seen out there at this late hour, anyhow!"

I moved to do so, gripping the heavy fabric and drawing the curtains as near shut as I could get them, though a gap still remained between them, exposing a shaft of night. This produced an unfortunate effect on Ashbourne, who was at my shoulder so swiftly, it was almost as if he had taken flight. "Open them, please!" It was practically a sob, and he seized the curtains from my grasp and made to fling them apart.

I could see his face reflected in the darkened glass at that very moment when he let out a ragged gasp, and his expression darkened, as if finally admitting defeat and letting exhaustion take full possession of him. He looked almost to shrink half a foot when his entire body sagged into itself, and he released the curtains to my grip with a muttered, "Open them. Please."

I did as he requested, while he allowed himself to slump into a chair. After a moment, he poured himself a double measure of brandy, brought in by the attendant who, entirely unbidden but acting with those abnormally keen reflexes found in the better club employee, had also fetched dustpan and brush to clear away the remains of Marston's glass.

"My story," he began, "may come as something of a disappointment after your creeping terrors and blood-soaked curses. It may not actually qualify as a story at all, since it has no conclusion...unless you accept a man being driven to insanity an ending. There is no sudden, ironic twist, and no explanation for the events I shall endeavour to portray. Therefore, if it does not satisfy the criteria expected of a real story, I apologise. Though you may be assured that the terror I feel is very real. For now, I beg, please do not laugh when I state that I cannot abide partially open curtains during the hours of darkness." He need not have pleaded. There was no laughter to be heard nor smile to be seen.

"When I was a younger man," he said, pausing only to refill the brandy glass, which he had drained in one gulp, "though I am still, technically, young, despite feeling so worn down and tired... Well, before this premature decrepitude gripped me, I, too, was fond of seeking out these tales of the weird. Fond? I was fanatical! I scoured the bookstalls and libraries for anything I could find with a glimmer of the uncanny about it. My dear mother, a Christian and pious lady, was convinced that I was consigning myself to the pits of eternal damnation for inviting such 'devilry' into my life. Imagine, then, her relief when I made my vow to forego my beloved ghostly tales. Of course, she could not have been expected to realise that my reason for choosing to give up the literature of the macabre was that I had grown bored of it, with its avenging phantoms and midnight rides through haunted woods. These tales no longer held my fancy, and I no longer wished to read ghost stories. No, gentlemen. I wished to live one!"

"You went actively seeking the supernatural?" I challenged. "Surely, if you believed in such matters, you were aware of the dangers of such a course?"

The young lawyer sighed as he regarded me, then replied, addressing himself to the entire group. "I did not give a moment's thought to dangers. The young seldom do. All I cared for, at that time, was the thrill of seeking out a new experience, my thinking being that, if reading about phantoms produced such a pleasurable thrill of terror, how much more so would the feelings be intensified by actually encountering one?

"However, what you are no doubt waiting to hear, gentlemen, is just how I planned to make contact with the unknown. To that, I must answer with a query—how would you imagine I might make my attempts? With the spirit board and glass, of course, just as in the stories you have been exchanging all night.

"I was in university, by now, and I had made friends who were as keen to experiment as I, and not merely with tarot cards and the Ouija. One such friend managed to persuade me that our efforts to pierce the veil and commune with those on other planes might be rewarded if we were in a more 'susceptible' frame of mind...and thus began my flirtation, and subsequent love affair, with powder and pill. My student days passed in a hazy rush, and still my pursuit of the worlds beyond continued. Then came the day that my mother returned home to find me with the cards and the board, and I was in the street within minutes.

"Lodging with genuine friends, I was forced, slowly and painfully, to give up my twin addictions. And, with some difficulty, I managed to claw my way through my course with an almost respectable qualification, which led me to an almost impressive position with an almost successful firm of solicitors. In this new, respectable life, I would establish myself and prosper. Sadly, however, the firm to which I had entrusted my future to prosper, had a policy of accepting some clients and taking on some cases that other firms might not have welcomed so readily. One such case was the house at Greymarsh!"

Here Harlstane tapped his skull, attempting to dislodge a memory from its hiding place. "Greymarsh? That's in the North, isn't it? Over the border, even? I recall reading something about the town, and a house on the outskirts. An old priory, if memory serves."

"Your memory does serve," Ashbourne replied. "If you knew the full reputation of that old house, and what is spoken of it in that frightened little town, you would find it hard to forget. The Priory, long since empty, was being sold, with the purposes of turning it into a sanatorium. I accepted the task of providing a written report on the condition of the building, following the previous owners' unexpected departure."

"Still hunting ghosts?" Wickstaffe scoffed. "A fool's errand, boy."

"Quite the contrary. I knew all of the stories...well, many of the stories. I do not reckon that anyone living knows all of them. But I wanted to go to this dark, empty house, and tell the darkness that I knew nothing lived there. I would use this as my opportunity to face the shadows, and my own foolish past, and put them both behind me. And, to achieve this, I would spend the night in the haunted house.

"How would I describe that house? Brooding? Not a house, but a living thing? A great grey spider, crouching at the top of a hill, waiting to pounce on anyone or anything foolish enough to venture near?" A bitter laugh followed this description. "To my thinking it was merely stones and slates, and stones and slates posed no danger to me."

"I came equipped with candles and a small hamper, and set up my temporary billet in one of the many bedrooms, filled with the debris of a suddenly fled inhabitant. And thus I waited and watched to prove to myself that nothing unnatural was to happen there.

"Unfortunately, I was wrong!

"My lonely vigil had begun to weigh down upon me, and I had started slowly to drift off into sleep. I had drawn the heavy bed curtains tight around the four-poster, not wishing the light of my candle to be seen through a window by anyone passing and, in consequence, inadvertently adding fuel to the local legends about the place. I have no idea how long that I, cocooned within those curtains, had been drifting in and out of sleep. A few times, my eyes had fluttered open and registered that the candle had burned lower. On what may have been the fourth or fifth instance of this, I observed that the candle, now burnt almost entirely out, was guttering, as in a draught. I, too, was aware of a flow of chilly air that I had not encountered earlier. Still befuddled by sleep, and not remotely making anything of it, I turned idly and saw that the curtains at the foot of the bed were open, just a few inches, showing a sliver of the darkness beyond.

"I was just reaching a fumbling hand to draw them closed again when I registered the awful face that was staring at me through the gap!"

Some startled exclamations greeted this alarming image that our young friend had conjured up, and I am more than certain that, in that instant, each man listening had, in his own mind, pictured a particular awful face straight from their own darkest imaginings.

Ashbourne took a sip before plunging onwards with his weird narrative. "In an instant, I had thrown myself bodily to the head of the bed, as far away from this unexpected observer as my cramped confines would allow. I was unsure whether it planned to continue merely staring at me, or if it was going to advance on me with dread purpose gleaming in those dark, dark eyes. And, at that moment, just as the tips of withered and waxen looking fingers began to creep round the curtain edges, the candle went out, and I was alone in the dark with the owner of that curiously unformed face and those unfinished hands.

"Not waiting for this silent being to come scrambling across the mattress to me, I hurtled out of the bed and through the side curtains, nearly winding myself by stumbling over a bed-side chest of drawers, and landing in a heap in the corner. Looking up, fully expecting to see some pale thing bearing down on me out of the dark, I was relieved, then puzzled, then alarmed to note that I was alone in the bedroom, and that the curtains at the foot of the bed were drawn once more.

"Striking a 'Lucifer' and hefting the heavy leg of a broken table, I dashed forward and prodded at the bed hangings, in case my nocturnal visitor had made itself comfortable within the bed, and was awaiting my return. Eventually, I summoned up the courage to pull the draperies back. There was no-one or nothing within."

Marston laughed, a little more shrilly than usual, I fancied. "Is that it? You think you saw something when you were half asleep in a house that is believed haunted, and where your imagination was obviously overwrought?"

Ashbourne laughed, too, and his laughter was similarly shrill and close to hysteria. "If that was merely it, I should still be considering what an alarming experience it was, whilst also giving thanks that it was more than likely a nightmare, brought on, as you say, by my surroundings and their supposed history. However, since that time, I have seen that abominable face again on more than one occasion. In truth, gentlemen, I fear that I am being haunted by it.

"The event I have just described—that strange night in that strange bedchamber—took place rather over one year ago. In the months that have followed, I have witnessed that oddly ancient yet curiously smooth and featureless face staring at me countless times, and the frequency of these sightings is on the increase. And while, frankly, you...some of you, at least, may question my sanity, I assure you that I am quite sane. Though I am unsure if I shall retain that status throughout this Hallowe'en night!

"After fleeing the Priory, now convinced that its ranking as a haunted spot was well deserved, I had found myself at the village inn and, after rousing the landlord, who was none too welcoming, I procured a room and fell into a sound sleep which lasted most of the day. So it was that I rose when the sky was already darkening, and I was forced to take an overnight train back to London, if I wanted to avoid missing a day's work and a day's pay. I obtained a compartment, not wishing the company of strangers while my addled head tried to process the extraordinary events of the preceding night. I even found myself giggling, somewhat foolishly, at the thought of my prior attempts with incantations and occult matter to call up an unearthly spirit, all of which had ended in failure, while an endeavour to disprove the existence of such things had summoned a monster.

"Naturally, within my briefcase, I had a pencil and paper, and I began to make notes and memoranda concerning my visit to the town and that house. I must have been engaged in this for quite some time, since I recall glancing at my watch and seeing that we were already well into the new day. Standing to alleviate the cramp that had set in as I'd huddled over my legal pad, I fancied that a short stroll along the carriage's corridor would loosen me up a little. This was when I again caught sight of it—that pale face and those

strange hands, holding the curtains open on the compartment window, just wide enough to look in on me.

"A few moments of darkness followed, which were as terrible as those I had endured in the bedroom. But, again,
nothing assailed me and, when the train emerged from the
tunnel, I was alone and unobserved, though I could hear the
ticket collector chattering as he worked his way along the
corridor. I would have asked him had he seen anyone loitering outside the compartment, until I caught sight of
myself reflected in the glass of the doors and realised that
what I had seen was not the face itself, but its reflection. I
knew then that it had not been staring in from the corridor,
but was watching from outside of the train, following my
escape through the night.

"After this I began to find myself almost expecting to see
it, and it was frequently there. On visiting relatives, I would
glimpse it, immobile, beyond the parlour curtains, like some
ruffian hidden beside the garden path, waiting to cut me
down as I would leave for home. In the offices of my firm,
there is a cellar which is accessible only by passing through
a curtained alcove. I've seen it there and, as you may
imagine, I find it impossible to enter that cellar, even though
it contains the files on all our cases. The junior clerks have
begun to whisper about me, and my superiors, I know, are
watching over me. Hah! As if there wasn't already something
watching over me.

"You see, even after all this time, and even though I
expect to see it, I am still terrified by its every appearance.
And, just last week, I ran screaming from the gentlemen's
outfitters three streets away from my office, because they
expected me to enter a changing room behind a curtain,
where I could clearly see my silent follower waiting in the
gloom within.

"At least, it was silent. Until today, that is...

"Having finished my working day just as the sky was
darkening, I was hastening homeward through the usual
five o'clock crowds. I have made quite a habit of keeping my
head down when I am out and about, lest I should inadvertently look upon my follower looking upon me from some

new position. I realise ignorance of danger is no defence, but I do not think my mind or my heart could take the strain of discovering from just how many outlooks it can watch my progress toward my early grave. Therefore, I have become quite adept at moving through a flow of people while my eyes are fixed on the pavement directly ahead of me. So, accidents, like this evening's misadventure, were commonly avoided. But there, without warning, and thrust directly into my path, was the baby carriage.

"I was far from graceful as I ducked back to avoid the wheels of the perambulator and, even as I raised a hand to steady my fall, I felt the chill touch of some fabric, brushing against my extended wrist. Looking up sharply, I was horror-stricken to find that I was teetering back towards a set of dingy curtains that hung in the open doorway of a disreputable looking haberdashery.

"In a panic, I pitched myself forward, grasping wildly for some form of support that I might use to pull myself back from the gloom that lay beyond those curtains. My hand happened upon the handle of the perambulator, causing it to tilt violently and spill out an assortment of rattles and ribbons and other childish paraphernalia.

"I realised that I must have appeared like some wild madman, as I struggled to keep the child's carriage upright. The infant inside, as one might expect, did not take kindly to being jostled so vigorously and protested in a keening, high pitched shriek.

"I scrambled about for one of the scattered toys to pacify the child, oblivious to the actions of the mother, who was rocking the carriage on its springs and murmuring soothing tidings from behind her veil. I proffered the silver rattle, toward the infant. Then my hand was stilled as I looked upon that veiled lady. She was raising her hands, lifting the folds of the lace, parting it.

"Averting my eyes from the horror that I knew must be revealed before me, I turned toward the child... The child, concealed behind yet more veils and shawls, draped over the hood of the carriage to keep the cold October air away from what lay within—craning to face me through the gap in the curtaining, a pale hand stretching out between the gap, too long to be a child's arm. Too long and withered and waxen! And then, it spoke my name. Not in the voice of an infant. In a whispering gurgle, as though the darkness it nestled in was thick and liquid..."

"Ashbourne," I said, "Enough, now."

A few of the others murmured their agreement, though I would venture to say that their eyes betrayed a morbid fascination with the young man's progressively more frantic account.

"It doesn't just hide in the dark," he mumbled. "It can hide in the darkness inside people.

"I ran. I found myself here, where I knew there would be others, where I would not be alone with the darkness."

An attendant had come through, silently waiting with our outer coats. Bayliss took this as his cue, rubbing his hands as if cold, unmindful of the still blazing fire. "Time we good gentlemen were heading homewards." He cast a sympathetic glance at our broken and defeated member, whom I was helping into a threadbare overcoat.

"I'm relieved, at last, to have told you my tale," Ashbourne said, a game attempt at good cheer in his voice. "You cannot imagine the strain it has been, knowing that you are alone with such monstrous knowledge."

"You are not alone," I told him, leading him slowly down the great marble steps and through the reception hall. A discreet nod to our other companions assured them that our distraught cohort would be delivered safely to his home. As the remainder of the group drifted apart, they formed into coteries of two or more, making arrangements to share transport, with gruff statements that it would be "a damnable waste of money to take separate cabs going in the same directions." Thus they went, each of them unwilling to voice the dread of carrying Ashbourne's tale alone with them through the darkened streets.

"Never alone," smiled Ashbourne, grimly, as I flagged down a carriage. He merely glanced once at the curtained windows on the side doors, then lowered his gaze again, until I waved it on.

"I once saw the face in a carriage window," he confided, as we walked in the direction of his lodgings. "I was within, looking out. It was without, glaring in." He fell silent, and it was I who spoke throughout the rest of our walk.

"Science is obliterating the last dregs of superstition. Where once there was the belief in magic, there is now the confidence in technology, and the rational is replacing the irrational. The creatures of myth and folklore, the demons and the spectres, have little influence in modern man's world! Soon, there will be nothing left to fear."

We had entered the building where the young lawyer held his lodgings: a small set of rooms on an upper floor in a tall building. Even from the street, I had observed that the curtains were already drawn, permanently closed against the external darkness. Ashbourne unlocked the door to his rooms and, before entering, flicked a switch that was mounted just within the doorway. Electric light flooded the narrow hallway, so intensely bright that I had, for a moment, to shield my eyes against the glare, before joining him, uninvited but unbarred, inside his home. He had moved through to a compact sitting room, again filling it with the glow from a ceiling bulb.

"Here again is an example of what I was striving to describe," I intoned, indicating the glowing bubble of glass. "A dread atmosphere does not come with glowing filaments, rather in the fluttering shadows cast by candlelight. And, just as science and philosophy and alienists, with their studies of the human mind, are blotting out the ancient beliefs, so a thing like this, man's ability to harness a natural force such as electricity, is gradually keeping the darkness at bay. Before many years have passed, this power will illuminate the whole globe or, at the very least, those parts of it inhabited by humanity.

"And, if the darkness can be held back, then what of those things that dwell in dark places? There would seem to be no place for them in this newer, brighter world."

"I thought there was no place for them in the current world," said he, looking right at me. "I thought that, even as I entered one of those dark places and brought a passenger out with me."

I smiled at this term. "Some creatures will cling on most tenaciously to ensure their survival. And now, you have unburdened yourself. Your story is told. And your dread is shared, and it has multiplied."

"Is that what you think I have achieved?" he asked, a hint of a challenge in his tone.

"I know so," I told him, walking past him to the bay windows that took up half of one wall. "That is, after all, what I planned."

He nodded, to himself more than to me. "Then it is true, what I glimpsed over your shoulder, reflected in the smoking room window as you made to draw the curtains. It was only for an instant, showing up against all that darkness on the other side of the glass. Your real face was breaking through..."

I had no need for the disguise anymore. The body that had served as my host, a man with an enormous capacity for darkness within him—a man who had remained resolutely unaware of my frequent residencies within his form—would be discarded soon. Such men are easy to find.

"But why this masquerade?" he demanded.

"There were some places where even I could not watch over you," I admitted. "And I needed to be there to ensure that the circumstances were right for you to share your torment. This form, this fleshy clothing, has merely been a transport for what I really am." I used the hands of my flesh host to pull back the curtains and, in the gap that opened up before me, my own, more fearful face was reflected back. Then, drawing them wider apart, until the window was nothing more than an obsidian void, I beckoned the lawyer to me.

"You have kept me, for a long time, peering in from the darkness, waiting just beyond the veil that separates our different worlds. I have waited for you to seize the chance and throw back the veil...to face me and all that you fear. Now you must witness things from my perspective. Now, you are ready to find out what else we have waiting in the darkness."

He seemed to step toward the curtains almost willingly, until I allowed the mask to slip fully from my face, and my true features were revealed to him under the stark electric lighting. Seeing the face that had so haunted his mind for all this time had a dreadful effect on him, and he began to struggle. So I snapped his ribs, and pierced his heart with my fingertips, and dragged him through the curtains into the darkness beyond.

He would be found shortly afterwards, he and the remains of my host, impaled on the railings below, his chest torn wide. Some terrible accident would be supposed. A struggle would be suspected, and rumours would spread that the young man had been slowly losing his mind and had attacked his friend in a delusional frenzy.

But others, certain powerful and prominent men, would know that, really, something so awful that it defied description had visited that spot on that Hallowe'en night and had, perhaps, walked amongst them. And they, too, these most rational men, would draw their curtains tightly against the night time, and instil in their children the knowledge that something does exist beyond their own little pools of light.

And this knowledge is one that shall thrive, despite mankind's attempted advances out of the dark. Which is as it should be. For we that dwell in dark places do not wish to be forgotten. We like you to know that we are here, always, and to look to us occasionally.

Otherwise, we will be compelled to look in on you...

Author's Note:

Shedding Light on Dark Places

THE SHADOW IN THE STACKS

Although I've only recently realised it, M.R. James has been with me since my childhood. I can't remember now if my first encounter with his ghost stories came when I was nine, through a television series called *'Spine Chillers'* (in which the fine actors Freddie Jones, Jonathan Pryce, John Woodvine and Michael Bryant narrated uncanny tales for the nation's children), or if it was in the pages of an anthology compiled *'for readers of eleven and over'* by Kathleen Lines, *'The House of the Nightmare and Other Eerie Tales,'* which I borrowed frequently from my primary school's library; I was closer to seven than eleven at the time. Whichever the case, I certainly remember that first tale, *'A School Story,'* for I can clearly recall my drawings of creatures with that were *'beastly thin'* and *'wet all over'*.

I don't think I read any more of James's stories throughout my teenage years, (though I did enjoy a further series of televised readings with Robert Powell), and I may even have forgotten the name of the author of that story which had so fired my childish imagination. Then, in the early 1990s, the BBC began an annual repeat showing of the adaptations directed and, initially at least, written by Lawrence Gordon Clark in the 1970s under the banner *'A Ghost Story for Christmas.'* From my first viewing of these quietly menacing versions of *'The Stalls of Barchester,'* *'A Warning to the Curious,'* *et al*, I was hooked on M.R. James again, and I haven't been without at least one copy of his Collected Ghost Stories close to hand ever since.

Following the *'Imagination Theater'* production of my radio adaptation of *'They That Dwell in Dark Places'* I wanted my follow-up script not only to be Jamesian in nature, but also to attempt to capture the mood of those Gordon Clark films. In particular, I was taken with his creation of Dr. Black (played by Clive Swift in *'Stalls'* and *'Warning'*) as a substitute narrator for James himself. Thus was born Dr. Lawrence, the name being a tribute to Dr. Black's creator (though I envisaged Lawrence more as Michael Bryant in *'The Treasure of Abbot Thomas'*). The necromancer's name was borrowed from an unfinished earlier work of mine; at the time I did believe Sir Nicholas to be long-dead and buried. Yet some individuals, once invoked, refuse to remain still.

The Mound

The germ of this tale came when I lived in a flat which overlooked a long, wide communal back garden. It was my habit, late at night, to stand at the open kitchen window to smoke a cigarette, my then-wife 'being of that breed of woman who cannot abide, etc.' Looking out across that moonlit lawn, I would imagine something detaching itself from the shadows between the trees at the far end and moving slowly across the grass to where I stood. And, frequently, something (rather some *things*) did. However, hopping rabbits aren't altogether effective in the context of a supernatural tale – not even ghost rabbits – but the association of rabbits and burrowing gave rise to something subterranean making its relentless progress.

The story sat in my head, unwritten apart from the opening paragraph, for a few years. I knew this was never going to be more than an anecdote, and, as such, it seemed the ideal length for posting in the creative writing section on

The Vault of Evil – a splendid online forum for the discussion of horror anthologies and pulp fiction. From here, it was picked up by Rog Pile and Steve Goodwin for publication in issue 3 of *'Filthy Creations,'* the spin-off magazine from that creative section, where it was also very capably illustrated by Rog.

The flat is now long behind me. The rabbits, as far as I know, are still there, though I'm not convinced the sight of them will have the same morbid effect on anyone else standing viewing from the kitchen window.

The Beacon

Like *'The Shadow in the Stacks,'* this story began life as a radio script. I'd always believed a lighthouse would be a perfect setting for a ghost story, the isolation adding to the dread when something unexpected knocks upon the door. I've since discovered that I'm not alone in that belief, and that there are old dark lighthouse stories aplenty to be found in anthologies.

I first became aware of the real-life mystery immortalised in *'The Ballad of Flannen Isle'* thanks to the *'Dctor Who'* story *'The Horror of Fang Rock'* and Tom Baker's closing recitation of that famous poem. Despite my best efforts, my three lighthouse keepers still owe much to the three keepers in that *'Doctor Who'* adventure, while the thing that crawls up the stairs is my homage to Japanese horror movies like *'Ringu'* (itself a brilliant modern day Jamesian story).

I should also add that the story's doctor borrows his name from Rosemary Pardoe, who, through *'Ghosts and Scholars'* (and its successor, *'The Ghosts and Scholars M.R. James Newsletter'*) has published many excellent pieces of original Jamesian fiction, articles on James and his contemporaries, and even newly discovered drafts and fragments of previously unrecorded ghost stories by James himself.

"Shalt Thou Know My Name?"

My earliest attempt at this story began with the pretext of a narrative being formed from documents relating to an inquest into the peculiar deaths of two rival scholars. This framing device was abandoned once I decided to write it as a radio play rather than a short story, as a simpler set up which cut down on the number of narrators involved seemed more apt. And, since I already had an antiquary with a particular interest in the peculiar to hand in the form of Dr. Lawrence, the solution was simple.

My initial inspiration came when I read that a now-deceased film historian was given, in his famous movie guides, to creating factual inaccuracies in a bid to trap plagiarists. Now, what if this trap was a fatal one? The idea took shape...but it was a shape already familiar from 'Casting the Runes.' And the revenant conjured up was inspired by another M.R. James story, 'The Tractate Middoth' (more accurately, by the photograph of that story's phantom on the cover of the tie-in book to the 1960s television series of classic adaptations, 'Mystery and Imagination'). Clearly M.R. James was much in my mind as I wrote this one, as was Fritz Leiber's classic novel, 'Our Lady of Darkness,' though I wasn't aware of quite how much I was constructing a patchwork of James's ideas until others started to point out elements of a good half-dozen or more stories of which I hadn't been conscious while writing.

If this sounds a little 'methinks he doth protest too much', considering that here is a story in which a plagiarist is horribly done to death by some ghastly abomination, under the circumstances might it not be wise to over-plead my case?

The Wager

This one started out as a radio script, as yet unaired. While I was writing the play, I had the chance to view the 'Mystery and Imagination' adaptation of Robert Louis

Stevenson's *'The Suicide Club,'* and I noted certain obvious similarities to Vincent Style's adventure. What prevented me from abandoning the idea was the notion of the Club Tenebrosa's patrons, those unseen spectators in dark places. I did rethink my plans to have a mysterious black-clad woman guiding Style through the various games on offer; Hildegarde Neil makes a very alluring femme-fatale in that television version. In her stead, the butler emerged, and he, as the emissary for Sir Nicholas Hobsgate, has been pressed into service several times since. There may well be a story in the manner in which the butler entered into Sir Nicholas's employ. As it is, this was the also first instance where it became evident to me that Sir Nicholas was not only still very much active, but also liable to make his presence felt again.

THE CRIMSON PICTURE

This story began, appropriately enough, with a picture. Imagining the cover to a Fontana-style anthology, I sketched a man throwing his hands up to obscure his view of some dreadful thing. That something proved, after a burst of scribbling with a red pencil, to be a portrait of some malevolent subject. The idea swiftly followed of a visitor to an exhibition being greeted by a painting that would bring years of terror rushing out in an account of how, as a struggling artist, he had been given a mysterious commission. So, I had an image, the midnight appointment, and the subject who transpires to be deceased. And nothing more came of it.

I toyed with the idea of a non-supernatural solution, and using it as a basis for a Sherlock Holmes story. Here the artist is struggling because his style is outdated. Why has he been given the task of painting a dead man? Let's suppose an inheritance has been tied-up for decades because the rightful heir can't be traced. Should those who stand second-in-line happen to have the corpse of an unfortunate derelict on their hands, and the services of an artist who might provide a suitably antiquated portrait of the missing heir's father, might not the family resemblance between portrait and dead man convince the authorities that the heir has died, thus freeing up the fortune?

A long chat with my dearest friend Craig (who has since found his way into a story as *'Ferguson of Botany'*) convinced me to bring the focus back on the supernatural, and Craig (no mean artist himself) helped enormously in sketching in some of the reasons behind our painter's mysterious assignment, while some long-abandoned notions for a Faustian play, also involving an artist, gave me the rest.

It was here that I first became aware that threads were beginning to develop between certain stories, for it seemed appropriate to link the drowned lord here with the lord who I'd already drowned in 'The Beacon'.

RAGS

There is something unsettlingly eerie about the genuine Cloutie Well, which Ferguson of Botany and I encountered while driving across the Black Isle, just North of Inverness, back in 2001. The sight of trees by the roadside bedecked in thousands of different coloured rags was so unexpected that it was a tough choice between stopping to investigate or stepping on the accelerator in case we'd stumbled into some *'Wicker Man'* scenario. But the inhabitants of that part of Scotland would consider sacrificing visitors far too rude, so we stopped and had a look around – though we didn't stay long, just in case. On reading of the legend behind those rags, the idea of something nasty occurring to anyone removing them was born.

A few years later, the subject of ghost stories came up during a taxi-ride, and the driver told me of the night he'd spent in a Highland bothy where he wasn't entirely convinced that it was only his rucksack occupying the other bed in the room. And, late in 2008, when I was looking for new stories for this volume, those two memories collided and combined.

The Travelling Companion

I'm one of those people who can't happily travel anywhere without a book for company. Mainly it's the twenty minute bus commute to and from work four times each day, for which anthologies are a godsend. And, when I'm between books, I always have one of my inexpensive M.R. James editions ready to shove in a pocket – unfortunately inexpensive copies of H.S. Grace's collections are rather more difficult to come by, aside from that one I found by accident in a secondhand bookshop on one of my travels, which started the long, often frustrating task of completing the set.

So, in a way, Mr. Endicott is based on me. As are several of the incidents which plague him; the crawling newspaper, the streetlights extinguishing themselves one by one overhead, the black umbrella that comes scuttling alarmingly out of the dark, these are all things that have happened to me, though not, I'm glad to say, within the space of a single journey.

The original idea here was to have the haunted book be a collection of James' stories, yet the time period was wrong; James, although his output had slowed, was still writing ghost stories up until shortly before his death (his last, 'A Vignette,' was published posthumously). I was also slightly (make that *very*) daunted at the prospect of creating fake James extracts for the altered edition. But, when I was making arrangements with Dr. Grace's Estate for the inclusion of one of his stories, they were gracious enough to allow me to pastiche his style and were, in fact, amused by my interpretation of the events which led to his still unexplained decision to cease writing ghost stories.

I should also thank M.A. Allen for allowing me access to her transcript of the remaining fragment of 'Delve Not Too Deeply,' which is, of course, nothing like the short story I've included under this name as part of the plot, although my Dr. Grace does refer to the events contained within the genuine article.

A RAVELLED TRESS

Throughout my twenties I had very long hair, which I kept in a ponytail until, feeling that a change was needed, it was time for two feet of hair to go. Rather than simply chop it off, I was sponsored to have my head shaved for charity. The hair was pleated and bound, and a work colleague, Riona, made a small cardboard coffin in which to inter it once the scissors had done their work.

On happening to find that miniature coffin again in the back of a cupboard, I was amused by thoughts of how a future inhabitant of my house might react if they were to discover this peculiar casket and its contents years after I'd gone. At which point the characters began talking, I began to take dictation, and the first draft emerged complete in a single sitting. Fortunately when I submitted the story, Joe Morey at Dark Regions Press spotted the flaws in construction that my initial burst of enthusiasm had blinded me to, and the story is much stronger for my being urged to go back and look at it with a fresh eye.

Sir Nigel is named after Nigel Kneale, as there's a passing similarity here to 'Baby', a particularly creepy episode of his series 'Beasts,' in which a nasty hairy thing is found long hidden in a newly inhabited house. Oana, the young lady from whom Luciana borrows her dark, foreign beauty, shares none of that character's less pleasant traits, I'm relieved to say.

'AND STILL THOSE SCREAMS RESOUND...'

Thanks to technical difficulties with an old e-mail address, the proposal for this collection arrived later than anticipated and on the same day as an invitation from Charles Black (also late, due to the same technical problems) to submit a story for 'The Fourth Black Book of Horror' (the two previous Dr. Lawrence stories having made their debuts in the first and second volumes of that series, and I'm grateful to Charles for allowing the story's appearance here almost simultaneously with the publication of volume Four). Luckily I already had a story in mind, one that had its basis in an earlier project of mine...

Christmas 2000, and a group of friends (among them the very talented illustrator of this collection) are gathered for an evening of ghost stories, a suitably Jamesian pursuit. The plan was that each would write and recite their own story. Typically, as the instigator of this plan, I couldn't decide which story I wanted to tell. My solution? I would write them all, and let the audience decide which they would hear. What I presented was in the style of the old 'Choose Your Own Adventure' role-playing books. Those gathered would, in the character of an estate agent sent to investigate an old property, be allowed to choose which rooms they would visit in a house with a particularly long and unpleasant history, each choice leading to one of a number of nasty little scenarios. Thus was born Wraithvale Priory, a house on the edge of reality.

Months of work went into creating a mystery at the heart of the Priory that would, if the correct choices were made, reveal itself to the players. Except, of course, that the debut audience made the wrong choice first time round and got themselves killed straight away. (I won't reveal anything more concerning the Priory, as I'm sure that I will revisit it some day, and that there are more things behind closed doors there than I knew when I first set out to explore it.)

Following three stories in which Lawrence is presented with other people's experiences, the time had come to let him take centre stage. The opening, mentioning a few of the antiquary's adventures, is inspired by Conan Doyle's tantalising hints of untold cases of Sherlock Holmes, involving giant Sumatran rats and remarkable worms unknown to science.

What I hadn't expected was to discover quite how dark a tale the good doctor had been concealing, for it was only as the first draft was nearing completion that the revelation emerged that he possessed the means to rescue his former friend yet chose not to. Sometimes it's nice to be surprised by your characters and their actions (even if these aren't so nice), and this 'afterthought' is now one of my favourite things about the story.

THEY THAT DWELL IN DARK PLACES

AN UNWISE PURCHASE

It may seem odd that, in choosing one of Dr. Grace's stories to reprint, I didn't opt for one that I'd already mentioned in *'The Travelling Companion,'* but a couple of coincidences led to the selection of this story.

Firstly, Hartwell's childhood nightmare concerning the tin spiders is uncannily close to a dream I once had, in which the ceiling above me was undulating with thousands of these creatures. And, secondly, the ship which carried the murderous sailor back to England shares a name with an old friend of mine who happened to e-mail me on the day on which I had to confirm my final choice of story with Dr. Grace's Estate.

Luckily, before I sent the final copy to the publisher, my friend and colleague, Mark, alerted me to the fact that a glitch somewhere had lead to several pages (between Hartwell's visitation by the three monstrous monkeys and his final public descent) being omitted, which left the story feeling rushed and not totally comprehensible.

THE UNMASKING—AN EVENING OF REVELS AND REVELATIONS

This is the only story in this collection that I wouldn't consider submitting elsewhere, as it relies on familiarity with several of the stories that precede it. But, as this collection gathers all of the existing Lawrence and Hobsgate tales, it felt appropriate that the two should at least be allowed to meet face to face—though whether Sir Nicholas could actually be described as having a face, I can neither confirm nor deny...

It's also the story with the longest gestation period of any in this collection, the initial idea having been jotted down in 1999. The original version formed part of a proposed series of Young Adult novels set around the haunted town of *'Dark Harbour'* (think of a combination of *Buffy*'s Sunnydale, *Dark Shadows'* Collinsport and Lovecraft's Arkham, only set in

Scotland), which was where Sir Nicholas Hobsgate was also due to have made his debut. In the Dark Harbour series, a modern day incarnation of Hobsgate was to have been the recurring villain, hiding behind his respectable guise as chairman of the Hobsgate Executive Corporation, a company unduly interested in the strange goings on investigated by the intrepid teenage heroes.

In that version of *'The Unmasking'*, HEX Corp's sponsorship of a masked carnival would see the donning and removal of masks having drastic effects on the townspeople. In the current version, the three masks which reveal different views of the same tragedy, came from one of the incidents in that *'Choose Your Own Adventure'* story which provided the backdrop for *'And Still Those Screams Resound...'*

THEY THAT DWELL IN DARK PLACES

This was the first story in this collection to be written, and it came about due to my irritation at another Hallowe'en approaching with no plans set to celebrate. So, in 2004, with October 31st a day away, I decided to write a ghost story to e-mail to some friends. I didn't have any plot in mind, just the vague notion that it should have a Victorian or Edwardian setting, and that it should attempt to capture the feel of the Fontana Ghost Story anthologies and those Amicus portmanteau films beloved of our little group. Thus the traditional (okay, clichéd) clubroom setting and the telling of ghostly tales, which served a dual purpose; they had instant familiarity and, more importantly, if I couldn't think of a suitably scary story, I could at least drag in snippets of classical-sounding stories to add atmosphere.

As the night progressed, I turned to notice that the curtains were open, just a sliver, with the darkness beyond peering in. My own discomfort at sitting with that gap into the dark so close by provided the story I needed, though it wasn't yet fully formed. The true nature of what Ashbourne was to spy didn't quite come as quickly as that and, when it did, it was as surprising for me as I hoped it would prove for its readers. As to whether the theories on the need for ghost stories propounded here are my own, I'll just say that the narrator clearly believes them and, given what I know about that individual which I didn't when I started writing his story, I'm not inclined to argue with him.

The story was written in the space of that one night and e-mailed off to friends (the version included in this book is roughly ninety per-cent faithful to that first draft). I was so surprised that I'd not only managed to complete it, but also quite liked it, that I posted it on the forum of the *British Horror Films* website.

Not long after, the *B.H.F.* started its *'Your Creations'* thread for aspiring writers and artists, which led Chris Wood, the site's creator, to compile a good old-fashioned horror anthology, where *'Dark Places'* made its first foray into print, accompanied by a fine illustration by Lawrence Bailey.

Between the time of that first posting and the publication of the book, however, the story had already taken on a new life. My fascination with Sherlock Holmes had drawn me to *'Imagination Theater'*, which regularly airs new Holmes radio dramas. Since I'd long-wished to attempt something in the medium, I thought I'd try a ghost story—after all, ghost stories are traditionally meant to be listened to—and I already had a story about the telling of ghost stories. To my delight, they made it their Hallowe'en broadcast. The excitement of awaiting the broadcast, the experience of listening to the actors who had recorded my words half a world away and being so carried away by their performances that I forgot I'd written it and got a few frights along the way, and the unfailing courtesy of Larry Albert and Jim French are all things I'll never forget.

So, this was where it all started, and without Chris's decision to include the story in that anthology, or Jim's and Larry's enthusiasm for the script, it's unlikely that any of the other tales in this collection would ever have happened. And, since I'm going back to the start here, it is only as I write these notes that I realise that, although the story is not particularly Jamesian, it does owe an unconscious debt to one of his stories; with its gentlemen in their smoking room exchanging snippets of ghost stories, I'd returned to that tale which first introduced me to M.R. James, '*A School Story*'...which is, I believe, where we came in.

DANIEL MCGACHEY was born in 1970, and grew up in Kilsyth, a small town on the outskirts of Glasgow, Scotland. A steady diet of *'Doctor Who,'* *'2000A.D.'* comic strips, Rathbone and Bruce as Holmes and Watson, and the films of Hammer and Amicus left him with an abiding love of the frightening, fantastical and mysterious that, in later years, would lead him to the works of H.P. Lovecraft, Sir Arthur Conan Doyle, Nigel Kneale, and, most especially, the pleasing terrors of M.R. James.

He relocated to Dundee in 1989, and has remained there ever since, where he works in publishing, having written scripts for some well-loved children's comic strip characters in such titles as *'The Dandy,'* *'The Beano'* and, briefly, *'Bunty,'* more recently focusing on digital media and animation.

His ghost stories, which began as an amusement for friends, have appeared in *'The BHF Book of Horror Stories'* and *'Black Book of Horror'* series of anthologies, and *'Filthy Creations'* magazine, while his radio plays—some adapted from his stories, some vice versa—have been broadcast as part of the syndicated mystery and suspense series *'Imagination Theater.'* He is also a regular contributor of reviews of television and radio adaptations of M.R. James's ghost stories to *'The Ghosts and Scholars M.R. James Newsletter.'*

CPSIA information can be obtained at www.ICGtesting.com
Printed in the USA
LVOW07s1609281014

410890LV00005B/631/P